Praise for  ...novels

"Yasmine Galenorn ...e."
—Sherrilyn Ker... hor

"Erotic and darkly ... pas-
sion." —Jeaniene Frost, *New York Times* bestselling author

"Yasmine Galenorn is a hot new star in the world of urban
fantasy."
—Jayne Ann Krentz, *New York Times* bestselling author

"Yasmine Galenorn is a powerhouse author; a master of the
craft who is taking the industry by storm, and for good reason!"
—Maggie Shayne, *New York Times* bestselling author

"Spectacularly hot and supernaturally breathtaking."
—Alyssa Day, *New York Times* bestselling author

"Simmers with fun and magic."
—Mary Jo Putney, *New York Times* bestselling author

"Yasmine Galenorn's imagination is a beautiful thing."
—Fresh Fiction

"Galenorn's gallery of rogues is an imaginative delight."
—*Publishers Weekly*

"Pulls no punches . . . [and] leaves you begging for more."
—Bitten by Books

continued . . .

"It's not too many authors who can write a series as long-lived as this one and make every book come out just as interesting and intriguing as the last, but Yasmine Galenorn is certainly one of them . . . Her books are always enchanting, full of life and emotion as well as twists and turns that keep you reading long into the night."

—*Romance Reviews Today*

"Explore this fascinating world."   —TwoLips Reviews

"As always, [Galenorn] delivers intriguing characters, intricate plot layers, and kick-butt action."

—*RT Book Reviews* (★★★★)

FLIGHT
FROM
DEATH

YASMINE
GALENORN

BERKLEY BOOKS, NEW YORK

BERKLEY

An imprint of Penguin Random House LLC
375 Hudson Street, New York, New York 10014

FLIGHT FROM DEATH

A Berkley Book / published by arrangement with the author

ISBN: 978-0-425-27215-2

PUBLISHING HISTORY
Berkley mass-market edition / July 2015

PRINTED IN THE UNITED STATES OF AMERICA

10 9 8 7 6 5 4 3 2 1

Cover art by Tony Mauro.
Cover design by Rita Frangie.
Interior text design by Laura K. Corless.

Penguin
Random
House

Dedicated to
Samwise, again. My greatest cheerleader.

Revenge doesn't stop.

—DANIEL CRAIG

Love is like a war: easy to begin but very hard to stop.

—H. L. MENCKEN

ACKNOWLEDGMENTS

I want to thank my usual suspects here: Samwise, my husband, whose support means more than anything to me. I couldn't ask for a more caring, loving partner. I want to thank my assistants, Andria and Jennifer, for keeping me on track; my editor, Kate Seaver; and my agent, Meredith Bernstein, for believing in my work. Throughout the vagaries of this industry, they have all been so much help.

Tony Mauro, my incredible cover artist, deserves his due—his art matches my vision of my characters so incredibly well. Rita Frangic and the Berkley art department always does a lovely job on my cover designs. Together, they put into vision what I see in my mind when I'm writing.

To my spiritual guardians: Mielikki, Tapio, Ukko, and Rauni. My devotion, always. To my Galenorn furbabies: Calypso, Morgana, Brighid, and our new little Apple. And to the memory of my beloved Meerclar, Keeter, Tara, and Luna—I wish so much they could all be with me forever. My cats keep me smiling through the dark times, and the hard times.

And most of all, I want to take a moment to acknowledge how much you, my readers, mean to me. Your continued support and your willingness to take a chance on my new books—and especially, on the new series I write—means so much to me, as do your kind words on my blog, Facebook, and via e-mail.

Dear Reader:

I welcome you to my new Fly by Night Series. While it is a spinoff of Otherworld, this series can be read on its own. I had so much fun exploring the world of Alex and Shimmer in this book, and I am eager to see how this series develops and grows. I hope you have as much fun reading this book as I did writing it, and that you take the characters to heart as much as some of you have taken my other series to heart. *Flight from Mayhem*, the second book, will be out in July 2016.

The inspiration for the plot came when I was visiting Port Townsend with my husband. A beautiful town tucked away on the Olympic Peninsula, Port Townsend is rich with history—and the area is also rich in ghostly lore. As Samwise and I were eating lunch on the beach (the town is situated along the Strait of Juan de Fuca), I suddenly imagined Shimmer diving into the waters off the coast. And when we visited the abandoned military battery there, I could see the area being ripe for a ghost story. So I hope you enjoy *Flight from Death*, and stick around for Alex and Shimmer's further adventures.

Next up, this autumn, on October 27, 2015, you'll get to read *Autumn Thorns*, the first book in yet *another* new series I'm writing. In the back of *Flight from Death*, you'll find an excerpt of *Autumn Thorns*, the first book in the Whisper Hollow series, which follows the story of Kerris Fellwater, a spirit shaman who attempts to put the dead to rest. Kerris returns to her hometown of Whisper Hollow, Washington, after her grandparents die and leave her their home. Located near Lake Crescent on the Olympic Peninsula, Whisper Hollow is a town where spirits walk among the living and the lake never gives up her dead. And not only do monsters hide in the shadows, but so do secrets of the heart, and love can be as dangerous as anything else that lurks in the dark.

In February 2016, we'll return to Otherworld with *Darkness Raging*—book eighteen of the Otherworld Series.

For those of you new to my books, I hope you enjoy your

first foray into my worlds. For those of you who have followed me for a while, I want to thank you for taking a chance on my new series. Check my website, galenorn.com, for information on my newsletter, short stories, release info, and links to where you can find me on the Web.

Bright Blessings,
The Painted Panther
Yasmine Galenorn

CHAPTER 1

"**H**urry up, damn it! Get a move on, woman!" Alex shoved me toward the stairwell and jammed the door by shoving a wooden wedge beneath it, but that would only buy us a little time.

"I'm trying, but the camera's stuck!" I yanked on the strap, which had gotten caught in the door as we'd beat a hasty retreat from the apartment where we had been spying. We couldn't afford to lose the camera—we needed the pictures on it. Not to mention, if I lost it, the cost for a replacement would come out of my salary. I wasn't about to leave it behind.

"Oh for cripes sake, Shimmer. Just cut the bloody straps! For the love of . . ." Alex grabbed the straps out of my hand and yanked out Juanita, his trusty big-assed bowie knife. The blade glittered dangerously in the dim light. He sliced through the leather bands like they were butter, and *bingo*, the camera came free in my hands. I managed not to play fumble-fingers and drop it as we continued to beat a hasty departure. Someone was pounding on the door behind us, but we *knew* who was on the other side, and we weren't about to let him in because he wanted to do really bad things to us at the moment.

"Get your ass down to the parking garage." Alex bared his fangs, looking pissed out of his mind as he shoved me toward the stairs. I didn't protest, just raced down the steps with the vampire following.

We made it to the third level of the garage and piled into Alex's sedan that he used for stakeout work. As he revved the engine and we swung out of the parking spot, the door to the garage slammed opened and Jackaboy Jones came barreling out, his eyes glowing. He wasn't alone. His pack of good ole boys followed. They were shifting into wolf form even as we managed to swerve toward the exit. With the wolves racing behind us, we hit the streets of Seattle.

Lucky for us, it was two A.M. and there was no traffic to speak of. Alex made a sharp right turn at the intersection and we left Jackaboy in the dust, his cronies now gathered behind him.

I let out a long sigh and leaned my head against the seat. "That was close."

Alex grinned at me. "Not really, love." He still had a slight Australian accent, even though he'd been over in the U.S. for almost a century. It was charming, in a boyish sort of way. "I've been in far tighter straits. We have the pictures and that's what counts. His wife will be able to press ahead in her case, we'll get paid, and we have one more divorce notched on our belts."

With a twinkle in his eye, he began to whistle. "But next time you get the urge to wear a pair of stilettos on a case, maybe rethink the idea? I'm not advocating Birkenstocks, but . . ." He laughed and held up the broken heel from my sandals. It had come off on the stairs and I'd left it, but apparently Alex had noticed.

I had known better than to wear heels, but the truth was, I had been feeling a little blah and wanted to at least look good. Blushing, I tried to hide my embarrassment. "You're a dick, you know that?" I didn't really mean it, but I had to say something.

He just laughed again. "Oh, sweet pea, I've known that

for years. I'll grow on you. See if I don't." He switched on the MP3 player and AC/DC's "Highway to Hell" came blaring out. As we headed back to the office, I couldn't help but think that he was already growing on me, too much for my own good.

"Holy fuck, what the hell are they doing in there?" I grimaced as another crash interrupted my conversation with Bette. We were eating lunch—well, what passed for lunch. It was midnight. But since our office hours were 8:30 P.M. to 5:30 A.M., this counted as our noon meal.

Bette sat behind the receptionist's counter of the Fly by Night Magical Investigations Agency. A fine gray marble veined with rich gunmetal, the counter stood between the back office and the waiting room. Bette was our official meet-and-greeter, and as unconventional as she was, people liked her. She netted us a number of new clients just by the way she welcomed them when they came through the door. Something to do with pheromones, she said.

I sat beside her, counting the crashes. "That's how many? Five?" The sound of breaking glass and raised voices would have alarmed me and sent me running into Alex's office if I hadn't known who was in there with him.

Bette cackled. "Four. Something's got her knickers twisted, that's for sure. I haven't heard them go at it like this for a long time. In fact, this may be the worst fight they've had. Maybe if we're lucky, she'll leave for good."

"That's not nice." I tried to look stern but ended up giggling. "I admit, that would be a relief. Would certainly be quieter around here, for sure."

"When did I ever claim to be nice?" The older woman—well, she *looked* like an older woman, even though she didn't act it—grinned and winked at me. "Glenda's a real bitch when she gets worked up, and she doesn't like me. She gets worked up over little things a lot. Though lately, the fights have been nastier and more frequent."

She leaned over her plate and enthusiastically bit into the hamburger. Dripping with bacon grease and secret sauce, the sandwich smelled wonderful, and the look on the Melusine's face told me just how much she enjoyed it. We had that in common, at least. Snake shifters and dragons both were major carnivores. There, though, any resemblance ceased.

Bette was a sight, with her long gray hair curled into a bouffant and eyes the color of green leaves with sunshine sparkling on them. She routinely dressed like a biker mama. Today she had on skintight jeans, a glittering gold belt, a spandex V-neck T-shirt stretched so tightly over her ample boobs that the material looked ready to tear, and a pair of Doc Martens. All that was missing was a leather jacket, and *that* was hanging on the back of her chair. At least she didn't smoke while she was eating—that would have killed my appetite.

We made quite the pair. When I'm in my human form I'm short enough for my kind—only six feet tall, with long black hair streaked with blue and purple. The streaks are natural, not dye. My eyes are the same royal blue, leading to a lot of people asking, "Do you wear colored contacts?" It's easier to just say yes. Add to that I'm strong and muscled, and—like Bette—I have big boobs, and I get a lot of interesting looks and a few too many hands I have to slap.

As I finished my fish and chips, another crash split the air. This time it was followed by Alex shouting, and Glenda shouting right back at him. The argument was escalating, all right. Apparently it had reached flash point because the door to his office slammed open and the succubus came storming out, as fast as her form-fitting pleather skirt would allow her to walk. She glanced over at us, glowering.

"Don't say a fucking word, either one of you bitches. At least I don't have to pretend to be polite to you anymore." And then she barreled out the door, shattering the glass window as she slammed it shut behind her.

"Well, then. I guess she told us. I'll clean that up after we finish our lunch." Bette arched one eyebrow, then glanced over at the door to Alex's office. "Wonder if he's alive in there, or if he took a direct hit."

"You think we should go see?" I followed her gaze, staring at the silent door.

Bette shook her head. "No. Give it time."

Alex peered around the corner of the heavy steel door. "She gone?" The twinkle that usually sparkled in those frosty eyes was absent, replaced with a clouded scowl. This wasn't the first time the pair had fought up a storm, but tonight something felt different.

Bette nodded, licking her fingers. "Sure is, *precious*. I'll get a broom and dustpan after I finish my lunch." She paused. "You all right, Alex?"

He shrugged, leaning against the wall. "Fine. But keep an eye out. Glenda is persona non grata from here on out. I don't want her coming in and torching the joint—her temper's worse than mine and she believes in revenge."

"You two on the outs?" Bette lowered her voice, speaking cautiously. Vampires were scary dudes when they were angry. Even to a snakeshifter and—even to me.

"For good. We're done."

As he turned to disappear back into his office, I wanted to ask what had happened but took my clue from Bette and kept my mouth shut about it.

Before he could vanish behind the door, Bette cleared her throat. "Just a second there, sweet cheeks. A call came in while you and Miss Prissypants were occupied. Patrick Strand needs to talk to you."

Alex froze. He was about my height—six feet—and had wheat-colored hair that was always lightly tousled. It reached his shoulders, and a stubble of beard covered his chin. His eyes were frosty gray, and he was fit, with a fine spread of pecs and abs. I knew that from seeing him without his shirt a couple times. The fact that I wouldn't mind seeing him without his shirt again was a thought I tried to keep to myself. Alex was a vampire. And he happened to be my boss. He owned and ran the Fly by Night Magical Investigations Agency, and I had been assigned to him for a five-year stint, so I did my best to keep on his good side, even when he drove me up the wall. I didn't have a choice.

"*Patrick Strand?* You're sure it was him?" He looked puzzled. "I haven't heard that name for a long time." He gazed at Bette, his expression thoughtful.

"Twenty-some years, if I'm on my game." Bette polished off the last of her meal and wiped her hands on a paper napkin, then tossed the bag and container in the garbage. "The last time you two talked, it ended up with a major argument, if I recall correctly."

I perked up. I hadn't heard this story. I'd only been around a few months. And so far, with what I *had* heard of Alex's exploits, I had come to realize that I was dealing with someone as volatile and chaotic as myself, which was in itself a scary proposition. Although he could be a real charmer when he wanted to.

"What happened?" I had no shame when it came to butting in.

Alex glanced at me, a smirk on his face. "Patrick conned me out of a thousand dollars that I happened to need very badly—"

"Tell us another one, sugar. You know you lost it in a poker game. Patrick won fair and square. But you know that's not the real reason you two parted ways." Bette snorted as she tapped a cigarette out of the pack, shoving it in one side of her mouth. She smoked like a chimney stack and smelled like one, too.

"That was reason enough. Patrick cheated—"

"You choked!" Her laugh was raspy as she lit up. The No Smoking sign above her desk never detoured her. She ignored it, just like she ignored just about everything Alex told her. But she ran the company with an iron fist. There was no doubt who held everything together for us.

"You old bitch . . . I never choke." Alex snorted.

"Sure you don't, sugar. Sure you don't. But like I said, you know that wasn't the *real* reason you parted company. And I know you've regretted it ever since." She winked at him. They teased each other constantly. It was their pattern. "Why don't you run along and call him, Alex. Patrick needs your help, and you two need to settle up and put your differences behind you. It's not like it was with Julian. Trust me on this one. Isn't it time to let the past go?" She held his gaze and I had the feeling something unspoken passed between the two.

Instead of arguing, Alex let out a grunt. "Whatever you think best, then, love. E-mail me the number." He turned and went back into his office. And just like that, we were back to work.

So . . . I'm Shimmer, in case you're wondering. And I happen to be a dragon. A blue dragon, specifically. If you don't know what that means, here it is in a nutshell: I'm a water dragon. I'm connected to the element of water in more ways than you'd think, and I'm most at home when I'm in a lake, ocean, swimming pool. Hell, even a bath makes me feel more secure. I can sense heightened emotions, and tend to be a little volatile myself, just like Mama Ocean.

That's where my trouble came to play. I got myself in a really bad jam and—long story short—was exiled from the Dragon Reaches for five years and stripped of some of my powers.

The Wing-Liege—one of our main council members and the advisor to the Emperor—commuted what could have been a death sentence and sent me Earthside. He assigned me to work for his friend Alex Radcliffe. That the Wing-Liege even admits to *knowing* a vampire still boggles my mind. But friends they are, and so Lord Vine—the Wing-Liege—gave me two options. Accept the punishment, or face certain assassination at the hands of my enemies. Exile seemed the better option.

So I've been here about five Earthside months, and I'm slowly acclimating myself to human culture, but it's not easy. I don't understand a lot of the mores and customs, and I'm still not sure how I'm supposed to fit in. I don't even understand the other Supes very well. I miss the Dragon Reaches, but since I was never accepted there in the first place—another long story, best saved for another time—I decided to give Earthside my best shot. It's a chance for me to make a fresh start. One I'd never get at home.

Essentially, I'm on probation. I screw up, and I get sent packing to a fate that might well include my execution. And while working for Alex can be nerve-racking, it's not as frightening as the thought of having an assassin on my tail.

Oh . . . last thing. As to what I did? Well, let me give you one piece of advice: Never, ever steal from a white dragon. *Even* if you think he might have clues as to who your parents were. Even if his sons tortured and humiliated you. Being an orphan is rough, especially in the Dragon Reaches. Being dead? Even harder.

was just finishing up on the computer, entering some info on a case we'd recently resolved when Alex called me into his office. I made sure I had my iPad and headed in to see what he wanted.

Alex's office always gave me the creeps. The ceiling was high—which I *did* like. At about twelve feet, it gave the room an open, airy feel. But against one wall, a line of trophies faced the door. A rhino, a hippo, a giraffe, and a crocodile all jutted out in 3D living color from their mounting. Over his desk was a giant swordfish. Occasionally I'd hunted them when I was in dragon form underwater, but I never thought to stuff one and stick it on the wall.

At one point in his two-hundred-some-odd years, Alex had taken up big-game hunting and this was the result. He had told me when I'd questioned him that it had been during a time when things like sport hunting was accepted—almost expected in some circles. And he also said that while he'd never do it again, he wasn't about to disrespect the animals he'd killed by dumping the trophies in a thrift shop or just tossing them away.

"I keep them as a reminder that I really don't want to play judge, jury, and executioner anymore," he told me.

The rest of the office was a mixture of brilliant wall colors, old wood, and chrome and glass. Glass-covered cases displayed the numerous blades Alex had collected. He even had a bow and quiver of arrows slung over a coat rack. I wasn't sure if he could use it, but chances were, he could. Alex was rough-and-tumble. He'd never pass for a cowboy, but he sure could pass for Mad Max.

I slid into a chair opposite his desk, looking around. Two of the vases that I had liked were gone, and one of the panes of glass on the display cases was also missing. No doubt the victim of Glenda's temper tantrum. But I decided it best to tiptoe around that subject and leaned forward, readying my tablet.

"Ready. What you got for me, boss?"

He laughed, folding his hands against his stomach. He had a flat stomach. Nicely flat. Way too nice. In fact, I noticed far too many nice things about him. It had been quite a while since I'd paired up back home, and I was feeling the lack.

A grin spread across his face, showing the very tips of his fangs.

"What are you laughing at?" I squirmed a little. His gaze was cool and yet, since the first time we met, there had been an underlying heat between us that made me uncomfortable. Half the time, I wanted to smack the guy. Half the time I was tempted to push him up against a wall and rip open his shirt and run my hands over that smooth, cool chest of his.

"You. You're always so to the point when you come in here." He leaned forward. "You need to learn how to loosen up."

"I just . . . you're my boss," I muttered. Truth was, I'd almost staked him a couple months back. Granted, I'd been under a charm at the time, but the end result? I'd just about dusted my boss and any chance I had at making a go of things. I still was amazed that he wasn't holding a grudge.

"Yes, I *am* your boss. I also hope you consider me your friend. Okay, here's the deal. Patrick Strand? He's an old friend of mine. We go way back."

"He a vampire?" Usually vamps associated with their own kind.

"Actually, he is, yes. At least now. He wasn't when I knew him. He runs a B-and-B joint up in Port Townsend geared toward Supes—especially vampires. He bought it a couple years ago but just recently got around to converting it over.

That's when the problems started." Alex winked at me. "Patrick always did know how to pick 'em, whether it was women or houses or jobs."

Now, I *couldn't* resist. I set down my iPad and stared at him pointedly. "And *you* do? So what gives with Glenda? Your succubus girlfriend has anger management problems, you know. Bette won't ask you outright, because she probably knows better, but I don't have her filters." Alex had just claimed me as a friend, and I was used to being up front with the few people I had befriended over the years. I found it saved a lot of trouble and misunderstandings.

Or maybe not . . . As his eyes began to turn a dangerous shade of crimson, I thought maybe I had pushed too far. But a moment later, they faded back down and he slumped back in his chair.

"Truth? I couldn't take it anymore. Shimmer, that woman . . ." He paused. "I refuse to take orders from anybody regarding my business or who I associate with." He waved toward the door. "Make sure the door's shut, will you?"

I hesitated. Alex didn't usually open up to me; he usually talked to Bette when he wanted to mull things over. Something must have happened. I crossed to the door to make certain it was closed. "Okay, spill it. What did she want?"

Alex shifted in his seat, playing with a pencil. The squeak of his pants against the leather was the only sound in the room for a moment. Finally, he looked over at me. "What I say in here stays here. You understand?"

I grinned. "I didn't survive this long by opening my mouth at the wrong time, dude." The realization that I could actually smile about my past—at least to some degree—hit me. That was a lot more than I'd been able to do a few months back.

With a laugh, Alex threw the pen back on the desk. "No, I don't suppose you did. All right. Glenda ordered me to fire Bette."

I blinked. Bette was the glue that held the agency together. She made it run like a well-oiled machine. And Glenda . . . didn't have a stake in the business, so to speak. "Why the hell . . . Wait. Was it because you two were an item way back when?"

He nodded. "Glenda's insanely jealous, but she expects me to accept her nature without question. She's a succubus, for fuck's sake. I know I'm not enough for her. But if I accept her need to feed on sex from others, she's jolly well going to accept that I have women friends. I don't usually sleep around, not anymore. But I'm not about to kick out one of the best friends I've ever had just to make my overly possessive girlfriend happy."

Now I understood why he was talking to me instead of to Bette. "You don't want Bette to know about this."

He inclined his head. "Exactly. First, it would just piss her off, and a pissed-off Melusine is a dangerous enemy. Second . . . I think it would hurt her feelings, even though I told Glenda to fuck off."

"So you broke up with your girlfriend to save a friendship."

"No, I broke up with my girlfriend because I'm tired of batshit crazy. I can handle regular crazy. I can even handle temper tantrums. But I can't handle someone trying to run my life for me or dictate who I do—or do not—befriend or hire for my agency. If Bette asks, I just had enough. That's what I'm going to tell her. Just . . . one argument too many." He leaned forward, a pale smile on his lips. His voice dropped as he said, "I've been thinking for a while that it's time I moved on. Find someone more my speed, you know?"

His gaze was unwavering and I couldn't look away. Those frosty eyes were gorgeous, wide and luminous, and below them, the narrow, sculpted nose, and pale stretch of lips mesmerized me. The intensity of emotion that I felt rushing across the desk overwhelmed me—blue dragons were good at picking up on emotions—and I found myself wanting to reach out and touch those lips, to draw my fingers across them.

All too aware that I was breathing rapidly, I forced myself to lean back and clear my throat. "Yeah . . . I know."

I sucked in a deep breath and let it out slowly, trying to calm the heat that was beginning to work its way up my body. From the beginning, I had found Alex attractive, but I knew it would be a mistake to act on it. He and I were like oil and water. And he was my boss. And he had a jealous girlfriend.

Strike that last . . .

"Shimmer . . ." The corner of one side of those delicious lips began to curve upward. "Oh, Shimmer . . ."

Shaking off the images that cascaded through my mind, I very slowly picked up my iPad and forced myself to say, "Maybe you'd better tell me about the job we're going out on?"

And just like that, he paused, let out a soft laugh, and returned his attention to the papers on his desk. "Right. The job." Another pause, and the moment passed. We were back to business. "As I said, my friend Patrick owns a bed-and-breakfast up in Port Townsend and he's having problems."

"What kind of problems? And what's the name of the place?"

"The High Tide Bed-and-Breakfast. It was supposed to open last month, but a series of accidents forestalled that. There's more, though." Alex frowned, staring at his notes. "Patrick thinks he's being haunted."

Ghosts. Wonderful. I had very little experience with spirits and wasn't eager to add to my repertoire. "And what makes him think that?" I tapped in a few notes on my tablet.

"Strange noises, poltergeist activity . . . cold spots. Typical stuff. I told him we'd come up and investigate."

Annnnd . . . there we had it. A real case landing at my feet at last. Over the past few months, we'd taken on some low-key items, but nothing out of the ordinary. Mostly taking pictures for divorces or court cases. Supes were really good about knowing when they were being followed. It took another Supe with a good camera to record the necessary proof. But until now, Alex hadn't thrown me into anything major.

He had told me that business was in a lull, but I suspected he'd been turning away clients until I got my wings about me. Now, it appeared, he thought I was ready. The thought actually excited me. I was tired of hanging around the office.

Hell, I wasn't even used to staying in one place for more than a few weeks. Settling down was proving to be a lot harder than I thought it would be.

"Sure thing. Anything I need to bone up on?" I'd spent my life breaking into people's—well, dragons'—houses and rifling through their stuff. I had a decent amount of experience at getting myself into tight places, if not out of them, but working on a team entailed other skills.

Alex winked at me. "No worries, girl. We'll head up tomorrow night. Find the ferry schedules, would you? We need to travel from the Coupeville ferry over to Port Townsend. We'll leave first thing after sunset, so pack a bag for a few days. You might want to read up on the town. It's an odd place. Supposed to be spook central, from what I gather. I'm telling Ralph to pull out all the stops and bring our ghost-hunting equipment."

"Equipment? But . . . you're a vampire. Ralph is a werewolf. I'm a dragon. What do we need technology for?" I knew that the agency had a store of EMF meters and EVP recorders and whatever else humans had managed to create in their quest to prove that ghosts were real, but *really*?

Alex let out a snort. "Listen to me, Shimmer, and learn. *Always* go in prepared. We probably won't need this stuff, but better to have it with us than not. I may be a vampire, but that doesn't mean I know when there are ghosts around. Same with Ralph and you. Not all Supes are psychic."

He made a good point. "Right, then. Tomorrow night, we leave right after sunset. Bette can pick me up, I suppose." I still didn't have a driver's license but was doing my best to learn, though Alex refused to let Bette teach me. He was making me take lessons at the Supe Community Action Council, which was just fine. Somehow, the thought of speeding around Seattle in a two-ton metal cage just didn't appeal on any level. Even though, in dragon form, I'd dived five thousand feet down in the ocean, driving a car intimidated me.

"What do you know about the house?" I created a new section in my notes file.

"Patrick said the place belonged to a friend of his in his pre-vampire days. Guy by the name of Nathan Striker. We're going to need to look into its history, but I figure doing so might be easier while we're up there. Meanwhile, I guess I'll go home and pack up Glenda's stuff . . ." He let out a sound; whether it was disgust or regret, I couldn't tell. My bet was on the former.

"How long were you together?" The question spilled out before I could stop myself. I clamped my mouth shut and stood up.

He gave me an odd look. "Too long? Two . . . maybe three years? I don't know. I guess . . . it was easier to just stay with her than face the problems we had. Nobody likes to admit they've failed." With a sheepish duck of the head, he told me right there all I needed to know. It had been over for a while. He just hadn't gotten up the courage to end it.

I headed for the door, but then it hit me that we'd be away for the weekend. *Together.* Granted, Ralph would be with us, but a lot could happen in unfamiliar territory. I glanced back. "Alex . . ."

"Yes?" He looked up, already engrossed in his Werewyx Search—the newest Supe search engine.

I paused, my hand on the doorknob, but then decided against saying anything more. Shaking my head, I gave him a gentle smile. "Nothing. Never mind." As I closed the door behind me, I realized that I was beginning to care about Alex. Maybe a little too much.

CHAPTER 2

By the time I headed home it was six in the morning and the majority of Seattleites were just beginning their day. Because Alex was a vampire, we worked nights. Luckily, since I was a dragon, I didn't need as much sleep as humans and so I would stay up till around two thirty to run errands and get my shopping done, then sleep until seven, and arrive at work by eight thirty.

When the Wing-Liege had carted me off to Seattle, he'd provided me with enough Earthside cash to set myself up for the first year. I was able to buy a small house—albeit in a ghost-ridden district that still creeped me out. But my home was a comfortable two-story bungalow that had been built in 1938, and the lot was filled with indigenous plants. Over the months, I'd managed to cut back most of the tangle and now I had a tidy lawn, an arbor draping with moss roses, and knee-high ferns that gave my home a wild feel while still appearing cultivated. A trellised archway straddled the sidewalk up to my house, and I had pruned back the honey-suckle draping over it, so it was still thick but not quite so aggressive.

I'd also installed a security system after an old enemy of Alex's had kidnapped me a couple months ago. Alex promised that Julian wouldn't come looking for me again—he was too smart to try the same thing twice—but I wasn't so sure. Hence, security codes on my doors and windows, and Ralph had encrypted my computer to make it difficult for anybody to hack in.

As I unlocked the front door and punched in the code, I inhaled a long breath and let it out slowly. There was something that felt reassuring about coming home. I had never felt this way in the Dragon Reaches. I'd never had a home there.

I stopped by the giant aquarium I had installed across one wall—it covered two thirds of the space and gave me the feeling of living in a virtual ocean. My biggest concern had been making sure that all the fish I bought for it got along and wouldn't eat each other. Glancing around the room, I smiled softly. The tangle of plants gave life to my home, and the colors were soothing. When I shut the door behind me, it felt as though I'd left the city behind. I wasn't used to the crowds and the noise, and the feeling of being cooped up in a concrete cage still jarred me.

Dropping my purse, I picked up a bowl of popcorn I'd left on the coffee table the morning before. I'd been watching a TV series on Rentbox, trying to puzzle out relationships in this realm. Hell, I didn't even understand them very well among my own people. But *Sex and the City* wasn't helping a whole lot, other than reaffirm my notion that humans were far too hung up on who was sleeping with whom. Jealousy and possessiveness were well known in the Dragon Reaches, but more over *things* than *partners*.

As I nibbled on the kernels, I looked around the room. The walls were pale blue, with cream trim. All my furniture was in shades of gray, white, and periwinkle, and a painting of a storm crashing against the backdrop of ocean waves hung over my desk. My sanctuary was serene, and secure . . . and lonely.

With a sigh, I dropped to the sofa. "I never needed

anybody before. I don't know why I should feel lonely here."
Talking to the fish wasn't all that productive, but on the plus
side, they never argued back and all they asked for was a
clean tank and food. Setting the bowl aside, I leaned forward
and rested my elbows on my knees. I glanced at the tank.
The jellyfish was giving me an accusatory look.

"I don't know how to make friends, okay? I've never had
a friend—well, other than Chai, but I haven't seen him for a
long time. I can talk to Bette because she's a great broad and
she doesn't judge me, but I've never done the gal-pal thing.
And until now, men have just been something to toy with. And
you and I both saw just how well Carter worked out."

For a little while, after I arrived, I'd dated Carter—a
half-Demon, half-Titan who ran the Demonica Vacana Society. His job was to chart the levels of demonic activity over
Earthside. I knew enough about him to know that I wasn't
cut out for his level of play. We stayed friends, but only
because we had nixed the relationship.

Coolray wiggled a tentacle. I waved back. Even when I
was in human form, sea creatures and fish recognized me
as part of their world. They may not always have much in
the way of the brains department going on, but the familiar-
ity was there.

"As for Alex . . . I have no idea what to do about Alex.
Should I give it a try? What if it goes bad? I'll have to spend
five years coping with the results of a mistake. What then?"

The jellyfish paused, then, apparently bored with the
conversation, burbled away.

"Not much help are you, you little goober?" I laughed,
forcing myself to think about something else. As I debated
on whether to do laundry, pack for the trip to Port Townsend,
or watch a movie, the doorbell rang. As I opened the door,
a whiff of lilac perfume hit me.

"Hey girl, what's going on? I thought I'd drop by after
work and see how you were doing." Stacy was the one
human friend I had made outside of work. And she was *all*
human, with coffee-brown skin that glowed under the soft
light. She had short hair, braided against her head, and she

was wearing a pair of indigo-wash jeans and a white button-down shirt. I first met her when I started eating at Marion Vespa's Supe-Urban Café. They had been full up, so we had agreed to share a table.

Stacy worked as a security guard at a local nightclub. After her shift there, she pulled another shift—though shorter—at an all-night coffee shop. She was doing her best to keep her little brother afloat while he was in college, and to help out her mother, who was disabled. She also took weekend courses and was on her way to becoming a legal aide.

I motioned for her to come in. "Thank gods you're here. I was talking to Coolray again."

Stacy snorted. She never said a word about me naming my fish, including the jellies. Or talking to them. She also knew I was a dragon. I'd reluctantly told her, but she had been more delighted than anything else. And most important, she knew how to keep secrets.

"Yeah, well, just watch it if he starts answering back." She made herself at home on the sofa and leaned back with a long sigh. "The club was packed, and so was the coffee shop. I'm so freaking tired."

Grateful for the company, I retrieved a couple sodas from the refrigerator. "Drink. Relax. I was just about to forage for dinner," I called out from the kitchen. I rummaged around and found the leftover bucket of fried chicken and a package of cheddar cheese that I'd bought the day before. Carting everything into the living room, along with a pack of napkins and a couple of plates, I spread out dinner on the coffee table.

Stacy took a long hit off the soda. She let out another sigh, this time one of relief, and accepted the plate of chicken and cheese I gave her.

"You like your meat and dairy, don't you, girl?"

I grinned. "I'm a dragon. What do you expect? Just be grateful it's cooked and not still on the hoof." While I'd developed a taste for some sweets, my dragon instincts were still in full force.

"So, how's it going?" She gave me a long look. "Alex treating you right?" Stacy didn't like vampires very much, and while Alex was a good sort, she steered clear of visiting me at the office.

"It goes. And yes, Alex is fine." I thought about telling her what had happened but then decided to wait. She wasn't exactly thrilled about my secret crush on him—which I had mentioned from time to time. Now that he was free of Glenda, I had the feeling Stacy would be a lot less lenient. As I said, she didn't care for vampires.

She gave me a long look and shook her head. "I don't *think* so. Girl, you look like the cat that ate the canary. What gives?"

I swallowed a piece of breading off a drumstick, then shrugged. "No, really. Pretty much the same old, same old . . . But I do have a question for you. Do you know anything about Port Townsend? Regarding ghosts, to be exact." At that moment, I realized I'd forgotten to look up the specifics on the ferry, but I figured I could do that later. What more could we need than a time schedule?

Stacy blinked. "Port Townsend? Why? It's a beautiful town, but freaky. A lot of spooks up there, for sure. And ocean." She motioned to the aquarium. "The town sits on the Strait of Juan de Fuca, you know. Makes your aquarium look like a kiddie pool." She paused. "You'll be near the water. You can always go out, take a long dip in the strait."

I curled up on the sofa with my food and soda. "That sounds wonderful. It's been too long since I've shifted into my dragon form."

Closing my eyes, I could see the huge expanse of water. *The roll of the waves, the pull of the currents. The spray of salt water and brine . . .*

I drifted in memories of immersing myself so deep in the water that the light disappeared and all that I could see were the bioluminescent shrimp and jellies and other creatures so strange that no human had ever before seen them. The pressure of the depths was incredible—like the weight of the world pressing down on my shoulders. But blue dragons were built to handle it—at least in our natural form. The water, the depths, were an integral part to our lives. With a sudden pang, I realized how thirsty I was to dive deep again, to go swirling in the mad dance of waves and whales and dolphins that always came out to play. It had been far too long.

"Shimmer . . . Shimmer?" Stacy's voice echoed through my thoughts, and I shook myself out of the memories. "Where did you just go, sugar? You were really out there somewhere."

I blinked, glancing at the clock on the wall. It had been almost five minutes. "Sorry . . . I guess I really do need to be in the water. While I'm up there, I'll spend some time during the early morning out in the depths." I caught my breath, missing the oceans of the Dragon Reaches.

She poked at her chicken thigh. "Tell me what it's like. Tell me about your home. I can see it in your eyes, Shimmer. I can see how much you miss it." Glancing up, she smiled softly.

"You really want to hear?" I hadn't spoken to anybody about my home since I'd been here, no more than to say I came from the Dragon Reaches.

"I wouldn't ask if I didn't want to hear." She cocked her head to the side. "I don't know much about the Dragonkin, so take it slow."

I wasn't used to this—I wasn't used to trusting people. I didn't even know if what I felt *was* trust, but Stacy was safe. I knew that on a gut level. I could feel it emanating from her, in her words, her manner, the smile in her eyes. "The Dragon Reaches are at the top of the world. They're among the highest climes. We live where the air is thin, and the clouds roll below the tall peaks. It's always cold there—at least for humans it would be."

She slid her plate onto the coffee table, sitting up. "Like Everest?"

I pulled off my boots and tossed them to the side, then sat cross-legged on the sofa. "Not exactly. There are lakes and marshes up there, rocky crags, and oceans. My kind live in the water, most of the time. We make our dreyeries there."

Stacy frowned. "What's a dreyerie?"

"A dragon nest. Like a lair. Dreyeries are our homes. Silvers, whites, gold dragons—they mostly live in the tall peaks. Red dragons live in the lower elevations, where it's warmer. Shadow dragons live in the Netherworld—they're also known as black dragons. Green dragons live in the temperate areas . . . and we blue dragons? We live in the oceans." I watched her closely.

She frowned. "You don't intermingle much, do you? I get the feeling . . ."

I shook my head. "You're right. There's a strong caste system among my kind. Silver dragons are at the top of the food chain, and then gold. Silver dragons rule the Dragon Reaches. If you're half-breed, you belong to the higher class of your parentage. What matters most is your lineage. You cannot escape your family heritage. You can marry out of it, but you can't leave it behind." I stopped as a wave of anger welled up to catch me by surprise. I hadn't felt this upset since I'd come Earthside, and now the emotion was an unwelcome visitor.

"Shimmer, your eyes are glowing. I mean really, *really* glowing." Stacy slowly unfolded herself from the chair, and I realized she was frightened.

I tried to get hold of my temper. At the Lost and Foundling, where I grew up, they'd taught us hard lessons on controlling our emotions. We were wing-strapped when we overstepped the boundaries and harshly punished for any infractions, which is probably why my temper had such a quick wick now. Add to that, blues were the most volatile breed, highly moody and emotional, and I was no exception. But Stacy had done nothing to warrant my throwing a temper tantrum.

I let out a shaky breath, once . . . twice . . . then a third time. As the glow in my eyes faded—I could feel it subside—I hung my head. "I'm sorry. I didn't mean to scare you. The fact is, I don't talk about the Dragon Reaches much because of the way I was treated there." Stacy knew that I had been sent here to work with Alex, but I'd never exactly told her why.

"What happened to you, Shimmer? What happened to you that sent you Earthside?" She leaned forward. I realized she was genuinely interested—she wasn't just being nosy.

I held her gaze, for once not looking away. "What I haven't told you is that I have no standing in the Dragon Reaches. I was an orphan, washed up on the shores . . . I have no place, no caste, I don't even have a name. I don't really even exist there."

As the huge contraption trapped my wings, spreading them out so I was unable to fly, unable to even move, it pressed me flat on my belly. The Wing-Liege was on the dais above, in his dragon form, while the guards—who had shifted—tightened the screws on the Strap. One of them leaned down near my ear and laughed.

"No name. No family. No class. You're a pariah . . . you have no standing. You don't even exist. When the Wing-Liege gets done with you, you'll wish you'd never been born." His voice was harsh, guttural, and I realized that he was enjoying himself. I struggled again, but with every move, the Strap made my wing muscles shriek, pain lancing through me. I screamed, my voice hoarse from the beatings the guards had given me when they'd hauled me into custody. As I geared myself up for another round of punishment, a voice broke through the haze of pain.

"Stop. Remove the Strap." The Wing-Liege's voice was gruff, but soft.

Amid whispered questions, the Strap was removed and I fell forward, exhausted. Confused, I found myself shifting into my human form. I was naked, save for the tattoo that adorned my body. The blue dragon started at my waist, its tail curling near my hip, and worked its way around my right side, surrounded by waves. The head came coiling down my right arm, with more ocean waves on either side. It was the one thing they couldn't take away from me—and it would always remind me of who I was.

"Bring her to my office." Again, the softly spoken command, and the unquestioning obedience. As I stumbled forward, aching in every muscle, I wondered what could be worse than the Strap, and so very afraid that I was about to find out.

Once there, Lord Vine motioned for me to put on a robe that was hanging over the chair. I slid into the white silk, wrapping it around me, wincing as blood from the cuts on my back soaked through. Wing-strapping left marks, it left scars that never went away even when we were in human form.

"Shimmer . . . you have to tell me the truth. Why did you do it? Greanfyr isn't going to let this rest. Even if you are imprisoned here, he'll come for you and find a way to destroy you." The impenetrable gaze of the Wing-Liege held me fast, and I couldn't look away. He was third in line to the Emperor and Empress, in terms of law and rule, and he had the charisma to prove it.

I didn't want to answer. I wanted to just let them think I'd been stupid. But the realization that Greanfyr's clan would come after me no matter what slowly sank in. Finally, I sucked in a deep breath and let it out slowly. "Greanfyr's son . . . Slap-Happy—I don't know his society name. He and a few of his friends caught me near the shore. They . . ." I stared at the table.

"Did they rape you, girl?" The Wing-Liege shifted uncomfortably, and I knew exactly why. Dragons that were outcaste, or without caste, had very few legal rights.

"No, they did not. They talked about it, but decided I was too . . . unclean for that. But they humiliated me. They forced me to strip and parade around in front of them naked. They made me wait on them, crawling on my hands and knees. They treated me like a trained bear—like I was . . . their property. I may not have status in this realm, but I am no one's slave!"

The memory of Slap-Happy laughing as he made me do tricks like a carnival animal reverberated through my thoughts, and I suddenly leaned over the side of the chair, dry heaves racking my system. As the cramps eased, I was able to sit up again. The Wing-Liege was waiting patiently. I held his gaze, even though by law, it was against the rules. I should have looked down, but at this point I no longer cared what was acceptable and what wasn't.

He must have seen the pain, because he held up one hand. "Stop. I think I understand. So . . . because you had no other recourse, you chose to retaliate by stealing from them?"

I scuffed my foot against the floor. In truth, I'd intended to set up a few booby-traps, to hurt them if I could. Greanfyr was no better than his son. The whole lot of them were corrupt and vile. But I was smart enough to shrug and nod.

"Yeah, I guess that was the idea."

The Wing-Liege nodded, then pushed to his feet. "I think I know everything I need to." He motioned for the guards to enter. "Take her back to her cell. Make certain she has food and access to a bath and clean clothes. Tend to her wounds."

And with that, he gave me a long look, then left the room.

"**O**h my God. Shimmer, that's horrible. They strung you up like that for *stealing*? After you'd been tormented by those . . . I was about to call them boys, but that doesn't seem right." She searched my face, a look of pain in her eyes.

"Close enough. And, Stacy, you have to understand. In the Dragon Reaches, I have no standing. It's a harsh place. What I did? Stealing from my betters? I could have lost a hand. Or my life. Blue dragons may be higher ranked than white dragons, but since I'm an orphan and have no name, no lineage . . . I'm outcaste. I'm lower than dirt, regardless of my breed." The words hurt, but they were true and I had been long taught to admit my failings.

Stacy shook her head, the pain replaced with anger. She

let out a sound that I'm pretty sure wasn't complimentary. "We have words for that here. Bigotry and discrimination."

I shrugged. "It's a dragon thing, and it has been that way since the beginning. My people aren't going to change. I either agree and fit in the best I can, or . . . I do what I did and go against them. I pushed the envelope so many times it's amazing I wasn't caught before now. But I never hurt anybody—not anybody who wasn't trying to hurt me." I'd been in my share of strafing fights, but nobody had ever died, and I hadn't started any of them.

Stacy stood up and reached down to take my hand. "Up. On your feet. Get your coat."

"What? Where are we going?"

"We're going out. We're going to go out to eat a proper breakfast. Then we'll go down to the docks and watch the water. I'm prying you out of this mire before you fall in too deeply. And while we're out, we'll grab a map of the peninsula so you have some idea of where you're going."

And just like that, I shook out of my thoughts and focused on the day.

S tacy left to go home and sleep after we ate breakfast, went shopping, and then stopped for coffee. I decided to stick around the Mug 'n Brew—a Supe-oriented coffee shop—for a while.

She waved good-bye as she headed for the door. "Catch you later, and . . . Shimmer? Don't dwell. Please? It's not worth your energy. Over here, you can be just about anything you want, regardless of where you started out."

I smiled at her. "You're right. I'll call you when I get back from Port Townsend."

Stacy knew how to get in there and shake things up, all right. The woman was all business and no nonsense. If she said we were going to have fun, by gods, we'd have fun. And if we were going to get something done—it got done. In fact, she kind of intimidated me, especially for a human.

Dragons didn't usually bother with humans. Now, living among them, I was being forced to confront my own prejudices. Respect was harder to give when you could shift into a giant creature and squash just about anybody you wanted . . . but I knew what it was to be at the mercy of others.

And, when I'd been ejected from the Dragon Reaches, the Wing-Liege had pared down my powers to a minimal amount. Now I could only shift when I was in water—the source of my power and strength. Otherwise, I was stuck in human form, even though I had superhuman strength and faster-than-average speed. I still had some of my magical abilities, though not all, and the heightened awareness of emotions was innate—nothing could take that away.

After Stacy left, I gathered my packages and headed home. I needed to clean house before I left. I'd rigged an automated fish feeder, so that was one worry off my list. And Stacy had said she'd come in to check on the house and the fish a couple times while I was gone. But I still needed to tidy up, vacuum, and clear out the refrigerator.

As I was putting away the tea I'd bought—one of the delightful surprises I'd discovered when I came over Earthside was herbal tea blends—I heard a noise. It sounded like wood scraping on wood. Frowning, I turned around to discover that one of the cupboard doors I'd closed had come open again. The latch must be loose. Or had I really remembered to close it?

I softly pushed it closed, making sure the latch caught, then turned back to the fridge. I pulled three containers of leftovers out and set them on the counter. I could finish them off for dinner. They'd just go bad if I left them while I was gone. Using a damp sponge, I quickly wiped up one small mess on the corner of a shelf and then straightened up just as the scraping sound caught my attention again.

Turning around, I saw the cupboard door was open again. As I walked toward it, the door slammed shut and I heard a low laugh. I never thought I'd hear that voice again and I didn't know whether to laugh or be pissed . . . or both.

"Cripes. Chai, stop it. You just scared the hell out of me."

The laughter stopped, and a waver in the air told me where he was.

"Show yourself. Come on out."

Very slowly, almost like a game of peek-a-boo, a figure shimmered into view. He was tall, very tall. Seven feet at least. His skin was golden and he had eyes the color of sea foam. Broad shouldered and bare-chested, Chai was gorgeous. I raced over to him, throwing myself in his arms as he hugged me tight.

"Shimmer! Little Sister! I've been looking high and low for you." He brushed my forehead with a kiss. "Finally, someone on the Western Shore told me that you'd been expelled over Earthside by the Wing-Liege. I don't need to tell you how hard it was to track you down."

Laughing—seeing him made all my troubles melt away—I playfully slapped his arm.

"Trust me, Chai, that's a *good* thing. The harder it is to track me down, the safer I am." If *Chai* had trouble finding me, then it meant that Greanfyr and his clan would have an equally difficult time. And the harder I was to find, the safer I was.

He pushed me back by my shoulders. "Girl, what a mess you got yourself into. If you needed money, why didn't you just come to me?"

I shrugged, not wanting to spoil the mood with the story of why I had really broken into the white dragons' dreyerie.

"What can I say? You know me. Now sit down and tell me what you've been doing with yourself." I pushed him over to the kitchen table. My house had an eat-in kitchen nook, as well as a formal dining room, and I'd decked it out in a blue and white theme that reminded me of the water. The walls of the kitchen were the color of pale morning sky, just before the sun peeks over the horizon. The fact that a djinn was hanging out in my kitchen seemed delightfully surreal to me. The fact that I even *had* a kitchen seemed surreal.

"All right, all right. Don't get pushy, Little Sister!"

Chai and I had met when I was first released from the Lost and Foundling—the orphanage for abandoned dragonettes. The owners brought us up rough and harsh, to steel ourselves for our adulthood. Not every orphan survived the ordeal. We weren't exactly abused, but there were no vacations or holidays and not much playtime involved. I had learned early on just where I stood in the world.

When I left the orphanage, I'd headed out for the Western Shores, intending to track down information on my heritage. Family meant everything to me at that point. Instead, I had found Chai, sunning himself on a rock. We'd struck up a conversation, and somehow, in the twisted way of the world, we'd become close friends. Djinns were tricky and you could never truly trust them one hundred percent. But in the scheme of things? Chai was the best friend I had.

"So, have you been Earthside before?" I returned to cleaning the counters. "And do you want something to eat?" Djinns ate food the same as anybody else, though they didn't really need it to survive. And what they ate varied with the type. Most djinns had a connection to the element of fire, and they tended to prefer their food on the spicy side.

Chai shook his head. "I thought I might stick around for a while. I missed you. And I could be a useful go-between since . . ."

"Since I can't return to the Dragon Reaches right now?" I glanced at him as I drizzled a spoonful of honey over the leftover pancakes I'd tucked away yesterday. I didn't mind eating them cold.

He grimaced. "Yes. I wasn't going to be quite so blunt, but now that you mention it, I can bring you things you might need. I can also help you keep an eye out for Greanfyr. In fact . . . I took a peek in on him and his family before hightailing it over here. Girl, you have to be careful. He's on the warpath, and he's pissed as all get-out at the Wing-Liege for letting you live. He wants his pound of flesh, my girl. And I don't think he's given up hope of getting it."

That *so* wasn't what I needed to hear. If Greanfyr was

still on the rampage, that meant I'd have to watch my back. There was nothing preventing him from coming over here to hunt me down, and there were oh-so-many ways to make a death look like an accident.

"I'll tell Alex. He can talk to the Wing-Liege for me. I still don't know how those two became friends, and he won't dish on the details." I glanced at the clock. It was nearing eleven and I still had to pack before I slept. I made a snap decision. "Chai, I want you to stay for a while, if you can. I have to go out of town for a few days on a case, but you can use the spare bedroom. Just don't trash the joint. And no bringing home girls."

Djinns could be as bad as incubi when it came to partying. In fact, they could be a whole lot worse. Their wishes came with long, snarled strings attached. So, while I was comfortable asking Chai for little things, I never once had accepted his offer of a wish. And generally I *told* him what I wanted, rather than ask, and he either complied or refused.

His eyes glimmered as he crossed over to my side. We had never clicked in a sexual way, but he was there for me, and I knew with certainty the djinn had my back.

He draped an arm around my shoulder. "Sure, Little Sister. I'll stick around for a while. You can count on me."

B y the time Bette stopped to pick me up on the way to the office, I had settled Chai into the guest room, which he'd promptly redecorated, and had managed to catch enough sleep to refresh me. As I shoved my suitcase in the trunk and clambered into the front seat next to her, Bette puffed a cloud of smoke in my face. I coughed. Her car was an old Chevy Impala, and she'd tricked it out like a low-rider.

The rain had increased to the point of being a downpour, and Bette turned the windshield wipers to high. "So, you ready for the trip?"

I shrugged, my thoughts still on Chai's sudden arrival. "I guess. I got a surprise visitor this morning."

"Hunky and hung, I hope?" She cackled. The woman could turn into a water moccasin, and she had an alluring charm for humans. She might look like a grandma-from-hell, but she could shake it up big-time in the sheets from what Alex had said. They had gone out about a hundred years ago but discovered they made much better friends than lovers.

"Yes, but it's not like that. He's more like a brother than anything else." I told her about Chai.

She turned a cautious eye to me as we pulled into the parking spot Alex had reserved for her in the lot next door to the office. "Shimmer, you're a sweet girl—"

As I started to speak, she waved me silent. "Don't contradict me, you have no clue how old I am."

I grinned and shut my mouth. There was no good way to answer that one.

"I know you say he's been a friend of yours for years . . . but honey, are you sure you can trust him? The djinn are a tricky species. They twist words for fun and profit, you know." Her eyes crinkled and she reached out to pat my hand. "Please, just walk softly. He may seem like family but the fact is, you can't trust much of anybody right now. Especially when it's only been a few months since the Wing-Liege sentenced you. I just don't want to see you get hurt."

I ducked my head. "I know . . . but I have to trust *somebody*. I can't walk around paranoid all the time. I've spent my entire life looking over my shoulder. I'm tired of it, Bette." My shoulders slumped and I hung my head. "I'm just so tired of fighting."

She squeezed my hand. "It's not fair, and you're right. You shouldn't have to. All right then, but if anything seems off-base, you come to Alex and me. You hear me?"

I nodded. "I promise." As I pulled my suitcase out of her car and carried it over to Alex's rusty brown Range Rover—he owned several vehicles, but thank gods he hadn't brought his motorcycle for the trip—I thought about what Bette said. Chai's sudden appearance after not seeing him for so long *had* startled me, but I needed to trust him. Right now, I needed the sense of security he brought me.

"Ready, love?" Alex was in the driver's seat, with Ralph in the back. Apparently we were all riding up together.

I nodded and stowed my suitcase into the back alongside theirs. "Ready as I'll ever be."

Alex blew a kiss to Bette. "Hold down the fort. We've got our cells. Call me if anything urgent comes up."

"You've got it, precious." As she teetered over to the building in her five inch platform boots, we pulled out of the parking space, headed to ferret out a ghost.

CHAPTER 3

Our route took us up I-5 to Mukilteo, where we would take the ferry over to Whidbey Island. From there, we'd drive up to the other end of the island to Coupeville, where we would catch another ferry to Port Townsend. There were other routes, but this seemed the most expedient. I didn't tell Alex that I'd forgotten to check out the schedule. I knew most of the Washington State ferries had late sailings, so we shouldn't have any problem.

North of Seattle, western Washington opened out a little. Oh, the forests were still there, but the land felt more like shoreline, with windswept trees and bushes. To the east of the freeway, once we were north of Seattle, a long stretch of rolling berry farms lined the road. To the west, Edmonds, a small town with a vintage feel, led into Everett, which was solidly Navy. Past Everett came Mukilteo, named after a Native American word thought to stem from the meaning "good camping ground" or—alternatively—"narrow passage." Continue north, and the road wound through Bellingham and on to the Canadian border.

I had never been up this way. Hell, I had seen very little

of Earthside. So, as Alex drove, Ralph played tour guide. The sun was long gone, even though we'd decided to take off at seven since we wanted to make it over to Port Townsend before midnight.

As we exited the freeway onto Highway 526, also known as the Boeing Freeway, Ralph leaned forward, over the back of my seat. He was a good kid—though I knew he wasn't all that young, but compared to me? He was a baby.

Ralph was lanky and lean, and he wore round, dark-tinted glasses in the style of John Lennon. Shorter than both Alex and me, he topped out at five eight at the most, and he tended to dress in cargo pants, T-shirts, and sneakers. Brilliant, he was also a genuinely nice guy. And he had a crush on me. I knew it. Bette knew I knew. Alex knew I knew. The only person who *didn't* realize I knew it was Ralph himself, and I preferred to keep it that way. Less awkward in having to turn him down if he made a move, because—as sweet as he was— Ralph was not my type.

"So, I grew up around here. I lived in Everett until I was ten and my father moved us to Seattle." He brushed back a lock of unruly black hair.

Alex flashed a quick glance over his shoulder at Ralph. "I didn't know that. When was that?"

"Oh, sixty years ago, give or take a few. The area was a lot less crowded then. My father found a job down on the docks in Seattle when he got out of the military. He was in the Army during World War Two, you know. After that, when he decided to settle down, he had to age himself up with glamour magic that he bought from a witch. That was before the humans knew we existed." He laughed softly. "I remember the first time— oh, what, five or six years ago? I remember the first day when he felt like it was safe to come out of the closet and he went to work without the makeup. The guys were spooked, but since he'd worked with them for so many years, it didn't take long before they accepted him."

Weres aged the same as humans until they hit young adulthood, and then the process slowed dramatically. The longevity factor made for some hard feelings among a few humans, but the *otherness* was far more problematic. There were hate groups actively out to kill the Weres and Fae and vampires.

I glanced back at him. "What did you do before it was safe to come out as a Were? Did you use magic to age yourself?"

He shook his head. "No. I spent the sixties doing construction and I job-hopped a lot. During the seventies, I got fascinated by the emerging computer market. I supported myself through temporary jobs while going to school. In 1989, I got hired on by Microsoft. I came out of the closet when I moved to Google in 2007. Two years back, I quit to open my own consulting company. Shortly after that I met Alex and decided it would be fun to work with him. I don't really need the money—I got in on the ground floors of both of the giants and made a killing. But I like keeping busy and I have control of the entire network."

Listening to him talk wiped away some of the geek-boy image. Ralph was a full-on professional in his field, though he still looked, and acted, like a shy college student.

We took a right, keeping on Highway 526, and shortly after, another right onto Highway 525. The highway would turn into the Mukilteo Speedway and lead us right to the ferry landing. As we sped along, the sign for the ferry lane came into view. The shoulder was dedicated to those waiting to board, and during peak times it would be filled several sailings' worth of cars, all lined up single file along the roadside.

Trees and houses buttressed the speedway, but here, homes weren't packed close together, and they didn't directly sit on the edge of the street. The two-lane road was covered in mist, slick with rain, and our headlights cut through the rolling fog like a dim laser. As the ferry lane became the "ferry traffic *only*" lane, we edged into it.

"We're almost there. Looks like we lucked out and missed the backups that happen around this time of night." Alex hadn't spoken much, but then, he wasn't a talkative guy. Ralph's nose was back into his phone or iPad or whatever it was he was doing.

"I've never been on a ferry but if it has to do with the water, you can bet I'm going to like it." I paused as the road began to slope down on a stronger gradient. Up ahead, the first traffic light we'd seen in a while glowed through the mist and rain. Just beyond it, in the distance, I could see the faint glint of water, but even more, I could *feel* it. *Open water.*

My spirits rose and I rolled down my window to breathe in the scent of brine and seaweed and decay. I could feel it in my bones, in my blood. The scent of it intoxicated me in a heady, welcome-home manner. Suddenly aware of how much I had missed this, I practically bounced in my seat like a little kid.

"You can hear her, can't you? She's singing to you." Alex glanced at me as he navigated the road. "No diving overboard when we're on the ferry, mind you. Once we reach Port Townsend, you can go out and take a swim."

"I promise." The thought that by tomorrow, I'd be out swimming in my dragon form made me so happy that right now I would have promised just about anything.

As the road sloped even further, I could see the water even through the dark of the evening. At that point, Alex turned to the right into what appeared to be a giant parking lot guarded by three toll booths. He pulled up to one that had an OPEN sign on it and smiled at the woman in the booth. "Two passengers besides me. Heading for the Clinton Ferry."

"Eighteen fifty, please." She took his credit card, swiped it, and then handed it back. "Next sailing is in fifteen minutes. Park in Lane B, please."

We eased into the lane, which was empty, parking up at the front. Lane A was full. Across the street from us was an Ivar's, and to the right of the restaurant, the Silver Cloud Inn, directly on the water's edge. To the left, beyond Lane A, was an intersection. Left of the intersection was an alehouse and what looked like another hotel. The road leading straight ahead jogged around Ivar's to lead to the ferry terminal. The ferry was in, and they were unloading the last of the cars and foot traffic from the sailing.

Alex turned off the engine. "They'll probably start boarding us in five minutes. They tend to be fairly prompt on the sailing times. There are bathrooms aboard, so unless you have to pee really bad right now, stay in the car."

"I went before we left." Ralph's nose was still buried in whatever he was reading.

I strained to catch a glimpse of the water but from here, the buildings and other cars blocked my view. "How long is the trip?"

"This run? Not very long. Fifteen minutes . . . maybe twenty. It's not as long as some of them." Alex grinned at me. "You're excited. I can tell."

"Well, yeah." I paused, then ducked my head, returning his smile. "You don't know what it's like, being a water dragon stuck in a city. At least Seattle's on Puget Sound, but I haven't gotten up the courage to find an area where I can dive in and shift form. I'm just . . . a little out of my element still. In more ways than one."

Alex nodded. His voice softened. "Well, when we get back home after this trip, I promise you, we'll find a safe place for you to swim. I know several private coves where you can probably find water deep enough." The way his voice curled around the words made me think he was offering me more than just a friendly outing.

I glanced at him sideways, trying to gauge just what to say with Ralph in the car. Flickering my eyes toward the backseat, I hoped Alex would catch my drift. "You like to swim, then?"

He held my gaze for a moment, then slowly inclined his head as though he understood my meaning. "You might say that. When I was alive, I was a fairly good swimmer. I had to learn early on. What say we talk this over later?" Again, the smooth caress of his voice over the words, and my stomach took a leap into my throat.

"I think . . . I'd like that." A shiver ran down my back as

I wondered what I was getting myself into, but my mouth seemed to have a mind of its own, and right now it was slamming the door on the CAUTION sign flashing desperately in the back of my mind.

"Good girl." Alex turned the key and started the ignition. "We're about ready to roll."

The ferry guard—I wasn't sure what his full title was—had motioned for people to start their engines. He was blocking off traffic in the street as he motioned for the cars in Lane A to file through to the ferry terminal. Before long, we joined the queue. As we drove onto the ferry, we ended up next to the edge on the lower level.

Alex turned off the ignition and motioned to the railing. "Come on. Let's take a walk around the boat. Ralph, you want to join us?"

"Nope, I've got my book." Ralph seemed oblivious, immersed in whatever was on his e-reader. Both Ralph and Alex were big readers, and while I was getting used to the format—in the Dragon Reaches, we read but for different reasons—I hadn't really connected with the concept of storytelling yet. But it was growing on me.

I opened my door and stepped out. The ferry was huge, but apparently there were bigger ones that traveled through these waters. I crossed to the side of the ferry, stepping up on the wide side step and leaning on the railing. Alex joined me.

"How many cars does this boat carry?"

"Over a hundred cars. There's an elevator to the main cabin, and bathrooms on both levels. Do you want to go up to the cabin to watch from there?" He stared out over the water as the ferry began to chug its way out into the Sound.

I thought about it, then shook my head. "I'd rather stay here. Feel the wind on my face and smell the water, you know."

The side of the ferry was low enough so that you could stand against it, leaning on the rail, and watch over the water. I stared out into the darkness, all too aware of Alex's presence beside me. But then the glint of the water shone under the lights of the boat and the gentle rocking caught me up. I loved the feeling of motion. I loved dancing, running, swimming, sex, anything that set my body to moving. The waves were so close that I could almost touch them, and the feeling of deep water—not ocean deep, but deep enough—rushed over me like a wave. As the ferry chugged across Puget Sound, I stood rapt, caught in the soothing embrace of the Water Mother's song.

My nostrils flared as I caught the scent of kelp and brine. I leaned forward, staring at the ripples of water that rolled beneath the boat, longing to spread my arms wide and dive so deep that I never needed to come up. The water was a sensuous lover, all-embracing, all-encompassing. It strengthened me and made me feel whole. Inhaling deeply, I straightened my shoulders, feeling my energy rise from the close proximity.

"Shimmer?" Alex's voice intruded, low and sultry.

I turned to find him staring at me. "Alex . . . ?" I slid my hand along the rail toward him. The air felt so thick it was like breathing vapor.

He held my gaze as he reached out to place his hand over mine, his skin cold as ice, cold as the depths, cold as river wine running down my throat on a hot summer evening. I sucked in a deep breath and shifted as a gnawing hunger began racing up through my body, between my legs, into my breasts. I let out a low growl and stepped closer as he tightened his grip around my fingers.

"Please return to your cars . . ." The voice interrupted, echoing through the loudspeakers.

Startled by the intrusion, I let out a low curse. Alex licked his lips, but then let out a faint laugh.

"Time enough, love. There will be time enough." And with that, he let go of my hand. "Come, we have to get back in the car."

Grumbling, I followed him back. As I fastened my seat belt, I took a few deep breaths to calm myself. Blue dragons aren't just emotional, we're also the most sensual of all dragons. We like sex and a lot of it, in all forms and aspects. My love life had been difficult. Being outcaste was akin to being undesirable and I'd spent a lot of time alone, not by choice. As I forced myself to relax, it hit me. I'd as good as told Alex I wanted to hook up with him.

Ralph seemed oblivious, still absorbed by the book he was reading. Alex gave me one last glance as the lights of the Clinton pier appeared. He winked at me, and I let out a sigh, but grinned in return.

As we disembarked, we drove onto what turned out to be a continuation of Highway 525 from over on the mainland, I reluctantly watched the water disappear behind us.

The town of Clinton, on Whidbey Island, was more a pit stop than anything else, and the Coupeville to Port Townsend ferry terminal was a good half hour away. It was fully dark by now, and though the rain had let up, there wasn't much to see along the way except the road in the sweep of the Range Rover's headlights. I glanced back at Ralph, who had put away his e-reader and was now staring out the window, a thoughtful look on his face.

"You okay?"

He nodded. "Full moon was night before last. I'm still feeling a mild hangover. I went out to one of the pack's sanctuaries and ran all night long."

"What pack do you belong to?" At one point, Ralph had mentioned it, but I couldn't remember right now.

"Technically, I belong to the Glacier Peak pack, although my family belongs to an urban offshoot. But most of my relatives belong to the GPs. Our sanctuary is near Monroe, and we welcome werewolves from a number of different clans. The only rules are: One, you respect others, and two, the Glacier Peak pack makes the rules." He let out a sigh.

"I expected werewolves to be more . . . insular." From what I'd heard, werewolf clans were usually up there with dragons for hierarchy and kowtowing.

He shrugged. "We're different—at least my family's subgroup—in that we've broken a lot of traditional mores for werewolves. We have an alpha, yes, but women have full status in our pack, and we are making use of technology to keep track of our members. We also have a strong internal behavioral monitoring program to keep an eye out for troublemakers, and we get them into therapy when it's deemed likely they can be helped."

"The modern world of humans has certainly shifted things for all of us." I leaned back against the headrest. "Alex, what about the vampires? I never thought to ask if you're aligned with anybody."

"Well, the big chief around here is Roman. He's Blood Wyne's son—she's the vampire queen, if you didn't know that. And Blood Wyne is determined that vamps make inroads into being accepted in society. The Seattle Vampire Nexus is all about streamlining vampire-human relations. I finally joined even though I didn't want to. Menolly D'Artigo knew about me, and she's Roman's consort, although I think it's more of a business arrangement than anything. She's married to some werepuma. But if Roman discovered I was running a business without his official authority, I could be subject to expulsion from the area, so I caved and applied for a license. We're all legal now."

He sounded slightly disgusted. "I agree we need to learn how to coexist, but I'm not so sure how some humans are going to feel about this as time goes by. It's one thing when we're like the circus sideshow acts. Quite another when we buy the house next door and set up shop in the town square."

"Yeah, that's why dragons aren't so out and about. It's one thing to know your next door neighbor is a werewolf . . . quite another to discover you're landlord to a dragon who could not only destroy the entire apartment building but eat everybody in it." I was smart enough to keep my nature under wraps unless I knew I could trust someone. Stacy was used to Supes; she wasn't threatened. On the other hand, there were enough hate groups around to make us all wary, and they weren't silent in their opposition to our existence.

We were still debating whether the world was ready for

dragons when we arrived at the ferry terminal. But the line was huge—stretching back far along the road.

Alex frowned. "You sure that we're good to go? Did we just miss the boat? There's a lot of cars lined up here."

Uh-oh. Time to confess. "I have to admit, I forgot to check on the sailing times for this ferry, but I figured they'd still have a few this time of night, with commuters and all."

Alex gave me a long look. "And you didn't think to say anything before we got here?"

"I'm sorry, okay? Look, there's one of the ferry guards coming along now."

A woman dressed in a uniform, sporting a Washington State Department of Transportation badge, was walking up to the driver's window. Alex rolled it down.

"Good evening, love. Are we in time for the next sailing?" He smiled pleasantly, and I noticed his fangs were retracted.

She nodded at him—and us—and said, "That depends. Do you have a reservation?"

"Reservation?" Alex didn't sound so happy now. "We need a *reservation* for a ferry trip?"

She shrugged. "I'm sorry, but we always recommend reservations on this run. We run an average of eighty-five percent booked, and the remaining slots, if any, are first come, first served. I can guarantee you that you won't make this sailing, or even the next two. They're booked solid and the overflow from the waiting line here will fill them both up before you get near the boat. You *might* make the last sailing if you stay in line."

I wanted to slide under my seat. How could I have made such a stupid mistake?

Alex cleared his throat. "You're sure? We need to make it to Port Townsend tonight."

She nodded. "You can wait, but it might be quicker if you return to Mukilteo, drive down to Edmonds, then take the ferry over to Kingston. You can drive up to Port Townsend from there. At the worst, you'll probably get there at the same time as you would if you just parked here and waited."

Alex thanked her and rolled up his window. He turned to me. "Shimmer . . ."

I blushed again. "I'm sorry! I screwed up. I admit it, but there's not much I can do about it now."

"Of all the idiotic . . ." He let out a low growl, but it wasn't really a threat—I had heard him use it often enough when dealing with Glenda.

I let out a snort. "Oh, stuff it. You could have checked yourself."

"Check myself? All right, love, but remember, it was your idea." Again, the smart-assed grin and he reached for his crotch, stopping as I swatted at his hand.

"Stop that!"

He laughed.

I shook my head. "Fine, fine, it's all my fault. So, what do you want to do? Stay here or backtrack?"

He glanced back at Ralph, who was wisely keeping out of it. "What do you think?"

"Not my call—I'm just along for the ride." Ralph kept up his stance as Switzerland.

"All right, then. I don't feel like twiddling my thumbs on a *possible* chance of getting aboard a ferry tonight, so we're going to go back to Edmonds and take the ferry to Kingston like she suggested."

As he pulled out of the waiting line and we headed back the way we'd come, I decided to join Ralph for a strategic game of keep-my-mouth-shut. While Alex didn't seem all that angry, he definitely wasn't amused and given the shift between us, I figured silence was golden.

N ot quite two hours later, we were in Edmonds, look-ing for the ferry terminal. Numerous construction proj-ects and roadwork signs led us on a merry chase, but Ralph managed to navigate us around the chaos thanks to his GPS, and we lucked out by pulling into the terminal just in time to drive right onto the ferry. No waiting.

Ferry ride, take three.

By then, it was ten thirty. Thank gods the ferries ran late, I thought. Or I'd really have mucked things up. The ride was a little longer than the earlier one, and once again, I stood out on the deck in the chill night, which was misting lightly. The pull was stronger now that the wind and rain had picked up. It quickened my blood and made me long to change shape.

Suddenly, I was aware that, once again, Alex was standing by my side. This time, however, the sparks between us kept themselves at bay.

He leaned on the railing and stared at the water. "Pretty, isn't it?"

"Yeah. It's my element. My essence." I turned to him. "Listen, I'm sorry I didn't check the schedule." I didn't like mucking things up. All my life, I had learned that you screw up—you lose.

Alex shrugged. "Eh, it happens. Just a simple mix-up in the scheme of things. But next time, make certain you do the work. This time? It doesn't really matter. We'll be there late, but we'll get there. But . . . when others are counting on you to come through, forgetting your assignments can lead to disaster. You've never really had a job where you were part of a team, have you?" He glanced sideways at me.

"Teamwork? When you're an outcaste? Not so much. At the Lost and Foundling, it was every dragonette for herself. Survival depended on trusting yourself and only yourself. The wardens didn't care whether we lived or died, to be honest. They trained us, but if we fucked up, it was on our heads. And if you trusted somebody, chances were they'd double-cross you because the ones who did the best got the most food and the fewest beatings. Once I was on my own . . . I walked away and didn't look back. I've never had to learn how to work with anybody before." I shivered, remembering those hardscrabble days. "I swore nobody would ever get a leg up on me if I could help it. I guess . . . I'm used to fending for myself. I won't fail you again."

"You'll pick it up. Just remember: Do the work and when you need help, ask. When you screw up, tell me first thing. Everything will be all right." He reached out to gently wipe the rain—which was now slashing down against us—out of my eyes. Grateful for his understanding, I leaned my cheek against his palm and he traced his fingers down my cheek. "We'll be pulling into the dock soon. From there, it's a hop, skip, and a jump up to Port Townsend." But as he turned, he paused.

I had the feeling he wanted to say something else. "What is it?"

"Just this. The Olympic Peninsula is home to a lot of spirits. Not all of them are ghosts. Dragon or not, you don't want to be running around without somebody with you. Don't wander off alone when we get there. Take Ralph with you if it's daytime, and me when it's night. Trust me, it's not a place you want to tangle with. The forest is ancient, and very much alive."

As he spoke, it was as if I could feel the presence of the approaching land descend around us. I looked up to see that we were pulling into the terminal. And right then, an overwhelming feeling of *otherness* hit me. Alex was right, this was not a place to get lost from the pack, as Ralph would say. Because even if you were the odd person out, I had the distinct feeling that you wouldn't ever be alone. And right then, I knew that some of the beasties out there had a razor's edge to them—sharp, shiny, and waiting to slice open a vein.

CHAPTER 4

The drive up the inner side of the peninsula left me breath-less, even in the dark. Ralph was feeling it, too. He let out a noise suspiciously like a whine as he pressed his nose against the window. As we pulled away from the dock and onto High-way 104, the energy settled in, and the moment we passed the cross street of Lindvog Road, a brooding sense of watchfulness took over.

Alex seemed immune, but still, he totally focused in on driving, as if he was trying to tune out anything that might be a distraction. Ralph, however, shifted pensively in the backseat. He'd stowed his phone and iPad and silently stared out the window. I turned to watch the trees passing by. Now and then, there would be a spate of houses—usually on large lots or acreage—between the stands of forest.

"Watch for the junction, please. This road will turn into 307, and Highway 104 will turn to the right. We need to take that fork, or our drive is going to be a whole lot longer." Alex flipped the windshield wipers to high.

I peered out the window, but by the time I saw the sign leading to the turnoff, so had Alex. We swung right on the easy, broad curve and once again found ourselves on a two-lane road. Before long, I could see the glint of the port coming in from between the heavy tree line, especially in the areas that houses hugged the waterline. Then we were deep into the woods again. The farther along we went, the more I sensed something watching us. It didn't feel specifically focused—it wasn't watching us because of who we were . . . but because we were moving through its territory. Uncomfortable, I shifted in my seat.

Ralph leaned forward. "I have to take a leak, Alex."

I groaned. "You can't hold it?"

"Not unless Alex wants the backseat to have a wet spot."

Alex grumbled but motioned ahead. "There's a turnoff up ahead where we can park. The bushes will have to make do for now." He swerved to the right, coming to park against a broken rusty gate attempting to barricade a trail leading down to what I assumed was the port.

Ralph leaped out of the car and headed for the nearest pile of brush.

Alex turned to me and grinned. "Hope the boy doesn't get himself stuck in a pile of stinging nettles. Welts like that could ruin his fun for a while to come."

I snickered. "Yeah, it really could." Shading my eyes with my hand, I stared at the faint gleam of water coming through the trees. If I hadn't been dragon, I might not have been able to catch the shimmer, but the water was so near I could taste it on my tongue. "Mind if I walk down there for a moment? I won't be long."

Alex muttered something under his breath, but then motioned for me to get out of the car. "Go on, but don't be long and don't go off the path. And watch out. As I said, there are creatures in these woods . . . creatures that don't like intruders of any kind."

I slipped away from the car, softly shutting the door behind me. As I headed around the broken gate, I could hear Ralph finishing up his business behind a bush. A moment later, he was walking beside me.

"Mind if I come along?" He shivered, pulling his Windbreaker tighter against the blowing rain and wind.

"Sure." Actually, I was glad for the company. I wasn't really afraid—after all, *dragon*. Not so much can hurt us. But Alex's warning stuck in my head and my ego wasn't so big to think that I was invulnerable. Especially in human form, and especially since I could only change into my dragon form underwater.

The path wasn't all that long. We broke out of the tree line to find ourselves on an open stretch of land. The trail led to an embankment overlooking the water. It was hard to estimate how far down it was, but I decided it wasn't a good idea to attempt a recon mission. As we stood there, I glanced over at a thicket of trees.

"Can you feel them? Something's watching us."

"Yeah, I've felt them since we started. I don't know what they are—not Supes in the sense of you, or me. They feel almost . . . alien. Also, there are a lot of ghosts. Did you know that Port Gamble is the most haunted city in Washington State? We're almost there." He shifted from one foot to the other. For a were-wolf, he really was fidgety. "Shimmer, Earthside is a lot different than your home. I think . . . in the Dragon Reaches, you expect things to be a certain way because they've always been that way. But here, there are so many variables. Never take anything for granted here. And don't take anything at face value." He punctuated his warning with a smile, but it still felt like a warning.

I exhaled slowly, realizing that I'd been holding my breath for the past couple minutes. The skin on my arms had puckered into goose bumps, and the hair was standing up on the back of my neck. "What do you think lives out here?"

He shrugged. "Out on the peninsula? Old things . . . older than me—older than even you. Bigfoot lives here—Sasquatch. He's not from this planet, at least that's what a lot of Supes believe. And he's dangerous if you get too close. But there are things that make even Bigfoot look like your best buddy. When we're hanging around Port Townsend? It's best if you don't engage the local entities too much. We don't want them pinning a target on your back." And with that, he turned on his heel and headed back to the car.

I jogged to catch up to him, thrusting my hands in my

pockets. My breath came out in little white puffs thanks to the cold. "Ralph . . . what's the real reason Alex and Patrick had a falling-out? I think I know Alex well enough by now to figure out it wasn't over a thousand bucks."

Ralph glanced at me, then stopped before we were within earshot of the car. "I'm not positive, but Bette told me that Alex and Patrick were like brothers. Patrick was still alive at the time, and Alex liked him a lot. Then Patrick got sick and asked Alex to turn him into a vampire. Alex refused. He didn't want to be responsible. Patrick broke off the friendship and apparently found another vamp to help him."

"Sick . . . as in . . ."

"Sick as in terminal. Patrick didn't want to die, and he wanted to be turned before he wasted away. Bette says he was diagnosed with aplastic anemia. They aren't sure what triggered it—this was a long time ago. But he was dying." Ralph glanced at the woods. "We're being watched very carefully."

"I know, I can feel it." I could also hear the sounds of something moving around in the bushes. Whatever it was, was incredibly quiet. If I'd been human, I might not have noticed the noise. But the creep factor was incredibly high and I realized that I was shivering. "Here's a thought: Let's get back to the car and lock the doors."

"I like that thought." Ralph started to jog again, and I followed. A moment later, we came to the gate and hurried to the Range Rover. I slammed my door, locking it, and reached for my seat belt with a sigh of relief.

Alex searched my face. "You find out what you wanted to find out?" He turned the ignition key and we eased back onto the rain-soaked road.

I gazed out into the dark night. "Mostly, I guess." But inside, I realized that I wasn't even sure what it was I'd been searching for.

Before long, the forest opened out and we could see houses to the left and the port to the right. In the daylight, it was probably lovely. At night, there was a definite small-town weirdness factor. From what I could tell, the houses were historical in look. Most were probably as old as they appeared to be. I'd have to see them in the daytime to know for sure, but from what I could tell, they seemed to be kept up to snuff with almost fanatical attention.

As we slowed to match the speed limit of the town, I realized that I was seeing wispy figures along the roadside—every now and then one would pass by us.

"Is anybody else seeing—" I paused, not wanting to sound like a fruitcake.

"People in the mist? Yeah." Ralph was breathing heavier, and he leaned against the window as we came to what appeared to be the center of town. Not much farther, the land would end at the water's edge, but before we reached the shore, Highway 104 turned west and we curved with it. Another few minutes and we'd passed through what there was of the tiny city, and were back into woodland.

I turned to Alex. "How much longer before we reach Port Townsend?"

"We'll be coming to the Hood Canal Bridge in just a couple of minutes, and once we cross that—another half hour. Maybe forty minutes, given the rain."

I grimaced. "I really botched things with the ferry over in Coupeville. I'm sorry."

Ralph pulled out his iPad. A moment later, he said, "Not really. Even *I* didn't know you need reservations on it, and obviously, neither did Alex. From what it says here on the Washington State Ferries app, the next sailing that we'd even have a chance of making would have been the last one. The stats here say it was full. So if we had waited, we'd still have had to turn around and come this route."

I flashed him a grateful smile and he winked at me.

Alex noticed the interplay because he let out a chuckle. "Could have been worse, love. As it is, we'll reach the High Tide B and B before midnight, so no harm, no foul. It's not like Patrick's waiting on us so he can go to bed. At least not till sunrise."

The Hood Canal Bridge, like the 520 over Lake Washington,

was another floating bridge. Western Washington seemed to make good use of the pontoon bridges and had at least two of the world's longest.

"You do realize this bridge went down in 1979?" Alex grinned as Ralph let out a grumble.

"Wonderful. And yes, I just try to forget it. At least, if history repeated itself tonight, Shimmer would be fine. She could just shift and come up on the shore with no problem. I, on the other hand, am not quite so fond of swimming, especially in frigid temperatures."

"That's okay, Ralph. I'd save you." I was beginning to realize just how much Alex enjoyed teasing his staff, though I'd never seen him be cruel about it. In fact, if I was honest with myself, he got on my nerves mostly because I hadn't wanted to admit my attraction to him. The vampire had a wicked sense of humor and enjoyed using it.

Ralph, on the other hand, was staring suspiciously out the window at the water.

The bridge felt narrow as it stretched into the darkness. Even the streetlights that illuminated the roadway could barely pierce the fog that had risen to wash across the area. It only took us a few minutes to cross the span, which stretched out farther than a mile, but it felt like longer. But then we were on the other side and headed up the interior of the peninsula, and once again, the sense of being watched rested heavily on my shoulders. I distracted myself as much as I could, and finally, half an hour later, we entered the town of Port Townsend.

As we eased into the town, Alex plugged Patrick's address into the GPS he had his Range Rover retrofitted with. "He lives on W Street, right across from the front of Fort Warden State Park."

I had done a little reading on Port Townsend, enough to know that the old military fort had been turned into a state park. It sounded like a beautiful place, with access to the beaches where I could take a dive in and swim out enough to shift into my dragon self. I'd have to go at night or early in the morning, to avoid attention, but I was determined that I wouldn't let this opportunity pass me by.

Now that we were in the town, I realized I was actually excited. I'd been stuck in the city for months and this was the first time I'd had the chance to see any place over Earthside other than the Seattle area. The forest had been gorgeous. Spooky as hell, but gorgeous. The Dragon Reaches—even the temperate climes of the greens, and the jungles of the red dragons—had a far different feel. They were more open, and far fewer spirits had ever passed through them.

I leaned forward, examining the houses as we passed by them. Most were dark. By now, it was nearing eleven thirty, but in some of the homes, lights still shone and I could make out that a number of the houses were Victorian in style.

Walnut Street, which paralleled the water, curved to the left and turned into W Street. To the left were houses; to the right, the street bordered the park. We passed Redwood Street, then Ash, and then Alex swung into a driveway. A hand-carved sign that looked both rustic and artistic at the same time read WELCOME TO THE HIGH TIDE BED & BREAKFAST.

As we stepped out of the car, the front door opened and a man came out to stand on the porch. His eyes had a faint, pale shine to them. *Vampire.*

Ralph hauled his backpack and rolling suitcase out of the back of the Range Rover, then lifted mine out for me. I thanked him and picked it up. Though I wasn't anywhere near as strong as I was in dragon form, I could more than hold my own in a fight. Lifting a fifty-pound suitcase? I didn't even blink.

We followed Alex up to the door where he and Patrick—I assumed it was Patrick—stood, facing each other. After a moment, Patrick gave him a broad smile, fangs and all, and held out his arms.

"All water under the bridge?" Alex asked, sounding cautious.

Patrick nodded. "Blood under the bridge, more like it. I let it go a long time ago, bro. And I get why you refused. I understand now." He flashed Alex a war-weary smile. "I've had to say no . . . when I desperately wished I could say yes."

Alex moved in then and gave him a guy-hug. The *pound-the-back-but-make-no-mistake-we're-being-manly* type of hug.

Patrick opened the door. "Please, enter, Alex—and your friends."

His invitation was a courtesy only. Vampires could enter other vampire domains without an invitation, unlike houses belonging to the living, and they could enter domiciles such as apartments and condo towers and frat or sorority houses. So, even though Patrick hadn't officially opened as a business yet, and the house was still a private domain, since it belonged to a vampire Alex could come and go as he liked.

The house was typically Victorian on the outside—huge and at least three stories high. Inside, however, it had been completely renovated. Instead of choppy little rooms, most of the downstairs had been opened up into one giant room that felt spacious and welcoming.

Seating areas had been arranged so there were several intimate groupings, and yet there was room to create a semicircle of chairs for a larger gathering. The dining table was obviously custom made. An extra-long picnic table—only far less rustic—it had long benches on either side. The table could easily sit fourteen. The benches had been cushioned, just enough to keep the polished wood from being too hard on the backside.

I set down my suitcase and looked around. It was gorgeous, but as I stood there, I began to sense something odd in the room, and whatever it was didn't make me feel very welcome.

"Let me take you to your bedrooms. Then we can talk and I'll fix you something to eat." Patrick turned to Ralph and me. He had a slick, fun feel to him, and I could easily see how he and Alex had hung out together. Patrick wasn't as rugged as Alex, but he definitely had an edge. I suspected he'd had it before he was turned.

Wearing leather pants and a smooth V-neck T-shirt that was a deep cobalt blue, Patrick had shoulder-length curly brown hair and full lips. His eyes shifted toward the blue spectrum, but I suspected they'd originally been brown. Vampires' eyes always changed to frosty gray and silver over time—the cooler the color, the longer the time as a vamp. And their skin color, even if darker to begin with, faded. It would never fully fade if the vampire had been a person of color before they were turned, but if they'd been Caucasian? Over time, they would become albino. As I studied his looks, I realized that Patrick was pretty hot. He reminded me of a European rock star.

As I passed by him on my way to the staircase, he leaned close and let out a little purr. "I'm so glad you could come with Alex."

I glanced at him, startled. He was hot, all right, and he knew it. I wasn't immune to vampire glamour, that much I knew from experience.

"You're a lovely one. How did you happen to start working for good old Alex?" Patrick's voice was all golden honey, suggesting so much with so few words.

Alex quickly intervened, his voice just on the edge of growly. "Shimmer, meet Patrick. Patrick, back off. Shimmer is . . . she's my associate as well as a blue dragon. She could eat you for dinner without blinking. And I'm not talking about your dick, so get your mind out of your pants."

Patrick laughed, just a little edgy. "So she's yours, is she? No worries. Hands off."

Behind me, Ralph shifted uncomfortably. I decided the best tactic was to ignore the testosterone war and be congenial, but play it cool.

"Alex took me on as a project for the Wing-Liege." I shrugged. "Apparently, in the Dragon Reaches, I'm considered persona non grata so they sent me Earthside. Basically, I'm indentured to Alex for five years. So when the boss says jump . . ."

"You jump." Patrick eased over the words. He glanced over at Alex and I had the feeling something had passed between them. A scuffle or something, but then it vanished and, once again, we were headed up the stairs.

Ralph and I were given the rooms on the third floor.

"I still have to furnish the second floor," Patrick said. "Or rather, re-furnish it. I'll tell you more about that later."

The rooms were spacious. By their size, it was obvious a few walls had been knocked down in order to turn what must have been four bedrooms into two suites. Each room had its own bathroom, and the view from my window overlooked Fort Worden State Park.

"Put your things away and then join us downstairs. We'll be in my office or the kitchen. The office is off the hall that leads from the great room back to the kitchen and laundry. Meanwhile, I'll show Alex to his room—the basement has been fully renovated for my guests who require . . . less sunlight." Patrick motioned to Alex and they headed downstairs.

After the two disappeared from sight, I glanced over at Ralph, who sagged against the door. "What do you think of him?" I kept my voice low, just in case Patrick's hearing was extra-sensitive.

Ralph shrugged. "You know, I think he's trustworthy, if a little sleazy. Well, as much as you can get with any vampire. Alex is the only vamp I'd ever really trust. But then again, their kind and my kind have never gotten along very well. I'm not sure where the old feuds began, but you have to bet it was probably over something stupid."

I nodded. I was rapidly becoming aware of an entire subset of interactions that I'd never considered before. Supes didn't figure into the Dragon Reaches any more than humans did.

"When I really think it over, I really have lived an insular life. Up in the Dragon Reaches there aren't many other creatures. Oh, cattle, and wild animals, and some of the Northlands folks made their way into our realm and settled there. But I'm beginning to realize that, as a rule, my kind don't play well with others, let alone with each other. Teamwork isn't a concept we come by naturally."

Ralph moved to return to his room, but then paused. "I know the circumstances are less than ideal, but Shimmer . . . do you regret being here? Earthside, I mean."

I had to think about the answer to that one, because even

though I opened my mouth to say *Of course*, I realized that wasn't exactly true. I genuinely liked Bette and Ralph, and my relationship with Alex . . . well, that was on a swiftly evolving escalator. And then, there was Stacy.

"No, I'm beginning to think this isn't so bad. Ralph, my life in the Dragon Reaches wasn't the same as other dragons have. I think most dragons would kick and scream before letting themselves be sent over Earthside. It's rare to meet one who likes interacting with humans—the nature of the beast, you might say."

I felt like I was running around and around the subject, but it really wasn't an easy question. I was fighting a lifetime of training. I had been expected to have the same perspective as the rest of my people, while still accepting their disdain for me.

"I'm going to jump out on a limb here and say I think this might be good for me. I don't want to treat others the way I was treated back there, and so I want to lose what prejudices I had . . . or at least be forced to question them. How's that for an answer?"

Ralph patiently listened, then jerked his head toward his room. "I get it. Okay then, I'm going to put away my clothes, then I'll meet you downstairs." He shut the door behind him as he left.

As I heaved my suitcase up on my bed, I hoped that I hadn't sounded insulting. But Ralph hadn't given me an indication that I'd said anything offensive. I opened the top dresser drawer and unzipped my suitcase. As I began to lay out my clothes, a noise startled me—like something slamming—and I turned around. The drawer was shut.

I stared at the dresser. This time I suspected that it wasn't Chai announcing himself. "Okay . . . let's try this again." I opened the drawer. As I turned back to get my shirts, a scraping sound echoed through the room. I whirled around. The drawer was shut.

"Can you please not do that?" I had no clue who I was talking to, but I wasn't in the mood for games. "I'm staying in the room, I'm here . . . deal with it."

Normally, I knew it wasn't wise to be surly with ghosts, but we'd had a long ride, I still felt guilty over the ferry incident, and I wasn't in the mood to argue. I yanked open the drawer and stood back, staring at it. *Nothing.*

Still keeping my eyes on the drawer, I leaned around to once again pick up my shirts, then thrust them toward the opening. As I dropped them in, the dresser drawer slammed shut, catching the hem of one tank top as it closed. If my hand had been any closer, it would have smashed my fingers. Well, if I were human it would have smashed them. But dragon or not, it still would have hurt.

"Well, thank you ever so much. That's rude, you know. Now knock it off." I was feeling less inclined toward being polite as this little game went on.

The drawer opened again, and my clothes came flying out to land at my feet. I picked them up and put them back in my suitcase and zipped it closed, leaving it on the bed. I made sure my iPad and anything else that I didn't want broken was in my tote bag.

"If that's the way you want to play it," I whispered to whoever might be listening. "I can play this game, too. But you may not like the end result." And, with that, I slung my tote bag over my shoulder and headed downstairs to ask Patrick who the hell his freakshow ghost was.

CHAPTER 5

"**W**ho's the jerk trying to drive away your guests?" As I entered the kitchen, I saw that Ralph had made it down before me. He was sitting there, pancakes and sausage on his plate. Alex was relaxing with a bottle of blood— the microbottlers who provided bottled blood made sure the glass was dark enough so that the color didn't show through. In fact, it was hard to tell there was liquid in there at all.

Patrick dished up another plate and handed it to me, motioning for me to sit down by Ralph. The table was tucked into the kitchen nook. The window behind the table overlooked what I assumed was the backyard. I glanced up at the clock. It was twelve fifteen. A little past the Witching Hour.

"I take it you met one of our resident problems?" Patrick frowned and took his seat again.

"If by that, you mean the joker who didn't want me to put away my clothes and kept slamming the dresser drawer shut, yes. If I had been a little slower, I would have had some pretty damned bloody knuckles, if not worse." I stabbed a sausage and bit the end off it.

Patrick froze. "Yeah. One of my problem children, all

right. Well, I was hoping you guys would actually find something rather than having to just go on my word, so I guess I can put *that* worry to bed."

Ralph pulled out his iPad. "Mind if I record the conversation? It's easier than trying to take notes, and this way we won't miss anything you're saying."

"Sounds good to me, but I warn you—more than one phone conversation has been messed with, so you may just want to take some actual notes regardless. I'm not sure I can guarantee that whoever—*whatever*—it is will be so kind as to leave the recording alone." Patrick shook his head, looking grumpy.

Alex pulled out a notebook and pen. He was such a high-tech-gadget kind of guy that it told me he was taking what Patrick said seriously. "History first. When did you buy the house?

"Like I told you on the phone, a couple years ago. It belonged to a friend of mine named Nathan Strand. He died about ten years back, and his family decided to sell the house, so I bought it. I always thought it would make a nice little B and B, but I didn't get around to doing anything with it till late last year."

Ralph glance around at the kitchen. "Did you live here in the meantime?"

"No, I was wrapping up another business I had going and wanted to phase out. I basically hired a housekeeper to come over once a week to keep things tidy until I could make time for renovations. I also wanted to sell my condo first. I haven't been a vampire all that long, comparatively, so I haven't built up the wealth some of them do."

Alex let out a snort. "Some never do. Not all vamps are rich. I do fine by my business, and have accumulated a fair amount, but it's not a given."

"Yeah, I've come to realize that." Patrick shifted in his seat and rested his right ankle on his left thigh. "Anyway, Nathan died and I bought the house from his family."

"What did Nathan die of?" I asked. It seemed likely to me that the previous owner would be our first possible suspect in the haunting.

Patrick frowned. "I'm not sure, to be honest. His family said that he wasn't well at the end—he was losing weight, and unable to eat. I'll have to dig out the information."

Ralph was arranging a bunch of gadgets on the table. I recognized them as the ghost-hunting equipment. "We're going to set up sensors and cameras around the area. Shimmer has already seen evidence of ghostly activity, but we need to get a clear idea of what we're dealing with."

"Did Nathan ever tell you his house was haunted? Could this have started before you owned the house? It appears to be a historical place; maybe it came pre . . . ghosted?" I was still new to knowing what questions to ask, but I was trying to learn.

Patrick took another sip of his blood. "He never said anything, but then Nathan wasn't a man who believed in ghosts. While I believe this current bout of phenomena started after renovations began, the truth is I don't know. Since nobody was living here, I have no clue as to what might have been going on."

Alex motioned to me. "Shimmer, in the morning, you and Ralph check around town to see if you can find out anything about the house's history. Patrick, do you have the original blueprints for the house? And how extensive were the renovations you made?"

"Yes, I do—in my office. The renovations were substantial. We knocked out a lot of walls, steamed off all the old wallpaper so we could paint. I updated the kitchen and bathrooms and the entire second and third floors. The basement had been fairly small and unfinished, so I had the contractors expand it. We built what amounts to another entirely new floor plan down there. It took the men I hired over three months and they worked at a good clip. And that brings me to another item. Robbie and his men complained quite a bit about the house. They kept saying strange things were happening as they worked."

"What about a local witch or necromancer? You know of any? We might need her services, if you do. Ghosts that make nuisances of themselves usually aren't willing to leave.

We may need someone who can come in and perform an exorcism." Alex took a long pull from his bottle, then wiped his mouth with a napkin. He might be rough-and-tumble but I couldn't fault his manners.

Patrick nodded. "Yes, Tonya Harris. I have her card in my office. I'll be right back."

As he left the room, I dug into my pancakes. They were light and fluffy, and thoroughly delicious. It was easy to see how Patrick would be able to keep all his guests happy, both the bloodsuckers and those still living. Ralph was fidgeting with the monitoring devices, calibrating them he said, and Alex was making notes, when a loud clanging echoed through the room as the skillet flew off the stove, scattering grease everywhere as it sailed past Alex, missing him by a couple of inches.

Alex jumped, his pen and notepad flying. Ralph blinked and looked back at the stove. I set down my fork, distinctly unhappy that pancake time was over.

"What the hell?" Alex headed toward the stove as Ralph punched a couple buttons and held up what looked like something from the pages of the Techno-Geek catalog. It made me think of a sophisticated toy, actually, but it was blinking with an orange light and making some sort of noise, and I had the feeling that it wasn't just a cosplay prop.

"Alex . . . there's something in the room with us." Ralph pushed his glasses back on his nose. "And whatever it is, it's just the tip of the iceberg." His voice sped up as he stood. "Look at this—the reading is off the charts. I know we've seen some funky things in the Greenbelt Park District—that's the most haunted area in Seattle—but this is bigger."

Alex was at the stove, examining the burners. He tore off a couple paper towels while he was at it and began to wipe up the grease that had spilled all over the floor. Meanwhile, I gingerly picked up the skillet and carried it, along with my plate, to the sink. I followed Alex's lead and helped him clean up the trail of grease that had splattered out of the pan as it went flying above his head.

"What's going on?" Patrick entered the kitchen, business card in hand.

"Your ghost decided to take a swipe at me with the sausage pan. Made a mess with the grease and nearly bludgeoned me, it did." Alex tossed the paper towels. He returned to the table. "Let's get back to business, shall we? And if that's your witch's name, give it to Shimmer. Shimmer, please contact her in the morning, as well as looking into the history of the house. Ralph, I want this place *wired*. We need to find out where the strongest energy is emanating from—that's probably where the ghost is anchored."

Patrick handed the card to me. I glanced at it. Apparently, Tonya Harris owned a witchcraft shop in the Town's End Mini-Mall on Kearney street.

"Human, Fae, or other?"

"Human, but a damn sight more powerful than most. I dated her mother years ago, before I decided that I was better off with someone less . . . volatile. The Harris women are not known for their good natures, but they're good at whatever they choose to do, and Tonya is a top-notch business-woman and witch." Patrick crossed his arms, staring at the stove, looking as though he were debating what to say next. Finally, he picked up a sponge and began to wash down the range.

"The ghostly activity is picking up," he said, his face grim. "I haven't officially opened for business yet because, the two times I was about ready, something happened to stop me. One of the bay windows shattered . . . from the *inside*. A vase went sailing through it. I'd just gotten the window replaced and was about to open up the next day when I came upstairs to find a pool of blood on the ground and the mattresses on the second floor were shredded. Remember I told you that I needed to re-furnish the rooms on the second floor? It's because the ghost tore up the joint. That's why Ralph and Shimmer are staying on the third story. The rooms on the second are a mess."

Alex jotted down notes as fast as he could write. "Patrick,

I don't remember you being scared of much, but right now you look about ready to jump out of your skin. And when a vampire is frightened, you know there's a problem."

"I was scared of dying, but that's about it. You're right, though. I keep thinking . . . what if the ghost decides to slam a stake through my heart during the day? Or worse, what if I open up to guests and something happens to one of them? Then I'm not only legally liable for their injuries but morally liable for them as well. I don't know what to do."

Closing the notebook, Alex tucked it back in his pocket and nodded. "We'll do our best to find out what's happening and get a handle on it. I think we're ready for you to show us the rest of the house. Let's start where you first began renovations."

Ralph handed me one of the gadgets. "This is a thermomagnetic resonating unit. TRU for short. See this gauge? It tells you what the temperature is, and what it was two minutes ago, and ten minutes ago. That way you can see when it begins to fluctuate. This readout monitors how many degrees the temperature dropped or spiked, down to one-tenth of a degree. And this one? Tells you how quickly it happened." As he pointed out the various functions, Ralph's eyes sparkled. He was so at home with his geek self that it made me smile to see.

I nodded. "Do I have to write down anything? Or does it keep a record?"

"It's a wireless device, and it feeds into the software on my laptop, so as long as my laptop is on and I've got the program running, it will download the information that it's extracting. It also has a USB port which allows me to download the stored information if my laptop is off at the time." He turned to Alex. "And you, please carry the EVP recorder. We'll see if we catch any audible components to the haunting. I'll carry the full-spectrum camcorder and see if there's anything to record."

It all felt very *Ghostbusters* to me, but then again, *knowing* we were dealing with a ghost didn't ensure that we had all the information needed to handle the situation. So the gadgets and toys could only help us. I tried to remember what Alex had drilled into my head over the past few months: We could never have too much information on a case.

Patrick led us down to the basement. "We started renovations here, because excavating so much room in the basement was the biggest job. We had to shore up the foundation, repair it in several areas, and then expand and finish the entire basement. I needed an area large enough in which to house several rooms offering secure protection to guests from the undead set. I also decided to build my bedroom suite down here. There are four bedrooms including mine. Each is reinforced with steel doors that lock from the inside. I have the master key and I keep that with me at all times. The walls are faux stonework, and while not fireproof, they offer protection from the vampire-slayer-wannabes."

The basement had a luxe feel—the marble tile and gleaming white walls brought a sensation of light and air in, even though there were no windows. The lights mimicked daylight without the harmful effect sunshine had on vampires. Central to the four bedrooms, a seating area offered guests a chance to sit and read. A desk nearby held a computer and printer, and a big-screen TV covered one wall.

"My vampire guests can retreat here without feeling trapped in their rooms, which is important when it's nearing. The television has both DVR and DVD, and the computer is for guests to use. I thought of everything." Patrick frowned, sounding so defeated that I felt sorry for him.

Ralph looked around and whistled. "Impressive."

"Thanks." Patrick glanced around. "This took a massive amount of planning. I just want to make a go of this."

Alex clapped him on the back. "We'll do our best to help. Now show us where you started the reno."

"Over here—in this corner." Patrick led us over to the bedroom door closest to the back of the house. "Right here, where the edge of this door is? This was the original wall of the basement. We dug the rest of the way back, shoring up the foundation and creating load-bearing walls as we went."

"Can we see the blueprints for what the house originally looked like?" Ralph cleared some of the magazines off the desk to make room.

Patrick headed for the stairs. "Sure. I'll go get them. Alex, why not show them your room?"

Alex led us over to the closest door on the right. "Here, take a look. I have to say, Patrick thought of everything." The rooms were small, but tidy, and not only were they behind reinforced steel doors, but the bed itself was in a stone base—like a sarcophagus, with a comfortable and rather large mattress inside. The top was bulletproof and shatterproof glass, providing a difficult task for anybody seeking to get through to the vampire inside when they were asleep. Alex showed us the hidden emergency trip wire to open the luxury tomb if necessary. These rooms provided a tidy amount of security, as much as any public resting place could be safe for vamps.

"I'm really impressed by the level of workmanship that went into this rebuild," Ralph said.

"That's right, you said you put yourself through school while working in construction." I glanced around. The rest of the room made a tidy use of space—with a mini-fridge (which I assumed would contain bottles of blood), a microwave, a recliner, and a wardrobe. There was no mirror, which made total sense—vampires can't cast a reflection.

"Yes, and I will tell you, whoever he had working for him? They knew what they were doing. This isn't some quick flip here."

As Ralph examined the quality of the construction, Patrick returned with the blueprints. He spread them out on the desk and Ralph and Alex pored over them. I had no clue what I was looking at—I knew what blueprints were, but they weren't something I'd ever paid attention to. In the Dragon Reaches, the families building their dreyeries weren't exactly forced to log in their plans with the government.

"So . . . over there . . ." Ralph pointed to the area where the two back bedrooms began. "That was the original confines of the basement. You dug through there, and expanded what . . . a good twenty-five feet. And you expanded . . . thirty feet in the other direction. This was quite the undertaking."

"I've got the money, the house is gorgeous . . ." Patrick almost sounded defensive.

"No argument from me on that. Okay, let's start at the edge where the original basement ended. We'll set up equipment and see if there's anything there. You didn't find any bones, did you?" Ralph motioned for me to take the TRU over to the wall near the door leading into Alex's room.

Patrick shook his head. "No. Nothing like that. I haven't really looked through the attic, though, to be honest. I've been so focused on the renovations down here. As I said, my friend Nathan owned the house and I bought it from his family, so I didn't really expect anything to be out of the ordinary."

Alex turned around. "Tell us about Nathan. Did he die here? What was he like?"

"Yes, he did. Died in the master bedroom." Patrick cleared his throat. "Nathan . . . how can I put this? Nathan had two sides to him. One side, I admit, was a conniving bastard. The other side? He could be a real charmer."

"That sounds like a psychopath to me," Alex said.

"Not really—he wasn't deliberately cruel. Nathan was a financial genius, but I'll be honest, part of that genius was invested in knowing how to manipulate others. Nathan's primary focus was money and power. During the eighties, he was a whiz at day trading and, unfortunately, he was also good at convincing others to go in on his investments. Sometimes they panned out. Other times? Not so much. Usually Nathan emerged richer, even though a number of his acquaintances didn't make it through unscathed." Patrick shrugged. "He was ruthless when it came to money but had a real soft spot for his family and those he considered friends."

"White dragon," I muttered.

Patrick gave me a quizzical look. "What did you say?"

"He was like a white dragon. The whites are the worst when it comes to money and greed. They'd topple your financial interests in a second if they thought it would mean more for them, and then eat you for dessert if you complained. But they are extremely family-oriented, most of them, and usually protect their own." I shuddered, thinking again that the Wing-Liege was right. It was a good thing I'd come Earthside. Greanfyr and his clan were tight, and though what I took wasn't sentimental or very expensive, the very fact that I stole it was enough to set the entire dreyerie rampaging for my head.

Patrick stared at me. "It's really easy to forget that you're a dragon until you come out with something like that. But yes, I suppose . . . Nathan was like that."

"You said he got sick? That he was losing weight at the end and couldn't eat?" Ralph was frowning at his camera.

"Yeah, that's what I understand. By then, we weren't talking too much. I told you, Alex, that I understand why you refused to turn me when I asked. I'll be brutally honest—I'm glad that I managed to find someone willing to do it. I don't regret my choice. But I do understand why you wouldn't want the responsibility on your shoulders. I say that because Nathan asked me to turn him. I refused. We had a falling-out, but his family—they knew what had happened, and after he died, they thanked me for not agreeing."

Alex studied Patrick's face for a moment. "Why did you make the decision?"

"The truth? Nathan was scary enough when he was alive. The thought of a man that greedy who had vampiric powers scared the hell out of me. Even though he loved his family, the way he treated his enemies and those he thought were standing in his way . . . I decided no, I wasn't going to loose a vampire like that on the world. So I told him no." Patrick sat down on the love seat. "I guess I'm a hypocrite . . ."

"No, you aren't. Patrick, the last time I turned somebody, she ended up doing exactly what you were afraid Nathan would do. I never had a clue she had that in her, and it broke my heart. I swore that I'd never chance helping another friend become a monster. You've stayed true to yourself. I wish I had trusted you enough to say yes. To be the one to give you the gift."

Alex was about to say more when Ralph let out a yelp.

"Fucking hell . . . something just pinched me." He swung the camera around to face the brick of the back wall. "Holy crap—look at this." Backing up, he motioned for Alex and me to join him.

As we stared through the lens of the camcorder—which was on the full-spectrum mode, and which could record in total darkness—we saw a misty shape taking form near the back wall. It was large, and dark, and as I glanced up over the camera, I realized that I couldn't see it without the lens. Maybe there was something to the ghost-hunting gear.

Suddenly remembering my part, I held up the TRU and watched as the temperature in the area began to plunge. "Temperature drop of ten degrees in the last twenty seconds." Actually, it was ten-point-three, but the point-three seemed meaningless with that big of a drop.

Alex held out the EVP and we all quieted down. Patrick had joined us, and he was staring at the figure with a mixture of fear and curiosity.

"Who are you? Can you tell us your name?" Alex slowly began to move forward and was now in range of the camera.

"Alex, I'm not sure I'd do that if I were you—" Ralph's warning came a hair too late. As Alex approached the area where the misty figure was forming, it reared back and lunged at him, knocking him off his feet, then headed directly toward us.

Ralph stood frozen as it barreled toward us, but I jumped to the side with Patrick following me. We went rolling to the floor in a tangle of arms and legs, just as Ralph went flailing back as the thing blasted him. A voice, deep and resonant, filled the room.

"Get out. Get out now!"

CHAPTER 6

"Bloody hell." Alex had lightning-quick reflexes and was on his feet before the rest of us. "What the hell was that?"

Ralph groaned, rubbing the back of his head, but then he scrambled for the camera. "Oh please, don't let it be broken!"

Patrick gave me a hand and I accepted, gratefully. I wasn't hurt, but the startlement of being run down by a ghostly renegade had dazed me slightly. I brushed myself off and shook my head.

"Well, that was fun. *Not.*" Patrick offered me a chair and then slid into one next to me. "Is that my ghost? Is that Nathan? What does he want? Why is he so pissed at me?"

"All questions that we hope to answer in due time." Alex picked up the EVP and brought it over to the desk.

Ralph, satisfied the camera was still working, joined us. "I've dealt with a few ghosts before but I will tell you right now, whatever that was, I don't think it was your friend Nathan. In fact, I don't know if that's a ghost at all."

"Demon?" Alex asked. "I know that demons exist. I've seen a few of them over the years."

"No . . . I don't think it's a demon, but I'm not sure what the hell it is." Ralph frowned. "I'm not saying that Nathan *isn't* around, but . . . I don't think that was him. We need to know more about this house, including what was on the land before it was built and who owned it before Nathan."

"That I can't help you with." Patrick frowned. "However, the town has a directory of historical houses. They keep pretty good records on the history of the area. You and Shimmer can go there in the morning. You'll find it at the Port Townsend Historical League's offices."

"Check. We'll do that first thing. Do you know when they open? We'll need the address." I glanced at the clock. It was a modified digital clock, not only giving the time in regular format, but it also had the hours listed in military time. There was a date indicator on it, as well as when to expect the sunrise and sunset. "Did you make that?"

Patrick shook his head. "I've got some pretty clever friends. I commissioned it from one of my mechanically minded buddies." He brought up a browser on the computer. "I'll look up the info you need."

As Patrick tapped away at the keys, Alex wandered over beneath the clock and stared up at it, a bemused look on his face. "Ralph, can you make me one of those? Or rather, two? That would be handy to have around the office, as well."

Ralph shrugged. "Should be a piece of cake. I'll do it next weekend."

"Found it." Patrick scribbled down the address listed on the browser. "The Historical League opens at ten A.M. and they close at four."

"Is there anything else we need to do before we go to bed?" Ralph glanced over at me. "Besides getting you to a swimming hole?"

I thought for a moment, then shook my head. "Not that I can think of. I'd prefer to get into the water before much longer. It's already two A.M., and I don't want to be seen changing into my dragon form. I'll do that in the water, but it's much better if I go now. Do you mind, Alex?" I tried to keep the eagerness out of my voice, but it was no use.

Alex smiled softly. "I think we can make time. While Ralph keeps up work here, I'll take you to the beach. Then I'll return and help Ralph until it's time to pick you up."

"Thank you. I'm going to go get into my swimsuit—I can change form with my regular clothes on, but I would rather not. It's a quirk I have." I dashed up the stairs to the main floor, then up to my room. As I entered the bedroom, I paused. The dresser had been mighty unfriendly and I had no clue if whatever it was that had been playing with the drawers was the same thing we'd encountered in the basement.

"If you're around, just back off while I change, please." While challenging a ghost—or whatever it was—didn't seem like the brightest of ideas, I felt like I had to say something to acknowledge that we knew it was there and had gotten its message.

I unzipped my luggage again and pulled out my swimsuit, quickly changing out of my jeans and tank top. As I slid on my suit—a pale violet one-piece meant for swimming more than sunbathing—I kept a close eye on the dresser, but the drawers remained shut. However, the entire time, I felt there was something watching me.

I rigged my hair in a high ponytail and then pulled on my jeans and top again, over my suit. As I grabbed my jacket and tote bag, I glanced back at the room. "I'd really like to know why you're here and what's making you so angry. We can't help you if we don't understand. And we want to help."

As I hustled down the stairs, I tried to stay alert. We hadn't been hurt yet, but we had been attacked, and that was enough reason to keep our eyes open. I wasn't looking forward to sleeping, either. Not with both Alex and Patrick out for the day. The others were in the living room, waiting for me. Patrick and Ralph were starting to set up cameras as Alex and I headed out to the Range Rover. The moment I stepped out the door, I took a deep breath. It felt safer out here. As I shut the door and fastened my seat belt, it occurred to me that whatever was in there, it wasn't going to want to leave. Which meant that we were going to have to force it out.

The route from Patrick's house to the lighthouse at Fort Worden was a simple one. Alex turned the way we had come on W Street, then left when we hit Fort Worden Way. Within a few minutes, we were on Harbor Defense Way, driving between the beach and the park. The thought that I would be back in the water within minutes set my whole body to tingling. I opened the window and stuck my head out, closing my eyes as the tang of the saltwater breeze hit me.

"You really need this, don't you?" Alex wasn't making fun of me. In fact, when I looked over at him, I could tell he was stone-cold serious.

"Yes. I do. If someone wanted to torture me, they'd only have to keep me away from the water. It's part of my nature, Alex. Water dragons aren't just dragons who like to play in the water—the essence feeds and recharges us. The water calms us down when we're stressed, and revs us up when we need energy. The waves are part of our nature, part of our . . . soul . . . if you want to get transcendental."

He gave a little nod. "I'll make certain you get out as often as you can. Puget Sound isn't exactly open ocean, but the water comes in from the Pacific, and there are plenty of places deep enough for you to swim. I don't think I realized how much this means to you. I suppose I never *thought* about it really."

Touched by his concern, I let down my guard for once. "Thank you so much. And don't beat yourself up. There's no reason why you *should* have thought about it—it's not like you've hung around with blue dragons a lot. I'm still boggled by the fact that the Wing-Liege is . . ."

"Buddies with a vampire? You know what they say about strange bedfellows. Only take the bed out of the equation.

I don't swing that way." He laughed, then, lightening the mood. "I met Lord Vine many years ago when I was on safari. I told you I traveled the world. Well, I was high in the Alps. It's foolhardy for a vampire to go out where he might not find shelter during the day, but I was with a friend who understood my nature. He saw to it that I was protected during the daylight hours."

"You met the Wing-Liege in the Swiss Alps?" That made sense, in an odd sort of way.

"I did. I'm not sure why he was there—he told me at the time but I can't remember now, but we were in a remote area and one evening, I happened to see him fly down into a valley and land. We were close enough that I was able to hike it over to where he was before he left. He very politely decided to leave me alive, and we got to talking. After that . . . well . . . we've stayed in touch over the years."

Alex drove to the end of Harbor Defense Way, past several campsites. Two lone RVs were parked in the camping areas, but there were no lights and no one appeared to be up and about. I stepped out of the car, and Alex walked around to stand beside me.

He pointed to the lighthouse. "You'll have to walk around the lighthouse out to the farthest point—that's where the deepest water will be. You could try to cut through but if they catch you, you'll be booted. The lighthouse is off-limits. The good thing is that nobody else seems to be up and wandering around at this time."

I shimmied out of my jeans and top, tossing them in the back. "I'm leaving my tote bag with you—I don't dare take it into the water with me, and I don't trust leaving it on the shore. So, how long do I get?" The wind gusted past, and I shivered—just a touch. I was used to the chill; it didn't bother me so much as tease my skin.

"Well, considering that sun rises at around seven twenty, and it's two-thirty now, how about I meet you right here in three and a half hours? I know that's not long but—"

"I can come back before we leave, and that's plenty long

for a quick dip." I paused, then darted forward to press my lips to his cheek. "Alex, I really appreciate this." And then, before he could answer, I headed around the perimeter of the lighthouse fence, toward the beach. Though I didn't look back, I knew Alex waited until I vanished from sight.

While a lot of people *like* the water, for a water dragon, it's like coming home. I crossed the beach quickly—it was a thin spit of sand and pebbles—and stood at the edge of the Pacific Ocean. Well, ocean *water*. The Strait of Juan de Fuca cut a swath between Vancouver Island—British Columbia—and the Olympic Peninsula. It fed into Puget Sound, which filtered down to divide the Seattle-Tacoma area from several towns on the interior of the Peninsula. At some point, going north, the Strait of Juan de Fuca met with the waters from the Strait of Georgia. But it was all ocean water, tried and true, and carried the energy of the Pacific.

Every body of water had its own energy and personality. I had visited many, but mostly up in the Dragon Reaches and—a few times—down in Otherworld. This would be my first time connecting with an Earthside ocean. I'd stood on the edge of the sound a number of times, though, and the water, even in that channel, was primal. Here, I could feel the essence of the Pacific much stronger. She was a wild creature, she was, refusing to be tamed. She was alive and vibrant, and when I reached out, I could sense her song. The Pacific, more than most, had her sirens and her wiles.

With a sudden swish, an icy wave rolled to shore to crash against my foot. I steadied myself, readying for a deep dive. I could hold my breath for a long time, unlike mortals, and once I was in dragon form, I could dive to extremely deep waters for long periods without coming to surface. My night vision was stronger than human vision, and I could see the silvery waters rushing in, illuminated against the fog. The water seemed to blend right into the mist, and the chill prickled my skin. But one thing I generally didn't have to worry about was hypothermia—not at all in dragon form, and I was far more resistant to it than the normal human would be in human form.

I waded deeper into the foaming waves. They were strong, breaking around my thighs. It would be easy to lose my balance, but that didn't frighten me. To shift, I had to be out where I could immerse myself completely while in dragon form, but even if the waves did knock me down right now and drag me out to open water, I'd be all right. Really, there wasn't much chance for me to drown, not unless somebody held my head under water for a long time. And it would take somebody a lot stronger than me to do that.

High tide was coming in, so I sliced cleanly through the water and began to swim. Since I was going against the tide, it took me longer, but within a few minutes I was out far enough to test the depths. I dove beneath the waves and, kicking hard, worked my way out to the point where I knew I could shift. It had been so long since I'd been in my natural form that for a moment I panicked, terrified that everything would go wrong. What if the Wing-Liege had been lying? What if I could never change shape again?

But then the blessed sense of transformation hit. My body began to morph and stretch out in the most sensual manner. Unlike Weres, changing form didn't hurt in the least for me—in fact, it was luxurious, almost passionate, heightening every sense I had.

And then the dreamy wash of transfiguration slid away and I was in full dragon form, feeling so strong that I wanted to roar, to shoot out of the waters, into the air where I could streak through the sky and then barrel-dive back into the water again. But I held myself back—do that and it would be a quick and harsh shift back to human. Instead, I sank into the sensations around me. It would be so easy to swim out to the ocean from here, swim away and never come back. But the heady rush of endorphins began to settle and I focused on stretching my wings, on exercising my muscles.

Blue dragons had much smaller wings than most others—we mostly stayed in the water and didn't use them much except to steer with and propel through the water, like oars on a boat. We could fly, but our flight didn't come through the power of our wings. My forearms were shorter. While water dragons resembled the pictures of Nessie more than regular dragons, we did have the residual wings and we did have legs and arms. We were closer to what people thought Asian dragons looked like, rather than westernized dragons.

With long sweeps, I guided myself through the water, diving deep to settle against the bottom. The water rolled around me as the buoying currents soothed my temper. The waves recharged me, amping me up in a way that I hadn't felt since before my incarceration in the Dragon Reaches. I could live here, I thought. Camp out on the bottom of the inlet and sleep for months in the rocking cradle of the Ocean Mother.

As my eyes adjusted, I looked around. There were fish. I didn't know their Earthside names, but they were there, silvery and shimmering in the dim, dusky light. And jellies— luminescent—fluttered by. I loved the jellyfish. They were prickly, though their venom didn't bother dragons. Their glittering bioluminescence mesmerized me and I could sit for hours watching the great swarms pass on by.

After a while, I began to swim again, spiraling in loops through the water, playing chase with my tail. I plowed through a group of fish, not to hurt them, but for the delight of watching them scatter. Hunger rumbled in my stomach, but I ignored it. Right now, I wanted to just enjoy my time and not focus on hunting. Diving to the bottom again, I pushed off, spiraling till I almost broke the surface. I did a belly roll and occupied myself by playing with a piece of driftwood I found floating in the water. I nosed it along for a while. But somewhere, in the back of my mind, something tugged at my thoughts.

And then, I remembered: *Alex*. The vampire would be back shortly. My internal sense of timing told me it had been nearly three Earthside hours.

Reluctantly, I began to swim back to shore in the still-darkened morning. As I reached shallow water, I changed to my human form and dove through the last of the waves until I came up on the shore. I was tired. My entire body felt like I'd just run a marathon. But I was happy, if a little melancholy, and my nerves had been cushioned by the water.

Recharged, I started slogging my way back up the beach when I heard something. *A song.* It was distant, but definitely there. I also heard the sound of a boy laughing. I whirled back to the water to see a teenaged boy heading toward the waves. Nobody else was around. He must have come from one of the RVs at the campground. He wasn't dressed for swimming, and my guess was that he hadn't planned on taking an early-morning dive. No, the sirens were singing, and he was caught in their trap.

Here's the thing about sirens: There are different sirens for every body of water, and they vary in number and form. But the Ocean Mother's daughters are legion, and they extend into lakes and ponds as well. And they most definitely lure people into the depths.

The boy was at the water's edge and walking into the waves. I raced over to where he was just as a riptide swirled around his feet and yanked him off balance, swiftly pulling him out toward the open channel. Riptides, a local term for rip currents, were strong, narrow currents that cut through the waves, pushing toward open water. Trying to swim against the rip exhausted swimmers because the force was too strong, and the victims usually ended up unable to keep their momentum, and were swept out to sea.

But I knew how to navigate them. I dove back into the water, letting the current carry me toward the boy. He was gasping, trying to stay above water and turn himself around. I pulled him against my side, holding him with one arm, as I cautiously swam sideways—the only way to escape from the current. I let it carry us a little ways farther down shore until the force began to lessen, and then I put in a concerted effort and managed to skirt around it, heading for the beach. The boy was able to stumble out beside me on his own two feet.

He leaned over, coughing up water as I sat on a driftwood log. After a minute he joined me.

"Thanks . . . just . . . thanks. I thought I was going to drown. I dunno why I headed into the water. Jeez, that was dumb."

"You *would* have drowned if I hadn't been here. Listen to me: Always take someone with you when you go swimming, unless you're an experienced swimmer. Even then, be careful." But then, I stopped. The boy hadn't meant to go in the water. The sirens had lured him in, but I couldn't very well tell him that. "Just be careful out here, okay? Now, head back to your campsite and dry off."

"You want to come back with me? My folks are going to freak and I bet they'd like to thank you." He looked me over, his eyes lingering on my breasts, and then he blushed. Yeah, he was going to be just fine. Typical teenaged boy.

I flashed him a gentle smile. "I'm sorry, a friend is waiting for me. But—what's your name?"

"Brad. Brad Iverson."

"Well, Brad Iverson, listen to me. Be careful around here. This town . . . there are a lot of strange things that go on. Just watch yourself around here. Now you go get out of those wet things before you catch a cold."

I stood, waiting till he was away from the water's edge. As he headed back up the beach, he turned to glance back at me again. "Hey, what's your name?"

"Shimmer. Just think of me as your guardian . . . well beach bunny. Okay?" I laughed and waved him on, then looked back at the water. "Not today, Mama. Not today."

I jogged around the perimeter of the lighthouse. Sure enough, Alex and his Range Rover were waiting. As I approached the car, I found him leaning against the door, towel in hand and a grin on his face.

"Enjoyed yourself, then?" It wasn't really a question.

I accepted the towel. "Alex, I can't even begin to tell you how much I needed this. It was hard to come back, though. Whenever I get a vacation I'm going out and staying out for a couple of days."

I slung my tote bag over my shoulder and headed to a nearby bathroom, where I was delighted to find a shower. As

I rinsed off under the steaming water, I lathered up my hair and rinsed it out, then quickly braided it back so it wouldn't drip all over me. As I dried off and slipped into my clothes, I managed to bring my thoughts back to the matters at hand. When I was out in the water, time seemed to cease and nothing else really mattered, but now, I needed to focus on the job.

By the time I climbed back in the Range Rover, I was ready to rock. I wasn't even very tired—but then again, I still had a good five to six hours before I would start thinking about bed. I didn't feel like talking about my swim—that was private—but I did tell Alex about the boy.

"Today was his lucky day. Good thing you were there, that's all I can say." Alex started the ignition and turned on the heater so I could warm up.

"Yeah, he was lucky. Say, I'm hungry. Patrick have anything good in the house? I could eat a horse."

Alex glanced at me, grinning. "Have you ever? Eaten a horse?"

I blushed. Truth was, I had. The truth was, in dragon form? I'd eaten a lot of things. "Um, can I reserve the right to answer on the basis that it might embarrass me?"

"No need. That tells me everything I wanted to know. And more. But to answer your question, yes, Patrick has a well-stocked fridge. He went shopping when he knew that you and Ralph were coming with me." He paused. "Shimmer . . ."

I knew what was coming. I had almost hoped that I could avoid the conversation for now. I was so overwhelmed by my time in the water, the last thing I wanted to deal with were my emotions from the human side of the equation as well, but if Alex wanted to talk . . .

He shifted so he was facing me. "What's going on with us? I want to know. I don't want to do anything that makes you uncomfortable. You work for me, and the Wing-Liege has essentially handed you over to me . . . I would never take advantage of my position."

I let out a slow breath and met his gaze. "Alex . . . I know you just broke up with Glenda, but it's been over for a while, right?"

He nodded. "I didn't want to deal with her temper, so I just let it ride, but yes. Emotionally I pulled out of the relationship some time back. I know I should have just ended it then, but you know how it is—it's hard to feel like you're a failure in a relationship. I just wasn't ready to admit that we couldn't make it work. And Glenda can get so angry . . ."

"I think I knew that." I tried to phrase it right—I didn't want to say something that could be misunderstood. "All right, I'll just spit it out. I've found you attractive since the beginning. But I also hated being shoved over here like the family secret that you hide in the closet. I think I blamed you for that. I know you had nothing to do with it, but you're involved, you know? And yes, you have power over me with the Wing-Liege, but I've come to realize that you won't abuse it. You didn't tell him I almost staked you . . ."

Alex ducked his head, smiling. "You were under a charm."

"Yes, but don't you see? Back in the Dragon Reaches, that still would have bought me a death sentence. At the least, some time under the Strap." Frustrated, trying to say something that I had no clue how to say, I leaned forward and cupped his chin in my hands, staring deep into those frost-laden eyes. "Alex, I make my own decisions, as much as I can. And if I want to kiss you, it's my own choice—not because you're forcing me to."

The next moment, his arms were around me and his lips were on mine. They were full, cool as ice, but still they set off a spark in me that began to ricochet through my body. My pulse raced as he crawled across the seat, bearing down on me, and I spread my legs so he could lean against me. He pressed his mouth hard against mine as his tongue darted between my lips. Shifting, I tumbled into the kiss, a deep hunger racing through my body. His chest was against my breasts, and his strength surprised me—it matched my own. He broke away, laughing deeply.

"Oh, woman. You know I want you. Ever since you came to the agency, I've thought about you. Every time I touched Glenda, it was you I was kissing . . . touching . . ." He gazed into my eyes, his fingers stroking my cheek. "What do you want to do? We'll take this at your pace."

It felt odd that he wasn't breathing, that his skin was cold as ice. But then again, I was used to sleeping with dragons, not people. Carter had been an entirely different matter. Demons were a breed of their own, and demigods, even more so.

"What I want . . . and what we should do are two different things." My body was aching for more, but my brain was on overload. The swim, being in my natural form, and now this emotional exchange had me in a whirl. After a moment, I opted for breathing room. "Kiss me again . . . and then I guess we'd better head back to Patrick's, as much as I'd like to get your clothes off." Suddenly bold, I pulled him forward and we locked lips again. That was one thing he'd have to get used to: I wasn't shy.

A moment later, when we came up for air and had untangled ourselves, he fell back in his seat, a goofy grin on his face. "Shimmer, you just made me a very happy vampire." But then he sobered. "Unfortunately you're right. We'd better get back to the case, as much as I'd like to take this further. I'm worried, Shimmer." We pulled out of the parking lot, then zipped down the street out of the park and back onto W Street.

His tone of voice shifted so abruptly that I stopped smiling. "Why? Did something happen while I was in the water?"

Shifting gears, he nodded. "Ralph and I checked the EVP. The voice we heard? Yeah, it's there, but so are a number of others. That house is riddled with spirits, and none of them sound content. I have no idea of what Patrick's gotten himself into, but this job? It's not going to be easy at all. And there's something else . . ."

"Well, dish."

"There was a woman's voice and she was chanting. I have no clue what she was saying, but it sounded magical. When I heard it, I didn't think about ghosts, if that makes any sense. I think we're dealing with more than a haunting."

"I guess Ralph and I'd better go talk to Patrick's witch

friend, then. Because I know squat about magic other than my own."

"Ralph and I aren't any more versed in it than you are. Okay, I just wanted to warn you before we got back to the house. I haven't said anything to Patrick yet, because I want to know more about what we're dealing with before telling him."

I nodded. It wasn't a good idea to disseminate information to clients before we had all the facts, especially when a man's home and livelihood were in question. "Got it. But we'd better find out something pretty soon, or the High Tide Bed-and-Breakfast is going to close before it even opens."

"That's the truth of it." Alex started the car again and we headed back to Patrick's.

CHAPTER 7

Alex and I managed another kiss or two—in secret—before he and Patrick retired for the day, leaving Ralph with the keys to the Range Rover. We sat at the kitchen table, plotting out our morning before we headed to sleep.

"We need to talk to Tonya, then visit the Port Townsend Historical League. Where else do we need to go?" I was taking notes on my tablet while Ralph and I ate. Patrick had made a pot of spaghetti. I'd never met a vampire who liked to cook, and while Patrick couldn't sample his own food, apparently he didn't need to because it was excellent.

"We should look around the yard here while it's daylight. Maybe we'll find something. Also, we should find out what we can about Nathan Striker. Is his family still in town? I'm tired, but I think I have a few hours' steam left in me. And Flying Horse is my friend." Flying Horse was an energy drink that Ralph guzzled like it was water. How he handled that much caffeine eluded me, but he managed it without a problem. "We can't do much before nine A.M., though, so after dinner, I'm taking a nap." He glanced around the kitchen. "That is, if I can get to sleep. I feel like we're being watched."

"That's because we probably are." I shivered. "I don't like this place. Don't get me wrong. It's a beautiful house, and Patrick seems nice enough. But I don't feel safe here." I paused. "You realize when we go to bed this afternoon, neither Patrick nor Alex will be awake yet. You want to sleep in my room?"

Even though Ralph had a crush on me, it would be better to sleep in the same bed and be safe, rather than be isolated in different rooms where we wouldn't necessarily hear each other if something happened.

Ralph blushed, but ducked his head and nodded. "Sounds good. Are you going to take a nap, too?"

"I thought I'd do some research online while you slept. I'm not tired. But tell you what. Sleep on the sofa in the living room. That way I'm right here."

The werewolf flashed me a grateful look. "Thanks. I admit, I'm a little nervous."

"I think that's wise. Okay, go get some shut-eye, and I'll see what I can find out. I'll wake you at nine and we'll head out. I may put in a call to Tonya, to see if she's home."

Ralph curled up on the sofa and was instantly out, despite the caffeine. I sat at a writing desk near him, Alex's laptop in front of me. First things first. I glanced at the clock. It was a little past eight. Withdrawing to the kitchen, I put in a call to Tonya. She answered on the second ring.

"Harris's Emporium of Magic and Witchery. May I help you?"

I was almost surprised she answered—I didn't think she'd be open already. I introduced myself. "My name is Shimmer, from the Fly by Night Magical Investigations Agency. Alex, the owner of the company, is a friend of Patrick Strand. Patrick gave us your card."

"Oh yeah, he used to date my mother. What's up?"

I laid out what was happening. "We're not certain this is just a matter of ghosts. And even if it is, we may need someone to exorcise them. Would you possibly be able to give us your opinion? Patrick will pay for your time."

Tonya seemed brusque, but pleasant enough. "I can make

it over tonight. No money unless it involves more than me just nosing around a little. We can talk about that later. I'll bring my equipment. Eight thirty all right?"

"That would be fine. Thank you."

"Can you drop by this morning? I think it would be a good idea if we met first."

"Will nine thirty, ten o'clock be all right?"

"That's fine. Do you have my address?"

I double-checked her address against the card and then hung up. One thing off the list. Next, I returned to the living room and pulled up a browser, typing the names "Nathan Striker" and "Port Townsend" into the search engine. The result was a yield of links that I had not expected. Apparently Nathan Striker had been quite well known.

I began scanning through the links, looking to see what I could find. Quite a few were bios on his business practices, but I began seeing more and more references to how ruthless he had been with his financial dealings. Finally, I added a third parameter to the search—the house address. That narrowed the field greatly. In fact, I came up with a personal website from a family named Buckland, and, curious, I began searching through it. Sure enough, I found Nathan Striker's name.

It appeared that they had owned the house before Nathan. In fact, Terrance Buckland had been a business associate of Nathan's until, according to the website, Nathan had screwed him out of a major deal and Terrance's family had lost everything, including the house. Nathan had foreclosed on it—somehow he had become the lien holder—and moved his own family in.

The Bucklands had ended up in a ramshackle house on the outskirts of town, and they had, as far as I could tell, died out except for their son, who had erected the website. He worked for a local garage as a mechanic, but I had the feeling his life was a far cry from how well-to-do his family had been before Nathan got hold of them.

I sat back, contemplating what I'd found out. Was Terrance Buckland haunting the house? Had he come back to haunt Nathan and stuck around? Or was Nathan haunting his own house in a Jacob Marley sort of fashion?

Jotting down my thoughts, I returned to the search engine and typed in "Terrance Buckland" and "Port Townsend." That brought up a whole different realm of results.

The Buckland family had been of Gypsy descent, over from England not long before the turn of the twentieth century. They had journeyed west and ended up in Port Townsend during the early days when it was still a thriving town, hoping to be *the* port city of Washington. As the town took a nosedive, though, the Bucklands thrived. They managed to make it through the decades during which Port Townsend turned into almost a ghost town.

During the seventies, as the hippies discovered the jewel of a city, citywide renovations began to take place, pushing the town into a prime tourism destination. The Bucklands rode the top of the wave. But then Nathan Striker entered the picture, and in one fell swoop, during the late eighties, he had managed to destroy everything the family had built, foreclosed on their house, and the friendship between Nathan and Terrance vanished into the dust in a war over money.

So the Buckland family had every reason to hate Nathan Striker. I added Toby Buckland—Terrance's only living relative—to the list of people we should talk to, though I figured we might want to leave out the part about Patrick being Nathan's friend.

I glanced at the clock. Eight thirty. Feeling charitable, I rinsed off our breakfast dishes and stuck them in the dishwasher. As I was bending over, somebody pinched my butt. Hard.

Startled, I stood up so fast I clipped the top of my head on the counter. With a groan, I leaned against the granite, wincing. "Enough, already. Stop it."

A low laugh echoed through the kitchen and as I glanced into the sink, I saw a bubble of blood rising from the drain. "Holy fuck—stop it. Just stop it!"

The laughter continued and I slammed the dishwasher

door shut and backed away. As I turned around, a plate flew off one of the shelves and whirled past me, just missing me. I ducked as a teacup followed suit.

"Get out . . ." The voice rumbled low as the lights in the kitchen flickered off and on. Easing back, I stepped out of the room and waited. A moment later, the heavy atmosphere vanished and I eased my way back in. The energy had lightened and when I glanced into the sink, it was clear—no sign of blood.

I turned on the dishwasher and went in to wake Ralph. If we didn't do something soon, Patrick's vision of a bed-and-breakfast would remain just that.

The minute Ralph and I left the house, I felt a sense of relief. The looming presence that lingered in Patrick's place was already starting to wear on me and we hadn't even been there a full twenty-four hours. I told Ralph about the blood and the poltergeist activity and the voice.

"Are you *sure* we aren't dealing with some demonic force?" I knew that some ghosts could be real PITAs, but this seemed like overkill.

He shook his head. "There's a tendency to blame everything on demons, but honestly? Astral entities can be just as mean and violent. I think we're dealing with a ghost . . . well, mostly. But there *is* something bigger behind it, though I really don't believe it's demonic. I hope that Patrick's witch friend might be able to shed some light on the subject." He yawned. "The nap helped, but I'll be looking forward to a good rest."

"I'm still not used to working the night shift." I slid into the passenger seat. "And on another subject, I really need to get my license."

"You're coming along . . . it won't take much longer." Ralph fastened his seat belt and started the Range Rover. He was the one who got me signed up for driving lessons at the Supe Community Action Council, and he was taking me out for practice a couple times a week. Ralph had more patience for that sort of thing than Alex did, and it was safer for him to teach me than Bette, who was a speed demon and accumulated tickets like she did notches on her headboard.

"Good, because I'm tired of relying on taxis for things like grocery shopping." I settled back and played navigator as we headed toward Kearney Street.

During the day, Port Townsend felt like a different city. At night, it was eerie and felt full of ghosts. During the daylight hours, it seemed to have almost a costume party atmosphere. The sense of Victoriana was strong here, and the buildings were bright and cheerful, looking newly built in a number of areas even though a good share of them were over one hundred years old. The town had a vibrant feel to it, even beneath the cover of the clouds, and yet, it seemed to me that they were trying to impress the tourists too hard.

Ralph glanced out the window. "I like it up here, I love the beach, but honestly? The veneer of this town feels like a bandage over a deep wound. This whole area—not just Port Townsend, but the peninsula—is haunted. A lot of nasty things happened up this way, and so many spirits live in the forest. And I'm not just talking ghosts."

I shivered, thinking of the siren. "Yeah, I know."

"Tomorrow morning if we get the chance, let's drive out around the outskirts a little. I'd rather not go at night. And anyway, during the evenings we'll be working with Alex and Patrick so I doubt if we'll have time." Ralph grinned at me. "Bet you we can meet Bigfoot!"

"I don't *want* to meet Bigfoot." I wrinkled my nose. "I can't change into dragon shape to take him on if he gets nasty, not unless he decides to go swimming with me and I kind of doubt that he'd take me up on that."

Ralph snorted. "Yeah, probably not."

We had been driving south on San Juan Avenue and now we turned left onto Nineteenth Street. The windswept trees and foliage on either side of the street left no doubt to the fact that we were in a shoreline community. Nineteenth merged into Blaine Street, and shortly after that we turned right onto

Kearney. Another couple blocks and we eased into the parking lot at the Town's End Mini-Mall, a small strip mall boasting a bookstore, a fish-and-chips joint, a souvenirs boutique, a coffee shop, and Tonya's magic shop. Of the five, only the coffee shop and Tonya's place were open this early.

Ralph and I headed inside. A bell signaled our entrance, and I looked around, surprised to see how open and airy the place was, and yet—the shop felt enchanted. Plants draped from almost every shelf, and a striped ginger tabby cat curled up in a rocking chair over by a shelf filled with bottled herbs. A scale stood on a counter next to the shelf, along with bags and a scoop. Obviously it was help yourself. Bookshelves lined two walls, filled with titles, and a display case offered crystals, wands, daggers, and various other human pagan paraphernalia. Near the back, a curtain partitioned off a doorway.

Along the window in front, a sign pointed people to a window seat, a waiting area for people who were here to consult with Tonya herself. The counter, directly to the right as we entered, was staffed by a young man. He smiled at us, his hair neatly combed back into a ponytail.

"May I help you find something?"

"We're here to see Tonya. I'm Shimmer. I called earlier."

He nodded. "She mentioned you'd be coming in. See those curtains back there, just go on through. She's in the back."

I led Ralph toward the back and pushed through the curtains. They were a cheerful montage of blues against an ivory background, and they partitioned off the back section to the store. There were three other doors in the room. One door was labeled OFFICE and another RESTROOM. The third was labeled EXIT.

A table stood in one corner of the room, round and wooden, with a crystal ball in the center, a deck of cards on one side, and four chairs.

I looked around, uncertain what to do, when the office door opened and a woman entered the room. She was wearing jeans and a green V-neck sweater, belted by a thin brown leather belt. Her hair was tucked into a neat French braid, and she was carrying a packet of papers. She stopped when she saw us, obviously startled, but then immediately walked over, her hand out.

"Hello, I'm Tonya Harris. Are you Shimmer?"

I nodded. "This is my friend Ralph. We work for the Fly by Night Magical Investigations Agency."

She shook her head. "Normally, I wouldn't ask you to come in before I investigate a haunting. I like to go in without being prejudiced by information. But when you called this morning, something told me that I needed to meet you in advance."

It made sense from a magical point of view. She was a witch; she'd have hunches and intuition about the situation. She motioned to the table.

"Have a seat. If this is as bad as you say, I want to know more about what I'm getting into."

Ralph held out the chair for her, and then one for me. "Ms. Harris—"

"Tonya, please." She pushed the cards and the crystal ball out of the way. When we were settled, she leaned back, looking at us. "You're Supes, aren't you? You aren't human."

I grinned. "You nailed us there. And neither is Alex, our boss. Or Patrick, the owner of the bed-and-breakfast. Is that going to be an issue?"

She shook her head. "Not at all. Doesn't bother me. Hell, I've been seeing spirits since I was a little girl. I knew there were Fae before they ever came out of the closet. In fact, when I was a little girl, one of my best friends was a wood nymph who lived in the back acreage behind our house. My folks thought she was an imaginary playmate, but they were wrong on that one." She laughed then, and I wondered why Patrick thought her abrupt. She seemed genuinely friendly to me.

"I'm a werewolf," Ralph said. He cleared his throat. "Our boss, and Patrick, his friend, are vampires. That change anything?"

She raised an eyebrow but shook her head again. "Not as long as they keep their fangs off me. Actually, I already knew about Patrick. He dated my mother for a while. It did not end well, but neither did it end in bloodshed so I guess that's as good as it gets. For the record, she's the one who ended the relationship. He was the one who got dumped. I felt kind of sorry for him—she wasn't relationship material." She leaned forward and rested her elbows on the table.

I debated whether to tell her what I was, but figured I'd cross that bridge if she asked. "Here's the thing . . . we're not convinced the ghost is just a ghost. Ralph doesn't believe it's demonic, and I don't have enough experience to tell. But whatever it is, the consensus is that more is involved than a single spirit or group of spirits. Patrick suggested talking to you."

"What do you know about the house?" She picked up her deck of cards and began to shuffle them as she listened.

"Just that it belonged to someone named Terrance Buckland years ago. He was a business partner of a man named Nathan Striker. Striker was a ruthless businessman, and he pushed Buckland into bankruptcy, foreclosed on his home as a lien holder, and ousted the family. Then Striker moved in."

"How does Patrick figure into this?" Tonya began to lay out the cards in a straight line as I spoke.

"Only in that he and Nathan were friends for a while. Anyway, Nathan Striker died, and his family sold off the place to Patrick a couple years ago. Patrick just recently began renovations and all of a sudden, the place has been haunted—something wants him out."

Tonya picked up the first card. "The Emperor. This is about control. A pissing match. Who controls who—and authority figures. But it's influenced by the Moon—hidden factors and forces. There are sides to this situation that have not yet come to light. Until those are discovered, we won't be able to solve the problem. Here we have the Wild Man, a force of nature who is undeniable and feral—in some decks he's known as the Devil. He's the wild card, so to speak, in this. He's upset the order of things and thrown everything out of balance."

She turned over another card. "We have the Queen of Wands . . . a woman of fire, a woman of power. She is influential in the situation. And the five of Swords and ten of Wands? This tells me that betrayal and oppression weigh heavily in this haunting."

The Queen of Wands? So far we had heard nothing about a woman. I turned to Ralph. "Terrance was married. We're going to meet with his son today. Was Nathan married?"

He consulted his notes. "Not that I can see. His sister was the one who sold the house to Patrick."

Tonya frowned. "The woman . . . she isn't Terrance's wife—that much I'm picking up on. But . . . do you know if Terrance was a Supe?"

I shook my head and took a closer look at her cards, keeping my hands to myself. I knew better than to touch other people's magical supplies. "No, he's not part of the Supernatural Community—at least not that it showed in any of my research. He is of Gypsy descent, though."

Tonya coughed. "Oh hell. You're sure?"

Her reaction startled me. She looked almost frightened. "Um, yeah. Why?"

"I don't want to say yet—not till I come over tonight, but that makes sense with the Queen of Wands here. I'll see you tonight. I want to do some research of my own, and I also need to prepare so that I'm not at the mercy of whatever it is. But trust me, be cautious what you say when you go speak to Terrance's son. *Very* cautious." She escorted us out politely but firmly.

As we got back in the car, I turned to Ralph. "What do you think all that was about?"

He had a pensive look on his face. "The Gypsies are a powerful people. They have a long history of magic, and they have a bad reputation, most of it unearned. But as a rule, they tend to hold grudges and they do believe in retribution. I wonder if . . . well, let's wait and see what Tonya has to say tonight."

Next stop was the Port Townsend Historical League. The building was located in an old converted Victorian. An ornate but not ostentatious sign indicated we were at the right place, and we followed the winding path through the neatly tended yard to a ramp that sloped up to the door. It was their one concession toward accessibility, it seemed, because when we entered, I realized I sure wouldn't want to be disabled and trying to maneuver through the choppy rooms.

After signing in at the desk and asking for information on historical houses, we were pointed in the direction of the second floor, where two entire rooms had been turned into a library focused on the history of the buildings of Port Townsend. As we stared at the overwhelming number of old books on the shelves, Ralph jabbed me in the arm.

"We're saved." He pointed over to a long wooden table that had four computers on it. "The Net saves the day again."

He settled in to one of the computers and typed in the address of the High Tide Bed-and-Breakfast. A moment later, he pulled up the information and I realized that the books in the rooms were for show only—the organization had scanned in all the info.

"Here we go. The house was originally known as the Buckland House. I guess the Buckland family built it in 1902 to 1903. But . . . let's see . . . oh lovely."

"It wasn't built over a cemetery, was it?" I grimaced. That would be par for the course, from the movies I'd been watching with Bette.

"No, it wasn't, but it was built over what was originally a training area for the soldiers before Fort Worden was officially established. The land was sold to the Bucklands in 1901, and the house was completed by 1903. Let's see . . . the soldiers stopped using it when . . . it says a miscalculation by soldiers led to one of their practice mortars misfiring. The bomb landed in the yard and exploded, killing five of the soldiers there. That was the last time they conducted practice on that piece of ground, and a year later, the battery gun was moved into what would become Fort Worden proper."

"So . . . five solders dead there. Anything else? What about before the government commandeered the area?" So far we had one very unhappy ousted family, a man who had died in the house he took away from them, and five soldiers dead from a miscalculation.

Ralph frowned, flipping through screens. "Back in 1840, there was a family named Jenson trying to homestead in that spot. They vanished . . . nothing was ever found of any of them. No bodies, nothing."

"Robbery?"

He scanned the article. "No, apparently everything they owned was still in place, and the fire in the fireplace had burned out by the time that friends discovered the family was missing, but a pot of stew was still on the woodstove. A blanket that the mother had been knitting was in the rocking chair . . . outside, they found a doll the daughter owned at the head of a path leading into the forest. They found a shoe that they think belonged to the son. The guns were all in place, nothing missing but the family."

That was weird. "Any speculations as to what happened to them?"

"No . . . though some people thought Indians. But that doesn't hold water either, not with any local reports of native activity during that time period. Also, it says here that there were reports of strange creatures in the woods and odd lights dancing in the air. The locals had warned the family that there were local legends of dangerous spirits around the area, but they didn't believe the stories, of course. Before them . . . there aren't really many notations here. And the information doesn't go into what the legends were."

I sat back, thinking. That made people gone missing, accidental deaths, and a really bad end to a business relationship, all taking place in the same area. Maybe the area really *was* cursed. Or, sometimes a location just attracted bad energy—evil, if you wanted to call it—or dangerous. Some places in the world were magnets for crimes and accidents. And that was a truth that ran through all the realms. There were areas in the Dragon Realms that nobody—even the most powerful of dragons—would venture into.

"We've got a lot of puzzle pieces here." I frowned. "Can you print out all that information? Will they let you?"

He glanced at the usage rules. "For a dollar a page. We just take the document numbers up to the main desk and pay them, and they'll print it out for us. I guess that's all we're going to find out here."

"It's more than I expected to find, to be honest." I gathered my tote bag and we headed for the front desk. There, we signed out, paid for our documents, and showed them the inside of my tote and Ralph's backpack.

"Do people really steal the books from here?" It seemed ridiculous when you could just print out the information for a low fee.

The clerk behind the counter gave us a smile. "What can I say? There's stiff competition in the genealogical circles and it can get pretty nasty at times. We have to keep a close watch on all documents in here—the actual documents, not what gets printed and what doesn't. People like owning a piece of their past, especially those who are fiercely into hunting down their ancestry. Some of the country clubs require proof of lineage for certain levels of membership. It's a status symbol for many."

This was sounding a little too close for comfort, given the nature of my birth and my standing in the Dragon Reaches. I said nothing as I took the papers from her, and Ralph handed her over three dollars for three pages' worth of information. She waved us out and we headed back to the car.

"One stop left, then. I guess we go see Toby, then grab a bite to eat. Does he know we're coming?"

I shook my head. "I haven't called yet. I know where he works, and thought he might be more likely to talk to us if we just showed up." I shut the door of the car and hunted through my purse. I was hungry. I ate a lot in human form, but not nearly the amount I consumed in my dragon shape. And I burned it off. Luckily, I had discovered the joys of protein bars. As I opened a chocolate-chip, cherry-flavored one, I added, "We have to figure out what we're going to tell him, though, because I think Tonya's right. If he knows we're helping a friend of the man who destroyed his family's livelihood? You can bet he's not going to want to talk to us."

"Then we'd better think of a good cover before we go in." Ralph started the car and we eased out of the parkway, bouncing ideas off each other as I looked up the address for the mechanic's garage where Toby was employed.

CHAPTER 8

The En-Royale Garage was along the waterfront. We pulled around back. Toby was supposed to be working, although we could easily miss the mark and get here on his day off. But when we wandered into the reception area, Ralph nudged me and nodded toward a man in mechanic's coveralls. He was about five seven, with dark tousled hair and piercing eyes, and he was focused on some part of the engine. I had no clue what, but he was giving it a puzzled look that I recognized all too well as bewilderment. The smell of oil and gas hung in the air, and grease from the cars. I grimaced, not liking the smell at all.

We were about to head over when someone tapped me on the shoulder. I whirled around to see Chai looming over me. He was dressed, at least—and fully, in a T-shirt that stretched across those broad shoulders of his, and jeans. His hair pulled back into a high ponytail and the massive ring in one ear weren't the only things that made him stand out. Dressed to fit in or not, the fact remained that Chai was still seven feet tall, with eyes that could never quite pass for human.

"Chai, what are you doing here?" I glanced around, but there was no way he could vanish now without attracting attention.

Ralph gaped up at him. "Hello? I don't . . . think . . . Shimmer, who is this?"

I rubbed my forehead, suddenly tired. "Chai, meet Ralph. Ralph, meet Chai. Chai is a friend of mine—he's a djinn. He was *supposed* to be staying at my house watching after my fish."

"Chai. Like the tea?"

"Yes. I have no idea where he got the name, but you can ask him later." I pulled Chai to one side. "*What* are you doing here?"

"I got worried about you. I had the feeling something was wrong and decided to trace you down and check on you. Are you all right, Little Sister?" Chai reached under my chin and chucked it.

I batted his hand away. "So far, but I need you to leave. Through the door. Wait outside for us, okay?" As I pushed him toward the door, he just shrugged and sauntered off. After he left the building, I turned back to Ralph. "Sorry . . . he means well. He's a good sort—djinn or not. And he's exuberant. Kind of like a very smart, very large puppy."

Ralph was trying not to laugh. I could see it in his face. "Okay, then. I'll remember that. Puppies can bite, you know." He nodded at Toby, who had—for the moment   given up on whatever he was trying to do and now was cupping a mug of coffee, leaning back in his chair. "I think we should go talk to him now, while he's taking a break."

"Makes sense to me." I led the way over to the man. He was about thirty-five, maybe forty by the looks of him. "Toby Buckland?"

He jumped a little as I spoke. "What?" Apparently he'd been deep in thought. "I mean, yes . . . I'm Toby. What can I do for you? Are you being helped?" He glanced around, but the garage was so busy that nobody else seemed to have really noticed our presence, which could be a good thing, in our case.

"We're not customers, thank you. We wanted to know if you had a few minutes to speak to us? It's about your family and the house on W Street." As I spoke, a veiled look came over his eyes and he frowned. "I promise, we won't take up too much of your time. Please, it's important."

"Follow me." He nodded toward what looked like a conference room. Once we were inside, he shut the door. The half window allowed us to see what was going on out in the main garage. He motioned for us to sit at the table. "Okay, who are you and what do you want?"

I glanced at Ralph. We'd discussed our approach on the way over. "We're investigators writing a piece on the historical significance of houses in the area. We have noted there have been some strange goings-on reported where you used to live—on W Street? We were wondering if you could give us any history of the house or land."

He looked confused. "What the hell? I'm sorry, but no. I didn't live there very long, just when I was a little boy. My father lost the house in a business deal gone wrong and we had to move by the time I was eight years old. I don't remember much about it." He paused, his eyes narrowing. "That's not why you're really here, is it? You might get further if you just tell me the truth."

I glanced over at Ralph, who shrugged. "All right. But you probably won't want to talk to us after you hear what we have to say. And if you don't, that's fine—we understand. We'll leave."

That seemed to intrigue him, because the look of suspicion turned to one of curiosity. "Go on, then."

Ralph cleared his throat. "We're with the Fly by Night Magical Investigations Agency. It's true that we are investigating a haunting at the house you lived in when you were young. We were wondering if you had any idea of who the spirit might be? Was the house haunted when you lived in it? Or can you think of anything that went on there that might have been the source of a disruption?"

"Well, that's different. How much do you know the

history? And who owns the house now? The Striker family, still?" Toby gave us a smoldering look.

"No, actually, they sold the house to our client some years back after Nathan Striker died there, but he just now got around to renovating it and ever since he began renovations, odd things started to happen." I did my best to avoid mentioning that Patrick was Nathan's friend. If we could keep that under wraps, we might actually come out of this with some sort of information.

Toby held my gaze for a long moment. Then he slowly relaxed. "My father died destitute, you know. Striker broke our family. We never quite pulled together again after that. Ma tried, but she was sick with diabetes and it killed her. My father watched her go, and he couldn't do a damned thing. I was the only child on our side of the family."

He leaned forward, his eyes bright. "But my father, he got even. Or rather, my grandmother did. When she found out what Striker did to my father, she went to Anna Lee, and she asked Anna Lee to put a curse on the house."

I stiffened. *The magical chanting* . . . Could it be related to whoever Anna Lee was, and her curse? "Who is was . . . Anna Lee?"

"She was my aunt. She was a fortune-teller and witch. We're Gypsies, you know—and proud of our line. She was one of the Bucklands who lived the lifestyle. My father, he was ashamed of his heritage. He just wanted to fit in. Grandma was disappointed in him, but she never said anything."

"And so he went into business and bought the house . . ."

"He thought he could give us a normal life. But we're not born for it—not really. I don't even try. I work, but once I save up enough money, I'm hitting the road and traveling the country. I know there's a group of Bucklands still making the rounds in upstate New York. I might see if they'll let me join them."

And so there it was. There was a curse on the house.

"And Anna Lee, she was your aunt, you say? She's dead?"

Ralph was taking notes, and he seemed to have the wits about him to be properly respectful.

"Yeah, she died a few years back. She never married, but she had a string of lovers a mile long. She could dance, and sing . . . when she was younger, she lived in a caravan. But after she developed arthritis, she decided to settle into a small apartment. She told fortunes and cast spells for her living."

I didn't know a lot about humans and magic, but I knew that some of them could be pretty damned powerful when it came to spellcasting. There was quite a history of witchery throughout human culture, long before the neopagans found it. While some of them had tried to tame down the magical aspects of it, there were a number who still understood the strength and power of the forces they worked with.

Stretching, Toby yawned and glanced at the clock. "My break's over. I have to get back to work or the boss will be on my back." As he stood up, he let out a snort. "About your ghost . . . I don't remember much. I think there might have been something there, but nobody ever bothered me. Have you considered the idea that it might be Striker? He lived and—you say—died in that house. The curse might have kept him there." And with that, he opened the door, indicating our talk was over.

As Ralph and I left, Chai was waiting outside for us. He followed us back to the car and I realized he meant to hang around. *Wonderful.* How was I going to explain this one to Alex? And if he objected, well, I had no influence over what the djinn did.

"So Anna Lee Buckland put a curse on the house. We don't know what kind, but at least we can surmise what the chanting is connected with. So we need to figure out what kind of curse it is, and then we might be able to figure out if the spirit haunting the place is Nathan." Ralph glanced nervously at Chai. "He coming with us?"

"Apparently so. Just be polite and everything will be fine," I said with more confidence than I felt. Chai would never mess with me, but I couldn't vouch that he'd behave himself around Ralph and Alex. "Oh, and don't ask Chai for any favors. Trust me. The question is, why would Nathan haunt Patrick in such a nasty way? They were friends—"

"*Were* is the operative word, isn't it?" Ralph turned to me as I was fastening my seat belt. "Remember, Patrick said that he and Nathan had a falling-out. Nathan wanted Patrick to turn him so he wouldn't die. Patrick said no. Nathan's family was grateful Patrick didn't, but Nathan wasn't. Maybe he's trying to get back at Patrick for refusing him?"

"That would make sense. And if the curse exacerbates the energy, maybe Nathan's spirit has turned into some sort of a monster?" I glanced into the backseat. "Fasten your seat belt, Chai. The law requires it and we're not getting any tickets because of you."

"You want me to take care of this ghost you have a problem with?" Chai's voice rumbled from the backseat.

"Yes! Can you?" Ralph sounded all too excited.

"What did I just say about asking him favors?" I glanced back at Chai. "No, thank you. Absolutely, emphatically, do not do us any favors or grant any wishes. You do, and I send you packing." I glanced over at Ralph, worrying my lip. I could speak in front of Chai without worry, but there was a point where bluntness turned into being rude. But I had to make Ralph understand. "*Never* ask a djinn for a favor, or accept one from him. Do you know anything about djinn wishes?"

Ralph shook his head. "Can't say that I do. Just thought, if he could help us, it might be worth a shot."

"Djinns are bound by their natures to twist your wishes in any way possible. Even when they aren't chained to a person's will." I shot a glance at Chai in the backseat. He'd managed to avoid getting enslaved so far, and I hoped that never changed. The thought of him being subservient to somebody turned my stomach.

Chai cheerfully chimed in. "Shimmer is correct. I'm bound to make the offer, and then I'm bound to screw things up for you if I can. Nothing personal, you understand."

"What, is it in your union handbook?" Ralph snorted, but Chai laughed right along with him.

"Actually, yes. Well, the equivalent." He was able to sit in the backseat without too much problem, but his head still brushed the roof of the car. "These vehicles need to be bigger."

"Don't even go there. This monster is big enough as it is." Ralph put the car into gear and we swung out on the street. "Okay, it's almost eleven. We grab a quick snack and then I seriously need some sleep. Even with catching an hour of shut-eye this morning, it's been a long time since six o'clock last night."

I was starting to feel the strain as well. "Right. I'm not hungry, so if you just want to go back to the house we can. When we wake up tonight, we should get right to searching through Gypsy curses to see if we can figure out what Anna Lee did to the house. Maybe Tonya will have some clue as to what we're up against." I yawned and stretched, realizing that the thought of *bed* sounded really good. "Chai, I want you to stay awake while we sleep. There's a nasty spirit in the house and we're a little leery of what it might do while we're in bed."

"Won't that backfire?" Ralph darted a quick look my way, his voice decidedly nervous.

"Nope. I didn't ask him a favor. I told him what to do. He doesn't have to obey me, but if he decides to oblige, that's a totally different matter."

Chai muttered something under his breath.

"What?" Ralph glanced in the rearview mirror. "You say something?"

"Damned right," Chai grumbled. "Nasty buggers, ghosts. Can't stand them. I'll keep watch. No worries."

We drove back to the house and, once we made sure we'd written down everything we needed to remember, Ralph and I decided that staying in the same room might be the safest route. Ralph was shy, slipping out of his jeans, but he was wearing boxers that looked like swimming trunks. I'd brought a pair of PJs as well as a sleep shirt, figuring it might be drafty in the old house. So I changed in the bathroom and we settled into the bed, turned away from each other.

Chai stretched out in the recliner near the bed with a book. I couldn't read the language it was in, but he seemed absorbed by it.

After a round of good-nights, Ralph and I fell asleep, the alarm set for six thirty. If anything happened while we slept, Chai kept it from bothering us.

Ralph went back to his own room to shower and dress. Chai was still where he'd been when we drifted off to sleep, and I gave him a quick hug before hitting the bathroom.

"You smell a bit ripe, girl. Go shower."

"I love you, too, dude."

He held my wrist for a moment, staring into my eyes. "Something else is going on besides spooks and spirits. Going to tell me what it is?"

I never had been able to hide anything from him, but right now I didn't feel like talking about Alex. It was too new, and I wasn't sure what it would turn out to be, and I wanted to just focus on the case at hand at this moment.

"In a bit, once I figure it out myself." I grabbed a towel and my travel kit and headed into the bathroom. Fifteen minutes later, I was clean from head to toe and smelled like cucumber-melon. I brushed my wet hair back into a ponytail, where it would dry, and then quickly dabbed on some eye shadow, liner, and mascara. I liked makeup, but it hadn't fully become routine with me yet. I added a thin slick of pale bronze lip gloss and then returned to the room, where I dressed. Chai had seen me naked before, and if he had any interest, he'd politely kept it to himself.

I fastened my bra and put on a fresh pair of panties, then slid into a clean pair of jeans and tucked in my pale blue V-neck sweater. I added a black belt with a silver buckle, feeding it through the loops. After I slipped on a pair of sneakers, and tied them, I turned around to find Chai staring at me.

"You are comfortable here." He held up his book and it vanished from sight.

"In this house? Hell, no."

"I don't mean in this house—it's a malignant cancer right now. But in your human skin. You are more comfortable in this world than you think you are. I've known you for a long time, Shimmer, and I've never seen you so easy with yourself. I think coming Earthside has been a positive thing for you." He stood, and—just like that—his clothes shifted. Now, he wore a dark green polo shirt and a pair of black leather pants. His hair remained in the high ponytail, though, but he'd changed the earring from gold to silver.

I smiled, ducking my head. "You know, I thought maybe it was my imagination. I don't really *want* to be comfortable here—there seems something almost shameful about it, like I can't fit into my own society. But . . . truth time? I do feel at ease over here in a way I never felt at home."

"Not surprising, given the difference in attitudes here. It can be harsh and cruel, but your world, Little Sister? Is a cold and harsh one. Come, girl, introduce me to your master." Chai held out his arm, and I grinned as I looped my own through it.

"Alex isn't my master. He's my boss."

"Same thing, isn't it?"

"No, now you're mixing up your semantics again." We playfully argued as we headed down the stairs. I was surprised that I hadn't seen any paranormal activity since we went to sleep, but then, djinns were powerful, and having Chai around could only help matters.

As we approached the kitchen, Alex and Patrick were already up. They'd risen at sunset, and now I smelled waffles and bacon on the table. My stomach rumbled. As I entered the room, Chai hanging off my arm, they both stared at me like I'd walked in attached to an elephant.

"So, who's your . . . friend?" Alex blinked and slowly stood.

"Alex, this is Chai. Chai's a djinn and a longtime friend of mine. He popped over to see how I was. He was going to stay at my house and watch my fish, but I guess he decided to see what I was up to here. Chai, this is my supervisor—the owner of the company. Alex Radcliffe. And this is his friend and our client, Patrick Strand."

I held my breath and the men sized each other up. But then, after a round of shaking hands and greetings, both vampires settled back into what they were doing. Chai gingerly sat down in one of the kitchen chairs, making sure he was out of the way. I sat beside him and gratefully accepted the plate that Patrick handed me. It was overflowing with food—apparently Patrick had noticed my appetite. But then again, most Supes had higher metabolisms than humans and bigger appetites.

Ralph entered the kitchen, looking chipper and ready for breakfast. He pushed his glasses back on his nose—they were forever sliding down—and slid into a chair on the opposite side of the table. "I'm starving."

Patrick dished him up a plate. "Here you go. We were just getting to know Shimmer's friend." He poured more batter on the waffle iron. "Chai, I didn't expect another guest, but I'll fix you a waffle right now, if you like."

"I would appreciate that greatly, Master Strand." Chai gave him a courteous nod.

"We have news from today. We can talk and eat at the same time." I glanced over at Patrick.

"Do tell." He added more bacon to the skillet, turned it on medium, then moved over to sit at the table with the rest of us.

"First off, did you know that the Bucklands are of Gypsy blood? And they have—or rather had—an aunt who was apparently very good at putting curses on people. And things. And apparently, she put a curse on the house after Terrance Buckland's mother found out what Nathan did."

That produced a response, from both Alex and Patrick.

"Um, no. I didn't know any of that." Patrick slowly leaned back in his chair. "That really doesn't bode well for me, does it?"

"No, but more so, it doesn't bode well for the house. By

the way, we talked to Tonya Harris. She's really quite nice. She's going to come around eight thirty in order to scope out things. At least we can tell her what we think the magical chanting we heard on the EVP was. Ten to one it was Anna Lee Buckland, working her magic."

Alex cleared his throat. "Well, that's a kettle of fish, isn't it? You find out anything else?"

"Yes, we did, actually." Ralph told him about the soldiers who had died on this land, and then we filled him in about the Jenson family who had vanished while homesteading in this spot. "So we have several possibilities for what might be happening in your house. Here's the information we dug up at the Historical League." He laid out the pages we had printed off, and Alex and Patrick scanned over them.

I happened to glance up from my breakfast to see something move behind Patrick. A drawer opened and a meat fork—one of the large forks used with a carving knife—rose into the air. I slowly set my own fork down, staring at it, but before I could think to say a word, it sailed through the air toward Patrick's back.

"Halt!" Chai was on his feet and around Patrick in a blur of movement. And then he was standing there with the meat fork stuck in his hand. Another second and it would have driven itself right through Patrick's heart, from the back. Which would have been the end of Patrick.

"Oh man, you almost bought the farm." Ralph inched his chair back, looking around nervously.

Patrick very slowly turned around. Chai was still standing beside him, the meat fork embedded in his palm. He didn't look very happy, either, but the djinn very calmly plucked it out and the wound healed within seconds. He handed Patrick the fork.

"I think this was meant for you."

"Fuck. Just . . . fuck me now." Patrick held out the fork, staring at the prongs. "That would have . . ."

"Put an end to you. Yes." Alex motioned to Ralph. "Get the equipment. Let's see if whoever this is, is still around."

"I wonder if the curse plays into this? Is this Nathan,

driven mad by Anna Lee's magic? Or is it something bigger and badder who was summoned in by it?" I finished off my breakfast. No use letting good food go to waste, and I was hungry.

Ralph returned a moment later with the camera, the EVP, and the TRU units. I wiped my mouth and accepted the temperature gauge. As I held it out, the temperature read a chilly fifty-two. I wasn't sure what it had been when we started breakfast, but it had been a lot warmer than this.

Ralph flicked the switch, turning on the camera. He scanned the room, and I peeked over his shoulder.

"If anybody's there, please talk to us." Alex held up the EVP. "We need to know who you are and what you want."

Chai shook his head like he thought we were crazy, but he just backed away and let us work. Patrick inched over to his side, probably so spooked that any port in the storm seemed safer than standing out in the open as a ghostly William Tell target.

I glanced at my watch. Almost half past seven. Tonya wouldn't be here for another sixty minutes. A blip on the TRU caught my eye, and I watched as the temperature began to plummet again.

"The temperature just dropped another five degrees in the past ten seconds." I scanned the room. Every hair was standing up on the back of my neck, and my arms were puckering with goose bumps.

Ralph eased over to the drawer where the fork had come from. He paused, lowering the camera. "Ectoplasm—it's dripping off the drawer. I need to take a sample because it might have the energy signature of whatever is doing this." He motioned to Patrick. "Get me a container, please."

Reluctantly, Patrick darted to a cupboard, where he retrieved a plastic container and handed it to Ralph before hurrying back to Chai's side. Ralph scraped some of the ooze into the round bowl and fitted the lid on it and went back to scanning the room with the camera.

"Talk to us. Tell us what you want." Alex raised his voice.

The temperature dropped another two degrees. Before I

could say anything, the lights began to cycle on and off, the light switch rapidly flicking up and down, and my stomach lurched as the air grew thick, like it did right before a big thunderstorm. I stepped back, suddenly afraid.

"There's something in the room with us . . ." Suddenly wanting to be anywhere but there, I whirled, looking to run back into the living room. But as I did, the lights plunged off and stayed off, and a clawlike hand gripped my shoulder. The next thing I knew, it was moving up my neck for my throat.

CHAPTER 9

"Something's got me!"** I tried to shake it off, twisting around so I could see what was facing me, but the darkness was unnatural—pitch black so that even I couldn't see what had hold of me. I reached out, trying to push off whoever it was. The hand worked its way near my throat but I was strong, and I shoved, hard. Though my hands made contact with my attacker, another second and the form vanished.

"Shimmer? Where are you?" A brilliant light flashed and Chai was standing there, surrounded by a golden glow that infused every corner of the room. He closed his eyes and it intensified, driving back the darkness until the lights suddenly came on again.

I leaned against the door, shaking. Whatever had hold of me had meant business—there was no doubt about that. Those claws had been aimed for my jugular, and I knew it. Chai hurried over to me before the others could react.

"Little Sister, are you all right?" He gazed down at me with those eyes that swirled in sea foam green. He wrapped a protective arm around my shoulders and brushed back my hair.

I nodded as Alex joined us. "Shimmer, girl, are you hurt?" He glanced up at Chai, a worried look on his face. "She okay? Thanks, mate, for the light. We needed it, for sure."

"No problem." Chai gave him a long look and, with a subtle move, stepped back, allowing Alex to shift closer to me. "But you have serious trouble on your hands."

I wanted to ask Chai to help, to go find whatever this thing had been, but I didn't dare. It was one thing asking him to watch the fish—that wasn't a wish or a favor per se. But for something like this? We'd be stepping into a very gray area that could go very wrong. And it wouldn't be Chai's fault if it did. He was bound to his nature, as much as any of us was. Ralph had to shift into Were form under the full moon. Alex craved blood and needed it to survive. I had to have contact with the water. Chai—Chai was a djinn, and as such, he did what djinns do.

Ralph hurried over to the table. "I got something on the camera. Come look."

We gathered around him, and he set up his laptop so the camera fed directly to the screen. That way we could all see. As we watched, the video showed where Ralph had panned down to the drawer, capturing a shot of the ectoplasm dripping in streams. And then the camera moved up, and I was in the shot, the lights flickered on the recording, and the room was plunged into darkness. But because the camera picked up all spectrums, we were visible in the inky blackness, and so was a short, stocky figure that looked vaguely male. I could see the talonlike nails as he lunged for me. The memory sent a shiver down my back. The figure didn't look human, and as he swiped for my throat, a pale green glow shot out of his eyes. The next moment, my own voice rang out, and then Chai's light illuminated the room. The figure who had been holding me swung around, staring at the djinn, then vanished.

"Did that look like Nathan to you?" I turned to Patrick.

He frowned. "Not in the least. That . . . whatever that was, it wasn't human and Nathan most definitely was. To be honest, it's hard to imagine Nate haunting this place. He was a ruthless businessman, yes, but I can honestly tell you I don't think he ever killed anybody. And that . . . creature . . . looked capable of killing." He hung his head. "I have to get rid of it."

"There's more." Alex set down the EVP and pressed Playback.

"Stop him, please stop him! Mommy!" The voice of a little girl, sounding terrified, rang out.

"Peter, Peter—he's taking the children!" This time, a woman.

"Fire in the—no!" A man's voice layered in.

"Mama, are you there?" Another man's voice. *"I tried so hard, Mama. I hope I made you proud. Everything's getting dark . . ."*

"Why did you lock me up here? What did I do? I don't understand, Papa. Papa! Don't—don't . . . please . . ." Another woman, but different than the first.

And then, over the top of all of them—laughter. Dark, ugly, laughter. *"You're all mine."*

The recording ended.

We stared at the machine. "There are a lot of them here. I think . . . most are ghosts, but the last—that was the creature that attacked you, Shimmer. I know it." Ralph frowned at the recorder.

"This can't all be part of Anna Lee's curse. Some of those spirits have been around for decades—over a hundred years, if our guess is right. Long before she was even alive." I frowned.

"Layers of hauntings building on one another? Maybe playing off each other?" Alex mused. "How long till Tonya gets here?" he glanced at the clock.

"It's eight, so half an hour."

Alex crooked his finger at Ralph. "Let's not waste time. Let's have a look at that ectoplasm."

Ralph set the container on the table and removed the lid. Inside, a pile of gel was puddled at the bottom of the dish.

There were about three tablespoons of it, and it was translucent with the faintest hint of green to it. I leaned close. "It looks like viro-mortis slime."

None of the three of the men knew what I was talking about, but Chai did. He picked up the dish and sniffed it. "Looks like it, yes, but it's not the same. This smells like the forest, like mold and mildew and decay." As he held the bowl, the gel pulled back from the bottom of the dish, oozing up onto the side. He frowned. "I think it doesn't like me."

I poked at it but didn't touch it. "Chai, can you touch it? If it shies away from your actual touch, then there's something about you that makes the big spirit—creature—whatever attacked me—recoil. It vanished when you started your light show."

"Eww . . ." Ralph grimaced.

But Chai obligingly reached in to touch it. The moment his hand neared the gel, it spread out, trying to avoid his fingers. "Looks like whatever it is has no use for me. My feelings are hurt." He snorted.

"I wish to hell I could ask you to go after this, but I can't." I stared at him, feeling boxed into a corner. Djinn rules were warped and wicked.

"I know, Little Sister. I know. But I tell you this: I want to see this creature taken down. So, if I have an opportunity, I'll seize it." Chai frowned. "Whatever it was, it ran from my light. And my light isn't the same light that healers or exorcists generally use. My light comes from the elemental plane of Fire."

We cleaned up from our meal and decided to move operations into the living room, where there were fewer pointy things to go flying around the room. Though the ghost could likely send a knife from the kitchen out here, as well. As we settled around the coffee table, Patrick leaned forward, frowning.

"I had no idea that any of this was going to happen. When I first moved in last year, I noticed a few oddities, but it never really hit me that something was wrong until the renovations started."

"Maybe we should wait until Tonya gets here. She might want to hear all of this." I tried to relax, but the house was making it impossible. I was so ready to go home. We'd been here less than twenty-four hours but the trip was already wearing on me. It made me wonder if I was cut out for this kind of work.

I glanced up to find Alex watching me. He gestured for me to follow him out onto the porch. When we were alone, he leaned against the railing and motioned for me to sit on the porch swing. The wind was blowing up a gale, and the rain sleeted down, pounding the sidewalks.

"How are you holding up?" Alex shook his hair back. It fell to the side in a tousled mess, and I resisted the impulse to reach over and brush it back into place.

Shrugging, I hunched forward, resting my elbows on my knees. "Okay, I guess. I've never dealt with anything like this before, Alex. I'm not sure . . . what I'm supposed to be doing. Am I doing a good job? Is there something you want me to do that I haven't thought of?"

He grinned, a suggestive smile crossing his face. "Oh, I think you've thought of it already."

I started to blush but then snorted, lightly kicking my foot at him. "Dork. You know what I mean."

"Yes, I do, and Shimmer, you're doing just fine. This is the first big case you've been on. Things bumble along in some cases—in others, they run smoothly. We're walking into unfamiliar territory here and now I'm truly not talking about you and me. I may be a vampire, but that doesn't mean I've had much to do with the spirit world. Ralph? He's a Were. They tend to steer clear of magic. So we have to just take it one step at a time."

I joined him by the railing, folding my arms across my chest as I nervously glanced from side to side. "I really hate this place, you know? Yes, it's beautiful here, but there's something . . . that makes me feel like it has a rotten core. Like an apple that's rotting from the inside out." I shivered. "The whole town feels like it's buried on a thin veneer that covers a graveyard of bones and skeletons. The facelift it got in the 1970s feels like a mask over the true nature of what lingers here. The past doesn't stay in the past in this town, Alex."

"I think that's true of the whole peninsula here." He gave me a long look. "What are you feeling? Premonitions?"

I tried to sort out the onslaught of sensations that were creeping around in the recesses of my mind, then shrugged. "I don't know, but I can feel it, down to the core. Port Townsend is magical, but it's a dark magic that has taken root. I wouldn't go walking around after sunset. Especially not if you're alone." A gust of wind sprang up and rushed past us, and my teeth chattered. "The temperature's falling. Winter storm is coming in. The water tells me so."

And it *was* telling me so. There was a storm brewing out in the strait, and it would be on the town before morning. I could feel the rocking waves in my bones. They roiled and churned as they fed through the channel. The wind drove them along, and somewhere, out in the open ocean, I could hear Winter singing her battle song.

Alex slid his arm around me. "I'm here, love. I'm here."

I turned to him, once again filled with questions. "I think . . . we need an understanding. This time I am talking about *us*. I like you, Alex, as much as you drive me crazy. I tried to hold myself back because of Glenda, but she's no longer a factor. Or . . . is she? Is there any chance you'll be getting back together with her? I don't want to be your out-of-town rebound fling. I'm not asking for any long-term plans, but I've had so much upheaval in my life that if we start something—or take what we have already started further—I want to know that I'm not just a stand-in."

He paused, holding my gaze, then pulled me close and stroked my cheek with one hand, his fingers brushing lightly across my lips. "I'm done with Glenda. We were over months ago, but I don't think I was ready to admit it. I don't know whether you and I will work. But I want to find out." Slowly, he leaned in, his lips finding mine, and slid both arms tightly around my waist, holding me close to him as he leisurely, with a cool fire, lightly tugged on my upper lip with his teeth, then pulled me under in a long, dizzying kiss.

My breath caught in my chest as I wrapped one arm around his neck. With my right hand, I trailed my fingers down his back, the chill of his body startling me as I slid my hand up the tail of his shirt to rest it against his lower back.

The next moment, the sound of a car pulling into the driveway interrupted us and I reluctantly pulled away as a gust of wind shattered through, howling as it jostled past us.

Alex glanced toward the driveway. "Looks like Tonya is here. And you're right, the storm is rising. We'd better tell Patrick to fasten down anything that might blow away."

A woman emerged from the Mazda—Tonya. She was carrying a large flowered satchel, along with a five-foot-tall staff that had a clear crystal sphere attached to the top of it. As she ascended the steps, I moved forward to greet her.

"I'm so glad you could make it. We've got some more information that may be helpful before you start." I stared at the door, loath to go back inside. But we had a job to do. I introduced her to Alex, then turned the knob, and we gathered in the living room again.

Tonya set down her bag and I introduced her to Patrick and Chai. She stared at the djinn for a moment, grinning. "I've heard rumors of your kind but didn't know you really existed."

He blinked. "You know what I am, milady?" Chai was polite to women, that was one thing I'd say about him.

She nodded. "Yes. My mother studied esoteric magical systems and she taught me about djinns and ifrit and, of course, salamanders and all the Elementals. She was a talented witch."

"Then may fortune be on your home and I will not offer to help you." Chai grinned. That was the equivalent of someone saying, "I respect you enough that I won't try to mess you up." Which, in djinn-speak, was a compliment.

She turned to Patrick. "Strand, it's been a while."

"I was sorry to hear about your mother." Patrick held her gaze. "I really did care about her." He glanced over at me. "Tonya's mother was in a horrible car crash last year."

"She didn't make it out alive." Tonya's smile slid away as she sat next to Patrick. "It's all right. I always felt bad for you because Mother never treated any man right. I know she dumped you hard, and it hurt, but trust me when I say that you were better off without her. She was a great mother, but not a good partner. I saw more than one man's heart broken by her—men that didn't deserve the hell she put them through. Even though I loved her, I can admit that."

"Thank you for that." Patrick leaned back. "I wasn't sure how you'd feel about coming here tonight. But now that we're on the subject . . . this place is haunted and I have no clue what to do about it. *I'm a vampire, not a medium, Jim.*"

Alex, Ralph, Tonya, and Patrick all laughed. Chai and I gave each other clueless shrugs. One of those cultural references I routinely was left clueless on. One of these days I was going to set Ralph down and make him give me a crash course in geek culture.

We filled her in on what we had discovered since talking to her. "So, we not only have a Gypsy curse, but we have at least five dead soldiers and a missing family—and who knows what else went on around this area?"

Tonya opened her bag and set out a deck of cards, a crystal spike, her wand, a smudge stick and lighter, and several other gadgets, none of which I recognized. She closed her eyes, took a few deep breaths, then slowly opened them.

"All right. First things first. I need to get a feel for the house from top to bottom. And then I need to walk around the grounds. I'd like for someone to record my impressions—voice is always best. That way we don't lose anything in translation, and also, if something reacts to me—"

"I have the EVP recorder. We can record with that." Alex held up the EVP.

"How many people do you want with you?" I wasn't sure if we'd be too much of a crowd or not.

Tonya glanced at us. "Chai, please stay here. Your energy is so strong you may block out some of my impressions."

"As you will. In fact, I will withdraw to the porch to make things easier." He graciously took his leave—if a seven-foot-tall djinn can be graceful—and stepped out on the porch, shutting the door behind him.

We prepped the equipment. By now I found myself automatically reaching for the TRU. Alex double-checked the EVP recorder.

Ralph picked up the camera. "Do you mind if I film as we go?"

She shook her head. "Won't bother me. All right then, let's get this show on the road. I suggest we start at the top, with the attic. I'm sure you have one?"

Patrick motioned for us to follow him. "Yes, in fact I do. But I forgot to take these guys"—he nodded toward us—"up there, so this will be the first time we've checked it out." He shrugged at Ralph's stare. "What can I say? I don't usually think about the attic. I'm more interested in basements."

He led us up the stairs to the third floor. Tonya was directly behind Patrick, Alex behind her, then Ralph, and finally I brought up the rear. We stopped not far from the door to my room, and Patrick slowly rose to the ceiling—it still never ceased to amaze me when vampires did this—and unhooked the trapdoor leading into the attic space. He pulled down the ladder and it unfolded to the floor, then eased himself through the entry and waited for us, up top. Tonya carefully climbed the ladder, which was a simple step affair, and then once she was up, Alex, Ralph, and I quickly joined them.

Patrick turned on the solitary light—a single bulb hanging near the entrance. The attic was finished. If there was insulation or open flooring, we didn't see it, and the entire space could easily have been turned into a usable, if creepy, room. The ceiling was high and slanted in the middle, but fairly low near the edges of the attic. The exposed beams were heavy, old wood, crisscrossing the ceiling to create a lattice design.

The attic was full of furniture and trunks that looked like they'd been consigned here throughout the years. A mirror, freestanding and dusty, was pointed directly at the entryway, and it was disconcerting to only see Ralph, Tonya, and myself reflected in it. Alex and Patrick didn't show up, of course. An apothecary chest rested against the wall. It caught my eye, and there was something about it that made me want to take a closer look. There were several sections to the attic—not exactly separate rooms, but half walls that extended from either side to form partitions.

Tonya cautiously walked toward the mirror. When she neared it, she stopped, closed her eyes, and held her hands out, palms facing up. Ralph circled her with the camera. Alex and I were watching our equipment like a hawk. And Patrick, he stood back, letting us do our job.

The gauge had read sixty degrees when I entered the attic, but now it began to drop. Within seconds, it had plunged to fifty. "We've got cold coming in. Ten degrees in five seconds."

Ralph began to sweep back and forth with the camera, looking for what might be causing the drop. As he did so, Tonya shuddered and her eyes fluttered open. At that moment, a mist formed in front of her and literally shoved her toward the gaping hole leading down to the hallway. She lost her balance and stumbled toward it, but Patrick moved behind her and caught her before she went plummeting through to the floor below.

Tonya let out a startled cry as she righted herself. "I can feel the spirits struggling behind this force. The soldiers are here, and several others, but they can't get past. It won't let them pass on."

"What won't?" Alex moved toward me and I had the feeling he had just put himself on guard duty.

"I need to sit down. If this thing tries to possess me, get me out of this house. If something happens and I need help, Patrick—you remember Lionel? He works at my shop? Contact him and tell him to call Degoba." She settled herself on one of the chairs nearby. "I need to go into a deep trance to see if I can figure out what the hell this creature is. It's not demonic, but it's definitely stronger than any ghost I've encountered."

Ralph sidled over to me. "I caught the attack on camera. We have the mist recorded. Why don't you take a look around the attic while she's preparing herself?"

Alex frowned. "I'm not sure any of us should be wandering around here without a buddy. Patrick, you hold this while I go with her." He handed Patrick the EVP recorder.

We slowly began to maneuver through the cobwebs and dust toward the back half of the attic.

"How much have you explored into this room, Patrick?" I turned around to ask.

He shook his head. "Not much. I glanced up here several times to make sure everything was up to code—that we didn't have a fire hazard going on. But we didn't have time to go through any of the trunks, or even really get an idea for what had been stashed up here. I thought it would keep until later since we really weren't going to use it for the bed and breakfast."

Alex took the lead, stepping over several trunks to reach the first partition. I followed, grateful that the floor was finished. The idea of accidentally stepping between a couple of beams wasn't my idea of fun, especially when the result could be plunging through insulation and then drywall below.

We peeked around the back half wall. This part of the attic looked almost set up to be a bedroom. In fact, I had the feeling it had been just that. A bed was below one of the small windows overlooking the backyard. The window was barred.

"Look—bars on the window. What about the other windows in here?"

Alex took a quick look around. "From what I can tell, yes, all of them are barred." He stopped, then, looking at the half wall again. "Look at this—it's been renovated." He motioned for me to wait there, then hurried back, sending Ralph up while he took over filming Tonya.

Ralph examined the walls. "He's right. This was reno'd at some point. My guess is, from the looks of the beams and the walls?" He stood between the jutting walls and stretched his arms. He could just touch the edges of both partitions. "There was once a full wall from here, to here. It looks like it was created to set off this area as a bedroom."

I walked over to the dresser near the bed and opened it. There were several things inside. Old, delicate lace shawls, a skirt, and a worn, leather-bound journal, which I confiscated. From here, I could see a small nook between the outer wall and the bed, containing a toilet and pedestal sink. While they were still hooked up, the water in the toilet seemed to have evaporated away. A desk sat opposite the bed, and in the desk, another sheaf of papers along with what appeared to be a photograph album. I picked that up, too, along with the papers.

As I stood there, I began to sense a strong feeling of melancholy permeating the area. The sensation grew stronger when I felt a whisper touch on my shoulder. It was light, not at all aggressive, and the scent of lilac wafted past me, like the flutter of butterfly wings.

I turned back to Ralph and motioned for him to lead the way back to the others. Carrying my finds, I followed him.

Tonya was deep in trance when we returned. She was breathing with a slow rhythm, and her eyes were closed. She almost looked like she was unconscious. Ralph took the camera back from Alex, who joined me to watch over Ralph's shoulder. Patrick remained near Tonya.

A moment later, she opened her lips. The voice echoing out wasn't hers, though. "Help us. Help us—he wants to keep us. We can't leave."

"Who are you?" I leaned forward. "Are you the woman who lived in the attic?"

She paused, then said, "Lacy. My name is Lacy. I want to leave. There are others with me. He frightens us . . ."

"Who is he?" I decided I might as well play the interviewer. Tonya and I seemed to have gotten along.

"He's here . . . why did they do this to me?"

And then, before she could go on, the voice quieted and another took over. Tonya's eyes flashed open and she lunged forward, a hideous expression crossing her face. "*They're mine!* This is *my* land, and they belong to *my* stable. Get out or die."

She managed to move quickly enough to take a swipe at me, and her hands caught my throat, but she let go as Patrick yanked her off me. Tonya struggled but then—just as quickly—gave up and collapsed in his arms. I felt a gentle brush of fingers on my shoulder, but these were the same I'd felt back by the bed and once again, I heard the whisper of, "Help me . . . I want to leave."

We hurried down out of the attic. As Patrick pulled up the ladder, then lowered himself to close the door, Tonya leaned against the wall, wiping a cold sweat off her forehead.

"Okay, then. And that was just the attic. Let's go downstairs, I want to tell you what I found out." She led the way, but I had the feeling she was rethinking her decision to help us out.

We gathered in the kitchen, and I peeked out the front to call Chai back in. He was staring pensively at the yard.

"There's something out of alignment here. This house . . . it's built on bones, Little Sister. It's built on bones."

"What do you mean?"

He shook his head. "I don't know, really. But that thought keeps crossing my mind and it won't let go of me." He followed me back into the kitchen.

We sat around the table. Patrick boiled water for mint tea and handed me a box of Oreos to set on the table. As Ralph opened them, my stomach rumbled. I was hungry, too. Tonya reached eagerly for them.

"Pat, you have any cheese?" She glanced over at him. "I need protein and sugar after that run-in upstairs."

He brought out some sliced cheddar and Swiss, along with a package of turkey breast and a loaf of bread. I figured we might as well get out the condiments, too, so I followed him back from the refrigerator with the mustard, ketchup, and relish.

Alex rolled his eyes but brought over clean plates and knives for us, then rummaged in the refrigerator for bottled blood for Patrick and him. "Okay, impromptu picnic in the middle of a ghost hunt. Anyway, so what did you find out?"

Tonya accepted a soda, taking a long drink before she spoke. "As you suspected, there are a number of ghosts trapped in this house. At least three of them are the soldiers that were killed on this land. Then there's a little girl and, I think, her mother . . . I'm pretty sure they're from the family who disappeared. There are a couple others I didn't recognize, and there's a woman—she probably died in her midthirties, and she's very gentle."

"I felt her. I think she lived in that bedroom in the back of the attic. I found these." I spread out the journal, the papers, and the sheaf of photographs. "She kept asking me to help her, she said she wanted out."

"But he . . . whoever *he* is . . . he won't let them go. Whatever . . . whoever . . . this entity is, he was never human and will never be. But he's not demonic, either. I keep smelling the forest when I think of him." Tonya picked up the journal and shuddered. "Yes, this was her journal. Lacy . . ."

I sorted out the photos. There were seven of them. A pretty woman was featured in all of them, and they all appeared to have been taken in this house, though the furniture was far different than it was now. In fact, I recognized several of the pieces from the attic.

She was dressed in what looked to be a flapper-style dress, and she was wearing the same lace shawl I'd found in the dresser. She looked haunted, though, instead of happy. I flipped over one of them where the name *Lacy Buckland, 1931*, was written in a shaky hand.

"She was one of the Bucklands, then. But . . . so what happened? She said that they 'did this' to her? What did they do to her?" I frowned, trying to sort through.

"We can figure that room in the attic was probably a full

wall. Maybe . . . maybe they locked her in there?" Ralph pulled the papers to him. He flipped through them. "These are old but look—they're sketches. My guess is she drew them, given where they were found. And look what they're pictures of."

Each paper was covered with scribbled charcoal sketches of a dark figure with empty white eyes and a vicious mouth, ringed with teeth.

"Ten to one, that's the spirit we're dealing with. The creature who trapped them. So that means he—or one of his kind—was here even back then, and she could see him. But they were a Gypsy family. Why would they lock up one of their own?" Alex looked confused.

I knew the answer to that one. "Because whether it was this creature or another like him, he worked on them. He considered Lacy a threat, so he engineered her imprisonment. And . . ." I paused. "Tonya, is there a way to find out if Lacy died here? Maybe, if they were hiding her—locking her up—nobody else knew she was still around?"

Ralph, who had been hunched over the journal, straightened up. "You're right. Here   this was her diary. In this entry, she says, 'They forced me into the attic room today. It's hot and stuffy but at least the windows open. Screaming won't do any good though—the nearest house is too far away for them to hear, and Father belted me one when I tried. I have to figure out a way to escape because they told the nearest neighbors that I left for a trip abroad. He's doing it . . . I know he is. I don't know if I can fight him, though.'"

"Is that her last entry?" Alex rubbed the stubble on his chin. "Did she die the day they locked her up?"

"No, but the entries seem to get more and more incoherent after that."

Tonya polished off the last bite of her sandwich. "Let's go outside. I want to walk the perimeter of the lot before we go through the rest of the house. I have a hunch."

We followed her out into the rain and wind. As we worked our way around the yard, Patrick in the lead because he knew where the obstacles were and he was carrying a flashlight for the rest of us who couldn't see so well in the dark, Tonya suddenly pointed to a corner of the lot.

"Over there, beneath the maple." She hurried forward, Patrick keeping pace with her to keep her from tripping over any exposed roots or anything. She knelt by the base of the tree, frantically digging into the dirt with her hands. "Beneath here—you have to get a shovel and dig right here."

Chai stiffened beside me.

"She's here," I whispered. "All these years, and Lacy is still here, unclaimed and hidden."

"This place is built on bones," Chai said.

Tonya looked up at him. "Oh, yes . . . and there are far more bones than hers scattered around here. This land is littered with bones . . . and the secrets that hid them here."

CHAPTER 10

"We can't very well dig in the rain and the dark." Patrick stood back. "Well, I suppose we could. I have floodlights we could bring out here. I'll go get a couple shovels and lights."

"I'm right behind you." Chai followed him off to the shed around the corner of the house. I watched him go, hoping he'd stick around for a while. In fact, the idea of having him as a roommate was starting to play through my head. He made me feel safe and like I had actual family with me.

"We still don't know how the curse is playing into this. Tonya, what do you know about Gypsy curses?" I wiped away the rain that was pouring down my cheeks.

She slowly stood up, wiping her hands on her jeans. "Enough to know they're nothing to mess around with. The Gypsies have a lot in common with some of the Strega. They take their magic seriously and they do whatever is necessary. There's a lot of family loyalty in the clans—tribes if you will. You mess with one, you mess with them all. Nathan fucked up pretty badly when he screwed over Terrance Buckland."

"What kind of curse could be put on a house? Toby was specific about the fact that Anna Lee put a curse on the actual *house*, not on Nathan per se. Which I find odd, given the revenge factor." As I stared up at Patrick's house, a light flickered through one of the attic windows. "Look—up there."

The others turned.

"What the hell . . . that isn't fire, is it?" Alex started toward the house just as Chai and Patrick returned.

"I can make it up there fastest." Chai vanished without giving anyone a chance to say a word.

Patrick glanced at me. "That wasn't a wish-favor thing, was it?"

I shook my head. "Simple requests like asking him to see who's at the door, et cetera, aren't considered in that category. Neither are moments when he offers to help without asking you if you want him to do something. It's complicated and there are a lot of gray areas, but eventually, you get used to the nuances."

We waited, but it wasn't long before Chai returned.

"No fire. The light vanished when I showed up in the attic. Whatever your big spook is here, he doesn't like me and he's afraid of me. But I can't figure out why. I don't even know what he is." Chai picked up one of the shovels Patrick had brought and began to dig. Patrick picked up the other and joined him.

"Be careful—there are bones down there. I can sense them. We don't want to break them apart." Tonya knelt down beside the trunk of the maple. "Lacy was imprisoned and possibly murdered. I'd like to give her remains as much respect as possible."

Chai and Patrick slowed down, cautiously removing shovel after shovelful of dirt, working around the roots of the maple. A foot down, and there was nothing. Two feet down, however, proved to be the key.

"I see something." Patrick motioned for Alex to shine the large light down into the hole. There, showing through the dirt, an ivory hand protruded. Abandoning their shovels, Chai and Patrick began to dig by hand now, carefully scooping out the dirt. Patrick asked Ralph to run and get a couple trowels and a bucket, which made the work go faster. Ten minutes later, they had uncovered a skeleton, entwined in a cocoon formed by the roots of the tree. We all sat back, staring at the bones.

There were a few buttons around the skeleton, but no cloth. In the years gone by, it must have rotted away. I stared at the remains, thinking how, beneath the skin and shape, most of us were just bones. Dragon, human, Fae, elf . . . it didn't matter. It all came down to a scattered bunch of bones once the flesh and blood and water vanished from our bodies. But at least she wasn't fully naked and exposed. As the ground had accepted her body, the tree had given her a shroud of sorts with its roots.

"What next? Should we call the police?" I glanced up at the others. "She was human . . . they might want in on this."

"Technically, we should." Alex stood back, staring at the grave. "Patrick, it's your land and you'd stand to be in the most trouble if we don't report finding the skeleton. What do you want to do?"

Patrick grumbled. "Lovely . . . they come out here, launch an investigation, and this will ensure I don't open for at least another week. But if we don't call them and this comes to light, I could be hip deep in shit. In the interest of keeping vampire-human relations good, I'd better notify them."

We covered the hole with a tarp, then went inside to wait. I kept glancing over my shoulder, wondering if this was going to stir up the spirits even more. Tonya spent the time with her cards, trying to discern anything she could from her readings.

"I can tell you this," she said after a while. "Whatever this spirit is that's trapping them? It—or one of its kind— was here long before the Bucklands built the house. And I'll tell you one other thing . . . that curse that Anna Lee put on the house? Has nothing to do with the spirits. It's more financial in nature." She glanced up at Patrick. "Basically, until you figure out how to lift her curse you'll never make a dime off your bed-and-breakfast. She sealed it to the failure of business. My guess is that she meant to ruin Nathan and his family. Turnabout is fair play, I guess she was thinking."

He facepalmed. "This just gets better and better. But wait, does that mean this spirit isn't Nathan, or Terrance Buckland?"

"Exactly. Whatever this creature is, it's not a ghost, and it was affecting the Bucklands long before Nathan was born." She laid out another card and paled. "I think he was responsible for the Buckland family locking that poor girl in the attic and killing her. And I *do* think they murdered her." Tonya sat back, frowning at the layout on the table. She pointed to the Death card, crossed with the eight of Cups. "Someone under the influence of drugs or alcohol or . . . the creature . . . brought death into the equation. I'll bet you anything the police will discover evidence pointing to it."

"Then what do we do?" I asked, scooting closer.

"First, we figure out what this entity is and where he's from. Then, we get rid of him if possible, and then we deal with Anna Lee's curse. But it's not going to be easy because the spirit is tied to the land, not the house or a person in particular." She stopped as the doorbell rang.

Patrick went to answer and returned with a pair of police officers. He invited them to sit down. I eyed them uneasily. Given that Supes were out in the open, we didn't have to hide a lot from them, but that didn't mean they were going to be friendly either.

The police, however, seemed good-natured enough. One of them, when he saw Tonya, tipped his hat. "Ms. Harris—good to see you again. My grandma appreciated your reading."

"Thank you, Roger. Tell your grandmother I'm happy I was able to help."

We had to tell them why we were digging out in the yard, so I brought in the journal and photos, though I kept the sketches back, and we told them how Tonya had been guided out to the maple tree.

"Let's go see what you found." Officer Paris Veraday, a thin, wiry woman with dark eyes and hair, motioned to the door. "Please, lead us to the site."

We headed out to the maple, where Officer Roger Willis removed the tarp from the hole. We waited while the officers knelt down and shone their flashlights into the hollow. Their lights reflected off the bones, and Paris reached down and gently nudged away a little more dirt to show a skull.

"That's a body, all right, and buried deep. She's been there long enough for the roots to snarl around her, so it can't be recent—not with that much root growth. And buttons—the clothing is long gone." She lifted out one of them that had been lodged partway up the hole. "Ivory, or I'll miss my guess. Unless I'm way off base, this lady has been here a long time."

"I'll call the coroner. Even given the apparent age of the remains, we have to treat this as a homicide until we know for sure who it is and how he—or she—died." Roger radioed it in and they taped off the perimeter of the hole. "You'll have to leave the area alone for now, until we know what's going on." He motioned for us to return inside.

As we went back to the house, it felt unnaturally quiet, like whatever it was inhabiting the place was waiting to see how events played out.

"Until we know more about who's buried out there—and granted, I do think it's Lacy Buckland—I suppose we should focus on the main entity we're facing." I glanced out the window. "What will happen now?"

"The coroner will come in to examine the scene. If it's deemed a homicide, they have to figure out when she died. They'll sift that area for evidence. If it turns out to be Lacy, I doubt there will be much beyond that. While murder files never close, old ones? Back burner and often cold cases." Patrick looked so depressed that I wanted to do something to make him feel better, but there wasn't much we *could* do, except take care of the ghost problem.

Tonya must have felt the same way, because she let out a

long sigh. "I'd suggest trying a séance, but somehow I don't think it's a good idea. This entity has had enough of a say as it is. I think we should just proceed to an exorcism. It's the only thing I can think of right now. We have to dislodge him from your house and then maybe the others can leave. And after what I've seen tonight? The sooner we tackle this, the better. I brought what I needed, just in case."

At that moment, a tap at the door announced the presence of the police again. Paris Veraday entered the room. She motioned for us to gather around.

"The coroner has already verified that the roots that wrapped around the bones grew over them, so she—and it appears to be a woman—has been in the ground for a long time. Roots may spread quickly, but they don't grow that thick in just a few years. And from what the coroner can tell, she was murdered. There appears to be trauma to the skull consistent with bludgeoning, but nothing conclusive right now. We'll come out tomorrow and sift around for any other evidence we can find, but I don't hold out a lot of hope, to be honest. We've got enough to cope with given all the cutbacks in funding. It's all we can do to keep up with our current caseload. We do have the name you gave us; we'll check into the records, see if we can pinpoint any mention of Lacy Buckland."

She tipped her hat and headed to the door. "Just don't disturb the taped-off area, and we'll do our best to get out of your hair by the end of tomorrow."

Patrick saw her out. When he returned, we looked at one another.

"Okay, an exorcism. Are you up for this, Patrick?" Tonya held up a wicked-looking dagger.

He nodded, slowly. "I don't think I have a choice, do you? If we don't put a stop to this, either I'll get staked or somebody else will get hurt. If I open to guests without resolving the problem, nobody in their right mind will stay after word gets around about all the crap that's going on here."

"Let's get this show on the road." Alex looked frustrated.

While Tonya began to sort out what she needed, I motioned for him to join me outside.

We stood on the porch, staring around the side yard to where the crime scene tape glimmered in the glow of the porch light. The wind was whipping strong, and the storm I'd felt earlier was close to shore now. When I closed my eyes, I could feel the clouds brewing up thunder and lightning and jagged rain bands ready to slam the town.

"Alex, what's wrong? You seem agitated." I opened my eyes and turned around, leaning against the railing.

He sat down in the porch swing, his eyes pale and frosty, and draped one arm over the back. "I don't like this, Shimmer. I don't feel safe here, and when a vampire doesn't feel safe, then something is seriously fucked up. The idea of an exorcism scares the hell out of me, and I'm not sure why."

I stared at the front door. "I know. But it seems the only option we have right now. Otherwise, what . . . we give up and go back to Seattle, leaving Patrick to deal with this mess? Part of me feels we made it worse with our equipment and ghost hunting, but then I stop and think, no . . . the minute he opened for business, all of this would crop up and bite his ass."

"I'm glad you said that—I was thinking about the same thing, and frankly, I didn't want to be the one responsible for stirring up a nest of hornets." He glanced around the corner at the gravesite. "She was there for all those years . . . and nobody knew."

"Well, whoever put her there knew. And chances are, more than one person was in on it. I wonder if the name Lacy Duckland means anything to Toby." I thought about giving him a call, but it was almost eleven and I didn't want to disturb him if he'd already gone to sleep. I settled onto the swing next to Alex and nestled against him. I wanted the comfort.

"I'm glad Chai showed up. I hope you don't mind." I glanced at him. "He's really the only family I have."

"He seems a good sort, and handy to have around. I'll

remember not to ask him for any favors, though. At least none that require magic." He grinned at me, then impulsively kissed my forehead. "Sit back. Breathe deep. Relax while you can, because I have a nasty feeling the spirit isn't going to react well to the exorcism."

I tried to relax but was all too aware of his muscled frame pressed against me. While I'd had my share of dalliances over the years, most were brief. Every dragon I'd been with had turned his back on me, once he found out I didn't have a clan. There were a few rogues out there, the pirates of the dragon world, so to speak, but they weren't the type to settle down. And if we'd had children, they would have been clanless, suffering the same fate as us. Love and relationships hadn't factored heavily into my life.

My head on his shoulder, I glanced up at him. He leaned his head back, staring into the night. His body seemed so still, no breath moving his lungs, and his skin was cool, but once again, the scent of cloves and cinnamon, of spicy rum wafted past me.

"What are you wearing? That smells so good." The question just fell out of my mouth.

"Bay rum," he murmured. "I've loved it ever since I first began traveling back in my safari days." He paused, then added, "Glenda hated the scent. She wanted me to use something more up-to-date, but this . . . it's who I am. I never asked her to change perfumes."

I held my breath, not knowing what to say. Finally, I decided to be up front. "Why did you go out with her?"

He shrugged. "Sex. I guess. She was available and so was I. We met and hit it off. But from the very beginning, it was a volatile relationship. Glenda has a hair-trigger temper. Why did you stop dating Carter? He mess you up?"

That, I could answer decisively. "No. I like Carter. I want to *continue* to like Carter, and if we tried to make it work, after a while we wouldn't be friends."

"Ralph has a crush on you, you know?" Alex's voice was level, but I sensed so many undertones to the question.

I chose my words carefully. "I know. I like Ralph. He's

smart and sweet and . . . he needs a brilliant werewolf geek girl. Not a dragon with a troubled past."

"What do *you* need, Shimmer?"

Again, the question had so many layers that I could barely sift through them. I took a deep breath and exhaled slowly. "I'll be honest, Alex. I don't know what I'm looking for. But . . . I'm lonely. I've been alone most of my life, so this is nothing new."

Alex leaned forward, kissing my lips gently. "I know. So am I—even through the entire time I was with Glenda, I never really felt like I was part of a couple." He was about to say something more when the door opened and Tonya stuck her head out.

"We're ready. Come inside, guys."

I jumped up. "We're coming."

As she vanished back inside, I turned around, but Alex was back to business. I flashed him a smile, both regretting that Tonya had interrupted and grateful that she had. This thing between Alex and me was starting to move a lot quicker than I expected it to. I wasn't sure if that was a good thing or a bad thing. Alex held my gaze for a moment, then returned my smile and we headed inside.

"Exorcisms can be messy businesses, and with the way spirits work, they're not always easy. We need to dig a wedge between the spirit and his hold on this land, and that's going to be rough." Tonya set out a number of objects—a brass pentacle, a dagger, a chalice, a red candle, and a short handled broom. To these, she added several other items. I wasn't sure what they were.

"Patrick, do you have any kosher or sea salt? I need a cup of it. I also need a glass of water and some wine if you have it. Red would be best, but any is fine."

He disappeared into the kitchen and returned with the items while she cleared the coffee table of everything that wasn't hers. Tonya poured the salt into a pretty stained-glass bowl and set it in the north quadrant of the table, then filled another matching bowl with the water and set it to the west. The candle went in the south quarter, and the broom in the east. Then she filled the chalice with wine and set it in the middle, along with a pair of candles—one was black, the other white. She placed the brass pentacle between them and stood back. "We're ready."

"What should we do?" Dragon or not, I was starting to feel nervous. For one thing, I couldn't change into my dragon form out of water. For another, it *was* possible for me to get killed in human form. And for a third, I'd developed a distinct dislike of ghosts. Most of it recent.

Chai patted my arm. "Little Sister, it's okay. I'll protect you, you know that."

Alex and Ralph moved restively around the edges of the table. Werewolves didn't like magic to begin with, and Alex seemed to be uncertain as to whether the whole idea was a good one, and he voiced as much.

"You *certain* you want to try this? Patrick, this could stir things up worse than before." Alex frowned, turning to his friend. "I'm willing to go through with it, but make sure it's what you want."

Patrick shrugged. "What choice do I have? It's either this or just hand the house over to the spirit and walk away. I doubt if I could sell it—or maybe I could, but then I'd constantly wonder what plight I handed over to the next poor owner. We might as well give this a try."

Tonya took that for a cue and motioned for us to gather around the table. "In a circle, please, and hold hands."

Luckily the table wasn't that big, so the five of us—Patrick, Alex, Ralph, Chai, and I—were easily able to stretch around the perimeter. Tonya picked up the broom first and began circling us counterclockwise, sweeping the air with the broom. As she passed me, I could feel the energy stir and swirl.

*"With my besom, circle round, declaring this sacred
    ground.
Sweep away the shadows nigh, I call upon the
    Eastern sky.*

*Wind and breeze hark unto me, clear this space, so
    mote it be."*

Her voice lilted over the words as she sang, and the melody wove in a sinuous rhythm, pulling me in. A breeze ran through the room, and I thought I heard murmuring on the wind as it passed by.

Tonya replaced the broom and picked up her dagger. Her arm outstretched, the blade pointed straight ahead, she circled the other direction—clockwise. Starting in the north, she walked the circle three times around us, again her voice trilling over the chant as she wove her magic.

*"Maiden weave this circle tight, weave the web of
    glowing light.
Mother weave this circle strong, let it hold the whole
    night long
Old crone weave this circle true, none unwelcome
    enter through."*

Tonya stood at the north again, right behind Chai, and drew a large pentagram in the air.

*"By powers of earth, water, fire, by the winds of
    strong desire,
I seal this circle and this room, protected by my
    witch's rune."*

A hush fell through the room and I could feel her energy weaving through the air. I hadn't encountered much human magic before and was amazed by the soft flow as it worked its way around us. It wasn't flashy—not like other magic—but there was a strong foundation in its quietude. Impressed, and feeling a little calmer, I squeezed Chai's and Alex's hands. Chai gave me a soft smile.

Alex blinked, and it suddenly occurred to me why he might be nervous. He had incurred the anger of a sorcerer—now a vampire—many years back. Human magic might just scare him as a matter of course.

Tonya set the dagger down and motioned for us to drop hands. She moved in between Ralph and Chai and picked up the chalice of wine.

"I call upon the great goddess Hecate, triple goddess of the crossroads. Guardian of the dead, I call to you, asking your guidance as we seek to free the spirits trapped here this night. We seek to evict the shadow spirit holding the others hostage. Be with us, if you will." She drank from the chalice, then handed it to me. I took a sip, and then she handed it to Ralph and to Chai in turn and they followed suit.

Afterward, she set it back on the table and picked up her dagger in one hand and the broom in the other, then turned to us.

"As we walk through the house, I will be chanting. The rest of you follow with a contra-chant. As I finish each stanza, you will chant, *Hecate, so mote it be.* In unison, please."

We began in the basement and slowly worked our way to the attic. The chant she used for exorcism was a long one, to the point of where I lost track of anything but her words and the refrain we answered her with. Tonya's voice was hypnotic—as much as any vampire or Fae I'd ever met. She wove magic with her words, she infused her will into every note that she sang, and I found myself focusing solely on what she was saying, binding my own will to hers.

> *"Spirits of the earth and sky, spirits of the fire and*
> *   water,*
> *Free all trapped within these walls, I command as*
> *   Hecate's daughter."*

We walked the perimeters of the house, along each wall, skirting the furniture but leaving no corner untouched by the energy. We walked in single file, with Tonya at the helm, her dagger pointed toward the wall as she swept the air with the broom. Behind her came Patrick, then me, then Alex, then Ralph, and Chai brought up the rear.

As we slowly ascended the stairs toward the main floor, I thought I felt things begin to shift and move—and a crash behind us told me I was right. But Tonya kept firm control of the situation. She didn't acknowledge the noise—didn't even turn around. The rest of us took our cues from her.

On the main floor, we began making our way through the rooms, one at a time, with the same pattern. Circling each room, Tonya swept with the broom and used the dagger to channel her energy. I'd figured out that was what she was doing—infusing her energy through the blade and into the walls.

"Hecate on you I call, free the spirits within these walls,
Give them wings, let them fly, by the powers of moon and sky."

Again, a couple of crashes rang through the living room as vases toppled and a picture hit the ground. I tried to ignore it. Tonya's focus was absolute, and she needed us backing her. The fact that we were getting a rise out of the ghosts—most likely our nasty one—had to mean that something was working.

As we headed toward the stairwell I noticed shadows beginning to grow along the wall, moving on their own without anything there to cast them. Shivering, I pulled my attention back, pouring it into the energy of the chant, into my voice as I echoed the refrain.

The energy began to press down, heavily, as if attempting to muffle her song, and the air felt thick in my lungs, almost like I was breathing water vapor. Alex, who was right behind me, let out a low growl. Behind him, I could hear Ralph's breathing quicken, growing deeper as if he were trying to gulp down more air. The oppression grew thicker as we ascended the stairs to the second and third floors, and with each room, the shadows weighed heavier. We were being followed by a legion of spirits, it felt.

Where had they all come from? We hadn't encountered that many in the house. But they were there, watching us, following us, joining us as we moved from room to room. My nerves jangled, I tried to keep my focus from wavering. Tonya needed us and right now, I didn't want to see what might happen if things came unwound.

As we came to stand beneath the attic, Patrick moved forward silently and, once again, opened the door and brought the folding staircase down for us. I did not want to go back up there—that was the last place that felt safe—but we didn't have much choice. Tonya started up the steps, cautiously easing her way up the flimsy ladderlike structure.

As we entered the attic, the room seemed illuminated from something more than just the lightbulb. Everywhere, flickers of light dashed and darted across the walls, through the air. I realized that faint orbs were glowing. We were surrounded by them.

Tonya fell silent. She stared at the bubbles of light that were everywhere. "Spirit orbs," she whispered. "Look at all the spirits. They can't all be coming from this house—there weren't that many here."

"From the land? Is there a graveyard near?" Ralph's voice was hushed, as he slowly inched closer to Alex and me. I could tell the Were was afraid—werewolves really weren't fond of magic as a whole. And spirits? A little too close to magic for most of their tastes.

"I don't know." Patrick turned to Tonya. "What next?"

"Next, we do our best to send them packing." As she readied her broom and dagger, a brilliant streak of lightning cut through the night, illuminating the attic through the windows. Following right on its heels, thunder shook the walls, rumbling through like a freight train. The weather had broken, and the town was right below storm central.

CHAPTER 11

"**Crap, we'd better** get moving." That was the most nonlyrical thing Tonya had said since we'd begun. She motioned for us to form a circle around her. "Join hands and don't let go. Keep the circle tight at all costs."

The storm began to rage outside, with lightning striking right and left, followed by deep rumbling bursts of thunder. Tonya began to chant something and this time I didn't recognize the language. It could have been dwarven for all I knew. But the energy behind the words was incredibly powerful.

Tonya's voice dipped, low and forceful, and as I watched her, I noticed, in my peripheral vision, the spirit orbs were beginning to swirl and spin. They darted through the air, as though they were bubbles in water, churning at a full boil.

The temperature in the attic suddenly plunged, and a loud laughter rebounded off the walls as books and old dusty plates and cups sitting around began to fly through the air. The free-standing mirror suddenly toppled, crashing to the floor.

Tonya's voice rose and she was suddenly speaking English. "Leave this place. Leave this house. Go and never return. I command you in the name of Hecate the Mighty, Hecate the Goddess of the Crossroads, Hecate the Guardian of the Dead. Hear me and obey! Be gone now, I command thee—so mote it be!"

Objects whizzed past faster than in a centrifuge, but then—as the orbs vibrated to the point of being a blur of motion—there was another huge flash of lightning, the thunder echoed through the room, and everything . . . was suddenly silent, all motion stopped. The orbs were gone. Every object that had been suspended in the air was on the ground, dropping from where it had been. The room felt silent. I glanced around, warily looking for any sign that we were in for another round of ghostly attacks.

Tonya slowly broke the circle, standing back. "Is he . . . are they . . . gone?" She closed her eyes, searching for something.

I tried to send out feelers but was bombarded by the energy of the storm. "I have no idea. I'm caught up in the storm. The rain is coming in fast now, behind the lightning. It's going to be one hell of a blow tonight."

Ralph edged back toward a chair and gingerly sat down on it. "I guess we have to wait and see? Unlike Diablo 2, there aren't any pinging lights racing through the room to indicate we cleared it." He pushed his glasses back up the ridge of his nose and brushed back the tangle of curly hair, looking more like a frightened and tired geek boy than a world-wise werewolf.

Chai frowned. "I cannot tell. I don't think . . . I can't see through the storm, either. The lightning in it calls to me." He leaned down to me. "Little Sister, you're in need of food."

Tonya plunked herself down on the ottoman next to Ralph. "We're *all* in need of food. Patrick and Alex, you might want to . . . drink up. Even for a vampire, exorcisms will take it out of you. There's no telling what we'll be facing when the storm clears, but for now, I am going to cautiously advance the hope that we have booted his ass out the door."

"How will we know?" Patrick asked, glancing around as if he were expecting the bogeyman to jump out from behind one of the armoires or dressers.

"We'll know. If he doesn't return, it worked. I'll come

back later after I've had some sleep and check on things. Shimmer, Ralph—you'll be around at . . . oh, say . . . one or two in the afternoon?"

Ralph slowly nodded. "I don't see why not. Until we figure out whether this has done the trick, there isn't much for us to do."

"He's right," Alex said. "Shimmer, feel free to go swimming again if you like. It's . . . what . . . nearly five thirty. Patrick and I will be retiring to our beds in less than two hours. Meanwhile, I think we can all use a breather."

I was wound up. The energy had left me strung on a wire and I realized that I was not only antsy, but also horny. I enjoyed sex and it had been several months since Carter and I broke up. I'd gotten used to it on a regular schedule. Now, the hunger hit me like a fork of the lightning going on outside, straight out of the blue. I stared at Alex. But just then, Chai gently touched me on the shoulder.

"Your thoughts wander in dangerous directions, girl." He gazed down at me with those gorgeous eyes and once again, I wished that he and I could feel more for each other than the brother-sister energy we had. Chai would be safe and simple.

I turned my thoughts away from sex and cleared my throat. "It seems danger is all around me. It always has been, you know."

"Perhaps so, but vampires?" He kept his voice low, but I saw Alex dart a quick glance in our direction.

"Hush. And yes . . . even though it sounds bizarre. We'll talk about this later." I turned back to Tonya, who was wearily heading back to the ladder. "Wait for me. I'm hungry, too." I scampered over to her, eager to push away both my thoughts and Chai's observances.

Downstairs, the place looked like it had been ransacked. Not a lot was broken, but there were a number of things out of place, scattered on the floor or on tables and chairs. Several vases were smashed, and a number of plates, but thank gods Patrick said none of them were too valuable. All in all, we seemed to have gotten off easy.

Too easy, my gut warned me, but I was too tired to listen to my fears. I pushed the voice away and pulled out bread and cheese and sliced meat. Ralph grabbed the condiments, and Tonya found some plates and utensils. Chai helped Patrick and Alex sweep up the broken glass. By the time we had a stack of sandwiches made and a package of cookies opened, they'd cleaned up most of the living room and kitchen.

"We'll finish the rest of the house after we take a break," Patrick said, pulling a couple bottles of blood out of the refrigerator. "I need a drink." He looked at Alex. "You're looking pale. When's the last time you actually *fed* on someone?"

Alex blinked, staring at him. "Come on, mate, don't ask about that among . . ." He paused, glancing at Tonya, Ralph, and me, waiting to see what we'd say.

Ralph shrugged. "It doesn't bother us. *I* know you're a vampire—so does Shimmer. While she might not be used to it yet, I've worked with you for enough years to know that you need to drink from humans now and then."

Tonya cleared her throat. "I don't know much about vampires. Mother never said much when she was dating you. I thought you could go for years on bottled blood?" She sounded genuinely curious, not revolted like I'd expect her to be.

Alex, however, was obviously uncomfortable with the line of questioning. "All right. Here it is: Yes, we can subsist on both animal blood and bottled blood. But the hunger is there, the urge to hunt. Giving in to it every now and then can help to control it, unless your inner predator takes over and sends the hunting instinct into overdrive. Luckily, I've got a pretty good hold on mine."

I had the impulse to ask how many people he had turned, but then stopped myself. First—it wasn't my business. Second—that could be a very touchy subject and I didn't want to stir up any more tension than we already had.

I made another sandwich and then asked Patrick if I could heat up a can of soup. Hot food comforted me when I was tired and stressed.

He immediately jumped up to do it and when I tried to protest, he waved away my objections. "I'm your host. You're doing me a huge favor and I have no intention of making you wait on yourselves." He opened the cupboard. "What kind do you want?"

"Do you have cream of chicken?" I'd come to love the salty canned chicken soup that plopped out in the pan like a lump. I never mixed it with milk, just water, and I bought it by the case at this point.

He laughed. "Yes, I have cream of chicken. I'll make you some. Anybody else want a bowl?"

Ralph cleared his throat. "I wouldn't mind some of that."

"Me, too," Tonya said, laughing. "I haven't had cream of chicken for a long time."

In the end, Patrick opened five cans and made a huge pot, and we devoured all of it. Tonya finally pushed herself to her feet. "I need to go home. I'm exhausted. I'll be back around two o'clock to check on how things are going." She had already gathered her things together, before we ate, and so she carried her bag out to her car and drove off into the still-raging storm.

I yawned. "I'm tired, too. I want to go swimming but maybe I'll wait till morning. I'm pretty sure I can sneak out there without anybody noticing, and right now the storm might make it problematic. Once I shift into dragon form, it won't matter, but until then getting out into the strait might be an issue." Glancing over at Ralph, I asked, "Did you want to sleep in my room again?"

He frowned, then shook his head. "I think it will be okay. Get up around one? That will give us six hours of sleep and we can always catch a nap later in the afternoon if we need one."

"Sounds good." I wiggled my fingers at Patrick and Alex. "Be sure to tuck yourselves in before morning light. Night, guys."

They waved back and went back to talking. I hoped they were mending their friendship. They truly seemed to like each other, and Patrick seemed like a good guy. Hoping we had seen the last of the ghostly intruders, I took a quick shower and climbed under the covers, immediately falling asleep as soon as my head hit the pillow.

Ralph was up a little before I was, and waiting for me downstairs. He'd made toast and eggs and was setting the table. Even after the meal we'd had before bed, I realized I was hungry again. I glanced at the clock. One fifteen. There was no way I had time for a swim before Tonya arrived, so I'd go later.

Chai, on the other hand, was ready and raring to go. "I thought I'd pop back to your place and check on your fish. I have a couple other things I need to attend to, if you don't mind. I'll be back later."

"Fine. Go talk to my fish and make sure they're okay." I hugged him. "Thanks, Chai. Don't you run off on me, though, you big lug."

He chuckled. "No chance, Little Sister." And then, with a wave to Ralph, he vanished. Ralph blinked over the plates he was arranging on the table.

"How did you sleep?" I slid into the chair opposite him, eyeing the spread. It smelled delicious and my stomach rumbled.

"Uneasy." He handed me the jam for my toast. "I had nightmares about the attic." He looked tired, and when my hand brushed his from taking the jar, he jumped, but I didn't think it was shyness.

"You okay, Ralph?" I spread a thick layer of the black-berry preserves across the bread and bit into it, closing my eyes at the burst of flavor that filled my mouth. "Yum. We don't have stuff like this in the Dragon Reaches."

He grinned, then. "You mostly eat cows?"

"And sheep and whatever else we can hunt. We seldom eat in our human forms there."

"I bet this is a treat, then. And probably took you some time to get used to?" He paused, then leaned forward. "Shimmer, I don't think we got rid of the spirit. I just . . . I think there's still something in this house. My dreams were full of fire and ash and dark laughter, and when I woke up, I could have sworn I saw something leaning over my bed."

That made me stop. "What do you think it was?"

"I don't know, but I know it wasn't my imagination. I'm too logical to imagine stuff like that." He glanced around the room, then squirmed, shifting his shoulders. "Can you feel it? Like right before a big storm. The air feels charged. Something's waiting to break."

I put down my knife and the toast and sat back, closing my eyes. Taking a deep breath, I let it out slowly. There . . . what Ralph had described. I could sense it—like a rubber band being stretched to the limit, ready to soar.

"You're right. Maybe it's residue? Tonya should be here soon. I guess we wait till she shows up and see what she thinks? We can't very well ask Alex or Patrick right now."

The phone rang and Ralph picked it up. He spoke briefly, then hung up and turned around. "That was the police. Officer Paris? They put a rush on the skeleton from the yard. The coroner says the bones have been in the ground at least fifty years. Female, killed by a blow to the head. Whoever hit her broke her neck. They think it was murder because of the force of the impact and the trajectory."

"Is there a way to find out for sure if it's Lacy?"

"There might be, but even if they can, that won't tell them who murdered her." He frowned. "I want to talk to Toby again."

"Why?"

"He might be willing to provide a DNA sample that they could link to the DNA in her bones. If it's Lacy Duckland, they should find a recognizable connection." He glanced at the clock. "Want to run out to the garage before Tonya gets here?"

"Yeah, we can do that, but first . . ." I paused, thinking for a moment. "I want to go back in the attic first. I want to see if we can find anything from the rest of the family that would lead to an answer of what they were doing to her and why." The spirit of the young woman had been so gentle and so plaintive that I wanted to know her story and make sure she was set to rest.

"Are you sure you want to go back up there?"

I nodded. "Can you grab a ladder so we can reach the ceiling? Or a chair that's tall enough. I'm six feet, but the ceilings are pretty high."

"That they are. All right, I'll help you, but you have to promise me that if something starts to happen while we're up there you'll get the fuck out of the attic. I'm going to sit on the top of the ladder and keep watch both ways. The last thing we want is for the door to close on us and trap us."

"Good idea. And yes, I promise. I'll rinse off our plates while you go get the ladder." I peeked out the kitchen window. The cops were back in the yard, sifting through the area where we'd found the skeleton. "We've got company. Why don't you take them some coffee?"

"I could invite them in. We could ask them some questions. Maybe there's something else we can learn about the case?" Ralph headed toward the door.

"Sure, if you think that's a good idea?"

But he was back in a few minutes with the ladder. "They don't have time, but they send their thanks. They said that they'd be taking the tape down. There were several bags there of evidence—buttons and what looks like a few patches of cloth . . . they wouldn't talk about it, of course, but Officer Paris said that the bones will be kept for evidence. And because we already told them who we suspect it is, they're going to contact Toby about the possibility of the DNA match. After that, Paris said they'll bury her. Probably in an unmarked grave unless Toby agrees to attend to her burial arrangements."

I felt incredibly morose. "I hope Toby says yes. It doesn't seem right. Her remains should be laid to rest, and she deserves to be remembered. If he won't, maybe we can help out somehow." Following him up the stairs, I tried to push the idea of Lacy being buried as a Jane Doe out of my mind. Ralph set up the ladder and I climbed up to open the door. I decided to just ignore the folding ladder—I was able to get past it without opening it up. Ralph sat midway up the step-ladder, keeping watch down the hallway.

As I hesitantly turned on the lightbulb, a gust of wind shook the trees outside the nearest window and I stared into the bleak day. The sky was silver and rain-shorn, and everything seemed to mute into the same foggy color. But I loved the weather here, with so much rain and the winds off the ocean. Coming Earth-side had been hard enough, but at least I wasn't having to adapt to a desert or a jungle.

I started with the desk and dressers nearest me, opening every drawer, hunting through every niche. I wasn't sure what I was looking for, but if I found it, I'd know. As my toe nudged against one of the trunks, I decided I might as well go through those, too. There were at least four or five of them within reach, and more toward the center of the attic. It was as if every member of the Buckland family who had lived in this house had owned a trunk that had been secreted up here when they died.

The first was half full, and mostly souvenirs, though there was a birth certificate for Mia Buckland, who was born in 1925. That means she might have been Lacy's sister, if they had both lived here. There was nothing like a diary, but I was able to make out her story to some degree.

There was a packet of letters addressed to a Mia Buckland, from a Lt. Jacob Ayers, which were sent from Germany. The post-marks were from 1943 to 1945. I found a wedding album, with just a few pictures in it. The bride and groom looked incredibly happy and the names on the back were *Jacob and Mia, November 1, 1945*. Then, ticket stubs to *Brigadoon*, a Broadway show, from 1947. They were tied together with a red ribbon.

The next picture was of the couple in front of what looked like a large cruise ship. The banner across the ship read THE OCEANIC, and I glanced at the back. The picture was dated July 7, 1949. The next thing I found was a newspaper clipping. The *Oceanic* had sunk on its way to Alaska. Fourteen hundred people had been rescued; forty-six had died. As I skimmed over the list of the dead, I saw that Jacob and Mia Ayers and their one-year-old daughter, Tansy, were listed.

I stared at the papers, thinking about these people who had lived so long ago. If Mia had been Lacy's sister, then she must have known what went on. Had she done anything to stop it? Had she participated in tormenting her sister? I placed the items in a bag, slowly closed the trunk, and moved on to the next.

The second trunk was empty, as was the third, but in the fourth, I discovered a jumbled mess of papers and journals. I scooped everything into a bag, then checked the other trunks. I found a scattering of mementos that weren't just clothing or old dolls, so I loaded them into a third bag, then handed everything down to Ralph.

"I'm going to give Lacy's bedroom one last go-over to see if there's anything we missed." I headed back into the depths of the attic, the skin on my arms puckering as I did so. Whether it was from what we'd already been through, or if somebody was still hanging around, I wasn't sure. Seeing that I was up here by myself, I didn't really want to find out.

As I poked around and found nothing, I grumbled and sat down on the bed. The faint scent of lilac wafted over me again, and I froze.

"Lacy? Lacy, are you still here?"

The scent grew stronger. And then, the gentle touch on my shoulder. So much came through that single touch—regret, a gentle sadness, tears, and an overwhelming loneliness.

"I'm sorry. I'm so sorry." I hung my head. "I wish I could do more. Is there anything you can do to help us? Anything to help us find out who did this to you? We found your body . . ."

Suddenly, something was tugging on the hem of my jeans. I frowned, looking down, half expecting to see a hand reaching through the floor. But there was only the fragrance of lilac lingering in the air.

What was she doing? And then I realized I was staring at the floor next to the bed. What if there was something beneath the bed? I quickly crouched down, getting on my hands and knees with a flashlight. I flashed it under the frame and there, in the corner against one wall, saw yet another trunk. There were way too many cobwebs between me and that box, but I found a piece of wood and brushed them away.

After I'd cleared out some of the dust and cobwebs, I managed to snag hold of one of the handles and drag the square, flat trunk toward me. I pulled it out and made sure there was nothing else under the bed, then carried it to the front of the attic, where I set it on the surface of the desk. Cautiously, I examined the closure. It was locked, with no key in sight. But locks couldn't stop me—not anything this old. First, I was adept at picking them from my thief days. Second, I was strong. If nothing else, I could easily break the hinges on the box, because they were old and partially rusted from the salt that hung heavy in the air in the coastal town.

I fiddled with the lock. It wouldn't take much to pick, but for that I'd need my lock picks and they were in my backpack. I handed the trunk down to Ralph and then turned out the light and climbed down out of the attic, shutting the trapdoor behind me.

"What's this?" Ralph glanced at the trunk. "Should I put away the ladder?"

"Leave it, in case we need to go back up there. That's a trunk that I found beneath Lacy's bed. She's still there, Ralph. She hasn't left, and if she hasn't . . ."

"Then maybe the rest of them are here?" He frowned. "Are you sure it was her?" He carried the trunk over to the stairs.

"Just a second. Let me get my lock picks." I stopped in my room to grab my pack. As I paused, looking at the unmade bed, I thought I saw the covers move. But when I focused my attention on the blankets, they stopped. I glanced around the room. Nothing, but the feeling of unrest was growing and I let out an impatient breath. "I know you're still here," I whispered.

Rejoining Ralph, I took the trunk from him. "Yeah, I

know her feel by now. It was her. Listen, you go get all the equipment and our notes. Just do it. Bring them downstairs with us. I have a feeling . . . just, please humor me?"

He studied me for a moment. "You know the rest are still here, too, don't you?"

"Yeah," I said softly. "But I don't want to upset the apple cart right now. We have too much to lose with Alex and Patrick both sleeping."

"Then maybe we should just take all our suitcases downstairs?" Ralph gave a short nod toward my door. "What do you think?"

I paused, sussing out the energy as best as I could. It was whirling, like before a waterspout or a funnel cloud formed. "Yeah, good idea." Going back into my room, I grabbed my suitcase as well. I hadn't unpacked yet, given the unwelcoming nature of the dresser drawers when I'd first tried to settle in, so all I had to do was toss a few dirty clothes back in the case.

We met back in the hallway and helped each other get our gear downstairs. Once it was piled by the kitchen table, I felt a little silly but decided that I'd rather feel stupid than be sorry later on. I fished out my lock picks and began working on the ancient lock. It had rusted shut, but with a little oil and some adept jiggling, it didn't take long to jar it loose. Within five minutes, I'd popped the lid.

As I opened the trunk, Ralph held out the camera, intent on recording everything. I looked up at him, then back into the trunk. Inside was a bloody shawl. The shawl had been white, and the reddish brown liquid dried into the material could be nothing else. I cautiously reached out and opened the shawl, unfolding the corners. Inside lay a hammer—old and heavy—and also a pair of leather gloves.

"This was what killed her. The hammer—this is the murder weapon." I stared down at the box. I'd seen death before; I'd seen dragons murdered. But for some reason, this woman's life—and death—was touching me in a way I didn't fully understand.

At that moment, Tonya knocked on the back door. Ralph

let her in and she didn't bother with small talk, just dragged out a chair, sat down, and said, "They're still here. I dreamed it."

"Yeah, we know." I glanced up at her. "We're trying not to rile things up too much by challenging them. But we know. Look what we found today."

She peeked in the trunk. "That's what killed Lacy?"

"Yeah, and I'm pretty sure the blood is hers. We should get this to the cops. I guess they will be able to determine whether she was murdered with it. For whatever good it does. The murderers are long dead, unless they happen to be Supes . . . in which case . . ."

"They aren't. They're all too human." Ralph frowned. "We can drop this off at the station before you go swimming."

I shook my head. "No. I don't want to leave Alex and Patrick unguarded. We don't know what these spirits are capable of, and I'm too uncomfortable to let them prance around here while our friends are vulnerable."

"Good point. Well, then—should I call one of the officers?"

At that, I grinned. "Why don't you call Paris? I can tell you think she's attractive and hey, maybe she'd go out with you?" I couldn't help needling him. I'd smelled his phero-mones around her and it was all too easy to see that he had the hots for her.

Ralph blushed. "No! I mean . . . no. I don't want to bother her. We'll just drop this off later. When the guys are awake." He ducked his head in a boyish gesture that made both Tonya and me laugh, but we weren't being mean.

"I've met Paris before. She's a good sort, but she's mar-ried. So sorry to burst any bubbles on that one." Tonya glanced around. "Something . . ."

But before she could say anything else, there was a crash overhead. We jumped up as another crash sounded, and then the thumping of something large and dangerous thundered down the walls from the stairs, as if somebody were running past with a large stick, banging it against the sides of the staircase as they ran. The noise was enough to wake the dead, but unfortunately it couldn't wake Alex and Patrick.

Tonya let out a scream and I found myself on the floor as she body-slammed me to the ground. The next moment, I looked up to see a large chef's cleaver go sailing over our heads. She had managed to save me from an attempt at decapitation.

We struggled to our hands and knees as the kitchen suddenly became a veritable beehive of activity, with pots and pans flying every which way. Ralph had dropped to the floor, too, and now he cautiously popped up to grab the equipment and his laptop off the table, fumbling to stow them away as quickly as he could. I darted up and grabbed the trunk with the hammer in it, and we quickly crouch-walked our way to the door and managed to get everything out on the porch.

"Tonya, put these in the car and then get back here, but be careful. We don't know how far this thing's reach extends." I pushed her toward the backyard, then turned to Ralph. "We can't leave Patrick and Alex alone."

"I'll grab my bag of tricks and we'll see if we can calm them down with anything I've got." Tonya raced toward the driveway.

As we re-entered the kitchen, cautiously, I smelled something coming from the living room. "What's that?"

"What's what?" But Ralph stopped, his nose twitching. "Oh hell, come on!" He raced full-tilt into the living room, heedless of the chaos going on around us. I followed on his heels.

There, in the corner, near the gas fireplace, a thick cloud of smoke filtered up from one of the curtains as flames began to lick at the walls, engulfing the filmy drapes that covered the blinds.

I frantically ran through the water magic I still had available after the Wing-Liege had stripped some of my powers. I closed my eyes, calling on the moisture trapped in the air to form a rain shower over the flames. The air shimmered as my magic began to extract the water from the air, the globules beginning to coalesce. The sudden onslaught pinged toward the flames like bullets, but even though the air was laden with humidity, it wasn't enough. I couldn't seem to draw the rest forth. Something was preventing me from charming it to help us. I gave up and turned to Ralph.

"We have to get Patrick and Alex out of here!" I raced toward the staircase heading to the basement. Taking two stairs at a time, I leaped down the passage.

"They'll dust in the sunlight!" Ralph was right behind me, but I whirled, stopping him from following me.

"They'll dust if we let them burn to death, too. You call the fire department and tell Tonya to put blankets over the windows of the Range Rover so that it blacks out the light. I'll try to bring them up."

As I raced down the stairs, I prayed that I'd be able to get into their rooms. I knew they could lock from the inside, but I also knew that Patrick had emergency contingencies set into place. I only hoped that we could figure them out before the house ended up an inferno.

CHAPTER 12

The smoke hadn't reached the basement yet. Hopefully, I'd have a few minutes before the house was engulfed. And, if we were lucky, we'd save the building before too much damage was done. I darted over to the rooms Patrick and Alex were in and tried the doors. Nada. Locked from the inside. I knew Patrick wouldn't go leaving the keys down here, and I also knew that the doors were reinforced steel, which I *might* be able to break down if I tried.

I tried the door handles again, but they weren't budging. I could pick the locks, but that would take time that we didn't have. These weren't rusty and on a trunk that was going on eighty years old. The walls were stone, and that was harder to bust through than metal, especially since the doors were on hinges, which would give way faster. Standing back, I took aim and, just as Ralph came racing down the steps, charged into Patrick's door, ramming it with the full brunt of my force. As I did so, it shook and creaked, and I felt something give.

Ralph took one look at me, then joined me.

I stopped. "Are you crazy? You'll break your bones."

"Werewolf, remember? We have our fair share of superstrength, too. Jeez, why does everybody keep thinking I'm human?" He grumbled as he got into position, but then we both rammed against the door, and this time it bent a little. "I think we need to apply the most force against the side with the hinges. You go start on the other one, and I'll finish this off."

As he smashed against it one more time, the sound of tearing metal grated through the air and I winced as the door slowly broke open on the top. I helped him twist it enough to allow me to slip through the opening. There, sleeping in the semi-sarcophagus, was Patrick. I quickly wrapped his body in the sheets and handed him through to Ralph.

As I did so, I noticed a set of keys on the dresser. I grabbed those, plus his wallet, and climbed back out into the main basement. Less than ten seconds later, I'd found the master key for the bedrooms in the basement, and we were heading upstairs with both Alex and Patrick, as shielded from the light as we could manage.

When we entered the kitchen, Tonya was there, at the back door, frantic. She was holding the plastic garden tarp that the police had put over the hole beneath the maple.

"They'll both fit in this—come on. Hurry!" She spread it out and we laid the vampires down on it, then rolled them tightly. Even through the sheets, the light coming through the windows was having a bit of an effect. I could see little whiffs of smoke.

The blaring of sirens sounded outside as the fire department arrived. As we hustled Alex and Patrick into the back of the Range Rover, I saw that Tonya had, indeed, blacked out the windows with more tarps she'd found in the shed. They were taped across the glass with duct tape.

I left her and Ralph to manage the vamps and ran around front to meet the firemen. "It started in the living room—one of the curtains went up. There's nobody else inside that I know of."

They rushed inside, telling me to stand back. A lick of flames flickered against the bay window overlooking the front lawn. The entire living room was engulfed now, and who knew what other rooms were at risk? Unable to do anything else, I headed back toward the driveway, where Ralph had managed to pull the Range Rover out and into a parking spot on the street, farther away from the house. I knew why. Just in case the entire bed-and-breakfast went up, we didn't want the cars catching fire, too.

He made sure the windshield was blacked out, too, then locked all the doors. "That should protect them, and they don't need to breathe so even if it gets stuffy in there, it's not going to matter."

Tonya had parked on the street when she got there, so her car was out of danger. As for Patrick's vehicle, I had his keys so I handed them to Ralph. He moved the sedan to a safer location.

"We're going to have to stay somewhere else." Ralph turned to me. "This house is no longer safe. If it had caught on fire a few hours earlier, while we were all asleep? We'd all be dead."

That was a sobering thought. Though by now, I was beginning to think we weren't going to solve this problem and maybe it was better to burn the whole house to the ground. But would that clear the spirits out? Considering there were ghosts here from before the house was built, highly unlikely.

"You can stay with me," Tonya said. "I don't have a very big house, but I've got a basement that Alex and Patrick can sleep in, and I've got one spare room. Shimmer, if you want, you can sleep in my room with me—I have a queen-sized bed. Ralph can take the guest room." She paused and looked around. "Where's Chai?"

"He's back in Seattle, checking on my fish. I kind of wish he'd stuck around now, given all that's happened. How are we going to get Patrick and Alex over to your place without letting some light into the car? Whoever drives has to see out the windshield." I edged around, trying to see how the firefighters were faring, but it was hard to tell. The fire seemed to have spread to the kitchen, but even then, it was hard to know how much of the house it had gobbled up.

Ralph shrugged. "We could always stay here until they wake up this evening and then head over to Tonya's."

I glanced up at the sky. The clouds were heavy and it looked like we were in for a drenching soon. "We're going to get soaked. Oh, what the hell. I don't mind so much. I guess we could sit inside the car." But the prospect didn't thrill me. I didn't really have claustrophobia, but truth was, I didn't like being in small spaces. Ever since I'd been wing-strapped and locked up in the cell, I had developed a strong dislike to being shoved into tight, closed areas.

But we were saved from further debate by the arrival of Officers Roger and Paris. I wondered just how tired they were getting of seeing us. On the plus side, this meant we could hand over the trunk with the hammer in it, and nobody had to go down to the station. They stared at the house for a moment, where the firefighters were still fighting against the flames, and then joined us by the Range Rover.

"Tonya, can you get that trunk?" I leaned against the hood of the car. "Hey, officers."

"You want to tell us what's going on?" Paris glanced around. "And where's Mr. Strand and Mr. Radcliffe?"

I motioned to the Range Rover. "Safely tucked out of the light. We got them out of the house and jury-rigged a nest for them."

She nodded. "Good, good. So, what happened here?"

I told her about the ghostly activity, then about how we smelled smoke and ran in to see the curtains near the gas fireplace going up in flames. "We thought we might have put a stop to the haunting, but no such luck. And this morning, I found this in the attic. I haven't touched the hammer, but I did touch the shawl." I handed over the trunk.

Paris opened it and then wordlessly set it in the back of the police car. "Seems the Bucklands were busy beavers, doesn't it? By the way, Toby Buckland has agreed to come in and give us a DNA sample to see if we can match it to the skeleton you found. We'll test the dried blood on the shawl and hammer—if they match, that would cement the murder weapon. We still couldn't say for sure if the remains belonged to Lacy Buckland, but we could narrow it down to a member of the family if the tests comes back like I think they will."

The fire marshal came over at that point. "We think we have all the flames out, but my men will keep watch for a while to make certain. The living room is pretty much destroyed, as is part of the hallway and kitchen. But we managed to prevent the fire itself from going upstairs or into the basement. There will be smoke damage, though. I can't let you stay here. There may be structural damage to the floor in the living room, and to the ceiling over the living room. An inspector has to clear it before the house can be used as a residence again. Are you the owner?" He looked at me.

I shook my head. "No, he's . . . the owner is a vampire and can't talk to you until sunset. We're friends of his and are staying with him. We smelled the smoke and ran into the living room to find the curtains on fire. We got everybody out."

"The inspector will take a look at the point of origin today and figure out what went wrong for the report he'll need to send to the insurance company. I think you may be looking at a frayed wire in the switch that turns on the fireplace, but I can't make that call." He signed off on a form and gave it to Officer Paris. "My men will let you know when we're ready to leave the scene." He turned back to us. "I can't really let you go back in for belongings—"

"We have what we need for now, thank you. Our bags were in the car." Ralph smiled at him. It was a lie, of course, but it sounded better than us saying we'd brought our luggage with us because we were afraid of ghosts. That might just sound like people who wanted to set a house on fire.

Ralph looked over at Paris and gave her a strained smile. "You know, trouble doesn't always follow us like this." The joke was strained, but it gave us all something to laugh at, which helped relieve the tension just a little.

A thought occurred to me, and I quickly turned to Ralph. "If we had the car towed over to Tonya's house, we wouldn't have to stay here all day."

"What are you talking about?" Paris asked.

"We have Alex and Patrick safely hidden away from the light in the car. We can't very well drive it, because we'd need to uncover the windshield in order to see, and that would put them in danger from the light. So we need a way to get them over to Tonya's safely. I wish we had a couple of caskets," I jokingly added.

Officer Roger shrugged. "We can arrange that. We can bring the coroner's hearse down here, along with a couple body bags. Then we can drive them over to Ms. Harris's house."

"You can do that for us?" It sounded absolutely macabre and the perfect solution to our problem.

"Glad to help. The ME happens to be my cousin." He moved aside and pulled out his cell phone. When he returned, he was smiling. "Not a problem. He's sending his assistant, Jack, with the car. As he put it, nice to be carting around bodies that aren't going to stay dead for a change."

I cocked my head. The people of Port Townsend were odd ducks, but I kind of liked them. "How does he feel about vampires, seeing he's a medical examiner?"

Roger snorted. "He says it would make his job a lot easier if more people could get up and walk around after they'd been killed. Vinny's always been peculiar, but he's good at his job and he's got a mind like a steel trap."

Ralph was talking to Paris. I hoped he was asking her out, but then remembered that she was married. Ralph didn't seem like the polyamorous sort of guy. But when they returned, it was obvious they weren't talking dinner and a movie.

"So, Mr. Strand's house is haunted." Paris gazed up at it, a contemplative look on her face. "Ralph was telling me that whatever is in there, it's big and dangerous. I have to tell you, I don't normally go for ghost stories. So much around here is geared for tourism, but there are some odd happenings in the area. This house is right across from Fort Worden. And the fort? Has one hell of a lot of secrets."

The firemen began trooping out of the house, where they set up barrier tape.

"The inspector will need to come in," one of the men said, but it was almost a question and I sensed there was something he wanted to say. He paused, looking uncertain.

Tall and hunky, he had gorgeous brown eyes and tousled wheat-colored hair. He kind of reminded me of a short-haired Alex.

"Is something wrong?" Paris frowned, and I realized she could hear the undercurrent in his voice, as well.

"I know it sounds crazy, but I could have sworn there was somebody else in that house. But we checked every room. There was nobody else in there. Yet three of us saw shadows moving around. I thought at first you had an arsonist who had stuck around, but I guess it had to be a trick of the flames. Watch fire long enough and it seems to take on a life of its own." With that, he gave us a polite nod and headed back to the fire engine.

"The spirits are still there." I turned to the house. "And whatever that . . . that . . . *thing* is . . . he's holding the other spirits hostage. He's not about to let go of his hold on the house."

As the fire engine roared away, the ME's hearse pulled in. The attendant emerged, looking rather bemused, and promptly pulled out two body bags from the back.

I turned to Ralph. "Help him, if you would. I'll ride shot-gun with him to make certain nothing happens to Alex and Patrick. Tonya can drive her car, and you can drive the Range Rover. Do you have a spare key?"

"No, but I found Alex's keys when I was carrying him upstairs."

"Okay, we're set then."

Tonya gave the police her address and phone number, and we gave them our cell numbers. "We'll be there until further notice. When the fire marshal figures out what caused the fire, please let us know."

Paris tipped her hat to us. "Will do. And good luck. Don't come back here until we give you the go-ahead, even if you think you need to. Interfering with a fire investigation might invalidate Strand's insurance policy. The ghosts will wait for a day. And hopefully, they won't follow you where you're headed."

On that lovely thought, Roger and Paris returned to their cruiser and crept down the street. Ralph and Jack—the attendant—managed to safely get Patrick and Alex stowed inside the body bags and into the back of the hearse. I rode shotgun with Jack, while Tonya led the way, and Ralph followed the hearse in the Range Rover.

Jack didn't say much, other than, "You're not a vamp."

I grinned at him. "Obviously; if I were, either I'd be back in a body bag with my friends, or I'd be dust by now."

"What are you, then? Werewolf?" He grinned at me. "My girlfriend's a werewolf. She likes life on the wild side, for sure."

I really didn't want to get into the "I'm a dragon" discussion, so I decided that I needed to establish a cover once and for all. I thought for a moment and decided I could probably best pass for Fae. That way, I wouldn't be expected to shift under the full moon if somebody wanted to call my bluff, and there were so many types of Fae that what little water magic I could still do might be enough to pass.

"I'm Fae. A river . . ." Sprites were usually lithe and tiny. I frowned. "I'm a river nymph."

As I expected, he chuckled. "Nymph, huh?" But he didn't make the nymphomaniac joke I thought was coming next. "You're not exactly what I'd call nymphlike." He seemed to realize he might sound condescending and quickly hastened to add, "Not that you're . . . what I meant was, nymphs—seems to me like they'd be all airy-fairy and fluttery. You look like you could pack one heck of a punch if somebody gave you trouble."

I tried not to laugh. Truthfully, now that I thought about it, the idea of me passing as a nymph seemed outrageous. "Yeah, I'm a bit of a contradiction. And yes, I can pack a punch and I'm about as far from airy-fairy as you can get."

Jack, who had to be in his midtwenties and had long bushy hair, with skin as pale as a beluga whale, let out a long sigh. "I hope I didn't offend you. I'm used to dealing with the dead, not the living." And that one simple statement summed up his life right there.

Giving him a soft smile, I shook my head. "You didn't. It's okay. I imagine this isn't the easiest business to be in."

"No, but somebody has to do it. Hell, I'd like to think that when my gran went, somebody like me picked her up and took care of her. There are some real freaks in this business. Me? I respect the dead—even like your buddies here, who have passed through and come back. I don't think I'd ever want to be a vampire, but gotta respect the journey they've been on."

At that point, we eased into the driveway beside Tonya's house. It was a small cottage, pretty and tidy. Ralph parked behind us, and together, he and Jack quickly transported Alex and Patrick inside, after Tonya formally invited the sleeping vampires to enter. After Jack left, I helped Ralph carry them down to the basement, where Tonya opened the sofa bed so we could stretch them out. It was odd to think that now, within seconds, we could rid the world of two vampires and they wouldn't be able to fight back or do a thing. They wouldn't know what had happened till they crossed to the other side.

The realization of how vulnerable vamps could be scared me. At least when I was asleep, if someone attacked me, I'd have the chance to wake up, to defend myself, unless it was a sniper who was absolutely silent. But a vampire was absolutely vulnerable during his or her sleep. The thought made me want to protect Alex and Patrick, to shield them.

Once we got them settled, I carried my suitcase into Tonya's room, and Ralph took his into the guest room. Then we set up all our equipment in the living room and Tonya brought out a bag of chips and some dip and made a big pot of coffee.

"There's soda in the fridge if you want."

Ralph shook his head. Like most geeks, he was a caffeine junkie and he practically mainlined the stuff. I could take it or leave it, and to be honest, I preferred tea and lemonade to coffee.

"Do you have any tea? I especially like anything with lemon or raspberry in it." I poked around the tea caddy she had set up in one corner of the galley kitchen.

Tonya's house was small but the space was laid out smartly, and every inch was utilized in an intelligent manner. It wasn't cluttered, but cozy. Garlic braids and bundled herbs hung from the walls, and a wreath made of bay leaves was nestled on the wall above the kitchen table. However, nothing was dusty and there were no cobwebs in sight.

Tonya put on the teakettle and motioned to the cupboard. "Grab the tea bags out of there." She started taking down the garlic braids. "I don't think Patrick or Alex would appreciate having these around." She glanced around. "Otherwise, I think they'll be okay here."

I glanced at the clock. Almost four P.M. Another ninety minutes and Alex and Patrick would rise.

A few minutes later, we gathered around the table with our drinks in hand: Tonya and Ralph with their coffee, me with my tea, and a plate of cookies in the center. I brought out the bag stuffed full of paper and journals.

"We can look through all of this while we wait. You don't think the ghosts can follow us here, do you?" I glanced around, but nothing seemed out of place.

Tonya shook her head. "I have this place warded heavily. Not much can get in here, I think. Plus, that creature? I'm pretty sure it's tied to the land."

"You know . . . a thought occurs to me." I had been mulling over possibilities about what might be going on. The realization that we had been treating this all like just one big haunting stuck out. "What if we're on the wrong track? We've already decided this creature isn't a ghost. What if he's not even an astral entity? He can move things, throw things at us, cause fires. What if we are facing some sort of being that has the ability to displace itself on a spatiotemporal level?"

"What are you getting at?" Ralph cocked his head. "You have an idea, don't you?"

I nodded. "Consider this: We looked up the history of the house and found out about the soldiers and the family who vanished here. This thing has been around a long time. Suppose it's *physical*? An actual physical being that can move itself through space . . . maybe through time?"

"You might be on to something." Tonya stopped midbite and put her cookie back on her plate. "What if it can phase in and out of this realm at will? That might account for some of the shadows we saw. What if this creature exists here, in this same space, but in a slightly different realm or dimension, and crosses over now and then?"

Ralph paled. "I don't think I like that idea very much."

"I don't think any of us do, but it's a possibility we should consider." I leaned back, taking a sip of my tea. The infusion of raspberry and lemon settled deep in my body, radiating out. I stared out the window. "I'm not sure why the thought didn't come up before."

"Because we were too focused on the ghosts. But you're right, just because it has *trapped* ghosts, doesn't mean that it has to *be* a ghost." Tonya frowned, pushing back her mug. She worried the cookie into crumbs on her plate. "I'm making a connection and I'm not entirely sure what it is. Hold on . . ."

Standing, she began to clear the counters, and I could tell she was thinking as she worked. "What you're saying resonates, feels right, and it reminds me of something else, though I can't quite remember what. Something very familiar. A couple years back, I ran into something that had the same feel . . ." She frowned, concentrating as she stopped by the window and stared out into the growing dusk.

"Is there anybody in town who might know the legends of creatures and spirits that lived here before the town was established?" I carried my cup back to the kettle to refill it with hot water.

Tonya whirled around. "That's it! I know where I've felt this thing—or something very much like it! I ran into something similar at the abandoned battery." She motioned for us to clear off the table. "Set up your laptop here, Ralph. I want to show you something."

He obliged and once he was hooked to the Net, she took over and typed "Kinzie Battery" into the search engine. It brought up a string of results. She scanned through the links, then clicked on one. What came up was a picture of a brooding structure of concrete and steel.

It was obviously a military instillation of some sort, but it was equally obviously abandoned. The word *KINZIE* was emblazoned across the top, with the date 1909 on one side, and the date 1940 on the other. The building stretched wide, entirely in concrete, with double staircases on either end, and then staircases from the second story to the roof.

Two wide openings hid behind the center columns on the main floor, and either the doors had been removed or they were open so far I couldn't see them. They led into the dark bowels of the building. On the floor above, a similar setup with three openings peered out from between the staircases leading to the top of the roof. The paint had weathered away, though it still looked like it had once been painted with camouflage, and the structure appeared to have been graffiti tagged. The concrete looked old and dirty, and the staircases rusty.

"That looks about as inviting as the cell they had me in back in the Dragon Reaches." I grimaced. "What the hell was it used for?"

Ralph peered over Tonya's shoulder. "It was a fortification in Fort Worden, which, apparently, added a couple guns to the defenses. The battery was able to defend below the level of the fog—which was extremely important when you think about how an enemy could sneak in silently from the water onto the shore."

Tonya nodded. "Okay, so I went there a few years back when I returned to Port Townsend. I used to live over in Aberdeen on the far west coast of Washington. I moved there when I first left home, and only came back when my mother and I made up our differences. Anyway, I went out for a walk early one morning and ended up at the battery. Immediately, I began to get cold sweats. By the time I got there, I was scared out of my mind and afraid to go in."

"Did you see anything?"

She shrugged. "Shadows moving. I kept hearing a deep laughter in my head, and had the feeling that something was trying to pressure me to go deep within the building. Luckily, I had my personal shields up and I was able to resist, but there was something there that I *knew*—*I absolutely knew*— could influence people's actions. Some dark shadow creature."

"Lacy said that something was making her family do

what they did to her. Okay, let's say this shadow creature can influence behavior. Let's say, for the sake of argument, there's more than one of them. I know the battery is in Fort Worden, which is across the street from Patrick's house, but this spirit seems bound to the house and land here. Maybe they are territorial?"

"Or tied to their territory by some connection?" Tonya bit her lip and then let out a gasp. "Hold on. Let me look up something in my bestiary here." She crossed to a bookcase with locked glass doors, turned the lock with an ornate key, and pulled out an old book with a leather cover. As she sat down again and gently cracked the spine, the pages crackled. "Kindly keep all edibles and beverages away from me while I look through this. I can't afford to lose this."

I put my tea on the counter, and Ralph did the same with his coffee. I had the feeling we were in the presence of what was probably a very old artifact. As she slowly paged through, cautiously turning each page, I sensed something else and, leaning forward, I put the tip of one finger on the leather binding.

"*Dragon* leather . . ." I stared at the book, both fascinated and horrified. "Tonya, that's made out of dragon leather." The skin of one of my kind had been used to bind this book.

"I know." She didn't look up. "I'm sorry, but there's nothing I can do about it, and the leather is what keeps these pages intact. The magic from the hide slows the aging of the pages by an incredible amount. But even so, I'll have to recopy every page within the next few years and put the new pages in the binding. That's been done a couple of times."

"Where did you get this book? It's not something you can buy off eBay." Ralph frowned.

Tonya glanced up, grinning. "I found it on a dead wolpertinger out in the Hoh rain forest."

"A dead . . . what?" I'd never heard the word, but Ralph gave her a sharp look.

"Wolpertinger. A Bavarian chimera. When I found it, it had turned back into its natural form—a very large rabbit with antlers, wings, and nasty claws. But wolpertingers can shapeshift. And they are terribly nasty. When they shift into human form, they tend to be lowlifes and toadies for bigger, badder guys. I was out doing some wildcrafting—" She paused and gave Ralph a shake of the head. "Don't even *start...*"

"Start what?" I had no clue what she was talking about.

Tonya gave me a sheepish shrug. "The park officials don't appreciate those of us who might take it in our heads to do a little plant collecting. I never take anything even remotely endangered."

Ralph laughed. "Okay, then. We won't tell Paris and Roger."

Tonya stuck out her tongue at him. "Anyway, I heard a noise. It can be dangerous out there if you're alone. There are some freaks, yes, but the spirits of the forest are numerous and chaotic. So I hid. I saw this Fae—he was strong and lean and had pale blond hair—racing through the forest after another figure, a short, squat man who was barreling past like no rock or tree stump could stop him."

I stared at her. "You really do get around, don't you?"

"Don't you mean to add, *For a human?* And yes, I do." But she laughed. "I'm not sure what the ruckus was about, but the upshot was that the Fae caught the wolpertinger, killed him, and then something startled *him*, and he ran. I waited, but nothing showed up and so I meandered over to take a look at the body. The creature had shifted back into his natural form. I found his backpack, which he had tossed under a bush in their fight, and this book was in it. My guess is the Fae was after this book. But he left before he could find it, so I ended up with it."

I gazed over her shoulder. The language it was written in was foreign to me, but as she ran her hands over the runic symbols, I could somehow read them. Ralph gasped and backed away. *Of course.* Magic made him nervous.

"That's a wolpertinger. And next to it? The creature I think we're facing." She pointed to the page. There was a picture—hand drawn—of the wolpertinger, and as she said, next to it was a drawing of another creature. Its face was malicious, almost barklike in nature. *A forest wight.* Among the forest wight's various and dubious talents was the ability to control humans through subliminal suggestion. Also, the ability to move in blurred form, so quick that mortal sight wouldn't be able to see more than a dark shadow.

"They stake out territory and claim that land as theirs. They feed on fear, pain, humiliation, and anger, and tend to pick victims who are weak-willed by nature, using them to bring harm to others." Tonya looked up at me. "Forest wights hive. They are solitary within their lairs, but you'll always find them in groups within a given area. In other words, they won't be pals, but you can be sure that where there's one, there will be more."

I arched my back, stretching. "Then, if we're facing a forest wight, the question is: How do we kill it?"

"No, I think the question at hand is, what the hell is going on?" Alex opened the door leading to the basement and, carrying their body bags, both he and Patrick stepped into Tonya's kitchen. "What the hell happened and where are we?"

CHAPTER 13

"Alex, you're awake!" I was so happy to see that he and Patrick were all right that I practically smothered them both in a bear hug. Or dragon hug. Take your pick. Patrick gave me a boyish grin while Alex laughed and—without thinking—planted a passionate kiss on my lips. I heard Ralph clear his throat, and Tonya snicker, but neither said a word as we turned around, although Ralph had a crestfallen look on his face.

"As to where you are, welcome to my world." Tonya waved to them from the table and went back to the book, taking down notes. "You have Shimmer and Ralph to thank for not being two piles of dust right now."

"What are you talking about?" Patrick looked confused. I let out a long sigh and slipped my arm through his elbow, garnering an odd look from Alex. "Come over to the table and sit down. There's something we have to tell you."

Looking worried, both vampires silently followed me to the table. We settled in and I glanced over at Ralph, who gave me a nod.

"First, the exorcism didn't work. The spirits are still there."

"Wonderful, but what does that have to do—" Alex started to say, but I cut him off.

"The spirits are still there and they started a fire, and your bed-and-breakfast is now lacking a living room and part of a kitchen." I didn't like being so blunt, but it was cruel to pussyfoot around. And though I could be clueless at times, I wasn't deliberately mean.

They both stared at me like I'd grown another head or stated I wanted them to turn me into a vampire. I thought of saying more, but I'd just be blathering at that point and I didn't trust my sense of propriety not to say the wrong thing at the wrong time.

After a minute, Patrick managed to stutter out a few words. "My house burned down?"

"Part of it. The creature started the fire, though I imagine the fire marshal will find a more logical reason. But yeah, your house needs some major renovations. We managed to get you guys out, but it wasn't easy. You might want to install some emergency settings on those rooms in the basement so we don't have to bust the hinges off the metal doors." Ralph gave him a sympathetic look. "Truth is, you're lucky that the spirit picked a time when Shimmer and I were awake, or we'd all be toast now."

The men remained silent for a moment, so I decided to plunge on ahead with the rest of our news. "We found the murder weapon used to kill Lacy. It was under the bed in the attic. And I found a bunch of papers up there I want to go through. We might be able to figure out what happened to her through them. We also figured out that the dominant spirit, the one keeping the others trapped, probably isn't a spirit at all but actually may be a forest wight. A creature that lives between the realms. We think it's feeding off the fear and chaos its causing."

Again, they stared at me, silent. Alex cleared his throat and leaned forward. "So . . . we're not chasing ghosts . . ."

"We are," Ralph said. "We're also chasing this forest

wight, which can trap spirits. We think he feeds off their pain. And they're easier for him to keep under control."

"Now that we know what he is, we can probably figure out a way to trap him—" Tonya started, but Patrick stood, shushing her.

"I've had it. I don't want to trap this creature, or free the spirits, or look through a sack full of old papers. Right now, I don't care who killed Lacy Buckland, or why they buried her in my yard. My business is in the toilet. The High Tide Bed-and-Breakfast should have just burned down entirely—I'd probably be better off because then, at least, I could collect the insurance money and sell the land and leave without a problem." He jumped up and stomped over to the refrigerator, then stopped cold. "I don't suppose you have any bottled blood?"

Tonya winced. "I'm sorry—I knew I forgot to buy something this afternoon. I can run out and grab a six-pack." She started to stand, but Patrick shook his head.

"Don't bother. And don't get me wrong. I appreciate you guys saving my ass—our asses—but I'm tired of this. I'm tired of fighting an invisible enemy. I just want to get on with my life. For what it's worth anymore, at least." And that was a telling sentence because he dropped to the floor, back against the sink cabinet, and stared at the toes of his boots, looking terribly morose.

Alex glanced at me. I shrugged. I didn't have a clue what to say. Patrick was his friend, not mine. So Alex settled himself next to Patrick and leaned back, too, staring at the ceiling.

Ralph went back to whatever it was he was searching for on the Net, while Tonya studiously ignored the pair of vamps, her nose deep in her book. I wasn't sure what to do, so I leaned across the table to watch Tonya.

"Mate, what's eating you?" Alex spoke in low tones, but we could all still hear him.

Patrick didn't answer for a moment, and then he said, "This isn't the way I thought it would be. None of it."

"Do you want to take a walk outside? We can talk privately." Alex leaned back on one hand and quickly jumped to his feet. He was lithe and strong, and the buckles on his motor-cycle boots jingled a little as he steadied himself against the kitchen sink. As I watched him, I found myself wondering what he looked like underneath those jeans and boots. Determined that I was going to find out as soon as possible, I tried to steer my thoughts back to the issue at hand.

Patrick accepted his hand. He brushed off the back of his jeans. "No, it's okay." They returned to the table and sat down, Patrick mulling over whatever it was that stewed inside him.

Alex poked his head over Tonya's shoulder, frowning. "That's an old book, love."

She nodded. "Very old. And this is our spirit." She pointed to the picture of the forest wight. "He can move in a blur and a shadow. He feeds off pain and anger and can influence mortals to do what he wants them to. He's basically a fucked-up little sadist."

Patrick hunched his shoulders then, letting them slump, deflated in his chair. "Okay, we'll do this. I'm sorry I was so whiny. I'm just . . . I wanted to be a vampire for so long. Alex—he was the first vamp I met and he made it all look so easy. He was—is"—he looked over at Alex and smiled softly—"one of the coolest dudes I've ever met. When I found out I had aplastic anemia, I asked him to turn me. I didn't want to die. I was scared."

"Anybody would be." Tonya gave him a faint smile. "Mortal life? We're told we should enjoy it more, that it's more valuable because it's so short, but the truth is, that's a bunch of bullshit. Death sucks and most of us don't have any choice about the matter."

Patrick laughed then. "I love how blunt you are. You're your mother's daughter, all right, minus the part where she kept threatening to cut off my dick." He grinned at her and she returned the smile. "Okay, so yeah, I didn't want to die. I don't know if Alex has told you the rest . . ." It was more of a statement than a question— but we all shook our heads. Better he think we didn't really know anything about the matter.

After another pause, he continued. "I asked Alex to turn me."

"I should have helped you out, I realize that now." Alex interrupted him, a guilt-ridden look in his eyes. "I was being selfish."

"You were being kind. I had no clue what being a vampire would mean and you tried to tell me, but all I could see was that long dark journey into oblivion and right then, anything sounded better than going there."

Patrick leaned back and crossed his arms, one side of his lip tilted up in a half smile. "I should have listened, I guess. After you left, I spent a couple months partying really hard. A friend—or rather, a cocaine buddy—introduced me to Zera, a vampire. We partied at her place. I couldn't let them use me as a bloodwhore because I was so low on blood as it was, but then . . . she took me aside one night and offered me what I had longed to hear. The chance to become a vamp. She said she'd turn me and we could be together. I didn't care so much about the latter. Oh, I liked her enough, but what I really wanted was that immortality. That freedom from disease and decay and death—the three big Ds."

"So you let her turn you." Alex stared at him.

"I let her turn me. I put my affairs in order first, and then . . . I went to her. It was rough, bad—she made it hurt. That's when I realized she enjoyed the struggle. She got off on pain, but not so much from bloodwhores but other vamps. We spent three years together and every single day she made my life hell. She was really into pain."

"Sadist, was she?" Alex's voice was steady in that icy cold way that I knew meant his temper was up. If he ever found this Zera, she'd be toast. "How did you get away from her, then?"

Patrick shrugged. "It was actually easy once I decided to do it. Zera wanted to travel to Europe, so she booked passage on a boat. I was supposed to go with her, but instead of going to sleep in my coffin that night, I sneaked out and managed to evade her bodyguards. They never thought I'd disobey my sire.

They gave up and left and . . . well . . . I haven't heard from her since then."

"So here you are."

"So here I am. I took up a new business. I dropped in on my relatives, but once they found out that I hadn't died, that I'd been turned, they ordered me out of their house. My own mother and father moved away, refusing to acknowledge me as their son. They think I'm some demon from hell." He winced at that and I realized that Patrick had no family, either. Not any longer.

Alex glanced at me with a warning not to say anything. So I sat silent, just listening.

"Look, mate. You would have lost them anyway, once their time's up. In a way, consider it a blessing because you don't have to say good-bye to them. It's not a walk in the park watching everybody you love die around you, while you never age a day. I think that's harder than having no family at all."

Patrick shrugged again. "I wouldn't know. I'm still too new at this to know very much. But I do know that I want a bottle of blood while we discuss how to handle this critter who's taken over my house. I'll run out and get a six-pack."

"You want company, man?" Ralph jumped up. "I could use a mocha and some chips."

"Sure, come along, wolf boy, and tell me all about what your boss has been doing for fun the past few years." With a wink, Patrick caught his keys as I threw them to him, and he and Ralph headed out the door.

I let out a long breath. "I feel sorry for him."

"I do, too, love. I do, too." Alex scooted his chair back. "Why don't we put the discussion of how to deal with this forest wight on hold till they get back. I wouldn't mind a little fresh air. Care for a walk?"

At my look, he snorted. "I know I don't have to breathe, but that doesn't mean I don't like being outside, now does it? Remember, I came from bush country—"

"Yeah, how long ago? You've been in the USA a long time, so you should be acclimated to city life, I'd think."

Razzing him, I slid into my jacket and followed him outside.

A few minutes later, we were standing on the porch steps. The storm had abated, the waning moon was out, and the air smelled oh so fresh and clean. The call of the water stirred my heart and I let my head drop back and inhaled deeply, my blood rising at the thought of the waves.

"You love it. You absolutely love it. The water, the salt in the air. I wish we could be nearer to the actual ocean back in Seattle. I see you like this and I feel guilty about keeping you in the city. But we'll do everything we can to make it easier on you. I promise." He paused. "I also . . . it turns me on to watch you when you're caught up like that. There's something sensuous about your look . . . wild and rapt and wanton."

Our eyes met and he slowly reached out his hand. "Walk with me?" His voice was husky.

My breath in my throat, I extended my fingers to meet his and he curled his hand around mine. Turning, we silently walked down the porch steps and into the front yard. My heart was thudding so loudly in my chest I was surprised he couldn't hear it, but if he did, he said nothing, just ran one finger lightly over my hand.

When we came to the Range Rover he paused, then unlocked the back. The windows were still taped over. He stopped, staring at the tarps. "What on earth?"

"Like we told you, we had to find a way to get you out of the house safely. Tonya covered the windows with heavy tarps, and Ralph and I wrapped you and Patrick from head to toe and hustled you into the back of the car to get you away from the fire. Then we drove you here in a hearse, in the body bags you were wearing."

"You truly saved our lives." Alex stared at the blacked-out windows a moment more, then slowly walked me against the back of the car, pressing his chest against my breasts. "There's room in the back," he said, his voice husky. "Tell me you want me. You have to be the one to make the final decision."

Shivering, I could barely breathe. "Take me. Here. Now."

Alex spun me to the side and yanked open the rear door. Then he boosted me in. Bracing one hand on the side, he leaped in with one swift, sure movement and shut the door behind us. It was pitch black, but he took a slim flashlight out of his pocket and flicked it on, setting it to the side. In the dim light, he looked feral, and I could see that his fangs were extended.

"Alex . . . I don't want . . ."

"You don't want me drinking your blood."

"Not yet . . . maybe never. That has to be earned." A bolt of fear shot through me. What if his predator couldn't handle rejection? But then I stopped myself. I was a dragon. I might not be able to shift my form here, but I was damned strong. I could handle him if need be.

"Rules understood. My rule? No hard pointy things in the bed unless they're attached to me." With a rough laugh, he tumbled me back onto the pile of tarps, straddling me as he leaned down to lock his lips against mine. The feel of his tongue in my mouth, the scent of him and his chill touch, sent shock waves of hunger through my body, rippling in waves from my breasts to my pussy.

I moaned into his mouth, wanting more, so horny I felt like I was going to jump out of my skin. I shifted position beneath him as he held me down with my arms stretched over my head. His lips traced my face as he kissed my eyes, my cheeks, my mouth, then moved down to lick my neck with one long, luxurious stroke.

"Oh, Shimmer . . ." Alex shuddered, and I realized he was smelling the blood racing through my body. His eyes were turning crimson and his fangs were out, but he kept his promise, fastening his lips to my throat to suck hard without breaking the skin.

I was growing wet, so wet, and I let out a growl as I squirmed, spreading my legs so he could fully lean between them. The bulge in his jeans was rock hard against my leg, and he laughed, grinding against me.

"You like that? Can you feel me, love? Can you feel how much I want you?"

Panting, I struggled to reach for the zipper on my jeans. "Yes, damn it. Let me out of these things."

Alex pulled back and I unzipped my jeans, scrunching them down as he unbuckled his belt. In a frenzy, we were shedding our clothes, heedless of the cold, and then—we were naked, on our knees, staring at one another. I was panting heavily. His chest never rose, never fell, but his gaze was fastened on me and I could feel the hunger rising from both of us, like wild dogs hunting.

I slid into his arms, and his hands found my breasts, as I wrapped my fingers around his rock-hard cock. He moaned into my ear and then leaned down to lightly tug on my nipple with his teeth. A rising swell spread through my hips, making me ache as he flicked it with his tongue, then sucked hard—so hard that it almost hurt. I let out a cry as the ache spread through my body—the need to be touched and explored everywhere so strong that tears sprang to my eyes.

He drew me onto his lap, and I wrapped my legs around his waist as his cock hovered between my thighs. With one hand, he braced my back; with his other, he reached down to slide his fingers over my clit, pinching just hard enough to elicit another moan from my lips. I struggled, wanting him inside me, trying to slide forward, but he managed to hold me at bay as he toyed with me, slipping two fingers inside my pussy, which was so wet that he met no resistance at all.

"You like this, Shimmer? You want more?" The look on his face was one of triumph, of sheer delight as he locked my gaze.

I licked my lips, hungry and gasping as his touch set off a series of sparks, chaining like lightning through my body. "Yes, I want more. Please, fuck me. Please . . ." I struggled again, reaching for his hips, trying to urge him forward so there would be only one place he could go.

"Not yet. Oh, love, not quite yet." And then he pushed me down so I was on my back again, and his head was between my legs. His lips found my clit, and with long strokes, he worried it with his tongue, swirling the nub—at first so gently I shrieked and struggled to get away from the insistent tickle. But he held my hips firmly, and then the tickle turned into a rougher stroke, and he lightly bit down. The sharp pain sliced through the grating tickle and sent me spiraling. I gasped, tears filling my eyes, but then he was sucking steadily, and the rhythm sent a shock wave through me as I came, sudden and unexpectedly, crying out.

But through it, he never stopped, continuing, and as soon as the dizzying wave passed, I was building up again, caught in a haze of hunger and need. I came again, and once again as he plunged two fingers inside me with his lips still fastened to my clit. Then, he pushed himself up. As I propped myself up on my elbows, panting, he grabbed my wrist and flipped me over. I was on my hands and knees and he began kissing my back, trailing his lips down over the curve of my ass. Wrung out, drenched with sweat and so caught up in the hunger that was still not satisfied, I could feel nothing but the sensation of his touch.

And then, I felt him, parting the lips of my vagina with his fingers, spreading them wide as he plunged the head of his cock—hard and icy cold and thick—inside me just enough to tease me. He held it there, just stretching the lips, and the pressure in my stomach threatened to overwhelm me. Then, with one long, hard stroke, he drove himself deep, his thrust so hard it pushed me forward. I moaned, leaning down so that my butt was in the air and my breasts were pressed against the bed of the Range Rover.

"Fuck me, Alex . . . fuck me hard."

"Oh, yes, love. I'll give it to you as hard as you want." He grunted and drove forward, so deep in me that he was up to the hilt, and I could feel his balls slap against the back of my ass. With every thrust, I let out another cry, as I reached down with one hand to finger my clit. I rubbed, hard, as Alex continued to pump, the girth of his cock thick enough to stretch me wide. I let him set the pace, meeting his strokes with my own rocking.

As I lost myself in the fucking, the air grew thick with moisture. I could feel it in my lungs, against my skin. I was close—so close again. I rubbed my clit furiously. "Harder, harder . . . please . . ."

Alex groaned, his pace picking up as he drove himself over and over again into my body. "I'm going to come, baby. I'm close—"

I squeezed my clit at the moment he gave one final thrust, the head of his cock barreling deep. As he shouted, still pumping against me, I let go, spiraling into the tidal wave that swept through my body; the orgasm sent me into a fit of laughter and tears. Spent, Alex leaned against my back, still inside me. His skin remained icy cool but it felt good against the heat and sweat that covered me.

The next moment, I felt a gentle rain against my skin— soft droplets that swirled through the back of the car, softly falling against us.

"What? It's raining . . ." Alex pushed himself to the side, rolling onto his back. "Look!" His voice was filled with almost a wonderment as he pointed to the ceiling of the car.

I nestled in his arm as the dew covered us with mist and shimmering droplets and looked up. There, against the metal, was a swirling pattern, coiling like scrollwork, in sparkling blue and silver.

"I think . . . I think I caused this. My magic—Alex, my water magic. But it's never happened before like this . . . And I've had a lot of sex through the years. Mostly casual encounters, but—"

"Shush. Just accept it as something beautiful." Alex stopped my words with a kiss. He kissed me deeply, gently, and then—as we watched in silence—the pattern faded and vanished.

"How bad is Patrick's house, truly?" Alex stared into the dark street. We were dressed again, sitting on the tail end of the Range Rover. There wasn't much to say at this point about our tryst, and I had the feeling we were both privately processing our feelings about what had just happened.

"Not good. The house isn't totally trashed—it's not like there isn't anything left, but it's not going to be ready for the public anytime soon, spirits or not. If he doesn't get rid of that forest wight, I'm pretty sure he won't be able to sell the land. With the Gypsy curse bungling up finances, until we deal with all aspects of this problem, your friend Patrick might as well just walk away and abandon it if he decides he doesn't want to go through with the bed-and-breakfast idea."

"And you think . . . you and Tonya and Ralph . . . that we can tackle this?"

"I don't know. We were about to discuss that when you two woke up and joined us. At least we found the murder weapon that killed Lacy. And if Toby's DNA proves she's a Buckland, we'll have some form of identification for her."

"Will that change anything, though? It won't punish her murderer—he, or she, is probably long dead."

"I know." I caught Alex's gaze again and held it. "But don't you think she deserves a name? That she deserves to be recognized as someone other than a Jane Doe?"

He pressed his lips together, then turned to lean back against the car and stare up at the sky. A few stars were creeping through the cloud cover, twinkling down through the chilly night.

"Names mean a lot to you." It was a simple statement, but it made my cheeks flush.

"Yes, they do. Maybe it's because I don't have a name."

"You're *Shimmer*, love. Isn't that a name? And it fits you, you know. It fit you tonight." He reached out to stroke my cheek as he smiled, but I couldn't return this one. The subject hit too close to home.

"Alex, you know . . . you know that I don't have a name in the Book of Records. I'm listed as Shimmer, under the Lost and Foundling Registry, but I have no existence in the lineage of the Dragon Reaches. My mother didn't give me a name; therefore . . . I don't exist. I'm illegitimate simply by the fact that my parents are unknown. Until I find out who they were, I'll never have a respectable standing among my people."

And there it was in a nutshell. I didn't exist to the dragons in the Dragon Reaches, not in any proper manner. I wasn't suitable, or regarded in any fashion. I was lower than the lowest caste . . . A name meant everything—a proper dragon name, given in secret with only the mother and child ever knowing what it was.

"There's part of me missing, Alex. I don't know how to describe it, but it feels like there's a part of me that was left unborn the day of my birth. My clutch mates probably feel the same way, but I have no idea who they are or where they'd be . . . or even how many of us there were. The Lost and Foundling won't tell you that—they won't let you ever meet your siblings. They think it might promote rebellious attitudes. So I don't even know if I have any brothers or sisters."

Alex looked about ready to say something when headlights blinded us as another car pulled in. Glad I'd pulled myself together, I shaded my eyes from the lights till the car pulled up close enough for us to see that it was a police cruiser. Officer Paris again. She waved to us, a tight but friendly wave. We wandered over to her.

"Hey, Shimmer. I have some news. Can we go inside? It's a little cold out here for me." She shivered and I realized again just how fragile humans could be.

Tonya looked up as we entered, and pushed her book back. She offered Paris a chair.

Paris sat down but refused the coffee Tonya offered her. "Thanks, but I can't stay long. I wanted you to know tonight, though. The hammer checks out as the murder weapon. As for whether Lacy Buckland left the area, records are so spotty that there's no real way for us to check. But I asked Mable down at the library—she runs the local genealogy club—if she could do some hunting around. She's on the case with her group." Paris leaned back with a soft smile and looked around.

"Wonderful. I don't know what they can dig up, but the family-tree clubs tend to yield a lot of good information." Alex gave her a nod. "I've gone to them for cases in the past."

"They do, at that, and Mable? Avid researcher. She'll find anything if there's anything to be found. But there's another reason I came over tonight. I was hoping Mr. Strand would be here." She looked around. "Is he here? I don't see Ralph, either."

"No, they went to the store, but they should be back soon."

"Unfortunately, I really can't wait. I have to question someone about a burglary investigation. I'll tell you, and you can tell Patrick. The inspector found a frayed wire in the wall that led to the fire. Nothing suspicious about it—just . . . old house, old wiring. They've forwarded the information to the insurance agency." She stood and put her hat back on. "Give my regards to everyone else and have a good evening." And then she was out the door.

I looked over at Tonya. "Nothing suspicious, my ass. I know that the forest wight started that fire."

"Oh, I'm with you on that," she said. "But I'm glad it shook out this way. Patrick won't have a hard time with his insurance in getting money for repairs. That could be problematic if the report had listed suspicious activity—they might think he was torching his own place." Tonya shrugged. "*We* know it was the forest wight; the insurance company doesn't need to."

"True enough. It's not like there's much they can do about it. And it seems there might not be much *we* can do about it, either." Antsy, I reached for the bowl of chips Tonya had put on the sideboard and began to aimlessly munch my way through them. "Is there somebody . . . anybody . . . around here who might know more about these creatures?"

Tonya crooked her eyebrows. "Funny you should ask. I was just thinking we should talk to Degoba Jones. If anybody can help us, it will be him." She pulled out her cell phone.

"Who's that?" Alex leaned over and sniffed the chips. "Do you know that as long as I've lived, I've never had a chance to taste a potato chip? They weren't around when I was turned. Always liked the way they sound, though."

"You aren't missing a lot. They're filled with carbs and really greasy. Degoba is his nickname—I'm not even sure anybody knows what his real name is. He's a local legend. His mother was from one of the Salish tribes. Grew up over in the Quinault area. Degoba is the man to ask about local myths, creatures, urban legends from the area. He stores up stories like a vacuum sucks up dirt." She was on her phone the next minute, calling him.

Ralph and Patrick chose that moment to tromp back through the door. They were carrying several bags of groceries, though Patrick's turned out to mostly be bottled blood. He'd also bought a bouquet of flowers for Tonya, as a thank-you gift. She motioned for him to put them on the counter while she finished her phone call.

Ralph emptied a bag filled with more chips, chocolate, cookies, and crackers on the counter, along with a couple six-packs of Flying Horse. I stared at the energy drink and the image of a puppy on espresso crossed my mind, but I repressed the urge to snicker. Ralph didn't need me cutting his ego by suggesting he was still a wolf cub.

Tonya hung up. "Degoba said to come on over in an hour. He's just finishing his dinner now. Wow, Ralph, you really have an appetite."

He motioned to the pile. "Both you and Shimmer, feel free to dig in. I bought this for all three of us. Just leave my Flying Horse alone." His grin was infectious.

"I don't think you have much to worry about in that capacity." I picked up a package of beef jerky and opened it, sliding a couple of the pieces out into my hand. "So, this Degoba Jones . . . he'll believe us about what's happening?

"Oh, he'll believe us. That thing I told you about, that I met in the battery? Degoba was the first person I trusted to talk about it. He didn't say much but warned me to stay away from the area. I have a feeling he knew what it was but didn't want to scare me at that point." She set her book off to the side so no one could spill crumbs on it and meandered over to the counter, where she picked up the bag of oatmeal cookies. "Let's go relax in the living room till it's time to go over to his house. We all need a little time-out and we can tell Patrick the good news—such as it is."

We followed her in and, once we were all curled up on the sofa and in her armchairs, we told Patrick and Ralph what Paris had said. Patrick looked more relieved than anything else.

"I don't care if Puff the Magic Dragon flew down and lit the thing on fire, I'm just glad the actual cause of record is something that I can collect on. I'm beginning to hate that house. That sucks, actually, because I loved it when I bought it. It seemed like the perfect getaway . . ." He stared morosely at the bottle of blood in his hand, and I thought it was a good thing vampires couldn't get drunk because if he could, he'd probably be plowing through the bottles.

"So, this Degoba Jones . . ." Ralph leaned forward. "He's good at what he does? He's a shaman?"

"I don't know that I'd call him that." Tonya leaned back and put her feet up on the ottoman. She frowned. "He's . . . he can work energy, though he won't talk much about it. But he's . . . I think he's a spiritwalker."

"What's a spiritwalker?" I had never heard the term, and both Patrick and Ralph looked confused. Alex, on the other hand, was nodding.

"We had them in Australia. They walk connected to the land in a way that isn't witchcraft, nor is it some woo-woo white-light and fluff-bunny business. They are so keyed into the land around them that they might as well be part of it. Half the time they can blend into the landscape so well, you'd think they could turn invisible."

"I'm not sure they can't." Tonya wrapped her knees beneath her, tucking a light throw around her shoulders. The room wasn't cold, but the winter chill still hung in the air. "Degoba won't tell anybody about his birth, where he came from, or how old he is. I'd place him around fifty, but you never can tell, especially with someone in touch with magic."

"Is he married? Family?" Ralph was on his second Flying

Horse. He'd already had a couple venti cups of coffee and if I didn't know how much caffeine the werewolf normally downed during the day, I'd be worried about him. But I knew he could handle it.

"Not that I know of. If he ever did have a wife and kids, he never speaks about them. We can figure out our next step after talking to him." She shuddered. "Why do I have a feeling it may lead to a trip to the battery?"

A shiver ran up my spine as I remembered the pictures. It looked bad enough during the daylight. Visiting at night, even with two vampires in the mix? Not exactly what I would call a good time.

"Pretend you didn't say that and maybe it won't happen. That place looks as welcoming as a black hole. Worse, in fact, because most black holes don't have any consciousness. This one seems to." I finished off the package of jerky and reached over to snag a couple cookies from her.

Right about then, there was a rustle in the air next to me and Chai shimmered into view. He coughed and looked around, clearly confused. "Um, when last we spoke, wasn't I in somebody else's house? The vampire's?" He spotted Patrick and gave him a wave. "His house?"

"Yeah, there was a fire. The ghost set the curtains on fire and we had to . . . oh, never mind, it's convoluted and was one horrendous headache but the upshot is, we're staying here with Tonya. And in about twenty minutes, we're heading out to meet a . . . what did you call him, Tonya?"

She shook her head. "Spiritwalker. That's what he calls himself, so that's what I call him."

Chai scratched his head, then shrugged and cautiously eased himself down on one end of the sofa. He was a big man—djinn—and I knew that he was always a little touchy about furniture and whether it would hold his weight.

We puttered for a few more minutes, making small talk, but everybody was antsy. The energy of the town was odd— isolated. It covered us like a soft shroud that seemed to cut off the rest of the world.

Finally, as if sensing we needed to be on the move, Tonya stood. "It's almost eight. We can stop at Rayhill's Espresso on the way over."

We trooped out to the cars, sorting out that Patrick would ride with Tonya, and the four of us—Chai, Alex, Ralph, and I—would follow in the Range Rover. I stared up at the sky. The clouds parted briefly, and the icy shimmer of stars glittered down, cold and distant.

I climbed in the passenger seat, hoping to hell Degoba would have some answers for us. Alex put the car into gear and we eased onto the silent street behind Tonya, inching our way through the low-rolling mist that shrouded the road. The stars vanished as another army of clouds rolled in, ready to lay siege to the city. The feel of the rain-soaked air set in, and I shivered as the sound of a foghorn echoed mournfully in the distance. All around us, I could feel creatures hidden in the shadows, and they watched us as we crawled down the road. Not all of them were friendly, and some of them felt downright dangerous. The land here was old, and humans were young, and the creatures lurking in the shadows knew that they were truly the ones at the top of the totem pole. Sometimes, Earthside seemed even more daunting than the Dragon Reaches.

CHAPTER 14

Degoba Jones lived a ways out—not exactly in the country, but given the size of Port Townsend, he might as well have been rural. Tonya navigated the dark two-lane road like a champion and we made it there about fifteen minutes later. As we got out of the car, I realized that—had I not known about the town—I wouldn't have realized Port Townsend existed. A mere fifteen-minute drive had plunged us into the forest.

The lights coming from within the old farmhouse shone with a warm and welcoming glow. I shivered as we followed Tonya up the porch steps. The forest was thick on either side and I really didn't fancy being out here in the dark alone.

Degoba opened the door as soon as Tonya raised her hand to knock, ushering us in with a gracious smile. He was a tall, thin man, with long black hair that hung sleekly back in a ponytail. His eyes were brown, and his skin naturally tanned, and as I gazed into his face, I had the sense he'd been around a long time, if not in body—then in soul.

Alex and Patrick stood outside. Degoba looked at them closely for a moment, then solemnly touched the door frame.

"My house and I welcome you for this evening." Which meant that he was going to rescind his invitation after we left, not a bad idea given the nature of vampires and that he had never met either of these two men.

The living room was part cowboy style, part . . . *something.* A golden retriever lay curled in the corner. He looked up, then growled a little as Patrick walked in. Dogs and cats weren't usually very friendly with vampires, but the dog raced over to Alex and jumped up on him, his front paws bracing against Alex's shoulders.

"Brother Bear . . . get down." Degoba snapped his fingers.

The dog whimpered and, after giving Alex a big lick across the face, did as he was told. He returned to his bed in the corner, but he kept looking over as if to say, *You really want to pet me, don't you?*

"Brother Bear?" Tonya asked. "I didn't know you found a new dog."

"I didn't till recently. Brother found *me*—I call him BB for short. He was guarding a bear cub when I found him. A black she-bear had wandered off to forage for food, I guess, and her cub managed to get himself lost. BB was standing there, guarding the cub. I got too close and he growled, but I convinced him that mama bear would be back in a few minutes and guided the dog over to a bluff behind a huckleberry bush."

"Did the mother bear come back?" Stories like this always captured my interest.

"She sure enough did. Five minutes later, the mother meandered back, found the cub, and gave him a good talking-to. Don't you think that cubs don't get scolded. Then she firmly escorted him back to wherever she'd made her lair." Degoba smiled fondly at BB. "Brother Bear didn't have a collar and was mighty thin, so I brought him home. Vet said he wasn't microchipped and that he was a little underweight, so . . . here he is."

I glanced around. The walls of the house were wood—not like a log cabin with round logs, but they were composed

of long slats of what looked like light oak. Open beams reinforced the vaulted ceilings, and in the living room, big bay
windows overlooked the yard. The rooms were open and
spacious. I could see the kitchen from the living room and
the study, as well.

The art on the walls was a mixture of Native American
and Celtic, and felt like an eclectic—if appropriate—mix.
One entire wall was lined with built-in bookshelves, fash-
ioned around a tall window. A banquette was tucked beneath
the glass, cushioned with a rich red upholstery.

The place was cluttered in a tidy, busy way, as if nothing
here went unused. A stack of magazines were all marked with
Post-it notes throughout their pages, and a notebook sat near
them, with pages of handwritten notes neatly printed across
the paper.

The smell of beef stew—I could tell it was beef stew
because that had become a current favorite meal of mine—
hung heavy in the air. My mouth watered as I took a deep
breath, inhaling the fragrant aroma.

"You want a bowl, Shimmer?" Degoba's eyes crinkled
with laughter. "I can tell an appreciative sniff, all right. I've
got stew and fresh-baked rolls in the kitchen. Ralph, Tonya?
What about you?" He didn't bother asking Alex and Patrick,
and neither one seemed to take offense. Alex had told me it
wasn't considered bad manners to leave vampires out of
food offers, especially given that food made them sick as a
dog if they swallowed even a bite.

"I'd love a bowl." I stood. "Would you like some help?"

"No, sit and be at rest." He stood and headed for the
kitchen. BB raised his head, letting out a hopeful whine. "No,
Mr. BB, you may not help yourself to people food. Keep these
good folks company while I play host."

The minute Degoba was out of the room, BB jumped up
and launched himself at Alex, wriggling as the vampire
laughed and petted him.

"You remind me of my Goldy," Alex said, ruffling BB's
fur and giving him a good scrubbing on the side. "I miss
her, I do."

"You had a dog?" Tonya glanced up at him. "I didn't think most vampires kept pets."

"Most of us don't. They live such short lives and it hurts to lose so many. Then again, we can give homes to a long string of otherwise orphaned critters." He held BB's chin, gazing into the dog's eyes. "This is a right smart one, tell you that. Goldy, she was my best friend for twelve good years. She was my dog before I was turned. The person who turned me . . . killed her. I never forgave them that. I paid them back, too."

BB let out a little whimper and nosed Alex's hand again, licking it, then went back to curl up in his bed. The dog was clearly enchanted. Something about the vampire struck a chord in Brother Bear's nature.

A few minutes later, Degoba was back, stew in hand. He set the tray down on the coffee table and handed out thick mugs of stew, along with a tray filled with soft rolls and fresh butter. I lost myself in the scent for a moment, then in the taste. Even though we'd eaten, the stress must have gotten to us because I was hungry as hell, and both Tonya and Ralph seemed to be feeling the same way. Degoba waited for us to take the edge off before speaking.

"So, tell me what brings you here? You told me a little on the phone, Tonya, but I want to hear it from their mouths." He motioned for us to go ahead. Patrick glanced at us, then took the reins. He told Degoba what had happened up until he'd called us, and then we took over. Ralph had brought his laptop and opened it to show Degoba some of the pictures and recordings we'd managed to pick up. I told him about Lacy and discovering her skeleton and everything else we'd found out—including the murder weapon. We also filled him in on the Gypsy curse, and then about what we'd figured out tonight.

When we finished, he motioned for us to be silent while he wandered around the room, picking up first one object, then another. He paused over a rock that he was holding, staring at it as if he were listening to it, then moved on to what looked like a simple wooden wand, still possessing the bark of whatever tree it had been made from.

I polished off my stew and rolls, quietly carrying my plate into the kitchen. Tonya brought in hers and Ralph's and we rinsed the dishes and set them to dry on the counter. The kitchen was as rustic as the living room but still had a polished feel with up-to-date appliances and the obligatory window overlooking the side yard.

"I like him." I kept my voice soft so as not to distract him if he could hear us. "I like his thoughtfulness—he's deliberate. Not hasty."

"Degoba has been exceptionally helpful to my family and the crowd I hang with over the years." She frowned. "I think he's had some pretty rough tragedies in his past, but I doubt he'll ever tell us. He intrigues me." She paused, then caught my eye and blushed.

"You like him."

"He's old enough to be my father."

"Does that matter? Age is so inconsequential in the Supe community. Unless someone's way too young, I don't think that it should matter among humans either, do you? Look at . . . well, you don't know her but the receptionist who basically runs our agency? Her name's Bette and she's a Melusine."

"What's a Melusine? I'm familiar with a lot of Supes but . . ."

"She's a water-spirit who can change into a snake. She looks like . . . well, Alex calls her a biker grandma, but she's super-sexual and has a line of lovers a mile long. A lot of them ask her to marry them, too, but she's a free spirit. She and Alex used to go together until they discovered they made better friends than lovers." I grinned. "She dates everybody from twenty-two-year-old humans to, hell . . . I guess a thousand-year-old Fae?"

Tonya laughed. "I wish it were that simple among humans. They call women who date men a lot older than themselves gold diggers, and they call women who date younger men cougars—and it's not used in a complimentary fashion." Her eyes twinkled as she added, "What about you and Alex? How long have you been together?"

It was my turn to blush. "How did you know?"

"It's plain as the nose on your face, Shimmer. You and he are constantly giving each other 'the look.' You can't lie to me about your feelings for him."

I hadn't been aware of that. "Well, yeah . . . We . . . not long. Not long at all. When I first got here I was dating someone, but he and I weren't on the same page. We're friends and want to stay that way. Alex . . . from the start we were noticing each other but there was a complication, recently removed."

"What about Chai? You and he ever . . . ?" Tonya peeked back in the living room. Apparently Degoba was still meditating.

"Chai's the older brother I never had. He and I . . ." I shuddered. "Even thinking about kissing him that way feels just wrong. And I know he feels the same way about me."

"So that's why he calls you 'Little Sister'? I get it. I have a couple male friends like that." She paused as Degoba called for us. "Looks like he's ready. Let's go see what he has to say."

And with that, we headed back into the living room.

Degoba motioned for us to sit down. "I think you're right. You're dealing with a forest wight. They're mean, and nasty, and to be honest, if it weren't for it taking up residence in Patrick's house, I'd say leave the hell enough alone. The danger isn't a joke. But it looks like we have to try something."

"*We?*" Tonya asked hopefully. "Does that mean you'll help us?"

Degoba rolled his eyes. "Oh, child, I really don't want to take this on, but you've come to me for help and the spirits tell me I have to answer. Yes, I will help you. But the first thing we have to do is to break up the hive."

"Hive?" Alex didn't sound happy. "The word *hive* implies *swarm*. I don't like that thought."

"Yes, it does, but it's not quite so bad as you think. Forest wights hive together in the same area. They may not cluster tightly together, like bees, but they will stake out territory as a unit and strengthen one another that way. To disrupt the hive, you must strike at its heart first—the king bee, so to speak—or you won't be able to dislodge *any* of them. We have to find the king of the forest wights and destroy him. Only then will the others be vulnerable, and then we will be able to dislodge the one in Patrick's house." He paused, then turned to Tonya. "You know what I'm talking about, don't you?"

She paled. "Yeah, I do, though I wasn't altogether sure of the nature of forest wights. I have some old information on them, but it's not extensive and it doesn't talk about how to get rid of them."

"I know about them. They breed out in the forests. They're born out of the dark hearts of the ancient trees who hate humans, who have seen the mighty woodlands die at the hand of the axe. They can sense and manipulate spirits. Whenever someone dies in the forest, the wights have a good chance of capturing their spirits and making them work for them. They also feed on the energy from the spirit realm, so . . . yes, ghosts are food to them." Degoba patted BB. "They tend to leave animals alone, you know."

Alex leaned forward. "How come we don't hear more about them? I can tell you from being around for a couple hundred years, I've never heard of them."

Degoba laughed then, slapping his leg. "Alex, you've heard about them. You just don't realize it. When logging trucks have accidents? You can bet there's a good chance a forest wight arranged it. When hikers go missing in the woods, there's a reason they get turned around and end up dying from exposure. There's a reason why serial killers are drawn to hide in the forest to wait for their victims. As Tonya has probably told you, the wights can influence behavior, not just of spirits but of *living people*. They can be terribly cruel. Sometimes, it's in retaliation for the loss of land—they consider themselves at war. Other times . . . well, it's their nature."

We sat in silence, taking in the information. It made me think of the sirens who lured humans into the ocean. They were alien, distanced from humankind, and did not see what they did as anything other than hunting food. The wights were the same way.

Tonya shuddered. "They may see themselves fighting a war, but I think they're nasty enough to qualify as evil. Toying with others for your own amusement—"

"True. But humans follow the same path. Good and evil aren't relegated solely to humanity. If you're talking about hunting and sustenance, well, humans eat meat, they eradicate pests that invade their homes. The wights don't see themselves doing anything different. To them, we're a dangerous pest, and spirits are a food source." Degoba smiled softly at her. "It's all a matter of perspective. There's always more than one way to look at a situation. But yes, cruelty exists, and evil."

"But why would the wight want me out of my house?" Patrick looked confused.

"There could be several reasons. For one, there are a lot of spirits there—a lot of food. If you free the spirits, you basically open the barn doors and there go the provisions. Or perhaps, the wights claimed that area long ago and you happen to be latest in a long line of attempts to reclaim it. Why does a man pick one fishing spot over another? He sees fish there."

"Great. Okay, then. So you won't have an ethical problem helping us?" Patrick asked.

Degoba stood, arching his back. He looked like he could run rings around men half his age. No wonder Tonya found him attractive—he had both personality *and* looks.

"I eat beef, I eat pork. I've hunted elk and deer before. I go fishing. None of those animals ever did anything to me— but I still eat them. I've spent my life making a study of legend and folklore, not only from my people, but of what is *actually* out there. Creatures like the forest wights don't care if you're white or Native American or black . . . we're all just human to them. They have no ethical problem with destroying any of us. And spirits are just tools for them. So, will I fight them? Of course I will, to save my house, my friend's house, my town."

Chai, who had remained silent, spoke then. "The spirit-walker is right. There are things in the world that view humans as expendable. I come from realms where creatures would consider you a snack. Fast food. A Big Mac on the way to the game."

"Well, that's comforting," I snorted. "They wouldn't think of me that way once I got done with them."

"Little Sister, don't be so quick to consider yourself immune from creatures such as this. You may be a . . ." He paused, looking over at Degoba.

Degoba grinned, sitting back. "I know she's not human, and she's not Fae, regardless of what she says. I have no idea what she is, but it's easy for me to see that the girl is an ancient being compared to the likes of Tonya and me. But I won't pry."

I had the sudden desire to tell him. He was not the kind to panic, or to go off the deep end. "Dragon. Water dragon."

The spiritwalker's eyes widened, and he let out a whoop. "I knew your kind existed! Tell me—Nessie and others of her kind?"

I laughed and ducked my head. "Yes, water dragons who crossed over here long ago and who've forgotten where they came from and forgotten how to shift."

"We *must* talk—but first, we take care of this problem." His enthusiasm was catching.

I grinned. "It's a deal. But first things first. Where do we go from here?"

"We figure out a plan of action." Tonya stood and arched her back, wincing. "I've been sitting too long. But first, Degoba, for the love of Hecate, I need some fuel. Caffeine, please?"

"How many shots?" He headed for the kitchen.

"Quad, plus milk and sugar, please." She let out a satisfied little mew.

It was nine o'clock—still early for most of us but probably a little late for Tonya, given she worked during the day. Degoba had a state-of-the-art espresso machine. I'd seen it when Tonya and I were in the kitchen.

He fixed her a latte, and then we all gathered around the table that was crafted out of a slab of cedar. The tree it came from must have been huge. The table was carved from one solid slab, five feet long and three feet wide, sanded to show the silky grain and then polished with polyurethane to seal and protect it.

Degoba brought out a map of Fort Worden. "When Tonya first came to me about the Kinzie Battery, I told her to stay away from it. But, and Tonya doesn't know this, I've been keeping an eye on it ever since. I'm amazed that there aren't more accidents there, but then again, make the source of power too obvious and you can destroy the hive by calling attention to the core. The king of the hive lives there, deep within the battery. It's like a man-made cavern for him."

"Why would he choose there?" Alex frowned at the map. "Why not out in the forest?"

"Simple. To affect a town, you have to have a finger on the pulse of it. And honestly? Fort Worden is the pulse of Port Townsend—it's the main tourist attraction. Thousands of people come through there each year, not only to visit the fort but to camp there. Open access to the beach is a prized commodity in this state. There's a lot of privately owned waterfront property and so when you have an area that offers such easy beach access, it's going to be heavily used."

Tonya nodded. "He's right on that. So it's a great place to tap into energy, to tap into people, and to find a way to use them."

Degoba motioned to Patrick. "All right, you live across the street from the fort. Tell me, when you started renovations, how long was it before you noticed spiritual activity in the house?"

Patrick rapped his fingers on the table as he thought. "Let me see . . . at first everything seemed rather subtle. I guess it started a week or so after we first began tearing apart the house. A noise here or there, things seeming to move by themselves. Now and then a workman would complain of feeling watched. It wasn't aggressive, not at first. In fact, more often than not, I remember a melancholy feel to the place. I kind of thought . . . this sounds silly but . . ." He paused, ducking his head.

"Never discount what you have to say before you actually say it." Degoba stared at him. "You might just toss out the baby with the bathwater that way. So, tell us, what sounds silly?"

Patrick shrugged, a sheepish grin on his face. "I kind of felt like the house just wanted to continue sleeping and we were waking it up. I felt almost guilty for not letting it just decline in peace."

"That's not silly." Ralph had been studying the map, and now he snapped his fingers. "I have a thought . . . hold on for a moment." He pulled out his laptop. "Degoba, do you have Internet access I can plug into?"

Degoba nodded. "Here, let me give you the guest password. I change it out weekly." He crossed to his desk and glanced at a Post-it. "X-T-5-9-3-P."

Ralph tapped away and then flashed him a smile. "I'm in. Okay, give me another minute . . ." His fingers flew over the keys and I marveled at how fast he was. It was as though he'd been born with a keyboard in his hand—the words seemed to bypass his brain and go directly to his fingers.

"Okay, here we go. I thought so! Look at this." His grin was a mile wide and he looked like he'd just discovered gold. He pushed his laptop over for all of us to see. There was a map of Port Townsend with a series of lines sketched over it. Only they weren't in any regular pattern, though most of them seemed to radiate out from one point in Fort Worden—the lighthouse where I'd gone swimming.

"What are we looking at?" I leaned in closer, trying to make sense out of what I was seeing.

Ralph pointed to one of the lines. "Look . . . here's the battery. And see how this same line travels right through Patrick's house, across the bay, and then out into the forest eventually?"

I nodded but was still clueless on what it meant.

Tonya, however, cocked her head, studying the map for a moment. "Of course! That's why the forest wights chose your house. Look—if they're nested out in there in the forest, and they have a hold in the battery . . . see how this line runs through your property from the woods to the battery to the ocean? Ralph picked up on it! You're right in the middle of a ley line." She glanced at Ralph. "Am I right?"

He nodded. "Exactly! You got it. One of the great things about the Werewyx search engine is that it offers a lot more refined searches into paranormal websites. This is Ley of the Land—a website devoted to mapping ley lines. And the ley line that runs through the battery and out into the forest is one of the strongest in this area. The next . . . oh hell, over by Crescent Lake it's really thick but here—this is the one that seems to be the most predominant."

Degoba clapped him on the shoulder. "Brilliant, man. This is the missing piece. How far does it extend?"

Ralph traced it along. "Well, it crosses Discovery Bay and travels right into the Olympic National Forest. It looks like . . . yes, the Valley of the Silent Men and Lena Lake are right in its path. The ley line eventually runs to the Pacific on the coast."

"You say the Valley of the Silent Men? No wonder." Degoba jotted down few notes. He glanced over at Alex and me. We must have looked clueless because he cleared his throat. "People don't talk a lot in the valley. There seems to be a natural dampening field that cuts off conversation. It's not impossible, but people are quiet there, almost reverent. There's a sense of some overwhelming . . . almost sacred energy that fills the area. It's like being in nature's church— you can sense the depth of the planet there."

Ralph frowned. "So could the wights have their home base there?"

"Could easily be. The Olympic National Forest is about as primeval as you can get in this day and age. Oh, the Amazon and some of the jungles in Africa are more remote and wilder, but the Olympics, they have their secrets and they do not give them up easily. It's a temperate rain forest, you know, and the old growth is older than most of us can really imagine. There are parts of the forest that have never seen human traffic come through. The forest spirits there are ancient and brooding." Degoba studied the ley line. "Yes, this has to be the missing link as to how the forest wights sensed the spirits in your house."

A thought occurred to me. "When you said we have to wipe out the king of the forest wights, do you mean of this particular hive? We're not marching on the most powerful one in existence?" The thought of marching on the supreme lord of forest wights ranked right up there with some of the nightmare horror movies I'd sat through with Bette, who loved the creature features.

But Degoba put my fears to rest. "Right. I have no idea where the godfather of forest wights would even be found. I don't even know if there *is* one. I have no clue if they have a god, or a goddess, or an ultimate source of authority. Somehow, I can't imagine they are that organized. They're a chaotic bunch, and hives usually work autonomously, I believe. Like hives of anything."

"Okay, so we have to fight the king of this hive. Then, I take it we have to go after the one in Patrick's house?" Alex was now focused in on the map as well. He traced a line on the paper with his finger from the Kinzie Battery to Patrick's home. "Will the one in Patrick's house be weaker than the one in the battery?"

"Potentially." Degoba turned to Tonya. "From what I studied, they're all about the same strength, but when the core of the hive—the center pin—is removed, it weakens the outer arms and makes them vulnerable to being hurt."

"And we can't hurt the others without taking out the king, right?" Tonya was writing down notes, as well as Ralph.

"Right. That's how I think it works. I've studied these creatures for quite some time, and while I have no definitive proof to back me up, I am pretty sure that if you take out the king, then you can carve away at the others. But make no mistake: The wight at the battery won't be invulnerable, but trust me, this isn't going to be easy."

I wondered off in my mind as they talked. We had wights in the Dragon Reaches—not this kind in particular, but barrow wights and land wights. Most of the dragons considered them treacherous and killed them at every chance. But I had no clue if my people knew they were hive creatures. That could be useful the next time I talked with the Wing-Liege. Maybe he'd even take a few months off my sentence if I came up with some information that proved helpful enough.

"Shimmer? What do you think?"

I shook my head as Alex tapped me on the arm. "Did you hear me?"

"Sorry, I was off in . . . never mind. What did you ask?" I tried to keep focused.

"We asked if you had any water magic that might be useful? Forest wights are naturally immune to a lot of earth magic. Air—not much it can do to them. Water, we're not so sure about. And fire is their nemesis."

"Trees are used to getting rained on. I wouldn't count on the magic I have left at my disposal being able to help at all. I'm brawn in this situation." Then I laughed. "But Chai— he's a djinn! Fire's his best buddy."

Chai rolled his eyes. "Nobody say anything. Do *not* ask me for a favor—I offer my help freely, without a request."

A spark flickered in Degoba's eyes. "Djinn!"

"At your service, may I offer you a wish?" It came rolling off Chai's tongue as smooth as silk. He instantly groaned and slapped his head, but he'd offered and if Degoba took him up on it, there was nothing any of us could do. But we could warn him first.

"Don't say yes! Don't accept his offer. The politics of this are tricky—" I stopped, though, when Degoba laughed, slapping his thigh.

"I haven't enjoyed an evening so much in quite a while. First a dragon, and then a djinn. No, my fair genie, I will not ask for one of your wishes. I know all too well what it would mean. I'd rather . . . you have offered to help and we acknowledge that. Is that good enough?"

"You *can* say thank you without turning it into a favor, but yes, I understand your caution." Chai shook his head ruefully. "I really have to watch my mouth, but it's my nature. This is why more of my kind—the more pleasant-natured ones—stick to our own realm. The danger is too great for those we consider friends."

I nodded. "We spent a long time figuring out how to circumnavigate the chance of me ending up on the short end of the djinn wand."

"So back to matters," Chai said. "I have fire, and I'm not afraid to use it. Just point me in the right direction and I'm all yours. Tell me what to do, though. Don't ask me. I give you permission to order me around for a bit."

His laughter was infectious and broke the tension. And with that, we began to plan our attack on the king of the forest wights.

CHAPTER 15

The trip to the battery didn't take long, but the entire way all I could think about was that we were going up against a creature who could beat us sideways if we weren't careful. With that comforting thought, I preoccupied myself by staring pensively out the window until we got close to the park.

Ralph didn't seem too thrilled, either. He had managed to tear himself away from his iPad, but now he was rapping his fingers against his backpack in what could only be considered rhythmic by the most generous of music fans.

Chai, on the other hand, seemed almost jovial, and he was talking Alex's ear off as we drove the distance from Degoba's house to Fort Worden State Park. Chai and Alex seemed to be getting on pretty good and right now they were discussing Egypt, which apparently both of them had visited at some time in the past. I wasn't sure how I felt about them getting so chummy. Chai knew a lot of my secrets. Secrets I wasn't sure I wanted Alex knowing. Chai could make me cry—he knew what my buttons were and while he'd never once deliberately use them against me, I couldn't put it past

Alex yet. I liked Alex, I had liked sex with Alex, but I didn't fully trust him. Not yet.

I decided to dive in and divert the conversation. "You really think that this silver dagger of mine can stab a wight?"

Degoba had provided me with a silver dagger. Of course it wasn't one hundred percent silver, it would have been way too malleable, but it had enough of the metal in it to hurt a wight, the spiritwalker had said. And to hurt Alex, Patrick, and Ralph as well. I'd watched all three of them shy away from it when the older man held it out to me.

"I think it can bite the wight's butt, all right. And you just keep that pretty pointy stick away from me. You tried to stake me once, already." Alex snickered, glancing at me.

Ralph let out a guffaw. "Yeah, and she almost made it."

"I wasn't in my right mind, guys. You promised you'd never bring that up again!" Even through my protest, I was smiling.

As we headed into the park, behind Tonya's car—Patrick and Degoba were riding with her—our laughter fell away. Jokes were all well and good, but things were about to get real. What we were about to do was probably one of the most dangerous things I'd ever attempted. Oh sure, breaking into a dragon's house could be deadly, but there I knew the variables. Here, the unknown was . . . well . . . truly unknown.

It was nine thirty. Later in the year the area would be crowded, but now the few campers braving the winter elements were tucked snugly inside their RVs, out of the chill evening.

We trundled along Harbor Defense Way until we came to the turnoff into the parking lot near Kinzie Battery. Alex eased into a spot in the empty lot, next to Tonya's car, and turned off the ignition. I glanced out the windshield. Across a short concrete slab, a gravel path led along a small rise, shrouded on either side by thick undergrowth and shrubs tall enough to tower over our heads. In the distance, I could barely make out the looming presence of the battery against the night sky. As I stared at the trail, an unrest crept over me and I realized how very much I didn't want to go there.

"Okay, I guess this is it. Shimmer, you ready?" Alex unbuckled his seat belt.

"Yeah, dagger's at the ready. But what are you and Ralph going to use? Neither one of you can touch silver." I stared at my blade. I was quite capable of using it—but I hadn't been in a real scuffle in a long while.

"I'm a vampire. What do you think?" Alex bared his fangs at me, giving me a toothy grin.

I snorted. "What if the wight doesn't bleed?"

"I'm quite able to do massive damage with my strength and fangs regardless of whether a creature has any blood." Sounding almost offended, Alex opened his door.

Ralph cleared his throat. "I'll probably turn into my wolf form. That way if somebody does draw blood . . ." He paused, and I smiled quietly. Ralph had a little quirk. When he was in his human form, he fainted at the sight of blood, which effectively made him useless during a fight, unless he shifted.

Actually, it wasn't the sight of *blood* that did it, but a *bloody wound*. On the rare occasion when Alex had spilled a bottle of blood on the floor, Ralph had turned pale and looked queasy, but he'd managed to stay on his feet. I wanted to ask him what trauma had set off the response, but we didn't know each other well enough for me to pry into that personal an experience.

"Good thinking. That way we won't have to worry about you hitting your head on some sharp edge." Alex took Ralph's fainting episodes in stride, but he didn't mince words to try to make the werewolf more comfortable about them.

Ralph rolled his eyes and gave me an *Oh brother* look. Sometimes Alex treated him like a kid, and while Alex was definitely older than Ralph, Ralph had been around awhile. I was older than both of them by a long, long ways. But given that my life had been spent in the Dragon Reaches where time moved differently, time for me seemed nebulous. In relative terms, I was as young as Ralph. And in relative terms, Ralph was a bit younger than Alex. Chai was the oldest of us all.

As we headed over to Tonya, Degoba, and Patrick, I

patted Ralph on the arm. "Don't mind him—you know he doesn't mean to come off so abrupt."

"I know that, it's just his nature. But damn it, Shimmer, the whole fainting thing? Embarrassing enough, especially given I'm a werewolf."

"At least you're not a vampire. That would be really bad if you fainted at the sight of blood." I snickered. "Can you imagine the ribbing you'd get then?" At that, he laughed and we hustled on over to the others.

"So, what now?" Tonya shivered. She had brought a wand with her, and what looked like a pretty nasty piece of weaponry. She was also carrying a short sword.

"Ooo, pretty!" I gazed at the sparkly blade. It looked wicked sharp.

"You like?" She held it out.

The blade extended about sixteen inches, and the hilt was carved from an antler. It was flat and double edged, and looked relatively plain, but the edges were honed to a razor-sharpness—that much I could tell by looking, and it glinted as the moonlight filtered through the cloud cover to reflect on it. She moved back and swept it around in an easy figure eight. It was obvious she'd had training to use it as a weapon. This was no ritual blade, for looks only.

"Where did you get it?" I admired her ease with it. While I could use a dagger, and to some extent a short sword, I'd relied more on my wits than my weapons skills. I'd also relied on my brawn—I was pretty strong. All dragons were, and I'd gone up against more than one adversary in my days wandering through the Dragon Reaches, after being released from the Lost and Foundling.

"My mother was . . . you could call her a Renaissance woman. She had a lot of skills, including fighting. She actually learned from her uncle, and he taught me, as well. Before he died, that is." She made a sad face. "I miss him. Uncle Van. He was quite the character, though he liked booze more than was good for him. Like my mother."

I found myself wishing Tonya lived in Seattle. We could probably be good friends. As it was, I nodded and turned to see what Degoba had ready. Patrick, of course, would do the vamp thing like Alex.

To my surprise, Degoba held nothing in his hands—no magical items, no weapons. Just . . . two empty hands.

He saw my look. "There comes a point where some of us do better without an encumbrance," was all he said. The energy behind his words felt strong and sinister, and I let it go at that.

Degoba pointed toward the trail. "Let's head out. I'll take the front, along with Alex. Shimmer, you and Tonya come second. Ralph and Patrick, third, and Chai, would you take rear position?"

We quickly sorted out into two rows, then headed off down the path. Degoba and Alex were both quiet as they walked. In fact, I realized that Degoba was making less noise than the vampire, which was mighty unusual. He seemed to glide over the trail, the gravel barely shifting below his feet.

I, on the other hand, made my fair share of noise. The gravel crunched under my shoes, and it was wet so it was harder to keep traction. Walking in sand is the hardest, but gravel falls a close second in terms of feet sliding on the shifting surfaces. The rocks were slick, but at least I was wearing shoes, which kept the rougher edges from digging in. I'd walked on a lot of pebbled beaches in the past, so I was used to the feel, but I hadn't mastered anything akin to the way the men were managing it.

We came up over the rise and the path narrowed. We weren't far from the battery, but the path seemed to telescope in front of me. It had to be an optical illusion, or maybe it was the wight's magic, but it looked like the path disappeared into a dark mist at the end.

I glanced over at Tonya. "Is it supposed to look like this?"

She shrugged. "It is nighttime, which can play havoc with the line of sight, but no, really? I think the wight senses us near and he's throwing up his first line of defense."

Degoba coughed. He kept his gaze straight ahead, but his words were clear enough. "Listen, the energy is starting to move. Think of it like a magical haze, an unnatural fog rolling in. Be prepared for the forest wight to attempt to subvert us through illusions and influence. Its abilities to influence behavior aren't necessarily limited to humans, though it will be harder for them to affect those of Fae origin, or vampires. I have no idea about dragons, djinns, or werewolves."

Ralph grumbled. "Weres—especially lycanthropes—are definitely susceptible to charm."

I frowned. "I have no idea about dragons. I think you have to know our names to gain full control over us—but I can't be certain of that. It's not something that was taught to me at the orphanage. Except I'm susceptible to a vampire's charm, so . . ."

Tonya peeked over her shoulder at Chai. "What about you? Can you be charmed? And . . . do genies really have a bottle that controls them?"

He let out a snort. "Charmed? Not from something like a forest wight. As for bottles and djinns . . . I'm not Barbara Eden and this isn't the Arabian Nights. No, djinns are not brought under control by a bottle or a bag or a magical lamp, or any such object. However, we do have a trigger that allows the possessor to control us. Each djinn's trigger will be different, and none of us will *ever* willingly tell you what it is. I escaped seven hundred years ago and plan to remain free."

I'd known Chai for the past hundred years, and yet I'd never known he'd ever been enslaved. The thought made me queasy that someone had owned him. "It's like magical slavery."

"Of a sort, yes. And yet, our masters have to be cautious because . . . well, you know all about the folly of asking me for a wish or a favor. The same thing applies to capturing a djinn—be careful what you ask for, you *will* get it . . . But usually not in the form you hope for." The look on his face was dark. "When my kind realized long ago that we were vulnerable to entrapment, we evolved ways of making it as unpleasant as possible for those seeking to enslave us. Eventually, it became a part of our nature. Now we're born this way and can't undo what we set into motion."

We reached the end of the path by then. We were staring

across a swath of grass that ran along the front of the concrete walkway attached to the front of the battery. The battery rose three stories tall—the top story open to the night sky. Both the left and the right side had two stairwells, leading to a section on the second tier. And in the center, staircases ran from the second story to the third, meeting in the middle on a landing, looking like an inverted V. I wasn't sure what was atop the battery, but there was a center door leading into the enclosed sector.

On the bottom and the second stories, the openings into the battery looked like dark mouths, waiting for us to enter. The square columns spaced along the bottom soared all the way up to the third story, holding up the wide, open ledges that loomed over the ground floor. In the partial moonlight, the concrete took on an eerie glow, marred by what appeared to be camouflage. I wasn't sure if it was paint, worn and weathered, or if people had tagged the building, but it gave it almost more of a military look to the battery than if the building had been spiffy clean.

"Where do we start?" I couldn't decide if it was safer to go up top and work our way down, or to plunge right into the depths of the main floor, from where most of the energy seemed to be emanating.

Degoba stepped forward, holding out his hands. "The energy is highly restless. Tonya, do you feel it?"

She moved to the front and stood by him, holding out her hands. With a shudder, she lurched back. "It's grown much stronger than the first time I sensed it. The wight has had time to strengthen."

"He's had time to extend tendrils from this place—hiving out into the town. My guess is that your house, Patrick? Is not the only one with a forest wight. Especially since the town has so many ghosts." Degoba seemed to debate for a moment, darting glances at either end of the structure, and then he pointed toward the center. "Let's go meet the wight in its nest."

The moment he made a decision, he sprang into action and strode forward, gesturing for Tonya to return to my side.

Alex scrambled, and we were on the move again. We had barely reached the concrete when there was a rustling from behind us, from behind the bushes crowding both sides of the path.

I whirled around, as did Chai and Ralph.

There, behind us, emerging from the brush, were creatures that looked a lot like walking tree stumps. They were bare-branched, and their roots bunched up into legs, propelling them along. Their branches writhed—but they weren't the movements of wind through the trees. No, this was deliberate. There were at least twenty of them, about ten from each side, all aimed in our direction.

I squinted, trying to make out their faces—dark hollows that could be eyes, black maws that could be mouths. But it was hard to tell under the light of the night.

"Holy shit, guys—we have company!" Ralph stumbled back, against Tonya. She had stopped when I turned but hadn't yet caught a glimpse of what was coming our way. The next moment, everybody was facing the shambling trunks, with Chai in front, on the receiving end.

"What do they want?" My first instinct was to attack, but then I thought, what if they were forest spirits entrapped by the wight? We couldn't just start killing things at random, could we?

As if echoing my thoughts, Ralph said, "Don't attack till we know what they want. They may be friendly."

"Don't be so sure about that." Alex swung to the front, flanking Chai. Degoba did the same.

There was plenty of room, so the rest of us spread out so we'd have a better line of sight. A thought occurred to me that maybe we'd better have somebody guarding our backs, which were now facing the battery, but once again, Ralph was ahead of me. He moved a few steps toward the building and shifted into wolf form. The blurring of his transformation was so quick that my mind had a hard time taking in what I was seeing. One minute Ralph was there, a second later—a very large, snarling wolf. There seemed to be no point of in-between.

Satisfied that we now had some semblance of a warning

system, I turned back to the tree creatures. I'd read a lot in the past few months, and at first the thought of Tolkien ran through my mind.

"Ents?" But as I looked at them, I thought no—they couldn't be. For one thing, Tolkien *created* ents. And for another, if these creatures *were* ents, they were short, squat, and much nastier.

"Fae," Alex said. "Sapwalkers, to be specific. They belong to the same realm as floraeds, and they are highly volatile and dangerous Earthside nature Fae. But don't let the word *nature* lull you into a false sense of security. These guys aren't friendly, if I'm not mistaken. I haven't ever had to deal with them, but I know that nature Fae don't usually take kindly to mortals. Or what they *think* is mortal."

Degoba snorted. "That's the truth. No, Shimmer, don't delude yourself into thinking these are going to be friendly. Nature is fierce, and she's self-protective, and she doesn't give two hoots about us. But we need her to survive, we need her because she is the only thing that gives us life in these bodies. So we accept her capriciousness and respect the hell out of her. She's bigger and stronger than we can ever hope to be."

I blinked. That wasn't the way most Earthside pagans talked. But then again, Degoba was a spiritwalker. I glanced over at Tonya.

She nodded and readied her sword. "Not to mention the fact that I doubt these creatures are under their own control right now. No matter what they would—or wouldn't—do given their own volition, if the forest wight has control over them, we're in danger."

"How do we attack them?" The wind had picked up and now it riffled through my hair, blowing it back. I wished I'd pulled it back into a ponytail. I held up my dagger, trying to look menacing.

"Same way you attack anything else, except I have no clue where the hearts are on these things. I don't know if they even *have* internal organs. Not every creature does, you know." Degoba was rocking from one foot to another, looking for every inch like he was testing the ground around him. "It's muddy, be cautious when you move. Even the grass is slippery."

The tree creatures were nearly to us. We'd spread out into one long line, so that we'd all have a chance to attack. I grumbled. If the sapwalkers were being controlled, fighting them felt wrong. But we couldn't just let them walk all over us.

That brought to mind another thought. "Guys, what can sapwalkers *do* to us? Anybody know?"

"Unfortunately, I do know. They can whip those branches around your throat and strangle you. I think they can absorb your bodies, too, but I'm not sure just how." Alex didn't look at me, just answered the question.

That changed my mind—it was them or us, and I wanted it to be us. Strangulation attacks, hmm? That presented a host of potential problems, given that each sapwalker had at least five to seven branches and most were long enough to reach over our heads. That meant they could easily coil around our necks.

There were five of us facing the sapwalkers, with Ralph guarding our rear. Which meant there were at least four sapwalkers for each of us. But the creatures were large enough that only one of them could crowd in on each of us at a time, as long as we didn't spread so far apart that they could hem us in on all sides.

I caught a deep breath, held it a moment, and then let it slowly whistle out as the tree creature thudded its way within reach of me. As it waved one of its branches, I realized I was in attack distance. It sent its branch whistling through the air and I jumped back. With no one behind me, I was able to avoid the lash of its limb. I quit thinking and went on instinct, and my instinct told me to reach for the branch.

Lunging forward, I managed to catch hold of it. Rather than woody, the branch actually felt rough, almost like coarse hair over a pliable reed. Whatever it was, I brought my dagger down, severing a good three feet of the branch from the sapwalker. The appendage went limp in my hand, and a trickle of liquid orange gel—like dishwashing soap—began to flow out of the severed limb. The sapwalker let out a shriek that sounded suspiciously like a crow.

"Be careful!" Alex was grappling with his opponent. At least if it got its branches around his throat, he wouldn't die from suffocation. I couldn't see how everyone else was doing and I realized that if I took the time to check, I'd open myself up to attack.

I stared at the severed piece in my hand. Sapwalkers were so far from human—or dragon—that they might as well be aliens. I dropped the limb, shuddering, as another branch lashed out for me. What worked the first time, worked the second, and I had another piece of sapwalker on the ground in front of me. But that approach ended as the creature wised up to what I was doing.

It was impossible to tell if the sapwalker was angry or just in a haze of pain, but it lurched forward, driving itself closer as I stumbled back. Before I realized what was happening, it wrapped a branch around my feet and yanked, and I was down on the ground. Another branch caught me around my neck.

I almost dropped my dagger, moving to flail at the lignified collar, but then stopped myself. That would do no good, even with my strength. Instead, I used the fingers of my other hand to run over the sapwalker's body, searching for a vulnerable area that felt like it might be good stabbity-material. And then, there it was. I pressed against an area right above the maw that reminded me of a mouth, and the sapwalker shuddered. Shifting, trying to keep from passing out as it tightened its grip around my throat, I brought the dagger up and stabbed hard.

With a shudder, the creature let out another shriek as a warm surge of liquid spilled over me. *Oh wonderful.* Tree blood. Or sap. Or whatever the hell it was. I just hoped it wasn't sticky.

The sapwalker loosened its grip enough for me to use my dagger to cut away the appendage around my neck and I shoved it off. It was still quivering, but I had the feeling it was almost dead.

As I rolled out from beneath it and staggered to my feet, I saw that Chai had moved forward to stand between us and the remaining sapwalkers. He raised his hands, palms out. A blast of flame came shooting forth, and the sapwalkers stopped in their tracks, shuffling back, again, jabbering like blackwings—what we called crows in the Dragon Reaches.

The flames licked at the edges of their branches and they quickly went to trying to stamp them out, swatting their limbs against anything close enough to hit. It had rained enough that there were puddles large enough for them to drown the sparks, but Chai wasn't done with them yet.

Meanwhile, I turned to see Tonya, cleaving away with her short sword, hacking at first one branch, then another, and another. I made an impromptu decision that—once we went home—I was learning how to use a weapon that had more reach. The dagger was nice, but it was way too up-close and personal.

Alex had managed to take down his sapwalker, and Patrick, too. Degoba had done *something* to his—I didn't see it anywhere, or any part of it. And now Chai focused another round of fire on the ones nearest and they turned, beating against their comrades for space so they could get away from the flames. The fight turned into a free-for-all of flailing branches and shrieks. The flames coming out of Chai's hands flickered and faded, but the sapwalkers were too intent on beating a retreat from us to notice.

"Crap. I wish we could kill them all." I surprised myself with how bloodthirsty I felt, but the sensation of that branch coiling around my throat was still very real and very raw, and right now, in my mind, the only good sapwalker was a dead one. "They have a vulnerable spot below the hole that looks like a mouth."

"We can move in while they're afraid." Alex stared at what was now a mini-mob of tree creatures pushing toward the undergrowth.

"Let them go," Degoba said. "I think we may have broken the hold the forest wight has on them. Look." He nodded in their direction. We turned back to look at them. The sapwalkers were vanishing into the undergrowth, without a single glance back at us. They seemed to have lost all interest.

I looked over at the ones we had killed. They were melting into puddles of mud on the ground. "Is that all they really are? Mud and some magic?"

"No, Shimmer. They are far more than that. But not all physical forms hold their shape when death occurs. Dissolution comes quickly for some—more than with humans. The sapwalkers, once their soul—personality—whatever you want to call it—was gone, returned directly to their mother." Degoba sounded a little forlorn. "Too bad the forest wight had to impress them into service. They may be chaotic and wild, but they are part of this world on such an intimate nature. They probably wouldn't have come near us if they hadn't been entrapped."

I felt disheartened then, my anger dissolving along with my thirst for revenge. As I've said, blue dragons? We're a volatile emotional bunch. "I guess . . . I wish we hadn't had to kill them."

"All things die. The forest wight, however . . . make no mistake—he knows what he's doing. Don't let down your guard, no matter what he says or does." With a gentle slap on my back, the older man turned toward the battery.

Ralph glanced back. He was a beautiful wolf—white as snow, and with gorgeous, gleaming eyes. His fur was long and blew gently in the wind as he stood there, guarding our backs. He let out a little whine and Alex moved to his side, clapping him gently on the back.

"Thank you for keeping watch." The vampire stared at the wolf, and then an eerie silence passed between them. Alex glanced over at me. "He senses the forest wight and it's making him uneasy." Turning back to Ralph, he added, "You'd better stay in wolf form, mate. You'll have a better chance of escaping his thrall."

Ralph bobbed his head.

"I guess we go in, then?" I regarded the gaping doorway. Voluntarily entering the building wasn't on my bucket list, but after seeing the sapwalkers and how easily this thing controlled them, I realized how far its reach could extend. If we ditched Patrick and said we couldn't help, the problem would grow because the forest wight was looking to expand its territory. How many other wights did it have lurking in houses around here, causing problems, forcing people out of their homes or under the influence of the dark creatures' natures? And suppose we *were* managing to catch it before it had grown its hive widely? If we just left it, how long before it extended its reach?

"Yes, we go in now." Degoba took the lead again, Alex joining him. We fell back into line and headed toward the door. Ralph remained in wolf form next to Patrick. As we followed, the air seemed to grow thick and oily, and I found myself wanting to cough. I repressed the urge, not wanting to call attention to where we were, though truth be told, logic said the forest wight would know we were here. He'd just lost his army of tree creatures.

The second-floor walkway was overhead now, and I gazed up at it as Alex and Degoba entered the building. The concrete loomed, a threatening umbrella, and even though I knew the building had been built to last, the thought of all the weight over our heads made me queasy.

As I passed through the door, the darkness became pitch black—the walls of the bunker sucking up any light that might have entered with us. Our footsteps echoed from wall to wall. Dragons couldn't see in the dark, but we were good with echolocation and I could tell the room we were in was huge.

Alex flicked on a flashlight, and Patrick did the same. Degoba followed suit. The room was as big as I thought, perhaps not running the full length of the fort, but big enough to hold a couple of ballrooms' worth of people. It was hard to get any accurate representation of what the walls looked like, but under the beams from the flashlights, I could make out a number of doors.

"No splitting up," I said. "I don't want to find myself alone in here." In fact, a warning was echoing through my mind. *Don't get trapped in a room without a second exit. Don't let yourself get sidetracked off from the others.*

I was about to tell the others when Ralph let out a yelp

and raced off to the left as fast as he could run, loping like a white spirit in the night.

"Ralph—come back here! Ralph!" Alex followed him, yelling over his shoulder, "Stay here, I'll be back with him."

The *thrum, thrum, thrum* of a heartbeat began to reverberate through the room, but nobody else seemed to notice it. It was growing louder and louder, and the thudding in my head was starting to hurt. I sheathed my dagger and reached up to rub my temples, backing up a step, when there was a sudden flutter and I turned to see Tonya dart out of the room, crying. Startled, Patrick—who was closest—raced after her.

"Chai . . . Degoba . . ." My breath was shallow as the thundering drums pounding in my head increased, now echoing from all sides. I whimpered and moved toward the older man.

Chai roared out an oath—I couldn't understand the language—and swirled into the center of the room. "Come out, you coward. Fight me, and let's see how strong you are!" His eyes were blazing and at first I thought that he, too, was feeling the effects of the forest wight's presence, but then I realized this was Chai when he had had enough. This was Chai, pissed off.

As I watched him bellowing into the darkness, Degoba touched me on the arm. "Come with me, I have to show you something."

Still trying to shake the echo of thunder out of my head, I turned and followed him into the room nearby. As we crossed the threshold, Alex's warning filtered back but it was too late, because Degoba slammed the door behind us and softly laughed. And I knew that he was laughing at my expense.

CHAPTER 16

I jumped away, but Degoba was quick. He managed to grab my arm but luckily for me, and unluckily for the forest wight, I was a dragon and my strength was enough to break free. I backed away toward the wall, grateful that he was still holding the flashlight.

"Degoba, the wight is influencing you. Listen to me—you have to resist it!" I didn't want to attack him. Even with the wight's influence, I was still stronger than he was, and I could hurt him badly.

But Degoba was firmly in the grip of the forest wight's possession, because he raced forward, ramming me back against the wall. I pushed against him but, to my surprise, I wasn't able to shove him away. He let out a low rumble of laughter, his eyes flashing a dangerous green.

"I'll teach you to interfere with me." Degoba cupped my chin and thrust upward, slamming my head against the wall. Dizzy from the blow, I struggled to get out of his grasp, but the force of the wight gave him strength. He dropped the flashlight near us and raised his other hand, using his knees and body to keep me pinned.

I glanced at his fingers and in the faint periphery of the flashlight, I could see that he was holding something—it looked like the hilt to a knife. He flicked it open to reveal a nasty, sharp edge. He brought the blade toward my throat. If I didn't do something—anything—in the next moment, he would slit my throat. And dragon or not, when I was in human form that meant a very bloody death.

I did the only thing I could think of. My right hand was able to reach the sheath holding my dagger and I quickly whipped the blade out, stabbing directly into his thigh. The blade slid into his flesh with a horrible sound. Degoba shouted, pulling back to yank himself away from my blade.

Roaring, he swooped toward me, his knife aimed at my heart. I brought my dagger up to meet him as I jumped to the side. He passed three inches too far to my left, but this time, my blade clipped him in the side and—my mind clouded with fear and confusion—I shoved it deep, letting go as I backed away toward the door. Degoba gasped, then fell to the floor.

At that moment, the door slammed open and Alex ran in, Ralph behind him in human form, carrying a flashlight. He trained it on Degoba. As he saw the blood pooling around the spiritwalker, the werewolf let out a single squeak and fell to the floor in a dead faint, the flashlight rolling away.

"What happened?" Alex stared at Degoba in horror. "Blood—oh hell. Chai! Get the hell in here."

Chai and Tonya entered the room and Tonya screamed, dropping by Degoba's side. Alex hurried out and I could hear him telling Patrick to go outside where he could get cell reception and call an ambulance. Chai struck up a light between his hands so we could see.

Tonya pressed hard on the wound. "I don't dare pull out the dagger—it would bleed too heavily and he'd die. I need something to stanch the flow of blood—give me your shirt!" She motioned frantically to Chai, who stripped off his shirt and pushed it into her hands. Within seconds, she had pressed it against the wound and was holding it tight. "It looks like you missed the artery in his thigh, but this side wound is a nasty one."

A noise from the other room alerted us as we heard voices echoing. Chai's ball of light vanished, as did he. The next moment, the police burst into the room. We didn't recognize either officer and I realized we could be in deep trouble. *I* could be . . .

"Call for help—" one of the officers started to say, but Alex chimed in.

"We've already phoned for an ambulance."

"Who stabbed him? What happened?" The cops glanced around, their guns still drawn.

I began to cry, unable to register just what was going on. I stammered out the only thing I could think of that might make sense. "I did—I didn't mean to. It was an accident. I thought he was going to attack me." I started forward, but they motioned to me to stay still.

"Don't move. Put your hands in the air where we can see them—all of you." He glanced down at Tonya. "Except for you—continue to hold pressure on the wound. You'd better pray for your friend here that he doesn't die."

There was a whir of sirens from outside and then, amid harsh, brilliant flashlights, the medics came running in with a stretcher. They eased Tonya out of the way and took over, working on Degoba.

I wanted to go to him, but I realized that it wouldn't be a good idea for me to move right now, given the mood of the police. One of them stepped forward and motioned for me to turn around.

"What's your name?"

"Shimmer."

"Last name?"

"Just Shimmer—I'm from Otherworld." A cold sweat broke over me as I realized what they were doing. One of them was pulling out a pair of handcuffs.

"Shimmer, you are under arrest for assault. Put your hands behind your back." As the cuffs snapped on, he continued. "You have the right to remain silent. Anything you say or do can and will be used against you in a court of law. You have the right to an attorney. If you cannot afford an attorney, one will be appointed to you. Do you understand these rights as they have been read to you?"

Now I *was* scared.

Alex moved in. "She was defending herself—"

"And who are you? Did you see the stabbing?" The cop swung around, glaring at Alex.

Alex's gaze shifted to mine and I knew that he had to answer truthfully. He could lose his license to practice, and incriminate me even worse if he lied. "No, I didn't see her stab him. But I heard her screaming from outside the door. I'm Alex Radcliffe, owner of the Fly by Night Magical Investigations Agency. And Shimmer is one of my employees."

The cops stared at him for a moment. One said, "Vampire. Okay, then, we'll all take a ride to the station to sort out what happened. Everybody out."

As the medics gently hoisted Degoba onto a stretcher and wheeled him out, the officers pushed me forward. As we exited the building, I thought I could hear the wight laugh and I realized that, for tonight at least, it had won the battle.

A cross town from Fort Worden, the police station was nothing like the FH-CSI, the Faerie-Human Crime Scene Investigation Unit down in Seattle. For one thing, none of the cops appeared to be Supes. For another, I had the distinct feeling they weren't sure what the hell to do with me. They checked me over, searching me thoroughly. Even when I'd been chained in the Dragon Reaches, I hadn't been strip-searched in human form, and that was a humiliation I could easily go without ever experiencing again.

I grimaced as the matron told me to get undressed, and then to "Bend over and spread your legs." Blushing, feeling once again the lack of any control over my situation, I did as she bade, while all the while wanting to smash in her smug and haughty face. That over, she handed me an orange jump-suit that barely fit over my boobs and was about three inches too short in the legs. I put on the slippers they gave me in place of my shoes and followed her to a cell where she handed me a blanket and a pillow and pointed to the bunk.

"Park it and don't cause trouble. No television at this time of night."

Feeling terribly alone, I sat on the edge of the bunk, clutching the pillow. The room was small, probably six feet wide by eight feet long, and contained a TV fastened to the wall, a bunk, a toilet, and a pedestal sink. My thoughts kept running to Degoba and I wondered if he was alive. The memory of my dagger hitting his side kept replaying through my thoughts and I winced, hanging my head. I'd had no choice, and yet—and yet—if he died, it would be *my* fault.

Wondering what the hell was going to happen next, I stayed right where I was. I got my answer soon enough, when someone popped into the bunk behind me. Startled, I turned to see Chai, trying to scrunch up as inconspicuously as possible.

"Don't look at me, and don't stand up," he whispered. "Alex wanted me to check on you."

"You can make it into the cells?"

"Here I can—this is a human holding tank, not built for Supes of any nature, apparently." He poked me in the side. "Scoot forward just a little, I need to rearrange my arm."

I did, thinking that I should just ask him to get me out of here, but then I realized there was a problem on two levels with that. One, the cops would freak when I vanished, and that would leave us open to more questions than we needed or wanted. And two, that would be asking Chai for a favor and he'd be forced to fuck it up as much as he could. Sometimes having a djinn as a friend could be complicated.

"Is Degoba still alive?" I wanted him to be alive, and *not* just because I wanted to get out of this as unscathed as possible. Though, if he died, I'd be up the creek without a paddle. Without even the damned canoe.

"He was the last time I checked. I peeked in on him at the hospital before coming here. The minute the cops showed up, I vanished before they could see me, so they don't know about me." He paused. "What did you tell them you were on the intake form?"

"Fae. Works well enough and most of the humans can't tell one Supe from another." A thought occurred to me. Maybe, if this lasted too long, they would contact Chase Johnson down at the FH-CSI and he could oversee things. He would understand; he was used to freaky shit happening.

Noises in the hallway alerted us and Chai vanished. I quickly stood and spread out my blanket and pillow, turning as the matron appeared outside my cell. She crooked her finger.

"Captain wants to talk to you."

I meekly followed her as she unlocked the cell and led me to a room. A large window looked into the room from the hallway, and she gestured toward one of the chairs. "Sit. He'll be in shortly."

I did as she said, waiting. She struck up guard duty outside the door.

About five minutes later, a man hustled into the room. He was carrying a file folder, and he wore a black suit that was about a size too large for him. He looked tired and grumpy. Great, just what I needed. A pissed-off cop.

He tossed the file on the table and sat down opposite me. "Degoba Jones is conscious. He's hurt, but he'll recover. He says it was an accident."

I breathed out a long sigh of relief. "I was so worried. I'm so glad he's going to be all right." I stared at the officer. He was examining my face, and now he quirked one side of his face, as if thinking.

"He refuses to press charges, so we're going to let you go." Another pause. I kept my mouth shut, not wanting to antagonize him anymore than he already seemed. "You realize that we've been paying a lot of visits to you and your friends since you arrived in town. You've discovered a skeleton of someone who was murdered, a fire breaks out in Strand's house, and now one of his friends gets himself stabbed, and you're the one who stabs him. Tell me, Shimmer, what were you doing in the battery in the middle of the night? "

I decided to opt for a version of the truth. "We were ghost

hunting and something went horribly wrong. I thought . . . I thought Degoba was someone else, trying to attack me." I prayed that Degoba would have had the foresight to think of that—at least he'd said it was an accident.

For once, luck was on my side. The cop tapped one finger on the table, then cleared his throat. "That's what he said. He said he didn't mean to sneak up on you, that it was his fault for playing a practical joke. He said he was trying to scare you."

Not knowing if he was trying to lead me into a trap, I just gave a little shrug and kept my mouth shut.

"I imagine he won't make such a stupid mistake again." After another uncomfortable silence, he pushed back his chair. "You'll be released and given back your clothes now. I'd advise you and your friends to stop mucking around in abandoned buildings during the middle of the night. Next time, things might end up far worse." Still looking unsatisfied, he turned and strode out of the room.

Shaking, I waited until the matron returned. She led me to another room where I was given back my clothes and property and allowed to change. I had to sign off on a ledger when I left the jail, and I walked outside to find Alex waiting for me. I ran over to him and he wrapped his arm around my shoulders. He leaned forward, kissing me gently, then led me down the steps and out of the glaring lights shining down on the entrance.

The parking lot was nearly empty and I spotted the Range Rover easily. Alex hustled me into it, shutting the door for me, and then he climbed in the driver's seat. I glanced at the clock. It was nearly five in the morning. I'd only been locked up several hours but I still felt traumatized, and now I leaned forward, resting my head on my hands.

"Put on your seat belt, love." Alex tapped me on the shoulder. "There's a good girl. Do as I say." I blindly obeyed and he put the car in gear and pulled out of the lot, easing onto the street. "Are you okay? Did they do anything to you in there?"

I mutely shook my head. The fact was, they'd been relatively nice—far nicer than my captors in the Dragon

Reaches. No, the real trauma had been in the feeling of being locked up—of being out of control of my life and my body, and subject to the whims of somebody else.

"I'm okay," was all I said, though. "Degoba, he's really going to be all right?"

"He'll be fine, love. He's healing up. There's more to that man than meets the eye. You gave him a pretty nasty jab with the pointy stick. Anybody else would have been in surgery a lot longer, if not dead. Degoba, he's a tough bird, all right." Alex paused, then added, "I'm sorry I ran off from the group. I just wanted to corral Ralph before he got himself in trouble. I didn't realize that the forest wight would jump Degoba."

"Yeah, well, he did a good job of it. He was . . . the thing gave Degoba strength, Alex. It gave him power." Managing to pull myself together, I finally asked, "How's Ralph? Did he hurt himself when he fainted?"

"No, he's a tough lad. He's fine." Another pause, and then Alex pulled over to the curb. He put the car in park and turned to me. "We can leave. We can go home tomorrow—well, tonight, after I wake up if you want to. This may be too hot for us to handle. I think Patrick needs a spot-on team of ghost hunters instead of us." He reached out and took my hand, gently rubbing my skin with his thumb and forefinger. "It's okay, Shimmer. I don't want you in danger. Or Ralph."

I stared at my hand, at his hand covering it, and lifted it to my face, feeling the comfort of his cool skin against my cheek. It was tempting. I wasn't used to spirits and ghosts. I wasn't used to stabbing people I liked. Biting my lip, I wavered for a moment, then softly kissed his fingers.

"No. You promised we'd help, and I won't make you go back on your word. And now it's personal. That thing is just going to spread its evil through the town if we leave it be. We'll think of something. But thank you, Alex. For the offer." I forced a smile and shook my hair back out of my face as I straightened my shoulders.

He nodded. "I'm glad you want to stick it out. Patrick needs us, though I'm not sure how much we can help him."

He kissed me for a long moment, and then we headed back to Tonya's house.

The table was covered with pizza and sodas when we arrived. Ralph jumped up, a worried look on his face, and he hurried forward.

"Shimmer, are you okay?" He helped me off with my coat before I could say a word as Tonya pressed a plate into my hands and motioned to the pizza.

"Eat. We have cookies if you want, and we also have coffee if you need it." She looked exhausted, and her eyes were rimmed with red as if she'd been crying. I remembered how much she cared about Degoba, and the guilt slammed back double-fold.

I set the plate aside and gave her a long hug. "I'm so glad he's going to be okay. I'm sorry, Tonya—I'm so sorry. I hope he knows that I didn't mean to—"

She shook her head. "He knows. He understands what happened. If you hadn't stabbed him, he would have slit your throat. He knew exactly what was going on but he couldn't stop himself. He said at that moment, everything seemed colored and the only thing he could think about was killing you. He asked me to tell you he's sorry. I think he feels worse than you do."

"I should say so. I'm not the one with a wound in my belly!" I was shaking and smiling and wanting to cry all at the same time. Delayed shock can be traumatic on the body and soul, and I was deep in the midst of a deferred response to everything that had gone on that night.

"That's not what I meant!" She pushed me over to the armchair and made me sit down. "Ralph, get her some food. I think she's in shock." She turned back to me. "Degoba wanted me to ask you to forgive him. He thought he was prepared, he thought he would be immune to the wight's charm, but apparently it's stronger than we thought. But the good news is that he was able to tell me more about it, because it had touched his mind."

I jerked my head up. "Really? Well, that's the one saving grace out of this evening, then." If he could give us more input on what we were fighting, the whole night might have been worth it.

I paused as Ralph brought me a plate stacked with four slices of pepperoni pizza with extra cheese dripping off them. The smell made my stomach growl and I realized that I was starving. Another lovely side effect from shock: adrenaline rushes and the accompanying energy burn.

Ralph dropped into the chair opposite me, draping his arm over the back. "What guarantee do we have that the wight isn't still working through him and feeding us false information?" He sounded buzzed and I saw the three empty cans of Flying Horse sitting on the table. Somebody needed to take away that werewolf's caffeine fix.

"That's a good question." Alex pulled a chair closer. "Ralph makes a valid point. How *do* we know the wight has lost his influence over Degoba? Is there a test we can do?"

Patrick, who was sitting cross-legged on the sofa, rubbed his head. "I'm about ready to just torch the damned house and be done with it."

"Oh gods, no. Then the insurance agency will be breathing down your back and they'll think you tried to commit fraud the first time." Chai let out a snort as he emerged from the wall next to the vampire. We all jumped. No matter how often I'd seen the djinn enter a room, it always seemed to be in a new and different way, and I never knew what to expect.

"He's right," I said. "For the rest of the night, let it be. We'll start sorting out stuff when we get up. I think we're all exhausted." Frowning at Ralph, I added, "Except maybe caffeine-boy here."

He stuck his tongue out at me, then motioned to my plate. "Eat your pizza. Then we'll get some shut-eye."

"We've still got about an hour before we have to be in the basement. While you eat, I think we'll scout around the neighborhood to make sure nothing is lurking near the house." Alex clapped Patrick on the shoulder. "Come on, let's take a walk around the block."

As they headed out the door, I bit into my pizza, realizing how hungry I really was. Tonya's cell phone rang and she went into the kitchen to answer it. Ralph glanced over at Chai, then looked back at me.

"How are you, really?" The note of concern in the werewolf's voice touched me.

I felt bad, knowing that being friend-zoned wasn't easy. And now . . . now Alex and I were . . . well, we were *something*, that was for certain.

"I know about you and Alex, Shimmer. I just want you to know, I hope it works out." He held my gaze and I realized that he was begging me not to say anything more—not to apologize or even admit I knew how he had felt.

"Thanks, Ralph. I guess we'll see what happens. As to how I am . . ." I considered his question rather than waving it off with an *I'm okay*. How was I? Hungry, that I knew. Freaked, still. Wanting to go home but knowing that we needed to do the right thing. "I'm worn out. Tonight was so fucked up . . . it was beyond screwed. I really, really want to destroy that thing. And I still can't get the memory of stabbing Degoba out of my mind. I could have killed him. I almost did." Biting my lip, I worried the flesh until Chai noticed and tapped me on the shoulder.

"Neither one of you is to blame. He was possessed and you were defending yourself. There's nothing anybody can do about the situation. Once we arrived, the domino effect took over and tumbled us one by one. The wight set up the perfect storm, but he didn't expect you to be so strong. I honestly don't think he recognizes you for what you really are, even though Degoba knew."

I nodded, finishing the last slice. "Another, please? I'm still hungry."

While Chai took my plate over to the table, Ralph leaned forward. "We need to find out if that thing is stronger during the daytime or night. If it's stronger during the night, maybe it would be better to attack it by daylight?"

I frowned. "We'd be down Patrick and Alex, then. But you're right—it would be good to know. And if it's a lot more vulnerable during the day, maybe there's some way we can attack it that won't require putting ourselves in as much danger. I just hope the one in Patrick's house isn't as strong."

Tonya entered the living room, looking drawn. "I was talking to Degoba. He managed to sneak a phone in his room even though they wanted him to rest."

I caught my breath, hoping the news was good. "How is he? He didn't relapse, did he?"

She shook her head. "No, nothing like that. In fact, he sounds like he's just got a minor cold. I'm pretty surprised by how resilient he is. But he is insistent that he has information on the wight for us. I'll grab my cards and do a reading to see if he's still under its control."

She headed over to the desk while Chai brought me back a couple more slices of pizza. I dug in, plowing my way through them. I wanted a shower and sleep, not to strategize, but better we get this out of the way now and know what we were going to do when we woke up. Otherwise, sleep would come hard. I knew my mind. I overthought things a lot and could lie in bed tossing and turning half the night when I was trying to sort out a problem.

Tonya shifted stuff off the coffee table, with Ralph helping her. As she shuffled the cards, the energy in the room begin to spiral. Humans' magic was different than that of the Fae or of dragons or of any other species. It wasn't flashy, and it didn't usually bring a bunch of special effects with it, but nonetheless, it worked and it had its own special flair.

She laid out five cards. "The situation—eight of Cups. Degoba's part—the Hierophant. The wight's part—ten of Wands. Is the wight still influencing Degoba—ace of Swords. And lastly, can we trust what Degoba tells us—three of Wands."

Setting aside the rest of the deck, she ran her hands over the cards, skimming the air above them as if she were testing their aura. After a moment, she looked up, smiling. "The situation was one of leeching—the wight possessing Degoba. The eight of Cups indicates slimy energy, often codependence or addiction. In this case, it tells me that the wight did have hold of him—it was piggybacking him. But Degoba's card is the Hierophant, he's the master, the teacher in this situation, and he was ultimately stronger than the wight. The wight's energy is the ten of wands—oppression, violence, anger. The ace of swords tells me that Degoba's energy is clear again. He managed to shake it off. Lastly, can we trust what Degoba tells us? The three of Wands is virtue, walking the truth of one's heart. So yes, we can trust him again."

Relief washed over me. I'd been worried that the wight had done permanent damage to him in some way, but it sounded like he was well clear of it. "Good. So what did he tell you, then?"

She folded up the cards. "Degoba said that while the wight was in control of him, it couldn't shut him out from peeking into its nature. Sort of like, when you're in the belly of the beast, you get to see its innards."

Ralph grimaced. "Delightful visual, there."

"But apt," Chai said. "Go on, Tonya."

Tonya cleared her throat. "There is a lot he's not clear on, but he found out one thing for certain . . . the wight that's at the battery? He is the king, controlling the other wights in town."

"There's more than the one at Patrick's?" There was so much about that statement that we really didn't need to hear.

"Yes, but we knew there would be."

"How many wights are we talking about?" Just the thought of having to face more than the king and his buddy at Patrick's gave me the willies. I had no desire to go tramping around Port Townsend, knocking on doors, asking to come in and fix their wight problem.

Ralph groaned. "Please, don't get into the double digits."

"No, actually, we're pretty lucky. It's not nearly as bad as it could be. At least, not yet. If we leave the king alone, it will get worse, though. In fact, Degoba told me that if we don't weed them out, then the violence in the town will increase and tourism will drop—because apparently forest wights siphon off good fortune, as well."

Chai edged onto the arm of my chair, his hand draped

around my shoulder in a companionable way. I leaned my head against him. He made me feel safe, and I was grateful he'd stuck around to help us.

"So how many?" I set my plate on the coffee table.

"Three, including the king. While the king's been around for some time, the hive is still fairly new and hasn't had time to build up yet. They breed slowly and it can take centuries to build up a thriving colony. There's the king, the one at Patrick's, and then there is another somewhere around town. The good news is that we were right. Once the king is dead, the others will be easy pickings. The hive needs its king in order to be strong—kill him, and they won't know what to do."

I shook my head. That might be good news of a sort, but the fact that we were facing three wights made me want to dive for cover. "What happens if we kill the king but don't get the rest?"

"Then, as time goes on, there will be a skirmish for power. One of them will take control and become the new king and then start adding to the hive again. So you see, we have to go after all of them, because if we don't, the problem will be right back to where it's at right now. There will be a new king." She leaned back, rubbing her head. "As to whether they're stronger in the night or day? Degoba told me the night makes them strong. He said they are far weaker during the day. So I think, when we wake up, we'd better head out and take care of the suckers."

I stared at the carpet for a moment, following the patterns with my mind. Then, as we heard Patrick and Alex coming through the kitchen door, I lowered my voice. "Don't tell them. We do not want them to know because they'd insist we wait till they wake up. If the wights are a lot weaker during the day, then that's when we have to attack them."

The others nodded as the vampires entered the room. We all said good night, not telling Alex and Patrick what we'd found out, and headed to bed to get some rest before going out on wight patrol once more.

CHAPTER 17

We got to sleep around seven thirty, and by noon, I opened my eyes, not fully rested but enough to pop out of bed. Tonya rolled over and let out a groan, squinting at me as I stretched.

"You've got huge boobs," she said, pushing herself to a sitting position. "Do all dragons have them? Women, that is?" Pausing, she added, "And do you call yourselves *women*? Females? I never know what the proper terminology is for nonhumans. Obviously, most Fae are men or women but . . . oh hell." She yawned widely. "Don't mind me. I'm pre-caffeine."

I laughed, then sat on the edge of the bed. I was wearing a loose sleep shirt that came to the tops of my thighs, but it was sheer and I hadn't realized till now that she might be modest or embarrassed. I just didn't think of things like that.

"I'm sorry—I hope I'm not embarrassing you. I know humans are generally more reserved than Supes, but I tend to forget."

She shook her head and pushed back the covers, staggering to her feet. "No, it doesn't bother me. A lot of people, it might, but not me." She stared down at her body. She was wearing a pair of boy shorts and a T-shirt. "I usually sleep in the nude but thought that might be a touch too friendly for you. I just wish I could do something about this cellulite." She smacked one of her thighs, then looked at me more closely. "That's an awesome tattoo. I have several."

I slid out of my clothes to show her the ink. "Most dragons won't get ink. It's just not a part of the culture. But because . . . the circumstances of my birth make me an outcaste anyway so I got this long, long ago. It reminds me of who I am, regardless of what society thinks of me. It reminds me that I am all dragon, even though I was an orphan."

She moved closer to examine the work. "Exquisite and realistic." Her breath tickled my skin and I jumped a little, laughing. Tonya looked up at me, then, and a shy smile stole over her face. "You're beautiful. If I were into girls, I'd so be on you."

That made me laugh. "I'm into . . . whoever I decide I want at the moment, but mostly I gravitate toward men."

She nodded. "I get it. Hey, you want to use the shower first? Go ahead, if you like. I'll go make coffee and get some breakfast going. Lunch. Whatever you call it when you get up at noon."

"Thanks, I really need to drench myself." The pull of the water was strong on me this morning, and I wanted nothing more than to head out to the ocean and dive deep. Maybe I could do that after we dealt with the wight. That is, if we survived the encounter. Consoling myself with that thought, I slid into the shower and lathered myself up. Tonya's body wash smelled like rain and I noted the brand and name of it. On the way home, I'd stop and pick some up.

By the time I finished getting dressed, smoothed my hair back into a high ponytail, and put on some makeup, Tonya was back. She jumped in the shower for a quick rinse after telling me that Ralph and Chai had taken it upon themselves to make breakfast for all of us.

Following my nose, I headed out to the kitchen, where a stack of toast waited next to a pan of scrambled eggs and another filled with sausage. Filling my plate, I slid into a chair at the table next to Ralph, who was downing his third cup of coffee. Chai poured me a cup and then proceeded to rinse the pans and put them in the dishwasher.

Ralph's hair was wet. Apparently he'd taken a shower in the second bathroom already. He was looking up something on his laptop and seemed immersed in whatever it was.

"What are you reading?" I reached over and poked him in the arm.

He gulped the last of the coffee in his mug and turned the screen toward me. "I was trying to pinpoint the amount of ghostly activity here, to see if we could figure out where the other two wights are. But there's so many things that go on around here it's impossible to tell."

I stared at the chart that he'd created. He was right— ghosts, hauntings . . . they spiked all over the place. There were far more events than three extra wights could account for. Frowning, I leaned in, trying to puzzle out something that was playing in the back of my thoughts.

"You know . . . they aren't always associated with ghosts. We might think so, because of the situation at Patrick's house, but the truth is that wights feed off a lot of different energies—not just spirits. Fear . . . chaos. What about violent events? Brawls, murders, mayhem of any kind? Have there been any spikes in Port Townsend? High-crime areas that suddenly had an influx in criminal activity other than burglary or the sort?"

Ralph grinned at me. "We'll make a detective out of you yet, Shimmer. Good thinking." He pulled the laptop back and began tapping away, his fingers flying over the keys. If I could ever even reach a third of the speed he had on the keyboard, I'd be happy.

While he was busy with that, I turned to Chai. "And you, how are you this morning, big bro?" I grinned at him and suddenly realized that I felt comfortable. It felt good for a change to have this many people around. I might be a loner, but that was partially because I'd never had any choice in the matter. Truth was, I liked being around friends, I liked feeling the camaraderie that we seemed to have formed. And I was really going to miss Tonya when we went home.

Chai shrugged. "Good. I popped back to feed your fish this morning but almost startled some woman who was there."

Stacy! Oh gods, what if she saw Chai? She wouldn't know what to make of him. She might know that I was a dragon, but that didn't mean she would know Chai was a friend of mine, or that he was relatively harmless unless you pissed him off.

"Did she see you?"

He shook his head. "I was in the kitchen when she opened the door. I managed to pop out before she ran into me. I have the feeling she thought there was someone in there, so you may hear something about it when you go home, but I don't think she caught a glimpse of me."

"I forgot, I asked her to check on my apartment for me." I spread a spoonful of jam on the toast and bit into it, enjoying the buttery feel of the bread in my mouth. I was growing to like human food more and more, and it was nice to not have to go hunting all the time. I couldn't very well do that anyway, unless I dove into the water now, seeing that I had been barred from my dragon form otherwise.

"Well, she's there, so your fish are getting their breakfast."

Tonya wandered in, dressed in jeans and a sweatshirt. "If we're going back out to the battery, I'm not wearing my good clothes. I'll call Degoba and see how he's doing—" She was interrupted by the doorbell. "Damn. Will somebody fix me a plate, please?"

As Chai handed me a plate and I began to spread jam on toast for her and scoop up some scrambled eggs, Tonya returned. Behind her was Degoba, limping a little, and wearing a loose shirt over a pair of sweatpants.

I shoved the plate into Chai's hands and jumped up, running over to him. I was about to grab him for a hug when he held out his hands. "Whoa, missy. You squeeze me and you might reopen the wound. I'm healing up quickly but I've still got a line of ten stitches in my side."

"Oh hell, I'm sorry. I didn't even think." I settled for

leaning in and pressing my lips to his cheek. "I'm so sorry, Degoba. I really didn't mean to hurt you—"

"Girl, stop it with the guilt. It's over. We had a bad situation and there's nothing that any of us could have done. We got caught with our pants down and took a hard spanking." He winked and I blushed.

"Come, sit down. Do you want something to eat?" Tonya led him over to the table where Ralph hurried to grab one of the chairs we'd carried to the living room. He moved his laptop to a tray next to the table so there was room for all of us. I went back to my breakfast, and Tonya to hers, while Chai graciously filled a plate for Degoba.

I frowned at the djinn. "What about you? Did you eat?"

He nodded. "I stopped at McDonald's on the way back from your place."

Tonya turned to him. "*You* eat fast food?"

He snorted. "I'm a djinn, not a vegetarian."

"I know but . . . okay, whatever." She laughed.

For a while, the only sound was that of our forks clinking against the china, but finally we were sated. She pushed back her plate at the same time I pushed back mine. Degoba, on the other hand, was having seconds. Ralph was still poring through documents on the Net.

"So I did a reading last night on you." Tonya turned to the spiritwalker. "I had to make certain the wight didn't still have a hold on you." She told him what the cards had said, and he nodded.

"Good thinking. Never trust blindly. But no, it lost its hold when Shimmer stabbed me. In a sense, that was the best thing you could have done, girl, because it startled me so much that it threw my body into shock and that dislodged the wight. So don't feel so bad, please." He gave me such a kindly grin that I finally realized that he meant it—that the incident was behind us.

"Just never again, all right? I don't want to ever attack one of my friends again. This is the second time that's happened."

"When's the first?" Tonya stared at me like I'd suddenly confessed to being a serial killer or something.

"I was charmed by a sorcerer, a vampire no less, and he forced me to attack Alex. I almost staked him." I stopped, suddenly realizing that Degoba had been in pretty much the same position I had. "Oh man, that hits home, doesn't it?"

"Yes, well, we'll just figure out a way to keep that from happening again when we go after it next." Degoba motioned to the last piece of toast. "Anybody mind if I take that?"

"No, eat hearty. But you're not going anywhere. We're heading out today to fight it because it's weaker in daylight, and you aren't coming with us. Not in your condition." Tonya gave him a stern look.

Degoba let out a sigh. "You're right on that. I want to go, but I'm not stupid and I know my limitations. I could come but stay in the car. You're going to want me there."

"Not necessarily. Somebody refill me with coffee, please. Hey, look at this." Ralph shoved away his plate and turned the screen so it was facing the rest of us.

I was nearest the coffeepot, so I poured the last of it into his cup. "I think you'd better make some more for our Energizer bunny here, Tonya. What did you find, Ralph?"

As Tonya headed over to the sink to rinse out the pot, the doorbell rang again and she went to answer it. Meanwhile, Ralph pointed to a map of the town, with three circles superimposed over the top. One was right over the battery. Another was over Patrick's house. Another was in the south area of town.

"These are the areas where the most violence has happened over the past five months—" He stopped as Tonya returned, with Paris Veraday behind her.

"Afternoon, folks." She stopped when she saw Degoba, then gave a little shrug. "I wanted to let you know that Toby came in and we did a rush job on the labs. The skeleton? Buckland bones. Probably Lacy but there's no real way of knowing that. Not at this point. But they definitely belong to the Buckland family. He's going to claim her and give her a proper burial."

That made me incredibly happy, and it must have shown on my face because Paris broke out into a warm smile.

"Finding her family really mattered to you, didn't it?" She sounded like she understood.

I nodded. "Yeah, it did. Even if you don't know for sure it's Lacy, we're fairly certain of it, and at least one of her kin laid claim to her and will remember that she belonged to his blood."

She held my gaze for a moment, then nodded and stood up. "Mr. Strand is free to go in and start work on rebuilding his bed-and-breakfast, but he can't open till the damage has been fixed and the inspector signs off on it." She paused then, looking like she wanted to say something else. I wasn't the only one who noticed it.

Tonya set a cup of coffee in front of Paris. "What is it?"

Paris took a deep breath and let it out slowly. "I know there are entities in that house. I felt them when I was there. I felt them around the skeleton. I know what happened—officially—at the battery. I also know there's something in that place because the last time I was there, it scared the hell out of me. I can't speak as a cop . . . ignore my badge for now . . . but if you're trying to take care of whatever it is, please be careful. Whatever is going on in this town, it's dangerous."

I looked at Ralph, then at Tonya and Chai. It was better for everybody if none of this ever chanced creeping into government hands of any sort. And while I trusted Paris, there was always the chance she'd feel obligated to report it and we'd be in trouble.

"We simply can't verify that. I hope you understand—we can't talk about it. I'm not about to say you're wrong, though."

I really didn't know if I should be the one taking over the official spiel; Ralph had been with Alex a lot longer. But Ralph was far better with a keyboard than he was with verbal communication. It occurred to me that we needed to clarify the matter on who spoke for the company, once Alex was awake to make a decision.

Paris considered what I said, then nodded and stood up and put her hat back on, adjusting it over her hair. "I understand. If you need me—unofficially—call me here."

She handed me a business card. It was her personal one, with her cell number on it. Apparently, Paris was more than just a cop—she also made and sold quilts. As we showed her to the door, I tucked her card in my pocket.

When she was gone, I looked back at the others. "So, let's get this over with. Degoba, is there anything else you can tell us about the wight? Any other facts you might remember?"

Degoba leaned back and closed his eyes. "Tonya, can you regress me? It might help me uncover anything that got buried when I attacked Shimmer. Everything after she stabbed me is a blur."

Tonya glanced at the clock. "Yeah, but we shouldn't wait too long. Dusk comes early this time of year. Get yourself comfortable and I'll go get my pendulum."

Degoba crossed to the sofa and cautiously stretched out, propping himself up with pillows. He gingerly fingered his side where the bandage was and then, taking a shallow breath, let it out slowly. Tonya returned with a long crystal attached to a silver chain. As she settled next to Degoba, sitting on an ottoman, he began to breathe slowly and rhythmically.

Tonya held out the pendulum in front of his eyes and began to swing it slowly back and forth. Degoba followed it with his gaze, back and forth as she whispered to him.

"Follow the pendulum with your eyes. Let it guide you back in time. Follow it into the depths of your subconscious, deep into your memories. Let it lead you into the recesses of your mind where you have hidden your thoughts and impressions. Take three deep breaths and let them out slowly."

Degoba obeyed, and with each breath, he seemed to fade a little from the room.

Tonya waited for a moment, then continued. "Can you hear me?"

"Yes."

"I want you to search for whatever you can find about the forest wight. Reach out to your memories—and look for anything you may have forgotten."

Degoba let out one more breath and a pale mist seemed to surround him, feathery tendrils gently waving like reeds in the wind. Tonya waited for another moment, then spoke again.

"Can you remember the forest wight and what it felt like inside your mind?"

"Yes." Degoba shifted slightly, as if he was uncomfortable.

"I want you to examine the experience—from an observational level. I want you to look at every detail and tell us anything that you think you may have overlooked. Is there anything you notice that may help us?"

Another moment, and Degoba jerked a little. "I can see . . . I can see where he's hiding. I can see where his lair is."

Tonya pounced on that. "Where? Where does the creature make his home?"

"The battery—on the bottom floor, deep in the room farthest back on the left side. He's created a secret access panel to an underground lair in the rammed earth that surrounds the structure. That's where you can find him in physical form." Jerking suddenly, Degoba sat up, eyes flying open. "He almost felt me—I could feel him out there, watching and waiting. If I had poked around any farther, he might have made the connection. I think there's still some sort of link between us and while this didn't activate it, I'm not sure what might."

We looked at each other.

"The question is," I said, "if you can still sense him, can he deliberately seek you out?"

"We can't take the chance that he'll know we're coming. Is there something we can do?" Ralph asked.

Degoba nodded. "Yeah. There is. Knock me out with a sedative that will dull my mind. On the down side, you won't be able to call me if you need help. But it should keep him from being able to get a firm grip on me again. If he senses you around the battery, he may try to take a peek in my brain to find out what's going on. Even from here, I could cause some major havoc. But if I'm sedated and fuzzy-headed, he shouldn't be able to do much through me."

"What will work? I don't have any sleeping pills." Tonya frowned. "I don't think any of my herbals will work either. I do have some pot—you want to smoke some of that?"

I grinned. Humans liked their marijuana and it was quite legal in Washington State. But Degoba shook his head.

"No, marijuana won't actually knock me unconscious. I have pain pills and they can fuzz me up pretty good but they don't make me sleep. I know!" He snapped his fingers. "Do you have Sleepy-Cold?"

"What's that?" I wasn't familiar with a lot of the pharmaceuticals humans used. Most of them reacted quite differently on Fae or other Supes. And most of them wouldn't do a thing to me. Hell, it took a jackhammer to even get me tipsy—dragon liquor was a hell of a lot more potent, and even when I was in human form, my resistance was strong to anything except the harder alcohols.

"It's a liquid cold reliever. A decongestant that's primarily alcohol, but it's also a sleep aid. Can cause one heck of a hangover, and yes, it does fog up the brain. I have a bottle in the bathroom. I'll get it." Tonya vanished down the hall and returned with a bottle containing a neon green liquid. She opened it and the pungent smell made me wince. Oh, that had alcohol in it, all right, but other things, too. I had no idea what they were, but I could smell them clear enough. It reminded me of a thick, doctored cherry syrup.

Degoba stared at it, cupping the bottle in his hands. "Okay, listen up. The creature will be in the physical realm if you catch it in its lair. I think it's sleeping now, but when you get there, it will wake up. Once it wakes, you'll have to work fast because it can shift out of phase at that point. I believe—I'm not positive, but I think that when it sleeps, it's a lot like a vampire. More vulnerable. Stab it with silver. Ralph, you can't touch silver, so guard the girls here. Also, and this is from my connection with him—the wight king has a pendant. If you can get hold of it, you can destroy it and it will make it that much harder for the hive to re-form."

"But it wouldn't be impossible? If we destroy the

necklace, another wight can still take his place?" Tonya was jotting things down as quickly as she could.

"Yes, eventually. So dive in there right away and don't let him escape. If you do, he'll just move his lair, and this time he'll make sure we can't find him until the entire town is over-run." Degoba sniffed the Sleepy-Cold, and the look on his face made me laugh. "Damn, this stuff could knock out an elephant. Okay, bottoms up. I'll stay here. Your house is warded heavily and that will help keep the wight out of my head, too." As we watched, he slugged a hit of the cold medication, then another. By the time he was done, he'd taken at least three full doses of the stuff.

We gathered our things and made certain that Patrick and Alex were as protected as we could make them. Tonya had the idea to bring down every silver chain she had in the house—necklaces, but nonetheless, they were silver. We unfastened them and hooked them together into one giant chain, which we draped on chairs around the sleeper sofa. It wasn't a great deal of protection, but given that the wight hated silver, it might cause Degoba to pause if the creature should somehow manage to gain control and go after the vamps. It was worth a try, anyway.

When we re-entered the living room, Degoba was snor-ing loudly on the sofa. He was already asleep.

"That crap works fast," Ralph said, laughing. "I kind of wish I could take it on nights when my mind won't shut up, but OTCs have a notoriously bad effect on Weres, especially werewolves."

Tonya tucked an afghan around Degoba, then motioned to the door. "Let's get a move on. It's already one thirty and we don't want to waste another minute."

And so the four of us went trooping out the door. I just hoped it wasn't to meet our doom.

Fort Worden had a different feel by day. Once again, I found myself staring hungrily at the water, wanting to ditch everything else and go dive in. But as we approached the battery, the energy from the night before still pervaded the area and my focus returned to where we were and what we were doing. I looked around for evidence of our fight with the sapwalkers, but there was nothing to be seen—it was as if they had never existed. Then, out of the corner of my eye, I noticed a twig. It wasn't moving, in fact it was just lying there on the ground, but my gut told me it had been the branch that had wrapped around my throat. I walked over to it and picked it up.

"What's that?" Tonya leaned in to look at it.

"Sapwalker branch—the one that wrapped around my neck. I don't know *how* I know, but I do. I can feel it." Suddenly not wanting to touch the thing, I tossed it aside, shivering. "I wonder if those things walk only by night?"

Ralph shook his head. "I have no idea. And I don't fancy finding out."

I paused. I didn't want to bring up a delicate issue, but it could turn into a major problem, so I decided it was best to have it out in the open. "Ralph, can you keep it together in human form? What if something goes down and . . ."

He groaned. "And blood spills. Yeah, yeah, I know." With a heavy sigh, he shrugged, looking embarrassed. His cheeks flared with color. "I'm not entirely sure I can promise. But tell you what, the minute a fight starts, I'll shift. That should prevent me from fainting."

It was the best we could manage. Chai took the lead—he would be the hardest to hurt and the hardest to hit. Tonya and I came next, and Ralph brought up the rear. As we headed into the battery, it was still light enough to see our way around. We came to a sudden stop. A couple of college-aged boys were standing in one corner, eyeing the graffiti on the wall. A girl—about their age—was hanging back near the door, and she looked nervous as hell. When she saw Tonya and me, she flashed us a relieved, shy smile.

I sidled over to her. "Weird place, huh?"

She nodded. "I don't like it. My friends wanted to come out to look at it, but I'd rather just go home. Everything feels so . . . sinister in here. It's probably just my imagination, but . . ." As she drifted off, I realized that her friends were staring over at her, and the looks on their faces were harsh and glittering.

Shivering, I tried to think of some way to get them to leave before the men were caught up in the forest wight's energy. Then it hit me. I slipped over to Chai and wrapped my arm through his, pulling him off to the side.

"Chai, I am not asking a favor. Not at all."

He grinned. "Okay, that much is clear."

"You see those two men over there in the corner?" I waited till he nodded. "They need to leave this place *now*. I wonder, I wonder, maybe I should do something to get them out before they get trapped by anything nasty?"

With a low rumble, Chai shook his head. "Little Sister, you're good. Wait for a moment, before you do anything. I have an idea . . ." And then, he slowly meandered over in their direction. As he went, the temperature began to rise. It was getting unseasonably warm, especially near the djinn. In fact, it was downright uncomfortable after just a few minutes.

The college boys looked confused, and then, tugging on the necks of their collars, they slid their coats off. Another minute and they dislodged themselves from their position and headed toward the entrance. Both looked a little glazed over and neither looked like he knew what the hell was going on. The girl glanced at me and slowly nodded, then swung in behind them as they left.

"There's no way to lock people out, is there?" Tonya glanced around once they were gone.

"I don't have anything that can help—not really." My magic might froth up the waves and drive people out of the water, but it wouldn't do much good here.

Ralph shook his head. "I got nothing."

But Chai, once again, arched his eyebrow. "Be right back." He headed out the door and then, a few minutes later, returned. "The entrance is not so appealing right now. I could not fully make it invisible—well, I could but that would be an all-out granting-of-a-wish type of power.

However, I put up an aura of *don't come near* around it, so anybody thinking about visiting will think twice, and a third time."

"That will have to do. I guess we're good to go, then." I turned to the left. "Degoba said to head left, to the further-most back room, to look for the panel to the wight's subterranean lair."

"Joy of joys," Tonya said.

And with that, we headed into the bowels of the battery yet once again.

CHAPTER 18

The farther away from the door we got, the more I expected the light to fade, but there were still windows— actually big gaping holes   that looked out into the brush surrounding the building, and they let in the daylight, such as it was. We wound our way through the battery, now deserted except for us; until we found ourselves at a door leading into the back rooms. The building was longer and deeper than I'd thought, and we were going to have to let go of the light as we entered rooms that were windowless. As we plunged into the darkness, Ralph brought out a high-beam flashlight.

We kept quiet, following Degoba's instructions. Even if the wight was sleeping, best not to chance waking him up. The more time we had before engaging him, the more chance we had to kill him outright. In my most optimistic fantasy, we'd discover him asleep and destroy him before he could wake up and take us on. I knew that wasn't a likely scenario but hey, I could dream, couldn't I?

As we moved into the room where he was supposed to be hiding, Ralph trained the flashlight into the corners, but there was no sign of the wight. We'd have to find the access panel he'd created—not an easy task given the size of the room and the fact that it was pitch black in here except for the light from our flashlight. The last thing we wanted to do was to wake him up before we'd discovered his hideout.

"Where do we start?" I kept my voice low, whispering in hopes we wouldn't be overheard.

Tonya assessed the room, staring first at one wall, then another. "It can't be the wall behind us," she whispered back. "Or the wall to our right—that's adjacent to another room. So it has to be either straight ahead, or the wall to the left. I'm thinking . . . straight ahead. There's some force that feels like it's pulling me to it."

"Compulsion?" I stiffened, wondering if the wight was putting the moves on her now that Degoba was out. But she just shook her head.

"No, just a sense. The energy there is thicker and darker—like a murky veil. I think that's our best bet." She moved up to stand beside Chai and, giving the djinn a hesitant smile, started forward.

He kept pace with her, guarding the way. Ralph and I followed behind. I wondered if it wasn't best to spread out in a single line, but that would just give the wight access to more of us at once. At least this way, Ralph and I were the second line of defense. Not sure if that was sound thinking or just self-preservation, I decided it made logical sense. I sure wasn't the expert on matters like this.

As we moved forward, it once again occurred to me how weird my life had become. After I'd been released from the Lost and Foundling, I spent most of my time alone, making my way as best as I could. I'd always managed to get myself into sticky situations, but most of it was trying to avoid being caught. I'd stolen to keep myself alive, for the most part—although I did admit to taking a covert delight in outwitting so many of the dragons who wouldn't give me the time of day on the street. But mostly, I had just wandered through the Dragon Realms, drifting from town to town, occasionally dropping down into the Northlands where nobody questioned me about my house or my lineage.

And now? Here I was, Earthside, working with vampires, werewolves, and humans, sneaking up on a forest wight to put a stop to his reign of terror. *Surreal.*

Tonya paused, extending her hands palms wide. My guess was that she was trying to gauge the densest part of the energy—the central core. After a moment, she started forward again, toward the far right side of the back wall. As we drew closer, Ralph lowered the flashlight so it wasn't directly pointing ahead. Good move. If there were cracks around the panel, we didn't want to flash a light through them.

Another moment, and we were there, within arm's reach of the wall. Tonya leaned forward, still silent, then turned around and nodded. She pointed to the wall, then traced an outline in the air, her fingers a few inches away from the concrete.

I squinted. In the diffused light, I could see the outline of a rectangle, flush against the wall. But was it a door or a panel? I couldn't see any protrusions indicating a handle, but that didn't mean there weren't hidden indentations or levers.

Ralph motioned for us to move back. He handed me the flashlight, then pulled something out of his pocket that he clipped on the edge of his glasses. A faint light glimmered from it and I realized it was a clip-on flashlight, but the light was pale and not blinding. He crouched on the floor, using one hand for balance, as he closely examined the outline.

I kept the flashlight turned to the side. Nobody was guarding our backs at this point, so while Chai and Tonya watched Ralph, I turned around to nervously peer into the darkness behind us. Every sound we made in this hollow bunker echoed, down to the littlest scraping sound. How could we be here without the wight hearing us, unless he truly was asleep?

A moment later and Tonya peeked around to catch my attention. Grateful she hadn't tapped me on the shoulder, I gave her a nod and turned back to see what progress Ralph had made.

The werewolf had backed away, but he pointed to the far right edge of the outline. Trying to puzzle out what he was gesturing at, I shook my head. I just wasn't seeing it. Tonya and Chai did the same. Ralph motioned for us to back out of the room. As soon as we were on the other side of the door, in low tones, he told us what he'd found.

"There's an indentation about halfway down the edge, and a small button inside the hollow. From what I can tell, when you press the button, the panel will swing open. I got the impression of hinges on the other side, but I'm not entirely sure." Ralph shrugged. "If he's rigged any traps, that I can't tell. I'm a damned good lock pick, but we aren't dealing with humans here, or even normal Supes."

"I'm good at picking locks, too," I said. I'd made a long study of various locks while attempting to navigate through my earlier life. It had paid off, too, until the Greanfyr incident.

"Thing is, this isn't a lock. It's a handle of sorts—so we're stuck with either just going through, or not. There's no middle ground." Ralph looked at Chai. "You know, if the biggest, toughest one of us went first . . ."

Chai cupped his chin. "I wonder who you're talking about, Master Wolf. You're about as subtle as a skunk." He let out a chuckle. "All right, I will take the lead. You could have just told me, you know."

"I didn't want to incur a favor." Ralph shrugged.

"Telling me to go first isn't the same thing as asking."

"How was I supposed to know that? I've never dealt with a djinn before. Anyway, you go first, then. Whatever the case, the longer we stand out here bickering, the more chance we have for that thing to wake up and come charging out at us. And you don't want me to fall down in a faint because some-body spills a little blood." Ralph snorted. "In fact, before we head back in, I'm turning into my wolf form to stave off just that possibility."

He stepped back, then effortlessly shifted into wolf form. As with all Weres, his clothes changed with him. In Ralph's case, they seemed to shift into a bandana around his neck. I wondered what determined their final form, but this was neither the place nor time to ask.

Chai took the lead. Tonya unsheathed her short sword and fell in behind him, and I took my place beside her, dagger out and ready in one hand and flashlight in the other. Ralph closed in behind us. We headed back in.

As we approached the outline, Chai motioned for us to wait. He went ahead. In the glow of the flashlight, he ran his hand along the edge where Ralph had pointed, and the next moment there was a soft *click*, and then a *swish* as the panel swung inward. From where Tonya, Ralph, and I were, the darkness loomed thick inside the passage. We hurried forward.

Chai was already peeking inside when we reached his side. A corridor of rammed earth stretched in front of us. It wasn't very tall—about six feet, which meant that Chai would have a rough time, and I'd have to hunch a little. Either that or scrape my head along the top. Bending low, Chai stepped inside, and then I followed, with Tonya behind me. Ralph loped in behind her. We'd have to hope nobody came along and shut the door on us.

The passage was so narrow that the light from my flashlight illuminated the entire area. I hoped to hell the wight was still asleep, because that was the only way he wouldn't know we were coming. Trying to see around Chai was useless because he filled the space. Behind me, Tonya and Ralph slinked along, Ralph letting out very low growling noises. I'd noticed one thing about him—when he was in Were form, he tended to be a lot more aggressive. Ralph the geek boy had a definite animal edge to him.

We hadn't gone far—about four yards—when Chai suddenly straightened up as he stepped out into a chamber. Two steps and I was by his side as I moved out of the way to allow Tonya and Ralph to enter. I glanced around the chamber.

The hole—it was more a hole than a room—was about eight feet tall and about ten feet wide. A nest of leaves and forest detritus filled one corner, smelling like a rain-sodden forest. There was a chest near the nest that looked like it was made out of interwoven bones. And on the nest, waking up to stare at us, was the forest wight. The moment he saw us, he was on his feet.

The wight was bipedal, short but squat like the sapwalkers, and he was dark and bushy, and his skin was an ochre color, overgrown with big patches of prickly black moss or lichen. His eyes were dark pools of anger, above a mouth ringed with teeth. With massive arms as long as mine, he walked in a gorilla-like fashion, and his feet were wide and gnarled with knobby weals.

He lunged forward, eyes flashing, hissing at us. I spotted the pendant around his neck that Degoba had mentioned. We had to not only destroy him, but get hold of that pendant and crush it.

But all thoughts fell to the wayside as he aimed himself at me. Startled, I dropped the flashlight and brought my dagger up. At the gleam of silver, he paused, eyeing me closely. Chai chose that moment to dive in and ramrod the wight with his head, a move that surprised me but also proved to be relatively effective in dislodging the wight's attention from me. The creature turned to the djinn and his already angry glare turned murderous. Apparently, wights didn't like djinns.

Tonya pushed past me, swinging with her short sword. The blade caught the wight on the arm and nicked it—but though it drew blood, the wight let out a hiss and glared at her. He didn't look like he'd been hurt in the slightest. Apparently he was tougher than her blade.

I thought quickly. I was stronger than Tonya, even if I wasn't as good with weaponry. Maybe I could grapple him and hold him for her. I was about to leap on the wight when Chai—apparently with the same idea—crashed into him. But the wight somehow managed to tuck and roll as he fell. He avoided being pinned as Chai went down on the ground, grappling air.

"Gah!" That wasn't exactly what he said, but Chai roared something in a language I couldn't understand. As he pushed himself up, the wight came to his feet again. He was scary-nimble, and he was eyeing the entrance to the passage. Ralph was standing guard, but if the wight pushed off with one good leap, I could see how he might go flying right over the wolf's head.

Sheathing my dagger, I threw myself forward, body-slamming him from the side. The wight hadn't been paying attention to me and I managed to surprise him. As soon as I wrapped my arms around him, we crashed forward and I took him down. The fall wasn't pleasant and neither was the feel of the muscle-bound creature in my grasp—he felt slimy, like wet fungus—and he stank to high heaven.

He bucked below me and I tried to straddle him, attempting to use my body weight to pin him down. I grabbed his wrists with my arms, but that was a mistake because not only did he drag his knuckles on the ground like a gorilla when he walked, but he seemed to have gorilla-like strength in those biceps of his. Though I was strong—dragon strong—he was a creature of the forest and he was also a creature who walked more than one realm. That gave him a decidedly supernatural advantage.

Tonya scurried forward, her sword out. "Let me get a clean shot! I don't want to stab you."

Flashes of skewering Degoba ran through my mind and I leaned back to give her access. As I did so, one of the wight's arms slipped out of my grasp and he immediately closed his meaty fingers around my throat, holding tight. I began to choke—the width of his fingers spanned halfway around my neck.

Immediately, I dropped his other wrist and clawed at his hand, trying to pry his fingers away. I managed to wedge my fingernails into the crotch between his thumb and forefinger and dug in as hard as I could. Droplets of blood—whatever passed for blood in his veins—dribbled over my fingers. I had managed to pierce his skin. His grip loosened just enough to let me jam my fingers between my throat and his palm and, by doing so, I broke his hold. Forcing his hand back, I jerked my head back, trying to keep my throat out of reach.

Tonya had been dancing around us, trying to find access, but suddenly, someone was behind me.

"I've got his legs, Shimmer." Chai was holding him down. I rolled off the wight, away from his flailing attempts to choke me again. As I scrambled away, my butt landed on the floor.

An audible *crack* split the air as Chai broke one of the creature's legs. He had hold of the foot in one hand and was applying pressure to the knee with his other. In one swift move, he brought the wight's foot up while pressing down on the knee. Horrified by the sound, I sat on the ground, staring.

Tonya didn't seem to have any such hesitation. She jumped right in and brought her sword down toward the wight's heart. But the wight bellowed and lurched to the side, and the sword barely pierced its shoulder. Tonya yanked it out again as Chai turned his attention to the other leg. He seemed to be working on the *break-every-bone-in-its-body* theory.

The wight flailed again, this time managing to grab one of Tonya's ankles. He pulled hard and she went down, her sword clattering to the side. As he dragged her ankle toward those horrible teeth, I scrambled to get hold of her sword. I decided there was no time to plan how to do this—it was either hit him or watch him bite into her ankle, and I didn't want to see what those gnashing, razor-sharp teeth could do to her leg.

I sucked in a deep breath and plunged the sword down toward his belly as hard as I could. Tonya might be a better swordswoman than I was, but I had strength on her in spades.

The tip of the blade hit the wight square center, and I followed through, driving it with my weight. As the blade shuddered, resisting his woodenlike skin, I let my breath out and pushed harder. The blade sank deep then, driving through to pin him to the floor like a butterfly in a schoolkid's collection.

The wight let out another roar, shuddered, and was still.

Tonya yanked her ankle out of his grip. "Is he dead?"

"I think so . . ." I gave him a quick jab with my toe to see if he'd move, but nothing happened.

Chai stood up, staring at the creature. "I have a feeling this isn't quite over," the djinn said.

And he was right. The next moment, the wight's body

convulsed again, and then his mouth opened. I leaped back as Tonya scrambled away. Ralph let out a long howl as black smoke began to pour out from between the wight's lips. It roiled over us like a cloud, then surged forward out the passageway, over Ralph's head. He leaped up in the air and snapped at it. A loud crackle split the air, and Ralph whined and slunk away. The smoke boiled down the passageway and then was gone. The room felt empty.

"Fuck, I think . . . he's dead all right, but he's not dead," Tonya said. "I have a really bad feeling that he's still around."

Chai leaned over the body. "His pendant is still glowing. He's still alive."

"Will destroying his pendant destroy him?" In some cases like this, I knew it would work, but having never dealt with this kind of creature before, I didn't want to assume anything.

Tonya slowly reached out, her hand hovering over the necklace. Then, with one quick movement, she grabbed it and pulled, breaking the chain. The center stone—a mixture of azurite and malachite, I thought—glowed softly as she held it. She wrapped her hand around it, closing her eyes.

A moment later, she looked up. "He's still alive, but he's not in the pendant. I think he jumped to another host. If we destroy the pendant now, he may decide just to stay in whoever he's taken possession of."

"Who could he . . ." And then I stopped. Who was the one person the wight had had a connection with in the past few days? Who had he already taken over once? "Degoba."

Tonya jerked her head up. "But we . . . no, it could happen. The wight might be strong enough to break through my wards. And in a life-or-death situation, he might very well have barreled along the thread that connected him to Degoba."

"When you regressed him, the spiritwalker said he felt the wight on the outside, waiting. The channel must be open. Come on, we've got to get back to your house. Not only is Degoba there, but Patrick and Alex are in danger!" Chai grabbed up the chest that was on the floor. "I'll be along in a minute. Go!"

Ralph turned as I grabbed up the flashlight from where

I had dropped it. Tonya retrieved her sword. She shoved the pendant in her pocket and we headed out. A moment later, a rush of warmth gusted from behind us, and I smelled flames as Chai came barreling along behind us. As we cleared the panel, Chai turned and slammed it shut.

"I burned the nest. There may be some smoldering in there, but I wouldn't worry too much about it. I used a quick-burning flame." He was still carting the chest, and I wondered what was in there.

By the time we got outside, the day had gone from over-cast and breezy to an all-out storm. The waves were rolling in, breaking as they buffeted along the shoreline. I could hear the voices of the sirens, but they were far off and muf-fled by the crash of the water.

We hurried back to the Range Rover. Ralph turned the ignition and hurriedly backed out of the parking space. Chai was sitting in the backseat with Tonya, the chest on his lap.

"What's in there?" I glanced over my shoulder.

He shrugged. "Could be treasure. We won't know till we open it, but it seemed important so I didn't want to leave it behind. You never know what creatures collect over the years." Pausing, he laughed. "But then, look who I'm talking to, Little Sister. You're a dragon. Dragons are the biggest hoarders of all."

I blushed. He was right. Among the creatures of the world, dragons were most known for hoarding treasure and goodies. But the truth was, the white dragons were most likely to be that way. Most dragon families of any stature would be well off and have riches that would make most humans drool, but among the Dragon Reaches, it was all relative. Being born with no house, no name, no family meant I had absolutely no inheritance, which not only put me in the outcaste category but made marriage unlikely because a good share of marriages were financial and politi-cal liaisons, and there was nothing for a dowry for me.

"Yah, well, you've seen my trove. It's all in my apart-ment." Even though I'd stolen to get by a good share of the time, I hadn't stolen to get rich.

Chai reached forward and placed a gentle hand on my shoulder. "I know, Shimmer. You are one of the oddest—and pleasantest—dragons I've ever met. And I've met more than my fair share over the years. I just wish . . ." He let his words drift off, but I knew what he was thinking.

The djinn had more than once lashed out on my behalf. He didn't like dragon culture, and the way I was treated just fueled his irritation at the entire structure of the society into which I'd been born. I'd listened to him pontificate more than once on the subject, mostly because I agreed with him.

Ralph cleared his throat. "Not to interrupt, but if the wight has possession of Degoba, what are we going to do? It's not like the creature has a body to return to now. We took care of that."

I frowned, thinking. "Can we make him jump into something else? Not *someone* else, mind you, but an object? Is that even possible?"

Tonya snapped her fingers. "That's it. I know what we have to do. But . . . listen. We may need to make a bargain with the wight. If so, we need to keep whatever promise we make, so be very careful before we agree to something. When I make oaths, the gods pay attention and hold me to them. That's just the way my practice works. I'm a fam-trad witch—it's hereditary. We're pledged to a goddess who honors vows and oaths, and if I strike a deal and then break the bargain, she's going to be pissed."

"Then we think before we speak." I didn't want Tonya in trouble with her gods. That would be worse than me being in trouble with the Wing-Liege.

We pulled up in front of Tonya's house and hurried to the front door. But Tonya paused before she inserted the key in the lock.

"Listen, Degoba has a lot of power up his sleeve. If the wight can get hold of that—well, I don't know what all a spiritwalker can do. Degoba never has fully told me the extent of his abilities, but just . . . be careful."

"He was hopped up on Sleepy-Cold, though. That may make it harder for the wight, if he's taken control. Degoba took several doses and that's going to affect both his thoughts and his coordination." Ralph shrugged. "Who knows, the wight might be drunk for all we know."

Somehow, the thought of a drunken forest wight didn't comfort me any. Alcohol usually fueled belligerence. But then again, if Degoba was doped up enough, the wight might not be able to function either. Hoping for the best, I followed Tonya into the house as she unlocked the door.

It didn't take long to get our answer. Degoba was sitting on the sofa, and the expression on his face was one of confusion. There was a cunning look behind the bewilderment, but it was obvious that the cold remedy had affected him. He looked up as we entered the room, and tried to stagger to his feet.

"Stop." I pulled out my dagger. "Recognize this?"

He flinched—whether it was Degoba in control at that moment or the forest wight, I wasn't sure, but his hand went to his side automatically.

"Crap. We can't let him attack us. He'll hurt Degoba in trying. Probably pull his stitches if nothing else, and we don't want that wound bleeding again." I glanced over at Ralph. "Do you think you can hold him down?"

"I probably can, but you and Chai are stronger than me. I think you should be the one to do that, just in case . . ." He sighed. "My thing with blood."

"Got it." I was beginning to see why Alex didn't take Ralph out with us on more cases. The guy was a whiz with computers and hacking, but as much as I liked him, he could be a big liability in the field. I started to hand him the dagger but he flinched away and I quickly sheathed it. *Damn it, werewolves and silver.* There were so many things to remember.

Tonya held her short sword steady, aiming the tip at the spiritwalker. He was trying to stand up.

"Chai, you take the right side, I'll take the left." I moved forward, Chai mirroring my actions.

"You don't want us to hurt the body you're in." I didn't know if reasoning with it would do any good, but I might as well give it a try. "If we do, there's nowhere for you to jump. We're protected and you can't control us." I was hoping he wouldn't be able to influence Tonya—she was holding the sword—but so far, he hadn't seemed to touch her.

I glanced over at her and she winked. "I'm wearing my grandmother's pentacle. It protects me against spirit possession. I'm a really good medium and she gave it to me when I was a little girl so I would be safe."

Apparently it worked against wights as well as spirits. I turned back to Degoba. "Once we have him down, how the hell do we get him out of Degoba's body?"

"I have an idea. Just get hold of him." Tonya motioned to Ralph to join her. As he did, I edged toward the sofa, around the coffee table. Chai took the other side. There was nowhere for Degoba to go. He tried to step onto the sofa, heading toward the window behind it, but apparently he'd taken enough of the decongestant to make movement difficult, and he stumbled, dropping back on the cushions. Chai took that moment to pounce, gaining hold of his wrists. I grabbed the afghan that had been covering Degoba and swiftly wrapped it around him, forming a makeshift straitjacket.

"Now what? We've got him."

Chai was holding him firmly, and although Degoba was still freaky-strong, between the medicine and the blanket and the wound, it was obvious that he wasn't going anywhere at this point. Degoba hissed—or rather, the wight hissed. But he said nothing, just struggled and growled.

Ralph and Tonya approached. Ralph held up the pendant. He must have gotten it out from Tonya's pocket. She still held the sword, aimed at Degoba's heart.

"You can't keep possession of the spiritwalker," she said. "You know that, don't you? We can't let you go free."

The wight stared at her through Degoba's eyes. After a moment he opened his mouth and said, "I can kill him if I have to."

"You do that and you kill yourself. I have a bargain to make with you." She nodded toward the pendant. "You vacate his body and enter your pendant, and I give you my

vow as a witch, on the honor of Hecate, that I will not destroy you. We will leave you and the pendant unharmed."

I stared at her. *Not destroy him?* Wouldn't that mean the
other wights would still bow to his energy? But I said nothing, figuring she knew something I didn't. We had to get
him out of Degoba regardless of the cost.

A moment passed, then another. Finally, the wight let out
a long sigh. "You give your word on your life?"

She nodded. "I do. If I break my word and I destroy your
pendant, may my goddess strike me down." A rumble filled
the living room. I had a feeling that Hecate was listening
closely. Tonya really was tuned in to her lady.

Another moment, and a flash of light filled the room as
a shadow flew out of Degoba and into the pendant. Degoba
stopped struggling. The wight had fled his body.

Tonya immediately knocked everything off her coffee
table and set the pendant on it. She dropped to her knees
and, hands over the necklace, began to chant in a loud,
clear voice.

> *"Spirit hidden in this jewel, I seal you forever within,*
> *Let no one free you, nor any tool allow you to access*
>   *this realm.*
> *Dark forest spirit, rest at peace. All your violence now*
>   *shall cease,*
> *You are trapped, never to flee, By Hecate's will, so*
>   *mote it be."*

Another flash of light and the gem flared with a sickly
green light, then paled to a soft glow.

I stared at it. "He's in there?"

She nodded. "He is. He'll never get out unless someone
breaks the gem."

"What about his influence on the other wights?" So Ralph
had been thinking the same thing I had.

Tonya shook her head. "That ended when we killed his
body. His spirit still lives, but the magic through his presence on the physical realm was what was holding them.

We're ready to pick them off now. They won't be terribly difficult at this point."

"We should get the other one before heading over to Patrick's. We don't have a lot of time before dusk." I glanced at the clock, then back at the pendant. A thought crossed my mind. "Before I leave Port Townsend, I can take the pendant out into the deep water of the strait and dive to the bottom and bury it there. Chances are good no one will ever find it then."

Tonya smiled at me, gratefully. "Thank you. That means my part of the bargain is done. If it's out of my house then I won't chance ever destroying it."

Degoba was snoring loudly—apparently only the wight's possession had woken him out of the drug-induced haze. We tucked him back on the sofa, making certain the wound was still covered and not stressed, and then I picked up the pendant.

"I don't feel comfortable leaving this in your house. Shall we take it with us? Is it safe to?"

Tonya nodded. "If we leave it in the car, there should be nothing that will happen to it. Just don't leave the doors unlocked so that anybody steals it."

And so, at three thirty, after a quick snack, we trooped out again to find the other wight.

CHAPTER 19

Ralph had the map he'd created with the potential lair on it. Our destination was a place called Kai Tai Lagoon. At the word *lagoon* I perked up, but Tonya put the skids on that mood.

"We've been working for years to turn it into a wetlands estuary. There's been a lot of push-pull from property owners nearby, and the city government, but it looks like we're finally making way in the battle." She shrugged. "In summer, it looks like hell in there and a lot of the water dries up, but the area is great for birds. Think swampy marsh, more than crystal-clear lagoon. Right now, the mists will probably be rolling through the area."

We drove past Tonya's shop on Kearney Street, then took a right on East Sims Way.

"When we get to Twelfth, take a right. We can pull into the Haines Park and Ride and get to the lagoon through there." She reached between the seats to point toward the turnoff. "Right there."

Ralph turned into onto Twelfth Street and then, shortly after that, he swung a right into the Park and Ride. Tonya directed him toward the back and we pulled into one of the empty stalls closest to the trees that indicated the start of the lagoon. He put the Range Rover in park and turned off the ignition.

"We will have to go through the underbrush, but it's not far of a walk. There are other turnoffs, but this will be the fastest to the area where you think the wight is hiding."

Ralph had marked an area near an inn that overlooked the lagoon as having reported the most brawls and fistfights, and a couple disappearances. It was a little jaunt, but not too far.

"How will we know where to find the creature? If it can hide in tree trunks or other nooks and hollows, isn't it going to take us time to ferret it out?"

Tonya shook her head. "I thought about that, actually. I'm going to wear the pendant. The wight can't get out—he's scaled—but it may lure this one out."

I stared at her. "Aren't you taking a chance? If it gets hold of you, then there's a chance it can break the pendant and free the king. Or try to take it and become king itself. But that would be a pickle, wouldn't it? We'd have wight fighting wight."

"It's a chance worth taking. Otherwise, it's just going to take us too long to find him. We want to destroy both this one and Patrick's wight before the night's over. Once they realize their king is dead, they'll be vying for power. But we've got luck on our side this time. Since it's still daylight, this one will be weaker." She gingerly slid the pendant around her neck and stared at it like she thought it was going to jump up and bite her.

After a moment, when it did nothing but hang there, she shrugged. "I can tell he's in there, but he's sealed away and his energy feels very muffled."

"Okay then, let's go see if we can lure out wight number two." Ralph took up his place in the rear, as usual. Chai went first, with Tonya and me behind him.

As we headed into the scrubby undergrowth, vegetation crackled under my feet. The surrounding growth had died back for the winter, and even with the rains, some of the reeds and bushes were still thick enough to crunch rather than turn into a pile of mulch. The ground was soft and I could feel the shift of the water nearby. It wasn't ocean water, that I could tell.

Lake and pond water had a distinctly different energy than free-flowing currents. It tended to be more resistant to outside interference. Mama Ocean was huge; nobody could take her down. But lakes and ponds were a lot like forests in that they worried about human intrusion and what it might do to them. Rivers, to some degree, did, too, but they had their own flow and power and they tended to ignore the surrounding world on their nonstop race to find their way back to the ocean.

I inhaled deeply. The scent wasn't fetid—not at all—but definitely had that still, quiet marshland sense about it. This was a place of refuge; the birds were active and seemed unperturbed by our appearance. As I tuned in, I could tell that the area was in the process of *becoming*. It was transitioning from something that was unwanted and ignored into a bustling avian metropolis.

"I like it here." I glanced around. "I hate to think of the wight getting his hands involved because he'll ruin it. He'll taint it. Right now, people are clearing away years of debris and neglect from this marsh. And the marsh is responding— it's evolution in action. But the forest wight will bring a blight to the area. He'll make people afraid of it and they'll destroy the marsh rather than live in fear. He'll cause the very downfall he's angry about."

Chai moved forward as we came out of the undergrowth to the clearing overlooking the lake. The ground here was like any marsh—tenuous and mushy. The water was still and a low mist was starting to roll off it.

"How are we going to find him?" I glanced around. There could be so many hiding places. I doubted he could exist underwater, but the vast amount of reeds and the thicket of shrubs provided an excellent shroud. Any duck hunter could easily create a blind out here, so it stood to reason a forest wight would have an easier effort trundling in with a burrow.

Ralph stood back. "I'm shifting form. I can run through the brush easier in wolf form, and I can look for any signs of him."

I didn't like the idea of splitting up, but Ralph's idea made sense. "Go . . . but don't put yourself in danger. The minute you find anything, get your ass back to us."

He nodded and, without another word, smoothly transformed into his wolf shape. Within less than sixty seconds, he was off and running through the bushes. I turned to Chai and Tonya.

"Either of you have any ideas while we're waiting?" I glanced at the sky. "Not long till dusk. I'd rather not still be out here then."

Tonya held out her hands and slowly let out a deep breath. "Let me focus . . ." Another moment and she began to slowly turn in a semicircle, edging out, feeling her way through the rising mist that now rolled past our ankles. "Over there," she whispered, nodding—still with her eyes closed. She had indicated a path to the left, which led to a large patch of scrub trees and undergrowth. "There's a darkness . . . it's unnatural. Like a shadow that has too much substance."

"Sounds like wight energy to me." I was getting more familiar with these creatures than I ever wanted to be and welcomed the day I could cross them off the to-do list for my résumé.

"Should we wait for Ralph?" Chai glanced over his shoulder. The werewolf had headed off in the opposite direction.

I bit my lip. Being the one in charge wasn't all it was cracked up to be, not when there were other people I was responsible for. It was one thing to be on my own: nobody's slave or servant or employee. It was quite another to be in charge of an operation that could endanger others' lives.

"No . . . yes . . ." I fought with the desire to just rush ahead and kill the wight if we could find it. But Ralph was out there alone. Finally, I made a decision and stuck. "We'll wait for Ralph."

"I think that's best." Tonya clapped me on the shoulder. "He's a good guy. I wouldn't want to see him in trouble."

But we didn't have to wait long. Within five minutes, Ralph was back, shifting seamlessly back into his human form. He shook his head. "I couldn't find anything."

"We think we know where the wight is." I nodded in the direction Tonya had pointed. "Tonya felt something over there. We were just waiting for you."

"The path is wide enough to go four abreast. Do we want to do that?" Chai frowned. "I'm thinking two by two is better, to be honest."

"Ralph, you and Tonya in back. Chai and I will go up front. Keep an eye out for anything out of the ordinary and don't hesitate to say anything. This isn't the time to worry about playing . . . who is it? The Boy Who Cried Lion?"

That made both Ralph and Tonya laugh.

Ralph sputtered a little. "The Boy Who Cried *Wolf*, the story is. And no, you're right. Better to be overly cautious than not careful enough."

As the afternoon light dimmed and the wind picked up, we headed forward. I had my dagger out, and Tonya, behind me, had readied her short sword. Ralph was prepared to shift form if anybody so much as got a scratch on them. And Chai—well, Chai was big enough that he really didn't need a weapon, not for a wight. But I hoped he wouldn't have to tackle this one. If we could just get in and out without a big fight, I'd count it a major coup.

As we approached a large thicket to the left of the marsh, Tonya let out a gasp. "He's in there. I can feel him—the energy reeks just like it did with the other forest wight."

With my breath caught in my throat, I very slowly turned toward the thicket. How far in would he be? It couldn't be very deep or we'd end up on the other side of the road. My heart thudding in my chest, I swallowed and looked up at Chai. He nodded and we headed into the brush.

The scrub here was windswept—all the foliage along the edges of the peninsula seemed bent and gnarled, and with good reason. The winds came blustering in off the ocean and the strait, and their stiff, steady breezes bowed the trees back. The tangle of knee-high yellow grass crackled against my jeans as I pushed through, and all the while my pulse was keeping a staccato beat. I swept my gaze this way and that, trying to pinpoint where we should turn.

Another few feet and Tonya's voice whispered, "Over there." She pointed past me to the right of where Chai was standing.

I shaded my eyes in the diminishing light of the late

afternoon. Sure enough, there was a dark hole leading into the brush—as if something had tunneled its way in through the foliage. There was a dank feel to it, and my stomach thudded as I stared at the circular tunnel.

"It's barely tall enough for Ralph in his wolf form. What do we do? I'm open to suggestions." I didn't want to go in there bent over, my face forward to whatever might be coming down the tunnel at us.

"I could burn it off but that wouldn't be a good thing for the rest of the marsh." Chai frowned. "I can go inside and find out. If I shift into smoke form, I can filter in and find out what we're facing. But if the thing sees me, it has a chance of trying to capture me."

I knew there was a reason Chai seldom shifted into the smoky form all djinns could, but until now, I'd never known why. That solved one mystery.

"Don't do that. I don't want that creature even having the remotest chance of trapping you. What else have we got? I suppose we could just take your short sword, Tonya, and start hacking away at the brush." I raised my hand to stop Ralph even before he could speak, because I knew what he was going to say. "And you aren't going through there in wolf form either."

"Then we all head in, I suppose. We hack and slash our way through." Tonya shrugged. "It might alert the wight, but one way or another it's going to find out we're here."

"Then we go full steam." Chai stood back and held out his hand. "I don't often have call to use this but . . ." As we watched, the air around his hand shimmered and a big-assed scimitar appeared. It was far bigger than Tonya's short sword, and the edge glinted, wicked sharp. "If you three will stand out of the way . . ."

We immediately backed away. Nobody wanted to be within striking range. Chai began to sweep the blade from side to side. The scimitar sliced through the vegetation, sending sparks into the air as it did. But nothing caught fire. The faint scent of the burning foliage only made me think of how much I'd rather be inside around the fireplace than here.

A couple of moments and Chai was five feet into the

tunnel. And one more moment and a rumbling sounded from back in a big mound of detritus. Then, the sound of a slow freight train, and Chai jumped out of the way as a bent and gnarled figure darted out through what was still left of the passage. The forest wight looked similar to the first, but he was shorter, and more hunched over, and his movements were erratic. I realized that he was focused on Tonya and remembered—she had the pendant!

"Don't let him near Tonya!" I pushed her behind me as he darted toward her. "Get back!"

"Give me—give it to me." The low voice hissed like leaves crackling on the wind and, with narrowed eyes, he kept his focus on Tonya as he rushed forward toward us. As he swept past, Chai whirled around and raised his scimitar. Horrified, I watched as he brought it down, whistling through the air, to catch hold of the single-minded creature and cleave deeply into his back.

The blade bit deep, splitting the wight's shoulders, and as he screeched, falling forward in front of us, the ooze that flowed from his body stank of decay and mold and mushrooms. The wight writhed for another moment, but Chai pried his blade free and struck again, beheading him. Smoke poured from his mouth as it had with the king, but this time, it dissipated as it hit the air, drifting harmlessly off like soot.

I glanced over to see that Ralph had fainted dead away. Tonya was trying to wake him up.

"Two down, one to go." Chai looked down at the creature with disgust.

I stared at the djinn. He hadn't been lucky—that had been all skill. In all the time I'd known him, I never knew he was so good with a weapon. He caught my gaze and held it, his lips set in a thin, grim line.

"You didn't mention that you're skilled with a blade." It was a statement, not a question.

He shrugged. "You never asked." And then, perhaps because I continued to stare at him, he added, "At one time, I was an executioner. Leave it at that for now, please." And with that, Chai turned and headed back the way we'd come.

Ralph sat up, moaning. Tonya flashed me a questioning look, but I just shook my head. Now wasn't the time or place to explore this. I could recognize Chai's moods by now, and he wasn't in the mood to talk. I'd have to walk the line cautiously and accept what he was ready to tell me.

"Let's get back to your house. It will be dusk soon, and we have to plan out our attack on the wight at Patrick's house." I glanced down at the body. It was already fading into the foliage—blending in with the sticks and dried grass and scrub brush, almost invisible. Within the hour, my guess was that if anybody came upon the body, they'd just think it was the remains of a small fallen tree trunk.

Ralph scrambled to his feet, still looking a little woozy. "I'm fine," was all he said when I started to ask him.

Turning, I took the lead and we trudged back to the Range Rover, where Chai was leaning against the hood, staring off into the distance. As I passed by him on my way to the front passenger seat, I reached out and slid my fingers along his arm. He patted my hand and smiled, but as we all buckled up, he was very quiet.

W**e made it** back to Tonya's without any problem, though we stopped at Jo's Chicken—a local eatery. As we pulled into the parking lot, I glanced at the clock. Nearly five thirty. Alex and Patrick would be awake by the time we got back to Tonya's house.

"Jo makes the best chicken around. She's a genius in the kitchen and one of the nicest people I know. You guys wait here while Shimmer and I go in—the place is small, it's always packed, and there isn't a lot of room to stand around."

Tonya led me into the restaurant and boy, was she right about the patronage. The counter was a spotless Formica blue, lined with bar stools. Every stool was filled with someone eating. There were three tables for eat-in, all occupied as well, and one long bench for people waiting for takeout. She motioned for me to take a seat while she went up to the counter to place the order.

I found myself next to a tall, gangly man with long hair draping around his shoulders. He was wearing a turtleneck and jeans, and he looked wiry but tough. He flashed me a smile and leaned over so I could hear him over the din rising from the number of people who were crammed into the joint.

"You had Jo's chicken before?"

I shook my head. "I'm not from around here. This will be my first time."

The man laughed and his voice sounded easy. "You're in for a treat. I'm Marty. So where are you from . . . ?" He held out his hand.

I accepted the handshake and answered the implied question. "Shimmer. My name is Shimmer. I live in Seattle. Just up here for a few days to help out a friend."

The side of his lip tipped up with a gentle quirk, and it made me smile back. His eyes were dark brown, and he smelled like cinnamon. He paused, and I knew he was looking me over, but the way in which he was doing so didn't feel invasive.

"You wouldn't have the time to maybe visit a few of the local attractions with me, would you?"

I shook my head. "I wish I did, but no. I'm actually on a job and there isn't much downtime." And then, without thinking, I pulled out my wallet from my purse and handed him my business card. "If you're ever down in Seattle, Marty . . . give me a call." At that point, I remembered Alex and wanted to hit myself upside the head, but then again . . . it never hurt to make contacts, did it?

He glanced at it. "You work for a PI? That's cool. I'm sure I'll be down there at some point." And then, before he could say anything else, the server called out a number. "That's me. Nice meeting you, Shimmer. Maybe we'll run into each other again." As Marty headed toward the counter, he pocketed my card.

"You just reel them in, don't you?" Tonya's laugh startled me and I realized she'd been sitting next to me for . . . I didn't know how long.

I let out a snort. "I don't try."

"You don't have to. You really are striking—your eyes are so blue they practically vibrate. And your hair . . . the blue and purple streaks look totally natural."

"That's because they are." I grinned at her. "Before I came down from the Dragon Reaches, my hair reached my knees. The Wing-Liege cut it as punishment." I sobered. That was a huge insult in the Dragon Reaches—having your hair cut off.

"Why?" Tonya sniffed as one of the cooks pulled a fresh batch of chicken out of the fryer and spread it out on a pan.

I glanced around but once Marty had left, nobody else was paying much attention to me. Everybody was busy texting on their phones or reading off their tablets. I saw one woman holding an actual book—it was a paranormal romance with a leather-clad woman on the front page.

With a soft sigh, I turned back to Tonya. "Watch my hair closely."

She looked confused but did as I asked. I closed my eyes and thought, *Untangle* . . . and my hair began to loosen itself. I could feel the leather of my jacket through it, I could feel the air pulsing by. I willed a strand to reach out and lightly touch Tonya's face, and I could feel her skin under the strands. Her eyes grew wide, but she giggled, sounding more delighted than scared.

"Our hair is part of our body. When I'm in dragon form it becomes my mane. We can feel through it. I could feel your face. It's very resilient and not easy to cut. And it grows very, very slowly. So having your hair cut? It hurts. It's painful, and while I didn't lose any sensation, if you see a dragon with shorter hair they've been either maimed or punished. It's an obvious stigma." I stared at the ground, feeling the shame rise up again. That had been a horrible day . . .

"**S**himmer, come here. Stand before me." The Wing-Liege motioned me to cross to the bench and stand on the spot reserved for criminals. He was in human form, as was I and the rest of the Council. His face was deadpan and

I waited, silent and brooding. Today, he would sentence me, and I'd find out if he meant what he said or if he had changed his mind and was going to hand me over to Greanfyr.

I took my place, hands behind my back and legs spread in the *obedience* pose we had learned at the Lost and Foundling.

"Shimmer, outcaste and dragon of no clan, you who stand before me in the Great Hall of Justice, I charge you with breaking and entering, theft, and disrespect for your betters. I charge you with defiling a class above you with your unrequested presence. I charge you with breaking the laws of this land. How do you plead?" His voice was even, calm, and collected. He stood there, his long silver hair perfectly still as he spoke, showing no sign of emotion.

I shivered. The coolness was more frightening than Greanfyr's wrath, and for that moment, I truly believed he was going to renege on his promise and have me executed, and there wasn't a damned thing I could do to stop it.

Shivering, I whispered, "Guilty, Your Lordship."

Lord Vine caught my gaze and—against custom and law—I held it rather than lowering my eyes. Regardless of what happened, I wanted him to know that I was watching him, that I—Shimmer—was standing on this pedestal, waiting his judgment.

"I sentence you to five years' exile from the Dragon Reaches. You will be sent Earthside in accordance with my sentence, and there you will spend these five years. You will not return to the Dragon Reaches until I summon you, and you will be stripped of the strongest of your powers. I also sentence you to Savarthi's Shame."

Savarthi's Shame . . . No dragon ever cut their hair—it grew ever so slowly, and it was as much a part of our body as any appendage. We could feel through it, sense through it, use it as we might another arm. Savarthi had been a dragon who had brought great shame on his family, and in the past—long past—he had threatened the Empress's life when she was young. Before his torture and execution, he was made to stand in the middle of the Great Hall, and his hair was cut, strand by strand, till it barely covered his head. Then, in an agonizing finish, his head was shaved. His screams were said to have echoed so long and loud that they became permanently embedded in the hall's very stones.

My heart skipped a beat. How short would they cut it? *Please, please don't cut it very short*, I pleaded in my heart. *Please . . . don't make me wear my shame daily.*

The Wing-Liege himself stepped forward, knife in hand. He crossed to me, and I struggled to stay standing. The weeks in jail had weakened me, the weeks away from water had drained me of strength. And now . . . this . . .

As he came near, he whispered in a low voice, "Do not faint. Do not show them your fear or your shame. Stand tall, girl. Stand tall."

I forced my shoulders back and waited as he lifted the first tendril of my hair. Trying not to flinch, I forced myself to keep my chin level. My lip trembled as he brought the knife up, but when it hit the hair—when the searing pain drove itself through my nerves—I stayed standing, letting the burning cut run through me like water. I closed my eyes but he yanked on my hair and I opened them again.

Again, he severed the strands, and again the pain ricocheted from nerve to nerve. And again, and again . . . and so he went, until my hair was up to my midback—a good two feet shorter than it had been. The strands were on the floor, curling and writhing, like an earthworm cut in two. They would be burned, while the remaining hair on my head would heal and once again begin to grow. But the shame of the cut, and the pain that had roared to life through my body, would never heal, and would never fade. That, I knew in my core.

Before she could say anything, the server called our number. We picked up our order and left the restaurant. Once we were out in the evening air, Tonya hesitated.

"I love your hair. But I don't want to bring up bad memories, so I won't mention it again."

I shrugged. "I have to deal with the memories at some point. But yes . . . our hair . . . it's a hard translation but . . .

it's just a part of ourselves that we rely on. We can use it as a weapon, or as rope . . ."

She snorted. "That would come in handy in bed." And then, as if realizing what she'd just blurted out, she colored up, blushing.

I laughed, though. "Oh, it does. Trust me. Depending on who your partner is and how they react to such play."

As we got back into the car, Ralph and Chai looked up. Ralph had been showing Chai how to play some game on his iPad. "You're back and that smells wonderful." Ralph handed Chai the tablet. "You can play while we're headed back to Tonya's house. Just don't break it."

The djinn let out a grumble, but he looked in better spirits than he had been after we had killed the wight.

Alex and Patrick were sitting with Degoba as we trooped through the door. Tonya and Ralph began setting out dinner while Chai and I filled them in on everything that had happened while they'd been asleep. Degoba still looked dazed, but he was awake enough to listen.

"You mean it got me again? I barely remember anything."

"If you hadn't drugged yourself up on Sleepy-Cold, we would have been in a lot of trouble and so would you, because I don't think the thing would have given a rat's ass about your wounds." I turned to Patrick. "The good news is that, given the death of the king wight and the other one, we can dispatch the one in your house and be done with it. It's weakened now, so I suggest we get a move on tonight and finish this job."

Alex frowned. "I don't like that you and Ralph put yourself at risk like this. I wish you'd waited for me."

"If we had waited, the king would have been stronger. And trust me, he was strong enough as it was." I didn't like arguing with my boss, but there were times it was going to happen and this was one of them.

He gave me a grumpy smile. "I guess I'm not going to be able to control you all the time. You've got a mind of your own, Shimmer, and never let it be said that Alex

Radcliffe doesn't like women with strong wills. We'll shelve this part of the discussion for when we return to Seattle. So, we go wight hunting tonight."

The thought of hunting down yet another wight made me queasy. I was tired of them and wanted to be done with it. "Yeah. After that, Tonya should be able to free the spirits bound in the house."

The doorbell rang as Tonya and Ralph finished putting the platter of chicken on the table, along with sides of mashed potatoes and gravy, and a green salad. Tonya went to answer it and when she returned, Toby Buckland was following her. He was smiling, holding something in a small bag.

"I wanted to thank you for what you've done. I'm going to call her Lacy, since that's who we think she was. I'm not sure of the whole story, though the cops told me you might have information that can help me sort it out, but the fact that you found a long-lost relative who had been . . ." He paused, emotion filling his voice. It was obvious that family meant everything to Toby.

I reached out and patted his shoulder. "We understand."

He smiled. "Thank you. I'm going to bury her remains in the morning before sunrise. I'd like it if you could attend." He handed Tonya a slip of paper with an address written on it. "I also brought you something." He held up the bag.

"What is it?" I was leery of bags and pouches and trunks by now.

"This belonged to my aunt, Anna Lee. The one who cursed your house, Patrick. It's a hex-breaker. She had several of them sitting around and I kept them. All you have to do is take it home and smash it inside the basement, and it will break her curse. Anna sold these to people she'd put curses on. It was her way of making a little extra cash from people she was mad at. Not exactly ethical, but then again, look at the family I'm from."

Patrick took the offered sack and opened it up. Inside was what looked like a large egg made from papier-mâché. As we stared at the colorfully painted oval, it vibrated lightly in his hand. He gently returned it to the sack and set it out of the way where it wouldn't be accidentally broken.

"Thank you, Toby. I truly am sorry about what Nathan did to your family. He wasn't my kin, but . . . it was wrong. He wasn't the type of man I would have befriended if I'd realized just how ruthless he was." Patrick offered his hand to Toby, who stared at it for a moment, then slowly reached out to take it.

"I appreciate that. His deeds aren't your deeds and there is no reason you should suffer from what he did." He paused, staring at Patrick's fingers against his own. "I've never touched a vampire before. You're very cold."

Patrick let out a snort, then laughed. "Yes, lad, I am very cold. We aren't all out for world domination or supremacy, you know. Some of us just want to open a simple bed-and-breakfast and make our way in a town we love."

Toby gave him a firm nod and then turned toward the door. "I have to go now. Please, if you can, come to Lacy's interment. I'd be honored if you were there. And if you have anything that can help me make heads or tails out of this . . ."

"We'll bring everything we found with us. I don't think you're going to like it, though—it shows some of your relatives in a very bad light." I let out a short sigh. "We think Lacy's parents killed her."

Toby pressed his lips together, hanging his head. Then, with a sad note in his voice, he said, "It wouldn't be the first time something like that happened in our family. Again, thank you and good night." As he shut the door behind him, Tonya let out a little sigh.

"Troubles follow families like that. There are some families destined to live in sorrow."

But Alex just shook his head. "No, love. Troubles follow *all* families. You can't show me one family that doesn't have its fair share of skeletons hanging in the closet. It's human nature, it is. The state of being who we are. Now, the four of you eat and then we'll head over and do our best to clear out Patrick's house. I'm ready to put a 'case closed' stamp on this file."

As we gathered around the table, I couldn't help but agree with him.

CHAPTER 20

The chicken was as good as Tonya had said it was. By the time we finished dinner, I really didn't feel like tromping out into the weather, but tromp we did. Tonya insisted the wight had to have built some access in the basement of Patrick's house, and so we decided to look there before we checked anywhere else. We left Degoba back at her house—his wound was still too dangerous for him to go adventuring. We decided to deal with the curse after we cleared out the wight.

The house was dark as we approached—no ghost lights anywhere. I wondered just how weak the wight would be without his king and hive mate, but it was foolish to underestimate him at this point. Hell, by this time, I wasn't underestimating the wayward moth that flew by.

Patrick's face crumpled as we neared the house. The smell of smoke and soot was still thick in the air, and there had been damage to enough of the sidewall that the rain was getting in. All the money and time he'd put into this place and he was going to have to redo a fair share of it and get city clearance before he could even think of opening.

We headed up the stairs and he slowly unlocked the door,

easing it open. The electricity was still working for part of the place—the circuit breakers had been turned off for the living room, office, and kitchen, but the upstairs was on a different circuit, as were the basement and the foyer. The downstairs hall bath had escaped damage, too.

But as we moved into the living room, avoiding the caution tape, he let out a little groan. What hadn't burned to cinders was heavily smoke damaged, including a good share of his books. Alex turned on a high-beam flashlight and between it and the glow from the hall lights, we could see just how bad the place looked.

The outer wall was charred black, with large gaping holes that allowed access for the rain and wind. The ceiling was burned, charcoaled timbers showing through in some places. In the unscathed areas, the smoke had turned the paint a dull gray. Most of the furniture was gone, piles of charcoal and melted plastic, and over near where we'd sat around the coffee table, the sofas were saturated with water. A fine layer of oily soot covered everything. The smell of smoke was thick, mingling with the smell of the rain, and mildew had already began to creep over the waterlogged upholstery.

"How can I begin to rebuild?" Patrick's voice was soft, mournful. He turned and led us into the kitchen, where we found the same state of shambles. The cupboards were smoke damaged, some charred by the flames. Food had spilled everywhere, and the appliances looked beat up and bruised. As I stared at the stove, I knew it would never see use again. Perhaps he might be able to save the fridge, but there were dents along the stainless steel doors where the firemen had trundled through, trying to put out the flames.

"You have the insurance money. You can repair this." Tonya's enthusiasm was forced, but at least she was trying.

I cleared my throat. "She's right. You're not going to let this wight get the better of you. We'll clear him out, break the curse, and then you'll be free to make this into the place you wanted it to be."

"Thanks for trying, girls. I don't know if I have it in me . . ." Patrick sounded so defeated I wanted to shake him by the shoulders, but I also realized that the odds had not been on his side, and it was natural to feel overwhelmed. He might be a vampire, but he was also human.

"I'll come over and help, and I'll bring some of my friends. We'll form a work party and clean up. Now, let's get the wight before it has a chance to do anything else to your home." Tonya seemed determined to keep up his spirits. I would miss her when we went home.

We made our way over to the basement door and Chai moved to the front, opening it. He turned to Ralph. "Little wolf man, you should change form. We can use you in back for a lookout, but we can't take a chance on you fainting on us."

"Got it." Ralph stood back, setting his pack on the floor, and within seconds was in his wolf shape. He wrinkled his nose and let out a whimper.

"Yeah, the smell would be worse in animal form," I said. "Okay, let's do this." With Chai leading the way, we headed down the stairs.

The basement hadn't received much damage, mostly from smoke and where Ralph and I had ripped off the doors, so that was one bonus. The wight wouldn't want to destroy his own home, but then again, I was beginning to think these creatures weren't all that bright.

As we cautiously descended the steps, Chai kept a close eye up front, and Ralph watched from up above. He waited at the top to make sure nothing came along and tried to lock us in.

A dim layer of smoke and soot covered the walls with a gray film, muting the light. Everything was coated.

"Where is he, then?" Patrick looked around.

"I can try to draw him out," Tonya said. "But I have the feeling his lair is against that back wall, behind an illusion." She stepped forward and withdrew the pendant from beneath her shirt. As she laid it against her chest the stone flashed and there was the sound of a shuffle from where she had pointed to. Another moment and the lights flickered out, plunging us into darkness.

I leaped forward and grabbed Tonya, hissing in her ear to keep still. "It's after you."

There was another flare as Alex's flashlight came on and tried to follow the scuffling sounds that darted around us. A pale gleam in one corner alerted me—the color of eye shine.

"I think it's over there—look!" But the shimmer of eyes vanished again as I shouted, and we heard the muffled sound of something opening and closing. From up above, there was a noise and the lights came on again. We turned to see Ralph, back in his human form, with his finger on the light switch at the top of the stairs. He backed away again, turning back into wolf form as we watched.

"Thanks, Ralph!" Alex called up the stairs. "Where the hell is it? Did the rest of you hear the sound of a door?"

"I did." I let go of Tonya, who slid the pendant back under her shirt.

"Thanks, Shimmer. Hell, I didn't think he'd be able to turn off the lights from down here." She adjusted her shirt and tucked it into her jeans. "What do we do now?"

"We find that panel. We tear apart the walls if we have to." I looked over at Patrick, who gave me a grim nod. "It's against the back wall, I'm certain." I led the way, with Chai and Alex on my heels. Patrick hung back, watching as we began thumping along the wall, listening for any hollow sounds that might indicate an entry behind it.

"The wight at the battery—the king—had quite the access panel into his lair. They're good at illusion, and good at creating seamless hatches." Chai grunted as he thunked his fist against one area of the wall. He paused. "I think . . . come listen."

Alex and Patrick had superior hearing—most vampires did—so they obliged him, pressing their ears against the wall. Chai gave it another good smack, and even I could hear the reverberation from behind the drywall and paint. But how had the wight managed to make it appear so smooth?

"Here it is." The djinn ran his hand over the edges, and a moment later the outline of a door appeared. "It was an illusion, and I can break some illusions. He has weakened, that much I can tell you, and it's probably because his king and hive mate are out of the picture. He has only his own magic to rely on now."

"How do we open this?" Alex prodded at the door.

"Look for an indentation. It will be faint, but there should be a hidden lever inside that releases the door." Chai took one side, Alex the other. Sure enough, a moment later Alex let out an "Aha!" and the door sprang open, revealing a tunnel dug into the dirt below the side yard. As far below ground as we were in the basement, nobody crossing the yard would ever guess there was a tunnel beneath it.

"Bingo." Alex frowned, staring at it. "Crap. I was hoping it would be simple, like a hole in the wall so we could just crawl in there, take care of him, and crawl out. I hate tunnels."

Given the fact that whoever went first was going to take the brunt of the attack, I agreed.

The problem with sending Chai first would be that any fire might blow back into the basement and cause even more damage to Patrick's house. If we set off any sort of explosion, the yard could cave in or, given our proximity in town, we could damage a gas main or water main.

"We can't use fire. We can't use anything that might damage the infrastructure around the house or the foundations." I worried my lip, staring at the tunnel, feeling like I should volunteer. But Alex jumped in ahead of me.

"I'll go first. Shimmer, you have my back. Chai, you next. Ralph, stay out here with Tonya. Patrick—you bring up the rear and carry the flashlight, would you?"

A thought hit me and I turned to Tonya. "Give me the pendant. I can play the same game you did with the other wight."

She lifted it from around her neck and handed it to me. "Here you go. Wear it in health and don't let him get hold of it."

As I slid the necklace over my head, I could feel the *thrum* from inside, but it was muffled, and the wight couldn't reach out to me. Satisfied that it wasn't going to turn me into a raving maniac, I withdrew my dagger. I was getting more comfortable having it in my hand than out of it.

Alex stepped up into the tunnel and began to creep through it. We all had to hunch over, though Alex didn't bother; he crouch-walked his way through. The tunnel was dank, like sour dirt, and circular. This passage was longer than the one the wight had created at the battery, but it still didn't extend that far. I figured we were well within the confines of Patrick's yard when, once again, the tunnel opened into a larger chamber. But here we found the remains of hundreds of rats and other small creatures.

Something about this wight was different.

I stared at the decaying and skeletal carcasses, trying to decipher why they were there. Wights fed on energy and fear and . . . a low growl startled me. Alex swung around, pushing me out of the way, and I went sprawling as something with four legs landed right where I'd been standing. I rolled to a crouching position as Alex moved in on it, Juanita gleaming in his hand. Patrick was holding the light steady on the creature, and Chai was aiming for it.

"*Wolfen*," Alex said, as he moved in. "Be careful, they aren't like regular Weres. They can infect you with a bite and can turn you."

I'd heard tales of the wolfen—werewolves born with severe defects. They were a vicious lot by nature, always taking the form of a misshapen wolf, and they were born with an ability other Weres didn't have—they could turn their victims. Not into Weres, but into wolfen like themselves.

"Stand back, Shimmer." Alex motioned me away and I stepped back. I was the only one the wolfen could infect. Vampires were immune to any contagion, and djinns . . . well, I'd hate to see the creature try to bite Chai and live. As Chai and Alex circled the monster—it was over five feet high at the shoulders—I backed up against the opposite wall.

At that moment, a hand landed on my shoulder, reaching for my throat. The forest wight! The damned things seemed to have an obsession with my neck.

I swung around before he could get his fingers on the pendant and stabbed his hand with my dagger. I managed to impale him with the tip, right between the knuckles, and he let out a roar.

Chai left Alex to deal with the wolfen as he raced to my

side. By now, the wight had moved out of the shadows as he attempted to grapple me. I kicked him in what would be his nuts, but it didn't seem to faze him. Maybe wights didn't have balls. Or a penis, I thought as he moved out of the shadows.

Idiot, quit looking for his junk and fight. My thoughts were a mad scramble as I yanked my dagger from his hand and tried to hit him again. I missed, and he managed to wrap his fingers around my wrist. He was dragging me toward him as Chai landed by my side, and the djinn backhanded him a good one. Unfortunately, the wight had a firm grasp on my wrist and I went flying with him. We landed in a tangle on the floor. Startled, the wight let go of me as we hit the ground, and I rolled out of his reach as Chai came barreling across the room at him again.

Alex was grappling the wolfen by then, and they were on the floor as Patrick still held the flashlight, a look of confusion on his face. I could tell that—vampire or not—he wasn't used to fights or rumbles or any sort of violent behavior. I scrambled up and raced over to him, grabbing the flashlight.

"Go help Alex—bite the damned thing and start sucking his blood or something." I shoved him toward the pair as they rolled along the floor. Patrick gave me one slightly frightened look and then dove into the fray. He landed atop the wolfen and dragged it back from Alex, who managed to right himself into a squatting position. Patrick was trying to keep hold of the creature as Alex dove for the monster's throat and latched on. A horrible sucking sound filled the chamber, and the wolfen whimpered and let out a low howl as Patrick fastened his fangs into the back of his neck. Together, he and Alex were draining the wolfen, and it didn't look or sound like they were making it pleasant.

I cringed as the three of them writhed on the floor, the wolfen sandwiched between the two vampires. There was a bestial, feral nature to the triad, almost sensual. Part of me wanted to watch—fascinated the way I might be when a spider was sucking her prey—but then my stomach lurched and I turned away. I was a predator—a dragon. But when we snatched up our food, we usually did so cleanly, with a quick kill. Vampires took delight in the sensation. Dragons were in it for the food.

Shuddering, I hurried over to Chai, who was in a full-scale tumble and roll with the wight. I dropped the flashlight so it was pointing toward the pair and dove in again, this time managing to grab hold of the wight's back as he scrabbled against Chai. I didn't have fangs, or big meaty hands, but I had my strength and I had a very pointy dagger that glinted with silver.

I struggled, managing to get my arm around the throat of the wight, who was now kicking and gurgling, and brought the dagger down into his back. He tried to roar and I tightened my lock around his neck. Pushing the blade in deeper, I buried the dagger up to the hilt in the wight's shoulder, and at that point Chai grabbed hold of the wight's head and, motioning for me to let go, snapped the creature's neck. With an audible pop, the wight went limp and the fire in his eyes died out. Chai let go and the wight fell to the floor, dead.

I pulled out my dagger and stood back, panting, as the creature's form began to fall into dissolution. The wight was dead—they were all three dead and gone. I thought I heard a sigh from the locket, but it had to be my imagination.

Just then, the wolfen gave one low muffled cry and as I turned, it, too, slumped into Alex's arms. He gently laid it down on the floor and then he and Patrick stood. Blood trickled down the sides of their mouths, and Alex pulled out a handkerchief from his pocket and wiped the droplets of red from his chin.

We stared at the bodies, and then Chai wordlessly went over to dig through the debris pile that mirrored the one in the marsh and held up a chest. More treasure. Or maybe, more trouble. It would be hard to know until we'd opened both of them. The body of the wight had already begun to decay, and the body of the wolfen was cooling rapidly. Dragging it behind us—the last thing Patrick wanted was a decaying corpse left behind—we headed back through the tunnel and into the basement.

Tonya and Ralph stared at the wolfen's corpse as we jumped out of the hole, pulling the body out behind us.

"A wolfen . . . I never saw one before." Ralph's voice was hushed as he stared at the body. "They're dangerous, and no Were community—especially werewolves—allows them to stay. Anybody born a wolfen is driven out shortly after birth. In fact, though it's not well known, we're usually instructed to put the newborns out for the animals to devour. Most parents who end up having one just hide them in the woods, though, and hope for the best."

The concept made me sad. "You don't stop loving something just because it's different." But then again, given their volatile nature, I could understand the need to isolate them from the general society.

"Right. I just hope there aren't any more near here, and I wonder how the hell the wight came by one anyway." Patrick cleared his throat as he looked around the chamber.

Alex shrugged. "A lot of strange beasts live in the forests out here."

"So what now?" Patrick glanced around. "Other than I start interviewing new contractors?"

"Well, the wights are dead so that problem is off our plates. I guess . . . we clear the curse next, using Toby's gift, then release your ghosts—Tonya, you'll have to be in charge of that. And then . . . I think we're done." I turned to Tonya. "That sound about right?"

She nodded. "I'd add that, after we clear out the ghosts, Patrick, let me cleanse and ward the entire lot and house. And fill in that tunnel before anything else finds it and decides to make good use of it. Right?"

Alex concurred. "She's right. You do not want something new setting up shop down here. And when you get your new contractor, dude—you need to have him create an out on the basement doors here. If Shimmer and Ralph hadn't managed to bludgeon their way through, we would have been toast."

"Good idea in theory, bad in practice. Yeah, that's on my list. Okay, so did we bring the egg thing that Toby gave us?"

Tonya nodded. "It's out in the car. Ralph, would you come with me while I get it? You guys had better let me handle this one. Magic is my department."

As they headed out to the car, the rest of us dropped into the sofas. They might be covered with soot, but they were still usable and they were comfortable. I didn't even want to think about the layer of silt covering the butt of my jeans. Soot could be washed off, and if not—they were only so much denim.

Tonya brought back the colorful egg, holding it gently. "Toby said all we have to do is put it here in the basement and then have Patrick break it—that should dispel the curse." She set it down on the coffee table and stood back. "I think you should use your fists to break it—skin contact might make a difference."

Patrick hesitantly moved toward the papier-mâché egg, staring at the brightly painted oval. It looked almost like stained glass, the colors were so bright, but when you looked closer, it was easy to see the imperfections that didn't mar glass. He glanced over at Tonya. "Should I say anything?"

"Toby didn't say you should, but I guess if you want to, you can say something like 'end this curse' or some such other statement." She frowned. "I don't think it's going to hurt anything if you do say something."

Patrick nodded. With his fingers interlocked, he formed a double fist and held it over the egg. "I ask Anna Lee to remove the curse she placed on this house and to free it—and me—from the . . . curse."

His words drifting off, he brought his fists down hard, smashing through the egg. A cloud of powder that it had been holding spread into the air, as if the egg were a bag of flour that had suddenly broken. A shimmer and a sudden *swish* of energy darted through the room, as visible as ball lightning. It built up static as it bounced from wall to wall, growing larger as we watched.

Unnerved, Ralph began to back away from it, but Tonya clapped him on the shoulder and he stopped. The ball of energy grew brighter and brighter and then—with a loud clap like thunder—it burst, filling the room with a pale warm light that rolled up the staircase. The timbers of the house let out a muffled "Ah" as if releasing a breath held for a long, long time. The entire house felt like it relaxed around us. A moment later the light dissipated, but the feeling of ease remained.

Patrick glanced around, staring at the walls as if he were expecting something else to happen. Another moment and he looked over at Tonya. "Is that it? Is everything okay?"

"Well, we still have to release the ghosts . . . but now I think they'll go easy. Come on, let's head upstairs for that." She led the way and we followed, with Alex carrying the wolfen's corpse. "What are we going to do with the body?"

I shrugged. "There's a hole out front where Lacy was buried, still."

Patrick quickly nixed that idea. "Oh no, I don't want anything to do with this thing. I want it off my property."

"We can deal with it later. Let's take care of your ghosts now. I'd like to see these poor souls freed." Tonya had also retrieved her bag and now, in the burned-out shell of the living room, she motioned to the remains of one of the end tables that hadn't fully been incinerated by the flames. "Can one of you lift that over here for me?"

Alex was still holding the wolfen's corpse, so Patrick quickly retrieved it for her. As soon as he set it down, she pulled out her sage smudge stick, a fan, a wand, a bell, and something that looked like incense powder. She handed me the bell, and she handed Chai the smudge stick and fan. She started to hand him the lighter, but he laughed and waved it away.

"I don't need a lighter, thank you. I'm pretty good with creating fire on my own." He held up one finger and a flame appeared on the tip.

"Right. I keep forgetting. Ralph, would you carry the powder for me? Have it ready to throw when I tell you and then just toss pinches of it into the air." She showed him how much she meant. He nodded.

"Okay, then, let's head outside first. I think the soldiers and the ghosts of that family are stuck in parts of the yard. Shimmer, if you'd keep ringing the bell as we go, and

Chai—light the smudge stick, please, and keep it lit, waving it around as we walk through the yard."

She led the way, with Patrick opening the door. We followed her as she sought for the ghosts. I watched her as we went. Tonya had been blessed at birth with power, and while she was human through-and-through, the fact was, she'd been born gifted.

The night was blustery but the rain had backed off, and we trundled through the wind, following Tonya as she felt her way through the yard. A moment later, she turned in the direction of a massive cedar that stood to one side, next to the fence dividing Patrick's lot from the neighbor's house.

As we drew close, I suddenly saw a glimmer—there were five men standing there. They were translucent and pale, shimmers against the night. They didn't notice us, but instead, they reminded me of mimes. Over and over, they appeared to be loading an invisible cannon and then setting it off. The next moment, their faces took on a look of horror and they dropped to the ground, mouthing silent screams. The next moment, the scenario began to replay.

"They're caught in time," Tonya said. "They're caught in an eternal loop." She motioned to me. "Ring the bell all around them. Let's see if they notice—it's been blessed by my coven mother."

I carried the bell up and began to vigorously shake it around the spirits. All of a sudden, they stopped and looked up. Tonya motioned to Chai. He carried the smudge stick up and began fanning the smoke toward them.

"Spirits of the night, spirits of the past, spirits trapped in time, I call you to depart this place and leave to your destinies. Lay down your chores, lay down your concerns, you are free to go. You are free from your duties, and your journey forward awaits. Spirits from the past, you have done your jobs well. Now depart and be here no more." Tonya was drawing some sort of symbol in the air. A moment later a golden light began to envelop the soldiers and then, in one bright flash, they vanished. The wind rustled by with a soft whisper of relief.

"They're at peace now." Tonya turned to us. "Now, for

the mother and child . . . they're over there—can you see them near the shed?"

We looked and sure enough, now that they weren't overshadowed by the wight's energy, we could see them standing there. A woman in a long dress that looked right out of a period drama, and a little girl with a sunbonnet tied beneath her chin. The woman was calling out something—we couldn't hear her, but she looked frantic and was obviously searching for something. The little girl was screaming and chasing after her mother, who couldn't seem to see her.

"Aren't they together?" I was trying to figure out how this worked. Dragon spirits were never trapped in the physical dimension. Once we died we went to stay with our ancestors. I'd never heard of a dragon ghost in my entire life.

"No, they're trapped in two separate realities—two different, yet overlapping, dimensions." Tonya frowned. "How to do this? I need to get them together so they can stop searching for each other." She thought for a moment, frowning.

Chai moved forward. "Let me help on this. I think . . . don't ask me or even say thank you." He handed the smudge stick—still smoking—to Patrick, along with the fan. After a moment's consideration, the djinn reached out and etched a glowing symbol in the air that looked for all the world like a door handle. He grabbed hold of the handle and pulled, and the sound of something shifting crackled through the air as realities collided. The little girl's face lit up and she stared at her mother, who was looking down at her, both alarmed and relieved.

"Tell the girl to run—now, I can't hold it open long."

Tonya held out her wand toward the little girl's spirit, aiming it directly at her. "Run to your mother, now. Run fast and quick, child."

The girl looked startled, then began to race forward. As if tripping over something, she fell, landing at her mother's feet. Her mother looked down and, with a shocked and delighted look, gathered the girl in her arms and backed away from the opening. Chai let go of the handle and the sigil vanished.

Tonya motioned to Ralph. "Throw several pinches of powder on the spirits." He did, as Tonya aimed her wand again and began to whisper something beneath her breath. A moment later, the mother looked directly at us, formed the words *thank you* on her lips, and she and her daughter disappeared into the dark of the night. With another gust, the wind blew away their memories and they were long gone.

"That just leaves Lacy." Tonya looked tired. "Let's go."

We made our way to the attic, where Tonya motioned for me to join her. "The rest of you can stay here." She brought her wand but shook her head at the bell. "You won't need that."

We crossed to the back of the attic. There, sitting on the bed, we saw Lacy. I could tell it was her—she smelled like lilacs, and a soft smile lit up her face. We sat down opposite her on the bench by the vanity.

I wasn't sure what to say, but Lacy said it for us. She rose, softly, and I could hear the *swish* of her dress as she knelt down in front of us. She laid a gentle hand on mine, and one on Tonya's hand. The weight was almost imperceptible, but a faint tickle told me she was really there.

"Thank you." The words rushed through on a breeze.

I felt like crying. She'd been trapped by her family, and killed, and then buried beneath a tree in the yard so nobody would know. It was then that I saw the matted blood on the back of her head. Yes, the skeleton had been Lacy's all right, and though we might never prove it for sure, we could tell Toby we knew it was her.

She looked at me and reached up to softly touch my face. Her smile was like a beam of sun as she touched my nose and then laughed. As she turned to Tonya, her smile was just as bright and once again, she whispered, "Thank you."

Then, standing, Lacy began to walk toward the window. At the window, she glanced back one last time, lifted a gloved hand to wave, and then vanished through the wall. A soft hush descended in the attic, as everything settled into place and the timbers fell silent.

Tonya and I returned to the others.

"The house and land are clear of spirits," she said. "As

soon as you have the repairs done, I'll come over and ward it so nothing can get through."

I stood at the edge of the wall leading back into the area in which the family had confined Lacy. Alex joined me. "What are you thinking about, Shimmer?"

My thoughts were running deep, and I turned to him. "Families. I have none, and I so long for one—it means so much to me. But then I see this . . . Lacy . . . her family locked her away and then killed her. I can't imagine that."

"Sometimes, family . . . some families are harder to bear than others. And that wight—we can pretty much be certain it was either him or one like him that caused them to do that to her." Alex seemed at a loss for words. "Don't build the concept of family up to be something it's not. Sometimes, Shimmer, the most loving families are those you make for yourself. Sometimes, your friends are the best family you can have. I know . . . trust me." He wrapped an arm around my shoulder and I rested my head on his shoulder for a moment. "Come on. Let's go downstairs and celebrate a case closed and the fact that Patrick has his house back."

"Not to mention that eight spirits were freed." I let out a small sigh. "Still . . . this was one hell of a battle. You have a lot of cases like this that I can look forward to?"

He snorted, then kissed my nose. "Oh, at times, love. At times."

Then we were with the others and trooping downstairs. There wasn't room to celebrate in the remains of the house, so—tossing the body of the wolfen in the back of the Range Rover—we locked the door and headed back to Tonya's.

CHAPTER 21

Early morning found us in the dark, in the cemetery, beneath a yew tree. Sunrise was still a long ways off, and a series of battery-operated candles surrounded the grave site. Real ones would have gone out in the wind that was blowing briskly. The cemetery had a lived-in feel, and I suspected a plethora of ghosts filled the fenced-in grave-yard. Though it might be the resting place for the dead, it was also their coffee shop and community center.

Toby was there, and Officer Paris, and Patrick, Alex, Ralph, Chai, Degoba, and Tonya. The grave digger who stood beside the open grave was none other than Jack, the hearse driver. When I gave him a questioning look, he shrugged.

"Town this small, a man has to have two jobs some-times." He gave me a soft shrug as if to say, *What are you going to do?*

There was no reverend there, but Toby seemed to be waiting for someone. I looked over at the casket—it was simple, a pine box, but it had been painted with runes and designs that gave it the feel of age and tradition. The symbols had meaning and power behind them.

I moved forward to look at it. The coffin was sitting on a small stand, rather than on one of the devices used to lower caskets into the ground. The paints used to draw the symbols were vivid, and they almost seemed to swirl as I watched them. On the ground, next to the casket, two long ropes rested alongside a basket filled with white roses.

Toby stepped forward to stand beside me. "I want to thank you again." He folded his hands in front of him, staring at the box, his voice solemn.

I glanced at his expression. He looked somber, though he wasn't crying. And frankly, it made me sad that those who *should* be crying over Lacy were long gone. I let out a long sigh. The world was a harsh place at times.

"I'm just glad we found her—and found out what happened to her. Did you read through the papers we gave you?"

He nodded. "Yes, actually I think I know who did it. I think you were right. Her father killed her. Her diary is filled with concerns about his mental stability, and after he locked her up, she keeps talking about him being influenced by the spirits in this area. There's no way to ever know for sure, I guess."

"I suppose not." I paused, then told him about freeing her spirit. I figured he'd believe us, given everything else that his family believed.

Toby smiled then. "Again, thank you. I wish I could have seen her, but I'm glad she's free and gone to her peace." He glanced over at the sidewalk. "There she is!"

I turned in the direction in which he was pointing, at first expecting to see Lacy. But instead, a flesh-and-blood woman was getting out of a taxi. She was dressed in a richly patterned dress, with a thick shawl pulled around her shoulders. Toby hurried off to greet her and escort her back, while I returned to stand beside Alex.

The woman turned out to be another one of Toby's aunts. She didn't have a fortune-teller feel to her, but there was something about her . . . Yes, Toby's family carried a lot of magical energy with them. After introducing us—her name was Kendell—Toby motioned for her to go over to the casket. He asked the rest of us to join hands as Kendell began to speak.

"Lacy Buckland was imprisoned in her own home. She was forgotten, and then murdered and buried alone at the base of a tree. But her life has been brought to light, and her death, and now we join her to lay her bones to rest, and wish her farewell."

Kendell paused, then placed both hands on the casket. She gave Toby a nod, and he did the same. "You were flesh of our family, blood of our family. We mourn your passing, mourn that death found you too soon. We abjure the one who did this to you and curse his memory. May our words reach out into death and drag him into fire for his act. May our words reach out into death and cleanse your passing, Lacy Buckland—we know and acknowledge you. We claim you, so that you may move on. Be at peace, even as your murderer finds his punishment."

Startled a little—I hadn't expected to witness a hexing at a funeral—I forced myself to stand still and not show surprise. Alex squeezed my right hand at the same time Tonya gave my left hand a little squeeze. Apparently, I wasn't the only one taken aback by this turn of events.

Kendell began to sing in a language I didn't understand, but the melody was lovely and it sounded like some sort of lullaby. At the end of the song, she and Toby removed their hands from the casket and moved back. Toby turned to us and motioned for Patrick, Alex, and Ralph to help him. The four men picked up the ends of two ropes and ran them beneath the casket. They then lifted the pine box into the grave, using the ropes to lower it into the gaping hole. Once it was in place, they let the ropes fall on top of the casket.

Kendell picked up the basket of roses and stood by the head of the grave. Toby motioned for us to follow him in a line, and one by one we passed by the grave site, each taking a rose from the basket and dropping the flower into the grave.

As I stood there, rose in hand, I closed my eyes and wished Lacy an easy journey, and peace. I let go of the rose and looked up. There she was, standing opposite me, watching.

She raised one hand, waved and smiled, and then vanished. Blinking, I looked around, but nobody else seemed to have seen her, and I moved out of the way. After the roses were scattered, Jack moved to fill in the grave as we walked away. Kendell and Toby thanked us and the service was over, and that was the end of Lacy Buckland.

While Patrick and Alex went back to Tonya's to sleep, Ralph, Chai, and I stood on the edge of the shore, near the lighthouse. Tonya handed me the pendant and, without a word, I headed to the water, wearing the sleek one-piece I'd brought. I couldn't put the pendant on—I didn't want to have to struggle with it in dragon form—so I clutched it tightly in my hand as I waded through the foaming waves crashing against the shore.

The sound of the water sang to me, and I dropped my head back and laughed, singing out to answer the waves. The sirens were out there, and the wild waves and the whales that came in from their time in the ocean. This was my territory, this was my joy.

By the time the water was waist deep, I struck out, swimming with the currents, letting them tug me out toward the open water. I dove deep as the water pulled me under, and then broke the surface again. My blood surged with life— the water knew me and I knew it—we were kin. I was part of the ocean and she was part of me and no matter whether it be a raindrop or a rogue wave, the same thread of the Ocean Mother ran through to connect them all to me and me to them.

Before I knew it, I was out far enough to transform and so I dove long and hard, deep, barrel rolling as I spiraled down, shifting form into my dragon self. The strength of my body overjoyed me, and the feel of the water became much more sensual as I drove through it, turning and spinning in joy. But then I remembered what I'd come for. The pendant was still in my hand and so I dove still deeper, down and down farther until I was at the bottom of the strait.

Once there, I rested on the silty floor. With the pendant in one front foot, I used the other to dig into the sand and rock littering the bottom of the strait. I dug quickly until I had a hole about ten feet deep. I stared at the glowing pendant. The forest wight king was trapped inside, and now, hopefully he'd be at the bottom of the strait forever. There was no guarantee that he wouldn't ever go free, but there were no guarantees in life, period. And this . . . this should hold him for quite some time. I dropped the pendant into the hole and began to fill it in. Once it was set, I looked around and saw a rather large boulder sitting on the bottom. I rolled it over to cover where I'd dug the hole.

That was it. That was all I could do. It would have to be enough. Free from my task, I spent the next hour playing through the water, enjoying my freedom. I was home—more than the Dragon Reaches, more than Seattle . . . the water was my home.

That night, we opened the wights' treasure chests. Inside, we found various treasures that spoke of the forest—beautifully polished river rocks, and polished pieces of wood. A curiously petrified bag of acorns . . . and we also found a beautiful sapphire ring in a platinum setting. Tonya and Degoba took the other items—they said they were good for magic—but Alex pressed the ring into my hand.

"It matches your eyes," he said, smiling softly. "Consider it a bonus for a job well done. You held up so well for the first major case we took you out on."

I stared at it, then slipped it on my finger, the metal cool against my skin. As I stared at it, I realized that it would help me never forget what we'd been through. What I'd learned about myself.

And then, it was time to say good-bye. We all gathered at Tonya's. Degoba was there, and Toby. Chai had vanished—he said he'd meet me at my place in Seattle, and the party seemed oddly empty without him. But the kitchen was overflowing with snacks and drinks and bottled blood for the two vampires, and before we knew it, it was time to make our farewells.

Tonya and I vowed to keep in touch.

"I'll be down in Seattle next month for a shopping trip, so maybe I can stay for the weekend." She frowned. "You guys have totally disrupted my life, but I'm going to miss you so much." She gave me a long hug. "You're so much fun to have around, Shimmer. And now I know dragons exist!"

I hugged her back, already missing her. "You call me, okay? Remember, I've got a five-year sentence here. I need my friends!" But even as I said it, I realized that maybe this wouldn't be so bad. There were places I could swim, and I could be who I was. And the fact was, Earthside people tended to be a lot more accepting than my own people. And, of course, there was Alex.

Degoba and I shook hands. I stared at his side. "I'm still so sorry about stabbing you—"

"You did what you had to. There is no blame, girl." He paused, cocking his head. "Your journey's just beginning, Shimmer. Whether you'll end up going back to the Dragon Reaches, I cannot tell. But I *will* tell you this: No matter what happens, you won't ever go back as the same dragon you were when you left there." He leaned forward and whispered, "You don't really need a family name, you know. You're creating one, even now. I promise you that." As he leaned away, his eyes flickered over to Tonya, and I caught a glimmer in them.

"Ask her out. Do it. I guarantee you, your interest won't be unwelcome." I pushed him toward her before he could start sputtering.

Patrick and Alex hugged, and Patrick offered us free lodgings anytime we were in town. "As soon as I'm good to open, you are welcome to come back whenever you want. I'll never forget what you did for me." He wrote out a check for our fees. Alex started to protest, but Patrick shook his head. "This is your job. I didn't expect you to help me for free, and you earned it. You all earned it. Just take the damned money."

"Well, seeing you owe me a thousand from that card

game, sure thing." Alex pocketed the check and then, it was six thirty and we had to make our good-byes before it got too late.

We gathered our gear and headed out to the Range Rover. This time, we actually had reservations on the ferry over to Coupeville, and I'd double-checked them before we left. The ride home would be a lot shorter, as long as we didn't miss the sailing. As we drove to the ferry terminal, I glanced back at the town. I'd grown to both love it and hate it—the place was a freakshow of weirdness and yet . . . there was something that called to me here. I let out a long sigh as we drove aboard the ferry. Yes, this had been quite a learning experience and it would stick with me. But it was time to go home.

The trip went smoothly, and as the freeway guided us back into Seattle, the lights seemed almost blinding. Culture shock, I thought; even just five days away had taken me out of the city mind-set. We pulled into the agency headquarters around nine thirty. I blinked as I got out of the Range Rover to the tune of sirens playing in the street. Only these weren't gentle songs, but whirring alarms. Somebody somewhere had done something wrong.

We trooped into the building. Bette was manning the desk and she jumped up, a grin a mile wide on her face as we pushed through the doors. Her ever-present cigarette was hanging off her lip as usual, and tonight she was wearing gold lamé stretch pants, a tiger-print V-neck shirt with ruffled sleeves, and a brilliant fuchsia pleather belt. Her four-inch stilettos were sparkling rhinestones and all in all, she looked like she'd stepped out of an ad for Frederick's of Hollywood.

"Good trip?" She bustled us into the break room.

"Yes, you lovely old broad." Alex gave her a quick kiss on the forehead and she smacked his butt. "Anything urgent go on while we were away?"

"Not exactly urgent, but I have two new clients wanting

to talk to you. They'll be in tomorrow night—I made appointments for them. Oh, and Glenda dropped off everything you ever gave her and said to fuck off and never call her again. She and I got into it, and I won't repeat what she called me, but I don't think she'll be back. I warned her to steer clear of me or I'd give her a taste of what my fangs can do. And a water moccasin's venom? Can affect a succubus." Bette chuckled, and I could tell she'd just love an excuse to sink her teeth into Glenda.

Alex waved her protests away. "I know, love. Don't worry. She won't be back." His gaze flickered over to me, just for a moment, but Bette caught it.

She snorted. "Well, finally . . . I've been waiting for you two to admit that there was an elephant in the room. Took you long enough!"

I blushed, but Alex just laughed.

"Hush, woman. Enough for now. We'll fill out paperwork tomorrow. Bette, you wouldn't believe what we went up against."

She tamped out her cigarette and took a swig of her coffee. "You underestimate me, Alex. But then, you always did." Laughing, she stood up. "Get your asses home now and relax. You all look exhausted."

As we trooped out the door, she caught my arm and pulled me back. "I need to talk to Shimmer a second—she'll be right out."

"I'm dropping her off at home, so I'll wait." Alex headed for the parking lot.

Ralph waved. "See you tomorrow night, Shimmer!"

I wrinkled my nose at him. "Sure thing, Ralph."

After we were alone, Bette turned to me. "Don't worry, I'm not going to ask if you bagged him in the sheets. I can see by both your faces that you're in that sex haze from the start of a new relationship. And I'm happy about it, before you ask. But what I do want to know is this: Did Patrick and Alex get things sorted out?" The concern was evident in her eyes.

I ducked my head, laughing. "Yes. Yes, they did."

She let out a satisfied sigh. "I'm so glad. They were best of friends for a long time. I don't wish bad luck on anybody but . . . if it brought them back together, that's a good thing." She gave me a keen look. "I think, Shimmer . . . you are going to keep Alex on his toes. And vice versa. And this is going to be a fun one to watch play out."

Then, I did blush. "It's so new . . . I don't really even know what *it* is."

"You'll figure it out. And you have me to talk to if you want." She patted my arm. "Go home now, and get some rest."

I glanced at the clock. "Yeah, I'm tired. And Alex is waiting, I'd better go."

"Mm-hmm," she said, a twinkle in her eyes. "Have fun, child." And then she gave me a quick hug and sent me out the door.

A lex parked the Range Rover in front of my house. "Here we are." He leaned back, staring at me. "It's up to you, Shimmer. Was Port Townsend a fluke? Or . . . is there more there for you? There is for me, if you're willing to give it a go?"

Now that we were alone and back in Seattle, I felt oddly shy. But I didn't have to think it over. "Let's see where this takes us. No promises, no guarantees. But we owe it to ourselves to give *us* a chance."

With a soft smile, he leaned forward, clutching the steering wheel. "I'm so glad you said that. I would respect whatever decision you made, but I . . ." He stopped, glancing sideways at me. "No, not going there yet. It's too soon. But, Shimmer . . . you're incredible. And I want you to know that I can't stop thinking about you."

I smiled softly. "I know. Listen . . . On the business side of things . . . I didn't muck anything up too badly, did I? On the trip? Other than getting us lost on the way there?"

With a laugh, Alex shook his head. "On the contrary, you were wonderful, Shimmer. You had a few moments there, but we all did. You're going to make a good team player. So don't worry about that. You'll get nothing but a stellar review to the Wing-Liege about this." He paused. "Will Chai be staying with you?" There was a tinge of something in his voice I couldn't pinpoint. Disapproval . . . disappointment?

I nodded. "He's a good friend, Alex. He can help us out at times. And . . . I need to feel like I have some touchstone here. As long as Chai stays, I have some sort of family. You know? Ralph has his family. You . . . you have Bette. I don't have anybody."

Alex reached out and took my hand, holding it as he caressed my palm with one cool finger. I looked up and he caught my gaze. His eyes glimmered, their frosty light flaring as he stared at me, refusing to look away. My breath tight in my chest, I suddenly felt dizzy as he leaned toward me.

"I have Bette, yes—and so do you, whether you know it or not. But you have me, Shimmer. Never think that you don't."

Before I realized what was happening, he whispered my name and his lips met mine. They were cool and insistent, pulling me under as the kiss deepened. I closed my eyes, parting my lips ever slightly to allow him access. And then, I was in his arms and he tangled one fist in my hair, holding me tight. His lips lowered to my neck, and he licked the skin softly. I could feel the edge of his fangs scrape against my throat, and then . . . and then . . . he pulled back, letting go.

Breathing hard, I stared at him. "Do you have time to come in?"

He let out a low laugh. "All the time in the world, love. Sunrise won't roll around for a while."

And so we went inside, and the house seemed much warmer and fuller than when I had left. Signs of Chai were everywhere, but he himself seemed to have vanished. I knew he was around but giving us our space. As I led Alex into the bedroom, eyeing his lanky form, I realized that I wanted this to work—all of this. Seattle. The agency. Alex. I wanted something in my life that wasn't transitory. Something real.

Alex took one look at the bed, then at me. "Come here,

you dragon wench." He took my hand and pulled me to him, trailing kisses down my cheek, onto my neck as he slid one hand up my shirt.

Fumbling for my belt and zipper, I began to strip, hungrier for him than the first time. This was new, like I had told Bette, and I didn't know where it was leading but I wanted to follow the trail and find out. As we slid beneath the covers and he began to explore my body, the sounds of city streets provided their own kind of music. Cars passing by, the thrum of the lights and the concrete.

"Alex . . ." I whispered his name, my thoughts whirling from the sensations of his hands on my body, of his cock thrusting deep within me. Yes, I was stuck here in Seattle for five years, but the future didn't seem as bleak as it had. In fact, maybe . . . just maybe . . . it might turn out to be something wonderful. Either way, I decided right then, I was going to enjoy the journey, and lost myself in the touch of his cool skin against mine.

THE PLAYLIST

I write to music a good share of the time, and so I always put my playlists in the back of each book so you can see which artists/songs I listened to during the writing. Here's the playlist for *Flight from Death*:

AC/DC: "Rock and Roll Ain't Noise Pollution," "Back in Black," "Highway to Hell," "Dirty Deeds Done Dirt Cheap," "Hell's Bells"

Aerosmith: "Walk This Way," "Dream On"

AJ Roach: "Devil May Dance"

Alice Cooper: "I'm the Coolest," "Go to Hell"

Arcade Fire: "Abraham's Daughter"

Asteroids Galaxy Tour: "The Golden Age," "Heart Attack," "Around the Bend," "The Sun Ain't Shining No More," "Sunshine Coolin'"

AWOLNATION: "Sail"

Bad Girls: "M.I.A."

Beck: "Cellphone's Dead," "Broken Train," "Qué Onda Guero," "Nausea," "Farewell Ride," "Emergency Exit," "Loser"

Black Angels, The: "Don't Play with Guns," "Evil Things," "Indigo Meadow," "Holland," "Young Men Dead," "Manipulation," "Bad Vibrations"

Black Rebel Motorcycle Club: "Fault Line," "Feel It Now"

Black Sabbath: "Paranoid"

Bret Michaels: "Love Sucks"

Broken Bells: "The Ghost Inside"

Cobra Verde: "Play with Fire"

Crazy Town: "Butterfly"

Dire Straits: "Down to the Waterline," "Money for Nothing"

Eels: "Souljacker Part I"

Fatboy Slim: "Praise You"

Foster the People: "Pumped Up Kicks"

Garbage: "I Think I'm Paranoid," "#1 Crush," "Queer," "Only Happy When It Rains"

Gary Numan: "Are Friends Electric," "Petals," "Down in the Park," "Cars (Remix)," "My Shadow in Vain"

Gorillaz: "Last Living Souls," "Hongkongaton," "Dare," "Feel Good Inc.," "Rockit"

Hugo: "99 Problems"

In Strict Confidence: "Silver Bullets," "Snow White"

Ladytron: "Ghosts," "I'm Not Scared," "Burning Up"

Little Big Town: "Bones"

Madonna: "4 Minutes," "Beautiful Stranger"

Marcy Playground: "Comin' Up from Behind"

Morcheeba: "Even Though (Acoustic)"

Pierces, The: "Secret"

Puddle of Mudd: "Psycho"

Rachel Digg: "Hands of Time"

Rolling Stones: "Gimme Shelter"

Screaming Trees: "All I Know," "Dime Western," "Where the Twain Shall Meet"

Sewn: "The Feeling"

Shriekback: "New Man," "Night Town," "Over the Wire," "Big Fun"

Stone Temple Pilots: "Sour Girl," "Atlanta"

Syntax: "Pride"

Tom Petty and the Heartbreakers: "Mary Jane's Last Dance"

Verve, The: "Bitter Sweet Symphony"

Turn the page to read a special excerpt from
the next book from Yasmine Galenorn . . .

AUTUMN THORNS

Coming November 2015!

ADVICE FOR VISITORS TO
WHISPER HOLLOW

1. If you hear someone call your name from the forest, don't answer.

2. Never interrupt Ellia when she's playing to the dead.

3. If you see the Girl in the Window, set your affairs in order.

4. Try not to end up in the hospital.

5. If the Crow Man summons you, follow him.

6. Remember: Sometimes the foul are actually fair.

7. And most important: Don't drive down by the lake at night.

Welcome to Whisper Hollow:
Where the spirits walk among the living
and the lake never gives up her dead.

The road twisted, curving through a series of S-turns as my Honda CRV wound along Highway 101. To my left, the forest breathed softly, looming thick and black even though it was still early afternoon. Mingled amid the unending fir and cedar, brilliant leaves—in shades of autumn bronze and yellow—whirled off the branches of maple and birch to litter the ground with sodden debris. October in western Washington was a windy, volatile month. The fact that it was a Sunday evening worked for me, though. There weren't many cars on the road.

To my right, waves frothed across Lake Crescent as the wind whipped against the darkened surface. The rain shower turned into a drenching downpour and I eased off on the accelerator, lowering my speed to thirty-five miles per hour, and then to thirty. The drops were pelting so hard against the asphalt that all I could see was a blur of silver on black across the road. These winding back roads were dangerous. All it took was one skid toward the guard rail, one wrong turn of the wheel, and the Lady would claim another victim, dragging them down into her secreted recesses.

It had been fifteen years since I had made this drive . . . fifteen years, a ferry ride, and about a hundred and twenty miles. I grabbed the ferry in Seattle over to Kingston, and then wound through Highway 104 up the interior of the Peninsula, till I hit Highway 101, which took me through Port Townsend, and past Port Angeles. Now, three hours after I had left the city, I neared the western end of Lake Crescent. The junction that would take me onto Cairn Street was coming up. From there, a twenty minute drive around the other side of the lake would lead me through the forest, back to Whisper Hollow.

As I neared the exit, I veered off the road, onto the shoulder and turned off the ignition. This was it. My last chance to drive past, loop around the Olympic Peninsula and turn my back on all of the signs. But I knew I was just procrastinating against the inevitable. My life in Seattle had never really been my own, and this past month, when the Crow Man sent me three signs, I realized I was headed home. Then, last week, my grandmother died. Her death sealed the deal because, like it or not, it was my duty to step up and fill her shoes.

I slowly opened the door, making sure I was far enough off the road to avoid being hit, and emerged into the rain-soaked evening. Shoving my hands in my pockets, I stared at the lake through the trees. The wind was whipping up currents on the water, the dark surface promising an icy bath to anything or anybody unlucky enough to be caught in it. The rising fog caught in my lungs and I coughed, the noise sending a murder of crows into the air from where they'd been resting in a tall fir. They circled over me, cawing, then headed north, toward Whisper Hollow.

Crows. I pulled my jacket tighter against a sudden gust of wind that caught me from the side. Crows were messengers. In fact, the Crow Man had reached out all the way to Seattle, where he summoned me with three omens. The first sign had been the arrival of his flock in Seattle—they followed me everywhere, and I could feel his shadow walking behind them, looming down through the clouds.

The second sign had been a recurring nightmare, for three nights running. Each night, I found myself walking along a dark and shrouded path through the Whisper Hollow cemetery, as the Blood Moon gleamed full and ripe overhead. As I came to the center of the graveyard, I saw— standing next to a headstone—Grandma Lila. Dripping wet and smelling of lake water and decay, she opened her arms and pulled me in, kissing me on both cheeks. Then she lit into me, tearing me up one side and down the other.

"You've turned your back on your gift—on your heritage. Face it, girl, it's time to accept what you are. Whisper Hollow is waiting. It's time you came home to carry on with my duties. It won't be long now, and you'll be needed. You were born a spirit shaman, and you'll die one—there's no backing down. Something big is coming, and the town will need your help. Don't let me down. Don't let Whisper Hollow down." Each of those three nights, I woke up crying, afraid to call her in case there was no answer on the other end of the line.

The third sign came last week, a day or two after I had the last dream. Signs always go in threes. Always have. Third time's the charm, true. But bad things happen in threes, as well. I was walking home from a morning gig at work, deep in thought, when I glanced at the store next to me. There, staring from behind the storefront was the Girl in the Window. A cold sweat broke over me, but when I looked again, she was gone. It *couldn't* have been her, could it? The Girl in the Window belonged to Whisper Hollow and she was never seen outside the borders of the town. Squinting, I craned my neck, moving close to the pane. *Blink . . .* it was only a mannequin. But mannequin or not, my gut told me that I had been visited by the sloe-eyed Bean Nighe, dripping wet and beckoning to me.

One of the rules of Whisper Hollow echoed back to haunt me. *If you see the Girl in the Window, set your affairs in order.* This was all the proof I needed. I went home and began to sort through my things. The next day, an express letter from Ellia arrived, informing me that my grandparents had gone off the road, claimed by the Lady of Crescent Lake. She was a hungry bitch, that one, and neither age nor status mattered in her selection of victims. The car hadn't surfaced, and neither had my grandfather's body—no shock there. But Grandma Lila had been found on the shore, hands placed gently over her chest in a sign of respect. Even the Lady knew better than get the Morrígan's nose out of joint by disrespecting her emissaries.

And now, a week later, I was on my way home to take Lila's place before the dead started to walk. I sucked in a deep breath, took one last look at the lake, and returned to the car.

"What do you think, guys?" A glance into the backseat showed Agent H, Gabby, and Daphne all glaring at me from their carriers. They weren't at all happy with me, but the ride would be over soon.

"*Purp.*" Gabby was the first to speak. She stared at me with golden eyes, her fur a glorious black, plush and thick. The tufts on her ears gave her an odd, feathered look, standard Maine Coon regalia. She let out another squeak and shifted in her carrier. Not to be outdone, Agent H—a huge brown tabby and also a Maine Coon—let out a short, loud, yowl. He was always vocal, and right now he was letting me know that he was not amused. Daphne, a tortoiseshell, just snorted and gave me a look that said, *"Really, can we just get this over with?"* They were littermates, three years old, and I had taken them in from a shelter after they were rescued from an animal hoarder. They had been three tiny balls of fluff when I brought them home. Now they were huge, and—other than Peggin—they were my closest friends.

Frowning, I squinted at them. "You're sure about this? You might not like living in Whisper Hollow, you know. It's a strange town, and the people there are all . . . *like me.*"

I stopped. That was the crux of it. The people in Whisper Hollow—they were *my* people. Even though I hadn't been home in fifteen years I knew that both they, and the town, were waiting for me.

Gabby pawed her face, cleaning her ears, and let out another squeak.

"Okay. Final answer. Head home, it is." With a deep breath, I pulled back onto the road, turning right as I eased onto Cairn Street. We were on our way back to Whisper Hollow, where the ghosts of the past were waiting to weave me into their world as seamlessly as the forest claimed the land, and the lake claimed her conquests.

'm Kerris Fellwater and I'm a spirit shaman by birth, which means I connect with the dead. I can talk to them, see them, and drive them back to their graves if they get out of hand. At least, that's the goal and job description, if you want to think of it as a profession. The gift is my birthright, from the day I was born until the day I die. My training's incomplete, of course, but instinct can take me a long way. And I've always been a rule breaker, so doing things *my* way seems the natural order of things.

As my grandmother was, and her mother before her, I'm a daughter of the Morrigan. Our matriarchal line stretches back into the mists, as do the spirit shamans. I can feel and see energy, and I can manipulate it—to a degree. Some people might call me a witch, but the truth is, most magic I can cast is minor, except when it comes to the world of spirits and the dead. There, my power truly blossoms out.

When I turned eighteen, after a major blowout with my grandfather, I decided to ditch my past, the town, and anything resembling family, so I took my high school diploma and the two hundred dollars I had saved, and headed for Seattle. I found a room for rent in the basement of a house, and a job at Zigfree's Café Latte. Over the years, I worked my way up from barista to managing the store, but it was just something I did to pay the rent on my shiny new apartment.

At night, I slipped out into the rainy streets to take on my second gig—one that made very little money, but that kept me sane. A few months after I arrived in Seattle, the headaches started. I knew what they were from, and the only way to stop them. If spirit shamans don't use their powers, the energy can build up and implode—not a pretty future, to say the least. At the best, ignoring the power can drive one mad. At worst, it can kill from an energy overload.

So I hunted around till I found a gig for a penny-paper that later turned into an online webzine as the Internet grew into something more than an oddity. I investigated haunted houses, and paranormal activity. On the side, I evicted a number of ghosts. The job didn't pay much, but that didn't matter to me. The coffee shop kept me in rent and food money, but the ghost hunting? That's what kept the headaches at bay. I spent all my spare time tromping through haunted buildings, looking for the ghosts who were troublemakers—the dead who were too focused on the world of the living to do anybody any good.

When I found them, I'd drop a hint to the owner and about fifty percent asked me to come in and deal with the spirits. And kicking their astral butts, so to speak, is what kept me from falling over the edge of the cliff into La La land. I began to create my own rites and rituals from the training Lila had taught me before I left home, and for the most part they worked. There were a few missteps, some of them embarrassing and a few downright dangerous, but overall, I managed.

In my personal life, I kept to myself. I had met a few friends but no one I felt like I could trust, other than keeping in touch with Peggin.

See, once people find out that I hang with spirits . . . well . . . it goes one of two ways: they're either afraid of me, or they glom onto me in hopes of gaining tomorrow's lottery tickets or finding out if old Uncle Joe had actually squirreled away money somewhere and forgot to leave a note about it in his will. Being a spirit shaman doesn't make for easy dates, either. When guys find out that I can chat up their dead sisters or friends and get the low-down on what they're *really* like, that usually ends the date. At first, their fear—couched as "It's not you, it's me"—bothered me. After all, the boys in Whisper Hollow had accepted me for who I was, quirks and all. So it seemed like a pale excuse. After a while though, I learned to ignore the brush-offs and eventually, I stopped dating, for the most part.

But now I'm going home, where everybody in Whisper Hollow is eccentric, in one way or another. Everybody's just a little bit mad. And I realize that I'm actually looking forward to it. Especially since my grandfather's dead and can never bother me again. At least . . . that's my hope. Because in Whisper Hollow, the dead don't always stay put where you plant them.

yawned, blinking. As I struggled to sit up, I wondered where I was, then it hit me over the head. *Home.* I was home. Stretching my neck, I realized that, for the first time in a long while, I had slept soundly. The master bedroom was on the main floor, but when I'd pulled into town it had been past seven. After stopping to grab a burger and fries and a few things at the local convenience store, I reached the house around quarter past eight.

I'd been exhausted, more emotionally than anything else, so I had set up the litter boxes in the utility room and locked the cats in there for the night. After I called Peggin—my best friend from high school and the one person I'd kept actively in touch with while I was in Seattle—to let her know I was back in town, I dropped on the sofa to think over my next step. The next thing I knew, I was waking up, still dressed, and morning was pouring through the partially opened curtains.

Stumbling to the bathroom, I showered, then sat at the vanity. As I leaned in, trying for a decent makeup day, I grimaced. My face looked as tired as I felt. Circles underscored my eyes, but that would clear up with enough water and another good night's sleep. My eyes were dark today—they varied from almost golden to a deep brown depending on my mood. Right now, they were mostly bloodshot.

I brushed out my hair and braided the long, brunette strands to keep them out of my face while they dried. At 33,

I had yet to see a gray hair, for which I was grateful. As I shifted, looking for my bra and panties, I caught the reflection of the mark on my back and paused. *A reminder of who I was. Of what I was.* It was a birthmark, though it looked like a tattoo—and it was in the center of my back, right above my butt. If it had been actual ink, they would have called it a tramp stamp. But I had been born with it, as had my mother and grandmother. It was the shape of a crow standing on a crescent moon, and it was jet black. It was the mark of a spirit shaman.

I slid into my underwear and then fastened my bra, shimmying to position my breasts in the cups. At a solid size eight and a 38F cup, I was happy enough with myself. I liked my curves—and I had plenty of them, in the classic hourglass shape. I hurried into my jeans and a snug V-neck sweater and patted my stomach. I did need to find a gym, though. I worked out a *lot*. I tended to favor weights and the stationary bike, though mostly for health and strength. Unlike so many of the women I met, I wasn't on a diet and I ate what I liked, preferring meat and vegetables and the occasional pasta dish. I ate my junk food, too, but tried to keep it to a few times a week.

Finally, I was ready to face the day. *You mean, face a new way of life, don't you? Fine . . . face a new life. Happy now? Yeah, I guess so.*

Snorting—I usually won most of the arguments I held with myself in my head—I headed out to the kitchen. Next order of the day: secure caffeine. Life always looked better after a pot of coffee and, as a former barista, I made a mean pot of java.

I wandered into the kitchen. Early light filtered through the kitchen window, silvery and gray with the overcast sky. The room was spacious, with an eat-in nook, and a large window by the table that overlooked the backyard. I ran my hands along the smooth, cool countertops. My grandparents had renovated during the time I'd been gone. The laminate had been replaced by granite, the white cabinets had been switched out for dark. All the appliances were now stainless steel, and tile on the floor had replaced the checkerboard linoleum. But the walls were still the same warm gold color they had always been—although the paint looked fresh—and the kitchen had the same cozy feel.

On the counter stood a shiny stainless steel espresso machine. Spotting a grinder and a container of beans next to the machine, I smiled. Grandma had loved her caffeine and I'd inherited her addiction. Grandpa Duvall had preferred tea—strong and black and bitter. I opened a cupboard at random to find neat, tidy shelves of packaged foods. The refrigerator, however, was empty and spotless. A few days ago, when I told her I was coming home, Peggin had promised to come in and clean it out for me. Apparently, she had managed to do so. I breathed a sigh of relief. One less task I'd have to deal with.

I pulled a couple shots of espresso and added some of the creamer I had picked up at the store the night before. As I carried my mug over to the table, the phone rang, startling me out of my thoughts. Who could be calling me? Peggin was out of town till Wednesday and she was the only other person who knew I had come home, besides my lawyer.

Hesitating, almost hoping it was a telemarketer, I picked up the receiver. "Hello?"

"Kerris . . . you're really back. Peggin called me. You got my letter, then? I'm sorry about your grandparents, my dear."

Ellia. She sounded shaky, but no matter how many years it had been, I would never forget the lilting sound of her voice. When I was little, I'd clutch my grandmother's hand as we followed Ellia into the graveyard. She would sing, leading the way, her violin in hand. I had been mesmerized by her songs.

I propped the receiver on my shoulder, shrugging to hold it up to my ear as I peeked in the various drawers, looking to see what might be there. "I was going to call you, but figured it would be easier to talk in person. I suppose we'd better meet. Grandma Lila came to me in a dream, she told

me there were things happening in town. What's going on?"
I knew I sounded abrupt, but Ellia had never been aces in
the diplomatic department either, and she didn't expect it
from anybody else.

"There have been stirrings in the forest for several years.
The Lady has been more active over the past couple of years,
as well. Spirits are on edge, Kerris. Lila noticed this before she
died and told me. We think Penelope's having a hard time
keeping them over on her side." Down to business, all right.

That didn't bode well. First, Penelope was usually pretty
good at keeping the Veil closed. That she was having problems wasn't a positive sign. And second, that the Lady of
the Lake was hungrier than usual meant nobody was safe.

"What changed? Has Veronica been at it again?" Veronica
could be friend or foe depending on her mood, though mostly
she was interested in her own agenda and tended to ignore
the living. But if she got her mind set on an idea and had to
turn the town on its ear to achieve her goals, she wouldn't
hesitate.

A pause. Then—"No. I have my suspicions, but I don't
want to discuss them over the phone. Let's just say that over
the past few months, things have begun to escalate. Your
grandmother started to investigate, but then . . . Anyway,
since her death, the dead have been walking more. I've been
doing my best to play the shadows to sleep but my songs
won't work right without a spirit shaman to lead the rites
for me."

I was nodding, though she couldn't see me. The night of
every new moon, the lament singers went out to the grave-
yards to calm the dead who had not yet passed beyond the
Veil.

The Veil was a world between the worlds—it was a tran-
sit station for the dead, in a sense. A nebulous place of mist
and fire and ice, where spirits wandered, not fully detached
from the world of the living, and not yet ready to cross the
threshold and move on to the Beyond. In most cities and
places on the planet, the line between worlds was highly

defined and it was easy for the Gatekeepers to guard the dead and keep them reined in, but in Whisper Hollow, things were different. The Veil was strong here, and so were the ghosts.

And now, with Grandma Lila dead—without a spirit shaman to perform the rites and escort spirits into the Veil to begin with—the lament singers' songs would not work. And while Penelope held the ghosts at bay as much as she could, until she was able to convince them to cross the threshold and leave behind all they had once been, the dead were still able to return and walk the earth.

Grandma Lila had been a strong woman—a stronger spirit shaman than I could ever hope to be, though Grandfather fought her every step of the way. I never knew why, but I knew that he wasn't her protector—in fact, unlike most spirit shamans, Grandma Lila had not been paired with a shapeshifter to watch over her. I wondered if that would be my fate, as well. She had never broached the subject during my training, and I had been too nervous to ask.

Shaking off my thoughts, I tried to push away my self-doubt. "When can we meet?"

"Tonight at my house? At six P.M. You remember where I live, don't you?"

I let out a slow breath. This was my job now, my heritage. I owed it to the town. "Fogwhistle Way. I don't remember the number, but I remember your house."

"That's right. 337 Fogwhistle Way. I'll be waiting for you. It's good to have you back, Kerris. I'm sorry about your grandmother. We needed her. And now, we need you." With that, she hung up.

I glanced out the kitchen window as a murder of crows rose into the sky from the maple in the backyard. They circled the house once, then headed out to the south. A storm was coming in from the north, off the Strait of Juan de Fuca. My gut said that it would barrel through the forest and hit us by afternoon.

Deciding I needed more caffeine, I pulled another couple

shots, then checked on the cats, setting down fresh food and water for them. They were freaked, of course, but they were safe and I'd let them out of their prison once I returned from shopping. I wanted to go through the house first to make certain there was nothing that would hurt them—no open windows, no rat traps.

With one last glance at the kitchen, I reached for my jacket and purse. As I paused, my hand on the doorknob, a wave of shadow rolled through. It reached out to examine me, cold and clammy as it tickled over my skin. Then, as I blinked, shivering, it vanished. Whirling, I glanced around the room, searching the corners. But the kitchen was empty.

Something was looming in the town, all right, and whatever it was, it knew I was back.

"I'm home, Grandma Lila," I whispered. "I just hope you'll be around when I need you."

And right then, I knew that—before whatever this was had ended—I was going to need all the help I could get . . . from *both* sides of the grave.

Don't miss the "erotic and darkly
bewitching"* series featuring the D'Artigo sisters:
half-human, half-fae supernatural agents.

From *New York Times* bestselling author
Yasmine Galenorn

WITCHLING

CHANGELING

DARKLING

DRAGON WYTCH

NIGHT HUNTRESS

DEMON MISTRESS

BONE MAGIC

HARVEST HUNTING

BLOOD WYNE

COURTING DARKNESS

SHADED VISION

SHADOW RISING

HAUNTED MOON

AUTUMN WHISPERS

CRIMSON VEIL

PRIESTESS DREAMING

PANTHER PROWLING

galenorn.com
penguin.com

BERKLEY | Penguin
Random
House

*Jeaniene Frost, *New York Times* bestselling author

M192AS0315